I0627207

Arrow of Fortune

BOOK 3 *of the* RAIDERS OF THE ARCANA

VAUGHAN WOODS PUBLISHING

ARROW OF FORTUNE

BOOK III
RAIDERS OF THE ARCANA

JACQUELYN BENSON

Copyright © 2025 by Jacquelyn Benson
Cover design by Selkkie Designs
Character illustrations by Averil
Cover copyright © 2025 by Jacquelyn Benson
Typeset in Garamond and Adorn Garland

First edition: November 2025

Library of Congress Catalog Number: 2025918547
ISBNs: 978-1-959050-29-2 (hardcover), 978-1-959050-27-8 (paperback), 978-1-959050-23-0 (ebook), 978-1-959050-24-7 (audiobook)

Published by Vaughan Woods Publishing
Hampton Falls, New Hampshire

Stay up-to-date on new book releases by subscribing to Jacquelyn's newsletter at JacquelynBenson.com.

Content warnings for Arrow of Fortune:
Contains instances of physical violence (throttling), fistfights, confinement in a dark space, field surgery (stitches), wild animal death, vertigo, racial exclusion, classism, death of a minor character. Contains references to sex, sexual fantasy, and parental emotional abuse.

For every woman whose history remains a secret, waiting for the day when we have the wisdom to rediscover it.

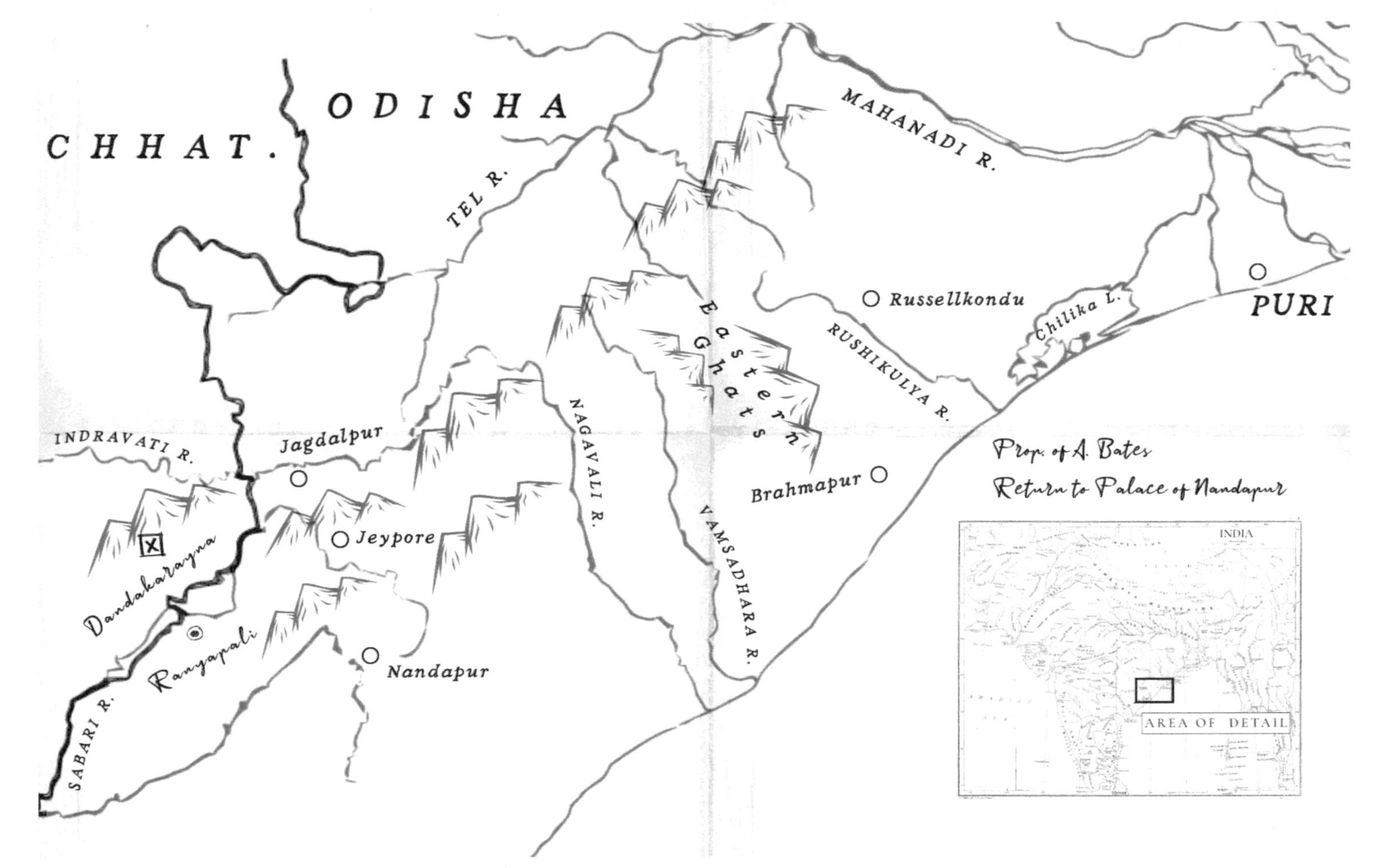

CHHAT.
ODISHA
MAHANADI R.
TEL R.
Russellkondu
Chilika L.
RUSHIKULYA R.
PURI
Eastern Ghats
INDRAVATI R.
Jagdalpur
NAGAVALI R.
VAMSADHARA R.
Brahmapur
Prop. of A. Bates
Return to Palace of Nandapur
Dandakarayna
Jeypore
Ranyapali
SABARI R.
Nandapur
INDIA
AREA OF DETAIL

No one knows where I shall go tomorrow.
I shall not apologize. I shall not be sorry.
I shall accept my destiny with a bowed head..

CHANDRABATI RAMAYANA, BOOK THREE
ENGLISH TRANSLATION BY NABANEETA DEV SEN

PROLOGUE

Late Afternoon
Third Day of the Month of Asadha
Kingdom of Kosala

THE RENOWNED SAGE Valmiki meditated under the dancing leaves of the banyan tree, his humble ashram sprawled below him on the banks of India's most holy river.

Valmiki's meditation was, in all honesty, a breath away from a nap. He was an old man, after all, and had lived a long, strange life. He was entitled to rest his eyes on a lazy afternoon heady with the breath of summer.

The warm breeze brushed against his weathered skin, rustling the leaves over his head and the grasses at his heels. He allowed himself to lean back against the nested trunks of the tree in the interest of better facilitating that nap.

Small, hurried footsteps pounded up the slope. Valmiki felt them as a subtle thrum of the earth against his aching bones. High, sweet voices called out through the clear air in tones laced with excited urgency.

"Maharishi Valmiki!"

The revered sage cracked open a wary eye.

A half dozen of the ashram's children gathered around him. They were led by one of the oldest girls, the dangerously quick-witted Iravati.

"There is a woman by the river," she reported authoritatively.

The wind shifted. The whispering leaves overhead seemed to echo the lilting melody of a song hummed by low caste wives as they drew water from the nearby well.

The moonlit night is here. Come, now, my beloved...

"She is draped in silk and gold," Iravati elaborated impatiently, hands braced on her bony hips. "She is either a princess or a goddess, and some warrior just left her alone here and went away with tears in his eyes. You must go to her and make sure that she is all right."

Valmiki, greatest of all living ascetics, who had found enlightenment among the anthills and received the tribute of kings, knew well enough when to give up.

"I'm coming," he grumbled, bones creaking as he rose.

He climbed down the hill, his feet long since hardened against the ground. His chest was bare save for a mala of ruddy, wrinkled rudraksha seeds and the white veil of his beard.

A woman stood on the banks of the river. She wore a sari of petal-soft silk in a hue like the pads on a hare's foot, the cloth draped modestly over her head.

Something about her arms drew the sage as he approached—the curve of her bicep as full and soft as a ripe fruit in a color like pearl dust over amber.

Iravati's impatient description echoed through Valmiki's mind.

A princess or a goddess…

His toes sank into the mud of the riverbank as he stopped at the woman's side.

Across the water, a nobleman rode away, dust rising from the wheels of his chariot. Even from a distance, Valmiki recognized his princely form and the dark, rich waves of his hair.

"That is Prince Lakshmana, son of Sumitra," Valmiki noted. "Why are his shoulders bowed with sorrow?"

The lady graced him with a sad, slender smile—an expression of such aching beauty that Valmiki felt certain it would pierce him like an arrow and leave him bleeding on the ground. When she spoke, her voice was the rush of water kissing a midnight shore. "Because he has left me here and ordered me not to return."

Wary caution shivered over Valmiki's wrinkled skin. "And does this order come from his lord?"

"It does," the woman confirmed.

Valmiki winced.

Lakshmana was ruled by his brother, the favored son of Dasharatha—the greatest king in the history of all India.

Lord Rama.

Valmiki found himself wretchedly certain of the identity of the woman who had just been abandoned on his riverbank by Rama's loyal brother—and fought back the urge to groan.

She was not just any princess, but the Jewel of Ayodhya—daughter of King Janaka, who could transcend the prison of his own flesh. The woman for whom Lord Rama had conquered and slain ten-headed Ravana and his entire army of demons.

His queen. *Sita.*

Was the king mad? Or was this bizarre act the result of a godly wisdom greater than any that Valmiki himself possessed?

Why? the sage moaned inwardly—the thought more a momentary indulgence in self-pity than a question.

The lines of Sita's profile were of unutterable grace as she gazed over the river at the puff of dust that marked the last sign of her retreating brother-in-law, her expression marked by an enduring, stoic grief.

Then Valmiki noticed the curve at the waist of her sari where the silk bent around the early swell of new life—and his knees started to wobble.

There must be some truly egregious sin in one of his past lives for the gods to have handed him this burden.

Fool, Valmiki cursed internally. Lord Rama, the great conqueror of demons, was a bloody fool.

"A great wrong has been done here today, Daughter of the Earth," the sage declared. "I will travel to Ayodhya and make your husband see reason."

Valmiki was quite sure that he could do it. He was not a sage for nothing, after all. He had once chanted a mantra so long and so deeply that he had come to live on nothing but the air itself and the earth under his feet, time itself slowing around him like a river turning to ice with the winter. He had danced along infinity, the wisdom of the space beyond the gods laid open to his wondering soul. And he had once been an adviser and companion to Lord Rama's father, King Dasharatha. Surely, he would be able to make the lady's noble husband see reason.

Valmiki expected that his promise might meet with a nod of regal acknowledgment or a sob of relief—but Sita's eyes remained on the land across the river, and her voice, when it spoke, was calm.

"There is an ashram of women hidden in the forest."

Valmiki jolted with surprise. "The existence of that ashram is a great secret, my lady. How have you come to know of it?"

She did not answer him, speaking instead with the quiet authority of a queen. "I will raise my children there."

The hairs at the back of the sage's neck lifted with a creeping chill as instincts born of a lifetime of study and meditation flared softly to life. Each word felt like a step through a quagmire. "A decision that reflects your great wisdom. A prince cannot help but grow into a better man among the ascetics and the wild than he would ensconced in the flattery and luxury of the court."

"Not one prince." The queen laid a graceful hand over the swell of her belly. "There will be two."

By the shape of her body, she could not have been more than four months gone. It was certainly too soon to have discerned through movement or pressure on the womb that she carried twins.

The uncanny chill on Valmiki's neck grew stronger, and the space between his eyebrows began to itch with an uncomfortable, electric tension.

His gaze shifted to where a bow hung over the queen's shoulder. The curved wood was elegant and supple, accented with slivers of carved bone— a warrior's weapon, unfussy and lovingly maintained.

Intuition tugged his attention down. In her other hand, the queen carried an object as long and thin as Valmiki's forearm, obscured by homespun wrapping like the tattered scrap of a vulture's wing. The black fabric rippled softly in the gentle breeze from the river.

"What is that you carry, my lady?" Valmiki asked through a dry throat.

"Something I demanded of Lord Lakshmana," she replied in a voice like silver. "Something that I would see kept safe."

The wind pulled again, and a corner of the dark cloth fell away from the burden in her petal-soft fingers.

Light flared from the slender gap in the frayed fabric in ghostly, whipping threads—blue and gold, silver and crimson. Hot wind buffeted across the plain, tossing the thick branches of the scattered trees like waves in a tempestuous sea. Pebbles bounced around the calloused soles of the sage's feet as the ground began to groan with the sigh of a rudely awakened giant.

Weathered flesh tugged against Valmiki's bones, pulling toward the lady's hand—and a freedom that could only mean death.

"My lady…" he pleaded, the word rasping like sand in his throat.

With a subtle shift of her wrist, she folded the cloth back into place.

The wind died. Little stones rolled to a crackling stop—and Valmiki realized what the Queen of Queens had taken from her brother-in-law into her keeping.

The knowledge twisted like fire in the sage's gut.

"I will give you Lord Rama's story, as you must tell it," Sita commanded.

Valmiki reeled at the woman's words. He was not a man prone to hubris—

he had, after all, spent a lifetime working to shed himself of his earthly desires. But Lord Rama's story was one of righteousness, betrayal, and wild adventure, threaded through with gods and saints, immortal monsters, and unexpected allies. To be the one chosen to record it was an honor beyond reckoning.

There were tales of ferocious battles. Of mountains moved across the night. Of the raising of the dead.

Of holy weapons of unimaginable power.

The sage's gaze dropped to the cloth-wrapped secret the queen held in her hand—and her final words echoed uncomfortably through his mind.

"As I must write it?" he pushed back uncertainly. "Will it not be the whole story, then?"

The woman on the riverbank turned her head to look at him.

Her face was the image of perfection, black brows soaring like the wings of starlings over cheeks warm and rosy as a summer sunrise. That beauty must have made a thousand hearts burn with regret that they had not had the good fortune to be born Lord Rama and enjoy the unimaginable splendor of this woman's favor.

Past lips like sun-ripened berries, lashes thick as the fall of evening framed eyes like those of a new-foaled fawn. But as the sage looked deeper into that still, relentless gaze, it seemed as though he saw past the flesh and blood that stood before him to a truth deeper than the reckoning of a single lifetime.

He tasted the bitter tang of copper on the back of his tongue. His ears rang with a sound like the clanging of gongs, and the shadow of another pair of arms fell over his soul.

A thought rose into his consciousness, echoing up from a place far beyond both space and time. Valmiki absorbed it with a wild sense of awe.

There have been skulls around her neck.

What had the child Iravati said when she had come up the hill to fetch him?

She is either a princess or a goddess.

The great sage, Maharishi of the Ant Hills, now knew with a trembling clarity exactly which of those stood before him on his riverbank.

"No story is ever complete," She replied, Her words ringing with all the terrifying potential of the space between the stars. "Because every story has its secrets."

"Shakti," Valmiki rasped through a throat dry as dust, falling to his knees in the mud at her feet.

ONE

Late morning
Sunday July 10, 1898
India

*F*IELDS OF JEWEL-LIKE green glided past the window beneath a rich gray sky as Eleanora Mallory curled up in a wingback chair, her nose pressed to the pages of a book.

The fields were speckled with brightly colored wildflowers and grazing cattle. The chair was bolted to the floor. The book was the third volume in Manmatha Nath Dutt's English translation of the Ramayana, an epic tale of love, exile, and war.

The landscape glided rather than staying put because Ellie was sitting in the elegantly furnished parlor of a private train car—a luxury she had never experienced before her arrival in India.

The car had been waiting for her and her companions when they had disembarked from their boat in Madras. Four servants in purple and gold livery had met them at the docks to guide them there, whisking up their luggage and carrying it the short distance to the railway station.

The servants, like the private carriage, belonged to Sir Vijayrama Chandra Devi, Maharaja of Nandapur—or Uncle Vijay, as Ellie's friend Constance affectionately referred to him.

When she pulled her nose out of her reading long enough to notice, Ellie had to admit that a private carriage was a very comfortable way to travel. The facilities included three cabins with berths for sleeping and a well-appointed washroom.

There were advantages to traveling as royalty—even royalty in a land dominated by a foreign empire.

The parlor, where Ellie sat, was appointed in European style, though the purple upholstery that covered the sofa and chairs was richer in texture and color than anything she knew from England. A wet bar in the corner glittered with crystal glasses and decanters. A small library was fixed to one of the walls, the volumes held in place against sudden stops by a raised ridge at the bottom of each shelf.

The other members of Ellie's traveling party were scattered about the room.

Constance Tyrrell lounged on the sofa, dressed for the day in a striped blouse and matching blue silk skirt. A natty red bow tie finished off the ensemble. Ellie's best friend was desperately excited to finally explore India, a land that constituted a quarter of her heritage. Though both her mother and grandmother had been born here, Constance knew relatively little of the country and was determined to soak up as much about it as she could.

She had spent most of the trip pressed to the window of the carriage, exclaiming over everything they passed as they traveled up the coast, from shipwrecks to roadside shrines. But as there was currently little more than farmland to gawk at, she settled for idly turning the pages of a magazine.

"What a darling hat!" She held the magazine out to the lanky tweed-clad gentleman who sat in the chair beside her. "Isn't this a darling hat?"

Dr. Neil Fairfax did not look up. Ellie's stepbrother was engrossed in his own reading material—namely, the second volume of Mr. Dutt's Ramayana.

"That's a reference to Indra, I believe," Neil commented distractedly as he turned another page.

Constance whacked him lightly on the shoulder with the magazine.

Neil startled in response, his round gold-rimmed spectacles going crooked around his green-tinted eyes.

"Hat, Stuffy." Constance snapped the magazine open again and pointed to the accessory in question.

"Connie, I haven't the foggiest notion…" Neil trailed off as Constance narrowed her thick-lashed eyes dangerously.

"Very nice," he offered uncertainly. "Excellent… brimmage."

"Brimmage," Constance echoed musingly, flipping the magazine back around to study the hat herself.

Neil warily returned to his reading. Over the last month, his comfortable life as a respected scholar and archaeologist had crumbled into a howling maelstrom of the unknown. He had been forced to raid his own excavation, escape from a luxury yacht, and fight with swords—not that it had been much of a fight, Neil not having the least notion how to use a blade.

He'd lost his job, and his academic reputation was in tatters, but at least he looked like himself that morning, with his soft brown hair neatly combed and his yellow bow tie in place. Ellie hoped that was a sign that he was beginning to adjust to his unconventional new circumstances.

Neil and Constance were getting along well, at any rate. Perhaps the time they had spent together back in Egypt had kindled a deeper connection between them than the one they'd shared as children. Back then, Constance had been a hell-raising terror, and Ellie's scholarly, easily mortified older brother had served as an ideal target for her more diabolical pranks.

Her musings about her brother and her friend fizzled as Mr. Adam Bates stepped out of the carriage's washroom, haphazardly toweling his freshly shaved cheeks. Of course, even a freshly shaved Adam Bates still looked on the verge of sprouting stubble along his rugged jaw. He was far more gifted in that department than Ellie's reluctantly youthful-looking brother.

Adam also found himself recently unemployed. He had originally taken a leave of absence from his job as Assistant Surveyor General to the colony of British Honduras when he and Ellie had run off to Egypt, but continuing on with her to India had meant resigning his post entirely.

Ellie felt a bit rotten about that—but then, Adam had already been struggling with his own uncomfortable questions about the job. He might very well have left anyway, even if he hadn't been hijacked into chasing dangerous magical artifacts across the globe by the lady scholar who had quite literally fallen into his lap.

Not that she would mind being in his lap again. In his shirt and braces, with his sun-kissed hair still tantalizingly damp, Adam looked absolutely delicious.

Before leaving Egypt, the pair of them had managed to steal two memorable opportunities to further the physical side of their relationship. Though they had put certain practical restrictions on the activities they had engaged in, Ellie had still made herself intimately familiar with more or less every single part of Adam Bates. And by God, she could not complain about any of it... except the fact that it had been damnably too long since she'd had a chance to further her explorations. Traveling to India with her uptight stepbrother, nosy best friend, and her nosy best friend's royal and all-seeing grandmother had thoroughly foiled any chance of arranging more illicit encounters.

Maharajkumari Padma Devi was the reason all four of them were now in India. She made her chair on the far side of the train car look like a throne as she spoke in rich, authoritative tones, handing letters back to the exceptionally well-dressed Sudanese gentleman behind her. "No reply. Schedule a call for this one. And this should be forwarded to my banker."

Mr. Mahjoud had graduated from dragoman to personal secretary as he accompanied Padma on their journey. He had adapted to the role with aplomb, mustering an exceptional air of dignity in his perfectly starched shirt and silk waistcoat.

Constance's royal granny must suspect that *something* was going on between Ellie and Adam. She hadn't made any comment on the subject, which Ellie took as a sign of tacit tolerance—but she doubted that extended so far as to condone Ellie sneaking into Adam's berth to do wicked things to him.

Not that Ellie could have done that anyway, as he'd been sharing that berth with Neil for the entire trip. The notion of asking her brother to make himself scarce so that Ellie could take flagrant and glorious advantage of his best friend was enough to make her want to hide behind her book.

It was all dreadfully unfair. Why should an independent-minded woman face such difficulty when all she wished to do was enjoy the company of the man who loved her without subjecting herself to the unjust shackles of holy matrimony?

Adam claimed the sofa beside Ellie's chair, sprawling across it with his customary ease. He was joined a moment later by an explosion of gangly fawn-hued limbs from the washroom. The animal skidded to a stop against Adam's legs, panting up at him hopefully.

Ellie had been somewhat less than entirely enthused when Adam had insisted that they bring his new dog—creatively named Kalb, the Arabic word for 'dog'—along with them from Egypt.

Admittedly, she wasn't overly fond of dogs in general. She had not grown up with them, as most dog-loving people had done. The animals seemed to be either clumsy agents of destruction or needy black holes for affection.

Kalb was no exception. There was something abstractly majestic about him during those rare moments when he actually sat still, as he was a slender dog with a graceful arch to his breast and a long-haired tail that waved behind him like a flag—but everything else about the beast was pure chaos. He chased everything that moved, regardless of whether that meant darting in front of a moving tram or into a sewer. He was obsessed with food and respected absolutely no boundaries when it came to getting it into his mouth. Ellie had seen him pull an entire pheasant off a table in a moment of distraction. He once ate through the side of a canvas bag of rice.

Even now, the dog had gone conspicuously still as it eyed the breakfast plates set out on the coffee table.

Ellie realized that his mouth was far wetter than even the sight of leftover scrambled eggs ought to have justified.

"Please tell me he wasn't drinking out of the commode," she pleaded.

"He'd never do something like that," Adam assured her without looking. "Would you, buddy?"

Kalb would absolutely do something like that.

In addition to chasing anything that moved and snatching food off the counter at every opportunity, Kalb was also afflicted with a startling lack of awareness of his own substantial size. When standing on his hind legs, the dog was roughly Ellie's height. He weighed a solid three stone. None of that stopped him from jumping on people when he got excited or thinking that he fit onto laps. Whenever Adam sat down for more than thirty seconds—which was admittedly not often—Kalb tried to sneak onto the man's thighs. He would start by setting his face on Adam's leg, then add a paw, and before Ellie quite knew what had happened, the dog would have slid entirely up onto Adam's body to start licking his ear.

Adam did not discourage this behavior in the slightest.

Kalb occasionally tried to do the same with Ellie, opening his negotiations by setting his head on Ellie's lap and gazing up at her with hopeful brown eyes. Ellie responded to this with the most discouraging looks she could muster. In response, the dog would press himself mournfully to the floor by her boots, whining like a badly tuned motor.

The beast moved his commode-dampened mouth toward Ellie's skirt. She was only saved when Adam casually tossed the dog a piece of toast from the table.

Kalb snatched the bread from the air with astonishing nimbleness.

"Good boy," Adam said, rubbing the dog between the ears as it panted blissfully.

He rose to fetch himself a cup of coffee from the urn. On his way back, he paused to lean over Ellie's shoulder and examine her book. She could smell shaving soap and a whiff of something rich and hot that was unmistakably and enticingly Adam.

"Any good?" he asked lightly.

The natural rumble of his voice so close to her ear sent a shivering little thrill through her.

The Ramayana was a Hindu epic ascribed to the great sage Valmiki, who played a minor role in the tale himself. It told the story of Lord Rama, a prince of the kingdom of Kosala, from his birth and marriage to his exile and ensuing adventures. The most famous of those was his quest to rescue his wife, Sita, after her abduction by the demon king Ravana.

The story read like a thrilling adventure novel, even across the roughly two thousand years since its composition. Ellie could easily see why it was such a popular and compelling tale—though she did have her own issues with the narrative, largely around the more dubious choices Rama made regarding his treatment of his wife.

"Rama's army is crossing the sea to Lanka." The breathless quality of Ellie's reply might have had more to do with Adam's proximity than the book.

"Huh," Adam commented thoughtfully.

The hand resting on her chair moved subtly, knuckles brushing secretly against the fine hairs at the back of Ellie's neck.

Ellie held tighter to the pages as a shiver moved across her skin at his touch. "I believe he's about to engage in his final epic battle with the demon king Ravana."

"Bet that'll be fun."

One of his fingers glided along the sensitive skin by the lobe of her ear. Ellie fought the urge to either pull him down into the chair with her or throw her book at him.

Neil looked up from his own reading with a frown. "Was our carriage just uncoupled?"

Ellie had barely registered the jolt, consumed as she was with the effort of not hauling Adam down to her by his braces. She welcomed the distraction now, glancing out the window at the sign for their current station. "Khurda Road," she read aloud.

Constance spoke up with an air of casual concern—though her eyes glinted mischievously. "Did you need us to open the glass, Ellie? You are looking a bit flushed."

Ellie shot her a glare, which Constance answered with an unapologetic grin.

Adam withdrew his dangerous hand, frowning thoughtfully. "Khurda Road's just south of Bhubaneshwar. I thought we were supposed to change lines back at Visakhapatnam."

Of course, Adam had already stuffed the geography of this region of India into his head. The thought filled Ellie with a rosy glow of admiration. Adam often made self-deprecating remarks about his lack of scholarly inclinations, but he had an absolute knack when it came to maps and directions.

He glanced over at Padma, his brow arched with a note of wry suspicion.

"Send this one a basket of fruit," Padma ordered, handing another missive to Mr. Mahjoud. She continued in the same tone without looking up from her correspondence. "There has been a change of plans."

"How can there be a change of plans, Aai?" Constance demanded. "We've all been on a train for the last eight hours."

"Do you think it is impossible to receive a message on a train, Kondi?" Padma retorted dryly, using her pet name for her granddaughter. *Kondi* was a local tribal term for a little pot—an affectionate dig at Constance's diminutive size. "There was a wire waiting for us at Samalkot. We are now stopping at Puri."

"Why Puri?" Ellie pressed.

"I suppose we will find out," Padma returned blithely, handing Mr. Mahjoud another letter. "Won't we?"

TWO

$\mathcal{L}$ESS THAN HALF an hour later, the private carriage jerked to a halt at another station. The platform was remarkably busy.

Padma handed the last of her correspondence to Mr. Mahjoud as she rose and headed for the door. One of the purple-and-gold-liveried servants opened it for her from the outside.

Constance snatched up her fashionable blue hat, throwing it on over the elegantly pinned waves of her ebony hair. She hurried after her grandmother, eager to set her kid boots down on yet another part of India.

Ellie put on her straw boater, then hesitated by the stairs, glancing at Adam and the lanky gold dog panting by his feet. "Might it not be a good idea to put Kalb on a lead?" she tactfully suggested, her mind filled with visions of the animal attempting to chase down another train.

"Naw," Adam returned easily. "I've been training him."

He gave the dog's head a vigorous rub. Kalb absorbed the gesture with obvious relish.

"If you're sure…" Ellie trailed off with a skeptical look at the animal.

"He'll be fine," Adam assured her.

Kalb skipped the stairs entirely in favor of leaping from the carriage to the platform, where he shook himself with alacrity.

Warm, humid summer embraced Ellie as she stepped outside. The scent of well-spiced food cooking somewhere nearby mingled with the honeyed sweetness of the flowering bushes that lined the tracks. The air buzzed thickly with the sound of myriad distant voices, punctuated by the pulse of dull drumbeats.

Kalb stiffened at the sight of a lizard perched on the platform wall, sunning itself with a lazy blink of its yellow eyes.

"Drat," Ellie burst out—and the dog bolted after the reptile, which moved from napping to a frantic scurry with remarkable aplomb.

"He's just stretching his legs." Adam set a hand to her waist, steering her over to join Constance, Neil, and Padma.

A gentleman strode forward to greet them with bright, quick energy. He was followed by a quartet of men dressed in the same purple and gold tunics that distinguished the servants in their private carriage. As he reached them, the stranger pushed back the brim of his white hat to reveal the features of a man of roughly forty with burnished amber skin and an elegantly shaped mustache that accented his gleaming white smile. His eyes were a lighter brown that danced with sparks of gold, and he was dressed in an exquisitely tailored suit of white linen with a dashing purple cravat.

The gentleman's English was Eton polished with just a touch of Indian warmth. "There you are! And not a moment too soon. Who knows how long I could have hung about while remaining incognito?"

A tall, lean man with a hawkish nose followed him at a more sedate pace, dressed in sober charcoal. "You cannot be incognito if you are dragging a liveried retinue about with you," he pointed out dryly.

"They aren't all in uniform." The dashing gentleman jabbed a finger across the platform at a young man who leaned against the wall in a white shirt and wrapped Indian trousers known as dhotis. "Just look at Dharmendra."

"I suppose everyone will be," his companion sighed with a note of affectionate exasperation, "now you've been so kind as to point him out."

Padma pressed her hands together and gave the purple-scarfed gentleman a graceful bow. "Good morning, nephew."

With a jolt of surprise, Ellie realized it was the first time she had seen Constance's grandmother make a gesture indicating that she was in the presence of someone who outranked her.

Which meant that the grinning gentleman in the dashing white suit was the Maharaja of Nandapur.

"Uncle Vijay?!" Constance burst out.

"And you must be Constance!" the maharaja exclaimed with obvious delight. "The last time I saw you, you were in nappies—and just look at you now, you splendid thing! Come here!"

He pulled her into a hug, which Constance enthusiastically returned, bouncing on her heels with excitement.

"But why are you here? Why are *we* here? What's going on in Puri? And why are you incognito?" Constance demanded in quick, happy succession.

Padma turned to Vijay's more sober companion. "Nawaz Chowdhury. I suppose I should not be surprised to find you here."

"An honor to see you again, Maharajkumari." Mr. Chowdhury bowed. "Felicitations on your return to India."

His accent was flawlessly English without even a hint of the foreign warmth that distinguished the words of the maharaja. Listening to it, Ellie might have thought she was on Bond Street.

"Mr. Chowdhury is your uncle's solicitor and close adviser," Padma explained to Constance—with an odd glint in her eyes.

"And very dear friend." Vijay emphasized the remark with an affectionate clasp of the stern lawyer's shoulder. "Nawaz has been at my side since our days at Oxford together."

"Is that your dog?" Mr. Chowdhury placidly inquired.

Ellie suppressed a wince.

Kalb was sprinting back and forth along the wall after the remarkably agile lizard, which turned on the dog with a hiss.

The lanky canine skidded to a halt, pulling his tail between his legs with a whine of alarm.

"Over here, buddy!" Adam called easily.

Kalb sprinted across the platform and barreled into the group, nearly taking Ellie out by the knees.

She glared at the dog. He returned the look with a wide brown gaze of unmitigated adoration, tongue lolling out of the side of his mouth.

"Let me fill you in while we walk," Vijay ordered.

The maharaja led them through the small station building, his distinctly attired servants opening doors and clearing their way. As they stepped into the street, the noise Ellie had been hearing since leaving the train rose into the distinct clamor of a crowd.

Ladies in bright-hued saris hurried past the storefronts, chattering excitedly. Children in loose gowns and sandals raced after a bare-chested ascetic. Young men laughed together with flower garlands draped around their necks, faces painted with ritual marks in saffron or vermilion. Most of them moved in the same direction, toward the source of the now-clear drumbeats.

Vijay pointed to Ellie as they plunged into the thick of it, heading up the road. "You must be Miss Mallory, archivist and historian." His attention shifted to Neil. "And this would be Dr. Neil Fairfax—though you're younger than I expected."

Neil gave a tired sigh. "I'm not, actually. It's just…" He waved a helpless hand at his admittedly boyish features. "I did try to grow a mustache."

"It was terrible," Constance helpfully added.

Vijay's attention shifted to Adam, who was reluctantly shrugging into his coat. Kalb loped innocently at his heels as though he hadn't just been trying to devour an unsuspecting reptile. "And you must be the surveyor."

"Adam Bates. Your… Highness?" Adam finished uncertainly with a polite tip of his battered flat-brim fedora.

Mr. Chowdhury arched a fine black brow. Mr. Mahjoud, following Padma in his excellently tailored suit, made a sigh of long-suffering disappointment.

"That'll do," Vijay returned with an amused twinkle in his eye.

They rounded another corner, the crowd growing thicker. Vijay's servants plowed through it with practiced ease.

"I believe Auntie Padma told you that we've been chasing rumors of the reemergence of a lost astra," Vijay prompted.

"She has." Ellie hurried along behind him, the racket of music and voices from ahead of them growing louder. "We've been reading up on it. I'm currently on the third volume of Mr. Nutt's English translation of the Ramayana, though I must say the text raises as many questions about the artifact as it answers."

"All of which I will be happy to address once we've sorted out a slightly more immediate difficulty," Vijay assured her.

"Which is?" Neil prompted, nervously adjusting his spectacles.

The maharaja and his solicitor exchanged a significant look.

"There are certain persons of interest here in India that Nawaz and I keep tabs on as a matter of course." Vijay's tone was careful.

"Persons of interest?" Adam echoed significantly.

Mr. Chowdhury answered him. "One does not survive as an autonomous state in a land ruled by a British imperial viceroy without constant vigilance."

He punctuated the remark with a pointed look at Vijay.

For the last century, the Indian subcontinent had been dominated by the British—first under the East India Company, and then under the Raj, a form of direct rule by the government of the United Kingdom where a viceroy served as the queen's royal representative. Within the Raj's vast territory lay several hundred smaller kingdoms. Known as "princely states," they possessed varying degrees of independence from the crown.

Nandapur was one such kingdom, technically owing fealty to the viceroy and the empire he represented while retaining some level of control over its own lands.

Ellie could imagine that such a position came with complications.

Vijay sobered. "One of the more *troubling* individuals that Nawaz and I have been monitoring is Colonel Charles Borthwick, the General Superintendent of the Thuggee and Dacoity Department."

"Thuggee and Dacoity Department?" Constance pressed, hurrying along at her royal relative's side.

"A prettier way of referring to the Raj's secret police," Padma explained flatly.

"What kind of secret police are we talking about?" Adam demanded.

"Legally, Borthwick can detain any Indian he chooses for questioning indefinitely," Mr. Chowdhury elaborated. "Along with their families."

Outrage snapped through Ellie. "Their families? *Indefinitely?* How is that legal?"

"Because it ensures the security of the empire, of course." The solicitor's words were edged with irony.

"Nor are Borthwick's methods of interrogation known for being over-gentle," Vijay added in what Ellie could already tell was an uncharacteristically grim tone.

"He uses every power he is granted," Mr. Chowdhury elaborated. "Charles Borthwick is the sort of colonial administrator who looks around India and sees nothing but threat."

The words sent a chill creeping over Ellie's skin despite the sultry heat of the day.

"When one of Nawaz's sources told us that Borthwick had shown an unusual interest in the temple of Lord Jagannath here in Puri…" Vijay began.

Mr. Chowdhury winced. "I do wish you wouldn't go about casually mentioning my *sources*."

Vijay flashed him a frankly unrepentant grin before continuing. "We looked into it—and learned that Borthwick's agent had been asking questions about one of the temple's well-kept secrets… a certain rare and important sixteenth century vernacular manuscript of Lord Rama's story, said to have been written by the famous poet Tulsidas."

"Why's a secret policeman interested in a sixteenth-century version of the Ramayana?" Adam pressed.

"Because it has an extra chapter," Vijay replied.

"An extra chapter?" Constance buzzed with excited curiosity—but then, a mystery chapter in a secret manuscript was just the sort of thing to fire up her prodigious imagination.

"It's appended to the end of the book," Vijay explained. "And was written in a script that hasn't been used for over a thousand years."

Ellie's interest piqued. "What script might that be?"

Vijay's look held a hint of challenge. "Brahmi."

Knowledge from past readings popped to life in Ellie's mind. "Brahmi was the script of ancient India, but knowledge of it was lost during the time of the Gupta empire. It was only deciphered again by British scholars fairly recently." She frowned. "No one would have been able to write in Brahmi in the sixteenth century!"

"Maybe the extra chapter is just a transcription of an older document?" Neil offered, mulling over the puzzle.

Padma cut in, her tone testing. "Tulsidas claimed to be a reincarnation of Valmiki."

"The original author of the Ramayana?" Ellie reeled from the suggestion. She had never thought too deeply about the Hindu doctrine of the reincarnation of souls—just as she'd never given much mind to the stories of magic rings and godly weapons that peppered historical documents.

Of course, she had good reason to give such matters more thought now that she'd spent the last two months tripping over powerful mythical artifacts.

She also found herself at a loss to explain how else a sixteenth-century poet could have written in a language that no one had been able to decipher for over a millennium.

"Let me get this straight," Adam began. "What you're saying is that a sixteenth-century poet reincarnated from a two-thousand-year-old saint used a lost script to record a secret message at the end of his book?"

"That more or less sums it up," Vijay agreed. "All we know of the contents so far is a single word that one of the priests at the temple was able to share with us."

"Brahmastra," Padma filled in with dark significance.

Ellie's pulse hitched at this mention of the mysterious arcanum that had brought them all to India.

The Brahmastra featured prominently in many of India's epic stories, including the Ramayana. It was one of several astras—supernatural weapons granted by the gods to those deemed worthy. Astras weren't singular objects like a mythical sword or spear. Rather, each one was a mantra—a set of secret ritual words that, when chanted, infused enormous destructive power into any object one chose.

Like a magic spell, as Constance had described it.

Ellie had tried to counter that abbreviated description with an explanation of the more sacred religious meanings of the astras—and then given up.

The Brahmastra was the particular weapon of Lord Brahma, one of India's supreme deities, who was meant to have helped create the universe itself. In the Ramayana, Rama called the Brahmastra into a humble arrow, which he then used to defeat the unstoppable demon king Ravana.

They stopped moving as the crowd thickened, packing up against an unseen barrier at the end of the road. The largest of Vijay's servants barked out commands with an air of habitual authority, forging them a path forward.

"The manuscript—the Ramacharitamanas—is kept in a secure vault under the temple sanctum," Vijay explained as they pressed through the close-packed bodies. "Except on a single occasion each year."

"What occasion?" Constance pressed.

"To accompany Lord Jagannath on his pilgrimage, of course!"

"Who's Lord Jagannath?" Adam asked. "Some local ruler?"

Kalb pressed closer to his legs, nose enthusiastically searching the air as the scents of food mingled with wet pavement, rich earth, and a great number of people.

"Don't be silly." Constance gave Adam's substantial bicep a playful whack. "He's not a ruler. He's a god."

"And he's right over there," Vijay added, clearly enjoying himself.

They pushed through another line of people to spill into a broad thoroughfare—and the noise Ellie had been hearing since she arrived in Puri rose into a roar.

The street was packed with shouting, singing, dancing, and chatting people of every age and background, from matrons decked in jewels to mendicant sadhus draped with mala beads. Flutes sang and drums pounded. Flower petals rained down from the balconies and rooftops of the buildings that lined the way.

In the midst of it all sailed a massive, brilliantly colored mountain. It took the shape of a tall, tapered pyramid, not unlike the distinct tops of the temple buildings that rose up behind the busy lines of shops and hotels. The structure was built from scaffolding covered in red and gold curtains, soaring forty feet overhead—which made it easily larger than Ellie's entire semidetached house back in Canonbury.

The silk-draped tower was set on a wooden platform with enormous wheels, which turned with ponderous grace as the entire contraption was hauled up the road by dozens of sweating, chanting worshipers clinging to thick golden ropes. Within the curtains, Ellie glimpsed a painted wooden god richly decked with jewels and flowers.

Another shower of petals rained down from above as a roar of approval rose from the seemingly endless crowd of celebrants.

"Jai Sri Jagannath!"

Constance squealed, jumping with delight. "It's the Chariot Festival! We're here for the Chariot Festival!"

"What's the Chariot Festival?" Ellie's question was a bit numb, as she was still reeling from the sheer scale and wonder of the display.

"Only the most important festival in all of Odisha!" Constance grabbed her arm, clinging to it with excitement. "Every year, Lord Jagannath undertakes a pilgrimage to the Gundicha Temple as part of a holy vow, traveling with his sister and brother. They're all loaded onto these chariots and pulled up the road."

She pointed back along the street, where two more of the massive towers trundled along, accompanied by the music and cheering of the crowd.

"And the Ramacharitamanas goes with them!" Vijay shouted to be heard as they plunged into the seething mass of humanity packing the thoroughfare. "Only not today—because the book went missing just before the start of the procession. It must have been stolen shortly after it was removed from the vault."

Neil squeezed past a group of silver-haired widows in white saris as he struggled to keep up with them. "Are you saying we need to find a single sixteenth-century manuscript in the middle of all this?" He waved a frantic hand, taking in the glorious chaos of the enormous festival.

"No!" Vijay called back over the noise. "We just need to find the man it was taken for!"

"Borthwick," Adam filled in grimly.

Mr. Chowdhury steered them into a lacuna in the sea of devotees beside a street vendor selling fried pastries that smelled of coconut.

"Is Borthwick part of it, then?" Neil pressed uncomfortably, able to speak without shouting now that they had found a place to gather more closely together. "That… Order of Albion?"

"He is a former associate of Lord Aldbury," Padma returned.

Aldbury. The uncomfortably familiar name made Ellie feel a bit queasy.

Adam cocked a skeptical eyebrow. "The Mustache's dad?"

Behind him, Kalb jumped up to snap one of the pastries from the edge of the cart, swallowing it in a single bite.

Adam automatically tossed a pair of coins at the vendor, which the man deftly caught from the air.

"The Mustache?" Vijay's mouth quirked with amusement under his own elegantly styled facial hair.

"Julian Forster-Mowbray," Ellie filled in awkwardly. "We had some deal-

ings with him in Egypt, where he was trying to get his hands on the Staff of Moses."

"He was also Neil's boss," Constance added helpfully.

Neil paled with mortification. "He wasn't my *boss*," he emphasized help-lessly. "He was just the local representative of the British Athenaeum for—"

Constance cut off Neil's protestations. "Well, we know Lord Aldbury must have substantial influence over the Order. There's no other way they would have given an idiot like Julian the job of trying to find an artifact that can darken the skies and turn rivers to blood." She made a face. "And to think I had tea with that man!"

Ellie startled. "You what?"

Constance rolled her eyes. "How else do you think Julian got pointed in my direction? Mother sought out connections to every eligible bachelor she knew to be in Egypt. She invited Aldbury over to size me up like a heifer at an auction."

"With such an attitude toward your potential suitors," Padma commented, "it is truly a wonder that you remain single. One might almost think you were opposed to marriage on principle."

"Not that there would be anything wrong with that," Ellie grumbled.

Adam coughed suspiciously.

"I'm not opposed to marriage, Aai," Constance retorted with a note of exasperation.

"One would hardly know it, looking at your record." Padma flashed Vijay an apologetic smile. "Our Kondi has been most exacting in her standards for a husband." Her eyes flashed back to her granddaughter with a dangerous glitter. "Perhaps a little *too* exacting."

Constance's cheeks drained.

Ellie had nearly forgotten that Constance's parents had threatened her with *consequences* if she failed to pick a suitor by her next birthday—which was only a few months away.

So far, Constance's formidable grandmother had appeared to be neutral on the issue. If Padma changed her mind, Constance would be in real trouble— not least because her Aai knew the vast majority of Constance's secrets and past transgressions. She had been the one to help Constance cover them up—and then add each and every one of those acts of assistance to her running tally of *favors*.

The same favors that had compelled them all here to India.

Should Padma decide to take Constance's parents' side on the marriage debate, she had more than ample leverage to force Constance to comply. The thought was sharply sobering.

"But there will be plenty of time to discuss all that later, once we have taken care of more pressing matters," Padma smoothly concluded.

Vijay cut in. "And on those pressing matters—Auntie Padma suggested that you four might be willing to assist us with this particular task, though it's not the welcome to India that I would've planned for you."

"Pretty sure we came out here to help," Adam pointed out.

"I'll admit there are some advantages to using you for the job as opposed to my own men," Vijay allowed. "I doubt Borthwick will suspect anyone is on to him about the theft, but if he does, he'll be watching for Indians, not Englishmen—or an upper-class lady in English dress," he added with a wink at Constance.

"And I'm guessing if he did catch any of your people, they'd be in a heap of trouble—that might point right back to you," Adam added darkly.

"You would be correct," Mr. Chowdhury replied with a significant look at his royal companion. "If any of you are noticed following him, you might simply pretend you meant to ask him for some sort of assistance."

"Which an Indian person wouldn't likely do, I suppose," Ellie elaborated uncomfortably.

"No," Mr. Chowdhury agreed with telling succinctness.

"Of course, we'll do it," Constance asserted brightly. "We're more than happy to aid in whatever way we can. Aren't we, Stuffy?"

"I can't claim to be very experienced with this sort of thing, but—yes," Neil confirmed, mustering up a look of determination.

Adam looked to the maharaja and his solicitor. "So how do we find him?"

"He's in charge of security for the procession," Mr. Chowdhury replied. "He will be here personally to oversee it. He's not the sort that leaves things to underlings."

"Likes to keep himself in the thick of it," Vijay added grimly.

Ellie's skin crawled with notions of what 'in the thick of it' might look like to a man who tortured the families of his suspects.

Mr. Chowdhury plucked a page from his briefcase, handing it to Ellie. "Here's his photograph."

She held an image of a man of roughly sixty, trimly built, with a stiff military bearing. He was dressed in an Indian Army uniform, epaulets loaded with the crowns and stars of his rank. A ruthlessly cropped mustache accented his lip under a hawkish nose and sharp cheekbones. His eyes looked pale against a complexion weathered by years of tropical campaigns.

"Find him and track him. Determine where he's planning to stay for the night," Mr. Chowdhury instructed. "I've looked into the usual spots, but nothing's come up under his name. He either hasn't made plans, or he's determined to keep them confidential."

"Perhaps because he's engaging in a spot of outright thievery," Vijay returned dryly. "If we know where he's hiding out, we can make a play for the manuscript then."

"Find the guy. Follow him to his rat hole," Adam summarized after a quick study of the print in Ellie's hand. "Got it."

"But where will you be?" Constance asked.

"I'm a bit too recognizable to go jaunting about the festival with you." Vijay's reluctant tone indicated that he would have preferred to plunge into the action. "And there are important reasons why I must be seen to be doing exactly what I'm expected to at the moment—which is gadding about with the upper crust as though I haven't a care in the world."

He punctuated the remark with a significant look at his solicitor.

"I will wait for you at the Hotel Jayadeva on Badasirei Road," Mr. Chowdhury instructed. "The rooms will be listed under the name Kazi."

"Auntie, you'd best stick with me," Vijay said. "Word's got out that I had my private carriage down to Madras, and you're the excuse. I'd rather Borthwick doesn't think I'm involved with Connie and her friends just yet."

Padma turned an eagle eye to the four of them. "Can I trust that you might manage this task without getting yourselves into too much trouble?"

Constance treated her grandmother to a blindingly confident smile. "Whatever would make you think we'd get into trouble?"

Mr. Mahjoud sighed eloquently. Padma arched a wry brow.

Constance thrust her hand through Neil's arm. "Come on, Stuffy."

Neil held back with a nervous look. "My luggage… please just leave it for me to manage?" He winced awkwardly. "It's… best if no one else opens it."

Vijay shrugged at the request, clearly puzzled. A maharaja with an enormous personal staff must have found it hard to fathom why anyone would want to burden themselves with unpacking their own things.

Mr. Chowdhury glanced at his watch, then snapped it shut. "You have your instructions. Find Borthwick and follow him. Return to me as soon as you know where he has gone." He fixed them all with a quelling, authoritative glare. "Do not involve yourselves any further than that."

A pair of uniformed constables turned the corner. They stopped, looking out over the packed crowd.

Vijay treated Constance to another quick hug. "We'll catch up properly soon, I promise. Best of luck—and stay safe!"

Mr. Chowdhury took Vijay's arm in a gesture that looked both quietly deferential and subtly proprietary, steering him into the luxury hotel that abutted the street.

Padma lingered behind them. "Do try not to disrupt this *very holy* festival in the process?"

Ellie considered her companions—the beaming and fashionable Constance, who almost certainly had knives strapped to her garters. Neil blinking behind his spectacles, his bow tie slightly askew.

Adam sneaking the dog another pastry.

"No disruptions," Ellie awkwardly assured her. "Ma'am."

Padma patted her cheek with a warm, dry hand. "I told you to call me Auntie, Jhia."

The request sounded like a warning.

She sailed into the hotel. Mr. Mahjoud followed after treating each of them to a glare that perfectly expressed his deep skepticism of their ability to stay out of trouble.

Neil looked from the photograph in Ellie's hand to the boisterous crowd that packed the street as far as they could see in each direction. "Where on earth do we start looking for one man in all of this?"

Adam's mouth tightened as though the figure of the pale-eyed colonel unsettled him. He scanned thoughtfully over the landscape of the festival, from the slowly rolling towers of the gods to the dancers, priests, and brash-voiced vendors.

Actors played on makeshift stages. Incense rose from roadside puja ceremonies. The wealthy crowded along the balconies that overlooked the festival, wearing Brooks Brothers suits and gold-accented saris.

Adam's assessment rose higher—and he sighed. "I think I have an idea."

"Why do you sound so unenthusiastic about it?" Ellie demanded.

"Because it involves the roof?" Adam returned queasily.

"Oh!" Ellie exclaimed with a burst of sympathetic understanding.

Adam did have a miserable time with heights.

"Maybe we can do the roof part, and you can… er… keep an eye on the dog?" she helpfully suggested.

"Sounds great," Adam readily agreed. He rubbed Kalb between his ears, the dog panting with blissful approval.

"Is your fear of heights really that bad?" Constance pressed.

"I'm not *afraid* of heights," Adam grumbled. "They just make me feel like the ground's turned into waves and somebody poured a bottle of bad hooch down my throat."

"You don't want him up there." Neil looked a bit pale at the notion. "I've seen what happens. It really isn't pretty."

"You and a dead emu, am I right?" Adam returned cheerfully, slapping Neil on the shoulder.

"A dead emu?" Constance echoed, gleefully curious.

Neil shot Adam an uncomfortable look. "Maybe we should save that story for later."

"Neil was reprimanded by the dean over it," Ellie added just a little wickedly as she recalled the scolding her stepmother had subjected Neil to over the incident.

"You are all being terribly unfair." Constance punctuated the remark with a pout.

"Just go up there and look for guys in khaki," Adam instructed. "Wherever you see the largest number of them all coming and going will be their headquarters."

Constance shrugged. "Sounds simple enough."

"Except for the part about getting onto the roof," Neil added.

"Oh, we'll figure something out," Constance breezily assured him, tugging him along.

THREE

$\mathcal{D}$RUMS PULSED AND trumpets blared. A cheer roared up as flower petals exploded from the rooftops—and Constance grinned with delight.

She was in *India*.

Her royal uncle—or first cousin once removed, if one wanted to be particular—had been as dashing, charming, and charismatic as she could possibly have dreamed. The hug he'd given her had been full of genuine affection, as though there had never been any question over her welcome into this long-distant side of her family.

Constance couldn't wait to get to know Vijay better, along with the rest of her Indian relatives—but first, she had a secret policeman to catch.

She scanned the surrounding buildings for a handy way to gain some altitude and spotted it in an incongruously familiar contraption attached to a European-style hotel across the way.

The iron fire escape was nearly hidden in the shadows of a narrow alley. Constance hurried over to it and made a jump for the ladder, which was tucked up against the lower landing. Her fingers fell just shy of the bottom rung.

"Stuffy!" she called out with an imperious wave as Neil pushed through the crowd to join her. "Give me a leg up!"

Neil looked from her to the ladder.

"Well?" Constance prompted impatiently, waiting for him to offer her a boost.

Neil's eyes glinted with an uncharacteristic spark of mischief behind his wire-framed spectacles. He reached up, grasped the lower rung, and easily pulled it down.

His expression remained conspicuously straight—save for a telling twitch at the corner of his mouth.

Constance glared at him. "Are you calling me short?"

"I never said a word," Neil protested innocently.

Constance considered this—and then curved her mouth into a smile. "I'm sure I can make it up to you later."

She made sure that the words were rich with threat.

Neil blanched. After all, he knew better than most just how creatively she could make good on it.

She set her boot onto the bottom rung—pausing as Ellie conspicuously cleared her throat.

"Perhaps Neil ought to go first?" Ellie pointedly suggested.

Neil's brow furrowed with confusion—until his eyes dropped to Constance's skirt.

The tips of his ears turned pink.

Constance's smile widened. Neil really was her favorite person to torment. He simply left one with so many marvelous ways to go about it.

With a burst of wicked triumph, she started to climb.

Constance was surveying the festival from the rooftop when Neil hauled himself over the ledge.

"It's a lot bloody harder to climb when you can't look up, you know!" he complained, resting his hands on his knees as he caught his breath.

"Is it?" Constance returned innocently.

He joined her at the front of the building. Ellie hopped over the ledge behind them, and Constance took in the sprawl of the festival.

The sheer scale of Lord Jagannath's party awed her. The street was packed as far as she could see in every direction. Even the men were dressed color-fully, decked out in long collarless kurtas in festive hues of emerald green or sunset orange. Others accented their dhotis and shirts with bright-hued scarves or painted gold and crimson symbols on their foreheads as signs of their devotion.

Tilak, Constance remembered her grandmother calling those ritual marks.

Like most proper English heiresses, Constance had been raised Church of England. She still attended services—if somewhat lackadaisically—but had always been fascinated by her grandmother's Hindu faith. Padma had made a point of making sure that Constance had at least some understanding of this part of her religious heritage.

Her Aai's quiet rituals were a world away from the celebration roaring below. Music came from everywhere, mingling with the sounds of mantras.

The smell of spicy chaat and syrupy pastries wove together with the musk of incense and crushed flower petals in the air.

Constance wondered if she had ever seen anything quite so splendid in her life.

Adam waited on the pavement below them, tossing another snack to his worshipful dog.

Returning her attention to the crowd, Constance easily picked out the khaki-clad policemen. Several of them walked alongside the chariots to guard them from interlopers, while others patrolled various places along the broad street.

She traced the movement of those distinctive uniforms through the crowd like tracking ants across the lawn.

Her attention snagged on a storefront to her left. The painted sign above the entrance was faded with age. It read *Chemist* in English, with the equivalent text in Odia script below.

Horses were tied in front of it in an area roped off from the crowd. A dozen or so policemen lingered nearby, smoking cigarettes. Others pushed out of the building as more moved to step inside.

"What about there?" She pointed out the place.

Neil leaned over the edge of the low wall to look—and Constance indulged in a frankly appreciative assessment of the lean lines of his figure through his tweed jacket.

And why shouldn't she? She'd been born with eyes for a reason, and there was nothing wrong with the way Neil Fairfax had turned out.

"It looks promising," Neil allowed. "But how can we be sure?"

Constance quickly schooled her features into an expression of placid innocence as he turned to address the question to her and Ellie.

"We get a bit closer, I suppose," Ellie suggested.

They descended the ladder—a bit more awkwardly, as other festival goers had discovered the route and were using it to secure themselves a better view. Collecting Adam and his dog, they set out to forge their way across the road.

Constance sparkled with excitement, soaking up everything around her. Vendors sold silver earrings and colorful cotton saris. A group of devotees sang to the rattle of a tambourine. A frankly gorgeous fellow dressed as Shiva, complete with tiger skin and topknot, laughed beside a gray-bearded sadhu with dreadlocked hair and a saffron robe.

A rainbow of languages rang through the air. Constance recognized both English and Odia among them. The others she could only guess at—perhaps Hindi or Telugu. One intimidatingly tall fellow with a thick black beard, turban, and scimitar was probably shouting in Urdu.

Young men dashed past her, laughing as they kept pace with the towering chariot. Others raised their hands in worship as the god moved by.

Adam stopped just shy of the chemist's shop, scanning the groups of loitering uniforms and patient horses. Constance craned her neck to look for the pale-eyed fellow from the photograph and failed utterly to see over the crowd.

Being short was dashed inconvenient at times.

Beside them, a makeshift stage had been erected at the side of the road. Neil stumbled back from a display of acrobatics by the foot of it as the actors stepped out from behind a curtain.

Ellie went oddly still as her attention locked on the performance. Her distant look gave Constance an itch of unease.

Adam noticed it as well. His eyes narrowed with concern and he put a hand to Ellie's shoulder. "Hey, you all right?"

"What?" Ellie shook her head as though surfacing through deep water.

"You went over a bit funny there," he elaborated patiently.

Ellie brushed off her skirt uncomfortably. "It's… nothing."

Adam clearly wasn't convinced, but he didn't press. "I'll take a closer look at that shop," he declared instead and slipped into the crowd.

Constance looked to the stage to see what might have made Ellie go over so strangely. Familiar characters strode across the platform—a muscular warrior with long hair and the mala necklace of an ascetic. A fellow with stuffed cheeks and a pinned-on tail, carrying a mace.

An even more impressive actor held up a bow, a quiver of arrows hanging on his back. His skin was painted a distinct sky blue.

"Oh—it's the Ramayana!" Constance exclaimed. She pointed at the familiar characters. "Lord Rama's the blue one. And that's Hanuman, his loyal monkey companion, with the tail. The skinnier fellow must be Rama's brother, Lakshmana."

The curtain shimmered, and another actor stepped into view—a woman with fair skin and a shimmering sari, her hair dressed with flowers.

"And that's Rama's wife, Sita," Constance added dryly. "Standing around doing nothing."

Constance had never been very impressed by Sita. She was supposed to be divine, just like Rama and his companions—an avatar of the goddess Lakshmi. But what did she actually do?

Nothing, so far as Constance could tell. She gave longing looks while Rama won her hand in marriage. Joined him like a piece of luggage when he was exiled to a demon-haunted forest. Then she let herself get kidnapped by the evil Ravana, sparking Rama's epic battle with the demon king.

What kind of goddess allowed herself to be kidnapped?

Not one that Constance was very impressed by.

A final player pushed through the curtain, his broad shoulders weighed down with ten maniacal faces.

The extra heads were all made of papier-mâché, cleverly scaffolded around the actor's face—not that Constance could see it yet through the undulating sea of humanity.

She pushed up on her toes for a better look. The bodies parted, and she found herself staring at a stranger—straight-backed, silver-haired, and sun-weathered with an officer's peaked cap and pale gray eyes.

The howling heads of the demon king framed the man so perfectly that for a moment, Constance was taken in by an illusion.

How odd, she thought, *that the demon king of Lanka would be played by an old white man.*

Neil grabbed her arm. "Hold on—isn't that Borthwick?"

Constance blinked away her confusion as the figure of Ravana straightened, revealing that a young Indian fellow actually wore the costume, his face painted to match the scowling papier-mâché masks braced on his broad shoulders.

It had been a trick of perspective. Borthwick, left behind, turned and slipped away into the mass of close-packed bodies.

"Adam!" Constance called out to where she could see his battered fedora near the entrance to the chemist's.

Adam pushed back to them, weaving nimbly through the crowd.

"We need to split up. Find out which way he's gone," Ellie determined.

"Neil and I can head back toward the Jagannath temple," Constance declared. "You two take the other way. Come on, Stuffy!"

She pulled Neil with her, moving against the current of the crowd. Here and there, she tried to push up on her toes to look for Borthwick over the heads of the people packed around her.

A Christian missionary railed about the evils of the "Juggernaut." A family cracked coconuts open against the curb for good luck. A shower of sweets rained down from a passing chariot, carrying the blessings of the god to his devotees.

Neil spoke up from behind her. "I've got him!"

The motion of the crowd jostled him into her back. Constance lurched at the impact, and Neil caught her by the shoulders.

Her awareness of the chaos around her was briefly overwhelmed by the press of warm hands through the fabric of her blouse.

Neil quickly let her go, pointing up the road. "Over there!"

Constance glimpsed a khaki cap and cropped silver hair—then grabbed Neil and whirled him about as Borthwick started to turn.

Risking a sideways glance, she saw the colonel's attention snag on her fashionable blue hat before he looked away again.

"Blast it," Constance cursed under her breath.

Her mind whirred furiously—and locked on a nearby cloth vendor's cart.

She yanked off her hat, tossing it at the old man inside. He caught it instinctively, blinking with surprise.

Constance snatched a length of richly patterned cloth from the shelf. Shaking it loose, she tossed it over her head, whipping the end over her shoulder.

She studied Neil with a frown, then grabbed his hat as well.

"Hold on!" Neil protested.

"We need to blend in—quickly!" Constance hissed.

With another assessing look, she grasped the end of his bow tie and yanked it.

The strip of fabric came loose, whipping out from under his collar.

Neil blinked at her.

"Put this in your pocket!" Constance ordered, shoving the unraveled tie into his hands.

She plucked a scarf from one of the wooden poles over the cart and threw it around Neil's neck. The shimmering fabric fell over the lapels of his jacket in a wave of gleaming saffron.

Constance quickly took in the overall effect—mussed light brown hair, round spectacles, gray tweed, and golden silk.

"It'll do," she concluded, tossing a generous handful of coins to the vendor and dragging Neil back into the crowd.

Borthwick had turned ahead of them, cutting across the road. Constance quickly mapped out a trajectory to intercept him, spotting what looked like a less-packed area in the sea of people that lay between them.

Neil stumbled in her wake as she tugged him after her. Music grew louder in front of them, the quick pulse of the tabla mingling with the twang of strings.

She reached the thinner spot she had been aiming for—and skidded to a halt.

The people there were dancing.

Some were members of a troupe dressed in traditional costumes. Others looked like festival goers who had joined on impulse.

The energy was electric—stomping feet and twirling bodies, all moving in sync to the rapid beat of the music.

Constance spotted Borthwick's straight-backed figure on the far side.

The dancers sprawled across half the road. The gathering was too broad for her to go around and hope to still find Borthwick when she got there.

A spray of golden flower petals burst from one of the balconies above, raining down like a fall of sun-stained snow.

Bugger it, Constance decided—and plunged into the dance.

Neil skidded to a halt at the edge of the crowd. "What are you doing?!"

"Just bounce along!" Constance shouted back to him. "We'll blend in well enough!"

She followed her own instructions—and found it surprisingly easy. Her hips swung with the rhythm of the drums, her arms rising up in time with those dancing around her.

"I don't know the steps!" Neil protested.

"Neither do I!" Constance retorted impatiently, eyes locked on where Borthwick had briefly paused on the other side of the dancers.

"Then how are you doing them!?" Neil pushed back wildly.

Constance realized that he was right. Her feet were pounding in perfect sync with the other dancers, her wrists twisting with a flourish. The music itself seemed to tell her how to move as though the tune was infectious and the dance an irresistible symptom.

Instead of answering, Constance grabbed the ends of Neil's scarf—and hauled.

Neil stumbled into the dance with a look of panic on his face.

"Keep moving!" Constance ordered as her feet continued to pound to the rhythm.

Neil muttered an unusually vibrant curse under his breath as he lifted up his arms—and started to move.

His shoulders pulsed with the stomp of his feet, body twisting in perfect time with the music.

He shot her a wild look through his spectacles—even as his hand rose to his head, elbow swinging. "How am I doing this!?"

Constance's wrists flicked as she circled her hips. "Does it matter?!"

Neil answered by clasping her hand and throwing her into a spin.

Constance whirled on the toe of her boot. She fell back—and hung there, suspended at the end of Neil's grip… just like three dozen other women around her.

The song froze.

Her eyes locked with Neil's surprised green look as they remained perfectly balanced, her back hovering halfway to the ground.

Goodness, she thought with an odd hitch in her chest. *I'm rather enjoying this.*

The beat of the silenced music carried on in the thud of her pulse. *One… two… three…*

The drum pounded, and Neil hauled Constance up. She caught herself against him, her hands going to his chest as his arm circled her waist.

She was vaguely conscious that everyone around them was doing the same thing, the entire crowd still locked in sync by the music—but only vaguely. The rest of her attention was consumed by the feeling of Neil's heart pounding against the surface of her palm.

Constance's cheeks flushed with summer heat and exertion. A bead of sweat slid down the line of Neil's jaw. His chest was firm under the light fabric of his jacket.

That's right, Constance thought distantly. *He is quite fit under all that tweed.*

Cold water blasted over her skin, dampening her blouse and kissing the heated skin of her neck. The packed festival goers broke out in cheers, raising up their arms to catch the moisture against the sultry afternoon.

A pair of young men held a fire hose nearby, aiming it out over the crowd as their friends furiously worked the pump.

Constance grabbed Neil's hand and dragged him through the roaring, cheering audience packed against the edge of the dance.

He caught her by the shoulders, whirling her to face him. "We just danced like we knew what the devil we were doing!" he burst out, pitching his voice over the roar of the crowd. "How could we possibly have done that?"

"Maybe that's just how it works in India!" she shouted back.

"Dancing when you shouldn't know how?"

Neil's spectacles were splattered with droplets. He released his grip on her to yank them off, wiping them quickly on his handkerchief.

More water—mingled sweat and damp—glistened on his skin above the vivid saffron of the scarf.

Constance's eyes locked there.

Neil put his glasses back on. "Connie?" he asked worriedly.

Constance shook off the odd fugue that had taken over her brain. *Must be the music,* she thought distantly.

A glimpse of silver and khaki flashed through the crowd ahead.

Borthwick.

"I have him!" Constance plunged forward as another cheer rose from the crowd.

Her pulse kicked up as she drew closer to her quarry, Neil pushing along in her wake.

Got you now, she thought with a burst of triumph.

Through the handful of people that separated them, she saw the colonel reach into his coat. He pulled out a slender wooden box, richly carved and accented with mother-of-pearl. It looked *old.*

Constance grasped Neil's arm, nodding to the box. "Could you fit a manuscript in there?"

"I… yes?" he answered uncertainly—and then caught her as she started to push forward. "Where are you going?"

Constance pulled her elbow free of his grasp. "He has the Ramacharita-manas with him! I'm going to get it!"

She turned for Borthwick. Neil's voice called at her back, low and urgent. "We're only meant to follow him, Connie!"

The carved box drew Constance like a lure, glowing in her mind. They could win their prize right here and now, before Borthwick even knew they were coming. How impressed would Vijay be then?

See, Uncle? I told you we could manage it…

"If I can just get a little closer…" Constance squeezed up to the final line of people that separated her from the prize.

A firm band snagged around her waist, hauling her back against a wall of tweed and saffron silk.

"Stuffy…" Constance seethed in warning.

Her hands dropped to his arm. She could break his grip if she wanted. She had practiced against just such a hold in her jiu jitsu classes—though admittedly Neil was broader and firmer than the Irish shopgirl who had tried to restrain her then.

His arm was stronger too, hard and immovable against the curve of her abdomen.

Neil's voice was a desperate rasp at her ear. *"He is surrounded by police."*

At Neil's words, the proliferation of khaki uniforms cracked through Constance's singular focus on the box. There had to be nearly a dozen men around the colonel, waiting to receive their orders.

As though sensing her attention, Borthwick turned toward her with a frown.

Neil swung them both around to face the dancers, the distant beat of the drum throbbing through the air.

"It isn't safe," Neil pleaded as the crowd shifted, forcing them even closer together. "*Please*, Connie."

The words were taut with worry—for her. Because she'd been about to try to pickpocket a ruthless spy chief in front of a full detachment of constables.

When one stopped to think about it, that did seem perhaps a bit over-risky.

"Fine," Constance conceded with a huff.

The pressure of his chest against her back shifted with his sigh of relief. His arm fell away from her waist.

"Follow me," he muttered.

He led her around Borthwick's coterie instead. Their pace was slow, Neil's body threaded with careful tension.

They stopped by a handful of worshipers conducting a fire puja by a roadside shrine. With a deliberate touch at Constance's waist, Neil steered her to look as though she were watching the ceremony—and an English voice drifted to her ears in a no-nonsense baritone touched with gravel and accustomed to command.

"And see this back to my safe at the club."

Constance risked a slight turn of her head—just enough to see Borthwick pass the antique box to an officer mounted on a black horse.

"Which club, sir?" the man returned in clipped tones.

"Which do you think?" Borthwick snapped impatiently in return. "Puri Beach."

The colonel dismissed the man with a wave, turning to another officer waiting nearby. "I want a dozen more men in front of Gundicha Temple."

The mounted constable jerked his head to two other men on horseback, and the three rode away. The crowd scattered to avoid their hooves.

Borthwick stalked off in the opposite direction, and Constance was torn by a moment of indecision, her heart still pounding with the thrill of the chase. Which way should she go—after the spy chief or the horses?

She was just coming to a decision when Ellie and Adam burst through the close-packed bodies, their dog scrambling along at their heels.

Ellie caught her brother's arm. "Did you find him?"

"Puri Beach Club," Neil blurted out automatically. "That's where he sent the manuscript. Wherever that is."

"Probably on the beach," Adam returned with a mischievous twinkle in his eye.

FOUR

Two hours later

ELLIE FANNED HERSELf against the heat as the tonga rattled along a quiet residential street. The open-air carriage was shielded by a canvas canopy and drawn by a single horse. It encountered little traffic as they rolled along, the business of the festival now concentrated around the Gundicha Temple, where Lord Jagannath would arrive later that evening. Ellie could hear only a distant rumble of noise from the celebration, the sound merging with the rattle of the tonga's wheels against the pavement.

Their party had been split, as the vehicles were too small to seat four. Ellie shared hers with Constance. Neil and Adam followed behind.

The Puri Beach Club, where Borthwick had sent the stolen manuscript, was a private membership establishment that catered to Puri's British population. It hadn't taken very long back at the hotel for Mr. Chowdhury to acknowledge that a group of English people stood a far better chance of getting access than any of his local agents. The solicitor had pulled a few strings to arrange for a temporary membership under Neil's name, deeming him the most respectable of the bunch.

Mr. Chowdhury had tried to convince Constance to stay back with her royal relatives—a suggestion she had flatly refused.

I'm the only one here who knows how to pick locks or throw a knife.

Adam had countered this, at which point Constance had quite reasonably noted that he could hardly get into the club with a machete strapped to his waist under his dinner jacket.

At least Mr. Chowdhury had accepted custody of the dog. Ellie could only imagine what sort of trouble Kalb might get up to in a private club.

Not that the solicitor had looked very happy about it—but then again, neither had Kalb. The dog had watched Adam leave with an expression of heartrending mourning potent enough that even Ellie had felt a bit bad about it.

Their mission—spelled out in no uncertain terms—had been to ascertain where on the property Borthwick was staying.

"And nothing more," Mr. Chowdhury had ordered. "Borthwick is inordinately dangerous. His Highness and I have resources that can take care of the rest."

Constance had looked perfectly content with this restriction—which left Ellie feeling suspicious.

Her friend sat beside her on the bench of the tonga, decked out in a dinner gown of gold silk with black lace accents and fashionably puffed sleeves. The color perfectly set off her complexion.

Ellie's gown was green with a wrapped bodice and narrow sleeves cropped at her elbows. She was lucky to have it, as she hadn't packed a dinner dress when she had left London several weeks earlier. Constance had arranged for this one with a seamstress in Cairo.

"They do dress for dinner on ships, you know," Constance had pointed out with a note of resigned exasperation.

"Not the one I took to British Honduras," Ellie had countered.

"That was a glorified freighter. You'll find Aai travels in a slightly more refined style."

Ellie had wanted the dress to have pockets.

It did not.

"I hope this place isn't dreadfully uptight." Constance flipped open her fan and cooled herself with it.

The sun was lowering to gold on the horizon, the light filtering over the rooftops beneath a thick layer of dark clouds. Odisha was rolling into its annual monsoon season, and the thick air was tense with the promise of rain.

"Of course, it will be uptight," Ellie retorted. "It's a private club."

"Not all clubs are dull. Some can be downright wild."

Ellie raised a skeptical eyebrow. "Since when have you been running off to wild clubs?"

Constance waved her fan airily. "I didn't say I'd been. I've just heard of plenty of them."

"I believe this one has a golf course."

Constance snapped the fan shut, grimacing. "Definitely uptight, then."

She grew uncharacteristically quiet as they rode past the tidy facades of some of Puri's finer houses.

"I suspect Aai might be preparing to join the fray over my marriage prospects," she offered at last.

The driver cheerfully ignored them. It had been clear when they were loading into the tonga that his English was limited to directions and monetary exchange.

"You're thinking of that comment she made on our way to the festival," Ellie elaborated.

Our Kondi has been most exacting in her standards for a husband... perhaps a little too exacting.

"It's more than that," Constance returned tautly. "I know when Aai's preparing to take sides on an issue. One can hardly grow up with her in the house and not learn to read the signs. It's more or less a survival mechanism."

"What does that mean for you?" Ellie pressed worriedly—because she *had* been worried for her friend ever since she had learned of the deadline Sir Robert and Lady Sabita had set for their daughter to choose a husband or risk facing *consequences*.

Pressure from Constance's parents was bad enough, but the prospect of her royal grandmother wading in was another kettle of fish entirely. Padma was formidable at the best of times—and she *always* got what she set her mind to.

Constance's mouth firmed into a grim, determined line. "It means that it's time to consider more extreme measures."

Ellie felt a thrill of alarm. "Such as?"

"An engagement with your brother."

Ellie's mind took a moment to catch up with her ears. Then she choked. "You... what...?!"

"Not for real!" Constance rolled her eyes. "Just for a little while. We'd find a way out of it when it was no longer necessary."

"How?" Ellie squeaked wildly.

Adam glanced up with a concerned frown from the other tonga, which trailed just out of earshot behind them.

Ellie gave him a wave, plastering a reassuring smile on her face.

"I haven't worked out all the details yet," Constance breezily dismissed.

Ellie fought down a low hum of panic. "And Neil is... amenable to this?"

"I'm sure I can talk him into it."

Ellie paled. "So, you haven't actually spoken with him about it yet."

"I haven't determined whether it's strictly necessary. Why alarm him in the meantime? You know how he can be."

Ellie knew how he could be.

"But why *Neil?*" she pressed desperately.

"If you hadn't noticed, we aren't exactly overflowing with eligible men in our traveling party," Constance pointed out. "It's not like I could ask Adam to do it. That would be terribly odd."

"It's not odd to ask Neil?"

"Not really," Constance returned lightly.

Ellie stared at her. The prospect of asking the next question made her wish she could squirm out of her own skin. "But do you harbor any actual… er… *romantic inclinations* toward my brother?"

"Don't be silly." Constance dismissed the idea with a wave.

"It's only that you did once suggest making him your…"

Ellie's throat dried up on the word.

"Lover?" Constance filled in easily. "Well—yes. But that was just a passing notion."

"So you aren't attracted to him," Ellie clarified hopefully.

"I didn't say that. Your brother cuts a reasonably fine figure."

Ellie wondered when the carriage had begun to spin.

"But there's a substantial difference between being attracted to someone and actively planning to lure them into bed," Constance finished helpfully.

"There… is?" Ellie frowned as she thought of her own sense of physical attraction, which had been roused from years of relative dormancy to raging, hungry life by Adam Bates.

It had most definitely involved luring him into bed.

Not that she had to lure very hard.

"I have no interest in making love to your brother," Constance asserted.

Ellie tried not to look queasy at her words. "Only to fake engage him."

"If it should become necessary." Constance cast Ellie a careful look. "You wouldn't mind, would you?"

"What on earth does it have to do with me?"

"You are my best friend," Constance pointed out. "And he's your brother."

A new dart of worry pierced through the mess of uncomfortable feelings roiling Ellie's gut. "You *would* make it clear to him that it's a fake engagement?"

Constance waved a dismissive hand. "It's hardly fake if only one of the parties involved knows it."

"Well, then," Ellie returned awkwardly. "It's hardly any of my business—assuming Neil is willing to participate."

"Why wouldn't he be?" Constance blinked with surprise as though the question truly hadn't occurred to her.

It might not have. Constance made her mad plans hard to resist.

Back in the other tonga, Neil was waving his hands enthusiastically as he chatted at Adam—which meant he was probably rattling on about the provenance of a historical place name or the ongoing effort to translate Cretan hieroglyphics.

Would Neil go along with a fake engagement to help Constance escape from the pressure to choose an actual husband?

Ellie wasn't at all sure that she knew the answer to that question.

"They do tidy up nicely," Constance murmured appreciatively beside her.

Ellie's focus shifted from her brother to the man beside him. "Adam hates jackets," she commented distractedly. "I'm surprised he had that one with him."

Adam wore his dinner dress well, the jacket hanging elegantly from his frame, but something about the sight felt wrong. Ellie fought against an odd impulse to shove the garment off his shoulders.

"Aai made him get one," Constance informed Ellie.

Ellie didn't answer. Her mind was busy picturing how Adam would look once she got the jacket off him. *Better,* she thought, conjuring up the precise gleam he'd have in his eyes as he gazed down at her in his shirtsleeves— deeply appreciative and tinged with lust.

"She has excellent tailors," Constance added, fixing Ellie with a knowing look.

The shirt wasn't right either, she thought distractedly. She really ought to get rid of that as well—tug loose each of the buttons one by one until she could run her hands over the strong, solid expanse of his chest.

"Have you considered talking to him?" Constance pressed.

"The tailor?" Ellie returned absently, imagining how she'd graze her nails over the curve of his biceps as he set her down on the dinner table.

"Not the tailor, Eleanora," Constance corrected her drolly. "Adam. About the fact that the pair of you are threatening to spontaneously combust with frustrated physical desires."

Ellie snapped open her fan, giving her flushed cheeks a breeze.

Had it been that obvious? Or just a lucky guess?

Surely Constance couldn't *actually* read minds.

Though admittedly, Ellie's thoughts had been tumbling into wicked places with increasing frequency since they had left Cairo, where she and Adam had last had a chance to enjoy each other's company in a private setting.

She thought of calloused hands pushing up her skirt under a sprawling desert sky. Of a curse on Adam's lips as his bare skin glistened in the lamplight of her room.

They had opened the door to all the myriad possibilities Adam's *improvisational skills* had to offer—and Ellie's brain refused to close it again. Utterly debauched notions kept spilling out of it at highly inconvenient times.

Like breakfast.

Constance's voice cut through the rush of Ellie's hotly tormented thoughts. "The solution to your problem isn't exactly a mystery."

"It's not?"

Her voice was edged with exasperation. "You just have to be fake married!"

"Fake married?" Ellie echoed uncertainly.

"It happens all the time," Constance assured her dismissively.

Ellie was skeptical of that—but knew better than to argue. She focused on more practical objections. "How would Adam and I even manage something like that?"

"You just start introducing yourselves as Mr. and Mrs. Bates. Who's to say that you aren't?" Constance gave her a skeptical look. "You two really haven't discussed it?"

Ellie felt as though the tonga had grown corners and she was backed into one. "We'd be lying to everyone if we did that."

"Only to a load of people you don't really care about. The ones who really matter would know, obviously. And what's the alternative? Live together in sin and be utterly ostracized by society, or keep going on as the pair of you have and die of sexual frustration?"

Ellie treated Constance to a quelling glare. "Nobody dies of sexual frustration."

Constance snapped open her fan, her tone dry. "You and Adam seem set on testing that theory."

"We haven't been *completely* deprived," Ellie pushed back desperately.

"You have since we left Egypt. Don't think that I haven't been keeping track."

"How could you possibly know?" Ellie protested wildly.

"Eleanora, it was quite clear in Cairo which nights Adam had slipped into your room to do wicked things to you. Just as it is very obvious when you two have not had the opportunity to… exorcise your sensual demons," Constance finished with deliberate tact.

Ellie stared back at her, stricken speechless.

"Not that I don't feel for you both. Aai is entirely too good at keeping track of us," Constance grumbled irritably.

Ellie let the mortification wash over her—as there was clearly no avoiding it. "This would all be so much simpler if the world would accept that two people can be legitimately devoted to each other outside of the unjust and coercive bounds of holy matrimony."

"If you're holding out for that, I think you'll be waiting a long time," Constance retorted. "You need to figure out how to live in the world as it is. And if you want my opinion, that's going to require a little creative fabrication. Or you can keep risking Adam breaking his neck climbing in through windows."

"I suppose that isn't entirely fair to him," Ellie admitted uncomfortably, thinking of a window in the Suez that had nearly led to Adam falling into the canal.

"Don't get me wrong—it's all desperately romantic," Constance assured her. "But what are you going to do when you're staying in a room without a window? You need to *talk* to him."

"How can I talk to him when I don't know what I ought to ask him to do?" Ellie protested.

"Be fake married," Constance replied flatly.

"I can't just tell Adam that I think we should become… *fake married*." The words were uncomfortable in her mouth.

"Why not?"

"For one thing, it's a further level of commitment than what we've discussed to date!"

"Oh. You mean that it would be a bit like asking him to marry you for real." Constance leaned back, thoughtfully swinging her fan. "But shouldn't a liberated suffragist think a woman ought to be able to do that?"

"Of course."

"What's the trouble, then? You know perfectly well how he'd respond."

Ellie was rather certain that she did know how Adam would answer if she asked him to marry her in earnest. She was less certain of how he'd respond to a proposal that they merely *pretend* to be.

Her temple began to throb. "This all just feels like it's happening terribly fast."

"How long do you think other people spend being engaged? Maybe a month or two. You've been with Adam for as long as that now."

"That still seems like a precipitously short period of time for assessing whether someone could be a compatible partner for the rest of one's life," Ellie asserted stoutly.

"We could argue that," Constance allowed impatiently. "But you and Adam don't seem too uncertain on that front, from where I'm sitting."

Ellie slumped back with a rising sense of helplessness. "I'd be proposing we spend our lives together bound by a falsehood. Adam doesn't really *do* falsehoods."

"Eleanora—he's an intelligent man," Constance returned patiently. "I'm sure that he's put all of this together himself by now. He must be expecting something along this line."

"Then why hasn't he said anything?" Ellie protested wildly.

"He's probably not sure where *you* stand on it. He's giving you time to think."

"He might try *talking* to me while I'm thinking," Ellie grumbled.

Constance whacked her lightly with the fan. "You are verging on the ridiculous. Tell him how you feel about all of it. Or keep torturing yourself— but do try not to set the bloody hotel on fire with your repressed lustful impulses while you're at it."

"It isn't *that* bad." Ellie's cheeks flushed again.

"It most certainly is," Constance countered. "You keep giving each other looks that you think nobody is noticing, only everybody's noticing, and it makes Stuffy's ears turn pink."

"Everything makes Neil's ears turn pink," Ellie pointed out—even as her own blush rose at the notion of her brother noticing any such looks between her and Adam.

"It does, doesn't it?" Constance sounded suspiciously thoughtful.

Ellie regarded her through narrowed eyes. "You're certain that your designs on my brother are strictly platonic?"

"What else would they be?" Constance dismissed with a wave of her fan.

The tonga slowed to turn into a gated driveway. Ten-foot-high stone walls marched to either side, disappearing into thick green hedges. The gate was open, framed by carved granite pillars. An Indian fellow in dark blue livery studied them as they pulled in but let both carts pass with a wave at the drivers.

"Goodness. It looks like a fortress." Constance craned her neck back to study the walls.

"Indeed," Ellie agreed with a pang of unease.

"Seems a bit much for a golf course," Constance complained. "Who are they trying to keep out?"

The tang of salt and a soft rush of waves mingled with the scent of flowers in the air as the club came into view. The sprawling two-story building was set on the edge of the sand, framed by flowering trees and soaring palms. It had been built in English style with painted shutters and striped awnings. A columned portico sheltered the entrance, lit by flickering gas lamps. Manicured gardens sprawled to either side, while morning glory vines tumbled over the ornamental boulders that distinguished an island in the middle of the circular drive. A pair of enormous stone lions flanked the stairs to the front door.

"It looks nice enough," Constance mused.

The club did look nice. So why did the sight of it fill Ellie with an odd sense of foreboding?

Clouds continued to gather overhead, and a soft gust of rain-scented wind danced over her skin.

The horse huffed out a frustrated breath as the tonga rattled to a stop. A uniformed footman came forward to help them down. Constance stepped daintily onto the carpet in a spill of golden silk and black lace. Ellie followed after her, wishing she wore boots instead of slippers.

Adam joined them. Even in dinner dress, he carried himself like a man who ought to have an eighteen-inch knife strapped to his belt.

Ellie's nerves wrenched. Had Constance been right? Was a fake marriage really the solution to her and Adam's dilemma? And what would Adam even think of such a suggestion?

Ellie studied his face as though she could read the answers there. His expression was uncharacteristically grim as he faced the elegantly illuminated building.

"What's wrong?" she pressed, keeping her voice low.

"Reminds me of somewhere I've been before," Adam commented quietly.

"In British Honduras?"

"In America," Adam returned shortly.

"Is that a good thing?"

His eyes darkened with worry. "Not really."

Neil tugged his waistcoat into place as he came to Ellie's other side, shoulders straight under his formal attire. Her brother had always cleaned up well.

Ellie found herself assessing how Constance reacted to his appearance.

Constance wasn't looking at Neil at all. Her eyes were on the gable at the far end of the clubhouse. "Look at all those birds by the roof!"

Dark, flickering shapes swarmed the eaves. The sight triggered an instinctive jolt of discomfort—along with chilling memories of ear-splitting shrieks in the gloom and the scrape of talons against stone.

"Those aren't birds," Ellie said carefully. "They're bats."

Constance frowned as she squinted into the growing twilight. "They must be roosting in the attic."

"Which would be a perfectly ordinary thing for perfectly ordinary bats to do," Ellie reminded herself aloud under her breath.

"Doesn't mean there aren't monsters here," Adam warned, slipping a hand under her arm.

An Englishman in a brass-buttoned uniform descended the stairs, greeting them with the sort of upper-class accent that only came through rigorous practice. "Good evening and welcome to Puri Beach. I am Mr. Sykes, the club majordomo. Whom do I have the honor of greeting?"

Neil stepped forward, managing to disguise his nerves under an air of casual authority. "Dr. Neil Fairfax. I believe my solicitor called ahead to make arrangements for us?"

Ellie saw the majordomo give a well-schooled blink of surprise at Neil's words. Her brother was cursed with looking a bit young for his age—but Sykes recovered quickly.

"Indeed, Dr. Fairfax," he returned smoothly. "If you'll accompany me to the secretary's office so that we might sign you in?"

"Jolly good." Neil flexed his hand as though actively resisting the urge to tug nervously at his bow tie.

The majordomo's gaze flickered over the rest of them, skimming easily past Ellie and Adam—then hitched on Constance as she peeked into her reticule.

The bats whirled up from the gloom of the distant gable, and thunder rolled softly in the distance.

"This way, please," Sykes directed, turning to lead them up the carpeted stairs.

FIVE

$\mathcal{A}$DAM BATES STARED up at the gilded facade of the Puri Beach Club.

Shit, he thought with a lurch of dismay.

He ought to have figured out what he was about to walk into back at the hotel. But when Mr. Chowdhury had tactfully suggested that Constance hang back from this particular mission, Adam had assumed the solicitor was showing additional concern for Constance's safety because she was a member of his employer's family.

He had been thinking of Constance as the charming heiress of a high-ranking civil servant or the firecracker partner-in-crime to the woman he loved.

The look the majordomo had just given her reminded him that she was something else as well.

The polished brass lanterns, the carpeted stairs, the manicured hedges—they all screamed of a world that Adam had lived in for years and never wanted to go back to. Pulling on his impeccably tailored dinner jacket earlier that evening had felt like forcing himself into an old, half-rotted skin.

Adam hadn't worn a dinner jacket since the day his father had disowned him.

He had never been to the Puri Beach Club before. That didn't matter. He knew how places like this worked—places with great big walls to keep the wrong sort of people on the outside.

Which meant he knew exactly what was going to happen next.

The majordomo led the four of them into the club. Adam didn't let that coax him into lowering his guard. The situation wasn't over. It was just being passed on for someone else to handle.

Shit.

They climbed the stairs to the club's public rooms, which were situated on the upper floor. More thick carpets muffled their footsteps as they passed walls of gleaming hardwood hung with dull landscape paintings. Potted palms softened the corners. The air rang with the clink of glass and a giggle of English laughter.

Waiters strode through the halls in picturesque uniforms, their white tunics and pressed trousers accented by bright red sashes. They were universally dark in complexion—but then they would be, wouldn't they?

Adam felt sick.

Thirteen years fell away, and Adam was in a different hallway echoing with the same sounds of privileged chatter and brittle crystal, where silent men carrying trays of champagne moved aside like ghosts as the silk-clad and glittering elite swept past without so much as a glance.

He remembered sitting on velvet with brandy on his tongue, forcing a smile as he endured the luxury of a world built on exactly who it kept out.

The underhanded innuendos. The backhanded compliments.

The crushing, impossible weight of his father's expectations.

Surely you can muster up enough intelligence to engage in a little polite conversation.

For a moment, it was hard to breathe. Sweat beaded on the back of Adam's neck. The dinner jacket was a vise closing around his chest.

This wasn't the same, Adam desperately reminded himself. He wasn't walking into the prison of that old life. He hadn't come here to try to force himself into a mold he would never fit—and to hear, over and over, how he was failing at it.

He would never do that again.

Adam tried to flash Ellie a reassuring smile. Her worried look lingered.

Well, maybe she should be worried, Adam reasoned grimly. This place was more threatening than the wilds of the Cayo. The opulence around him was its own sort of snake-infested jungle—one that Adam trusted far less than the kind he was used to, with actual snakes.

His hand twitched at his side, missing the reassuring feel of the hilt of his machete.

They passed a dining salon tastefully decked out with white linen and silver. Patrons in dinner gowns and jewels watched them pass, blatantly assessing.

The majordomo stopped at the door to an office that was dominated by a heavy wooden desk and a pair of richly upholstered club chairs.

"Mr. Secretary, Dr. Fairfax has arrived with his party," Sykes announced before stepping aside to admit them.

The secretary was a slight fellow, bald save for a fringe above his ears. He glanced up at Adam. "Dr. Fairfax?"

Neil stepped forward. "Ah—no. That would be me, actually."

The secretary frowned at Neil's youthful features. "You're a doctor?"

"Yes," Neil replied with a note of exasperation.

The man cleared his throat and recovered. "Apologies." He checked through the notes on his desk distractedly. "Your solicitor has already provided your references and deposit. You are paid up through July. Dues are invoiced at the end of each month, and meal tabs are settled weekly. Overnight accommodations are…"

His voice trailed off as he finally looked over the rest of their party—noticeably halting on Constance as she studied the mediocre art on the office walls with a frown of disdain, not bothering to listen to his monologue.

"…available," the secretary finished awkwardly. "But I do need to clarify that all overnight guests must be personally approved by the club council and are typically restricted to family members or business acquaintances visiting from another cantonment or overseas."

"Sorry?" Neil blinked at the man, clearly not understanding.

Adam understood.

Back in San Francisco, many establishments had made matters clear by posting signs in their windows.

No Blacks. No Chinese.

But those rules weren't always spelled out in big, bold letters. Sometimes the only sign read *Welcome*—but you weren't, really. Not if you were a certain kind of person.

Adam should have known he'd find that again here in India, where the majority of the power lay with an unwelcome set of foreigners vastly outnumbered by the people they ruled over. An arrangement like that only held if everyone Indian was resolutely shut out of the places where ruling happened, digging the lines between races as deep as battle trenches.

Constance—with her ferocious courage, her adventurous spirit, and her Indian blood—was on the wrong side of the trench.

The secretary was still talking. The words had a nervous edge. The man must be wondering whether the circumstances were about to go from merely awkward to something that qualified as *an incident.*

Adam wanted to make it an incident. He couldn't—not without sacrificing what they had come here for. And that wasn't his call to make.

"Other guests may be entertained in our North Dining Room, but we ask that they are kept clear of the rest of the club facilities." The secretary punctuated his speech with a look at Neil that was both hopeful and slightly belligerent. "Is all of that acceptable?"

It wasn't—not even remotely.

Adam answered anyway.

"It's fine."

At his uncharacteristically clipped response, Ellie shot him another quietly concerned look.

Then understanding snapped into place, and her expression fell into one of shock—quickly replaced by a hot, rising fury.

Adam took her hand and squeezed it in warning.

"Will you be needing any rooms for the night, then?" the secretary prompted carefully.

Neil opened his mouth to answer. Adam cut in first. "We're good."

Constance's brow furrowed as the unexpected tension in the exchange finally drew her attention.

It wouldn't take her long to figure out what was happening. When she did, it was going to hurt.

Helpless rage flared up inside of Adam once again. He choked it back.

He could do that well enough. After all, he'd had plenty of practice.

The secretary's posture softened with a subtle relief. "If you'll just sign here, then?"

He turned his book to Neil and handed him a pen. Neil signed the page, casting a questioning look back at Adam as he did so.

The secretary snapped the book shut. "Welcome to the club, sir."

"Yes. Well." Neil straightened awkwardly.

Adam walked out the door.

He spotted Sykes at the end of the hall, talking to one of the waiters. The majordomo glanced their way as though trying to discern how their conversation with the secretary had gone.

Adam wanted to punch him. The impulse was both irrational and overwhelming.

"Why did you tell him we didn't want rooms?" Neil pressed in a whisper as he joined Adam in the hall. "I thought we were going to stay in case it took a while to locate Borthwick."

"Change of plans," Adam returned shortly.

"But—" Neil clamped his mouth shut as Sykes approached them.

"I believe the club secretary will have related that your party would best be accommodated in the North Dining room," he offered with practiced courtesy. "Shall I direct you there now?"

At the majordomo's careful tone, Constance's expression blanked with mortified understanding.

Adam stepped between Constance and Skyes, a move that put him closer to the majordomo than was strictly polite. He pinned the man with what he knew to be a damned intimidating glare. "I think we can find our own way around."

The majordomo schooled his expression to blankness. He gave a short bow. "Very good, sir."

Adam watched the man go. Part of him ached for Sykes to turn around and make an issue out of it—one that he might've settled with his fists.

"I see," Constance said quietly from behind him.

The words hit like two short, breathless blows.

Adam burned with shame. He forced himself to face her anyway. "It's my fault. I know how places like this work. I should've steered you off back at the hotel.

"I doubt I would have listened to you if you'd tried." Constance's voice held a pale shadow of her usual wryness.

"Connie—" Ellie began, taut with anger and concern.

"I don't understand." Neil looked between them helplessly. "What's going on?"

Constance lifted her chin, her eyes flashing with challenge. "We're not taking rooms because I wouldn't be allowed, Stuffy. Because I'm part Indian."

Neil's face drained. "But that's… That's…"

His look hardened, shifting to an expression of heated fury that Adam wasn't sure he'd ever seen before.

Neil spun on his heel, stalking toward the secretary's office.

Adam caught him by the shoulder, forcing him to halt. "We do that now, we're getting kicked out of here."

Neil shoved Adam's hand away with a quick, violent gesture. "What, then? We're just going to stand around pretending it's fine that they're excluding people based on the color of their skin?"

"That's what places like this are for, Fairfax," Adam returned. "Keeping certain kinds of people out. That's why they call them clubs."

"Perhaps we should continue this conversation outside." Ellie's voice was a tense murmur.

Adam looked up the hall to see a cluster of guests pausing to stare at them. The women whispered speculatively behind their fans.

Ellie thrust her hand through Constance's arm and steered her to a door that led out onto the veranda.

Adam followed. Neil stalked behind him, anger emanating from every line of his stiff posture.

They pushed out into the thick, humid night. The veranda was deserted save for a pair of gentlemen puffing on cigars at the far end. Intimate tables lined the railing. Beyond that lay narrow gardens and the shadowy sprawl of a twilit golf course.

The lanterns that lined the walkway had been left unlit against the coming weather, cloaking them all in gloom. A rumble of distant thunder and a flicker of violet light near the horizon whispered of an evening storm.

"Do you know, that's never happened to me in England." Constance stared out over the golf course, gloved hands resting on the rail. "Isn't that funny? There are the occasional rude comments, of course, or the dowagers who are simply a little dim and warn me I'm spending too much time in the sun. But I'm not sure I've ever experienced something quite so…"

Her voice trailed off as though she didn't know how to finish the thought.

Hateful, Adam mentally filled in.

"Class matters more than color in England," he said. "You're descended from royalty. And you're an heiress."

"I suppose that's true." Constance's voice was uncharacteristically neutral, as though she were going through the motions of the conversation rather than actually having it.

That numb distance kindled a low, wrenching anger in Adam's gut.

"Well, it hardly matters," she concluded.

Neil whirled toward her from where he was pacing along the tables. His words snapped with fury. "Hardly matters?"

Constance's eyes narrowed. "I am fully capable of fighting my own battles, Stuffy."

Neil answered her with deliberate control even as his hands clenched into fists at his sides. "I know that. But those people in there think you're less than they are. And that's *wrong.*"

His voice cracked on the word.

Adam was surprised by the intensity of Neil's response—but only a little. Neil might be a quiet guy who mostly wanted to be left alone with his books, but there'd always been places where he chose to plant his standard.

And lord knew he could be stubborn as hell about it once he had.

Constance met Neil's look with a fierceness of her own, chin lifting. "But they're *not* better than me."

"Of course, they're not!" Neil burst out, throwing up his arms.

Ellie glared through the glass doors at the glittering, laughing bodies inside.

"Frankly, the whole business makes me want to burn this entire place to the ground… which wouldn't be all that hard to do, really. It looks quite combustible," she added with a hint of dangerous contemplation.

"Do you want to go home?" Adam pressed flatly.

Constance was startled by the question. "Home's a long way off," she pointed out with a hint of an edge.

"Back to your family," Adam countered patiently.

Constance returned to the rail, staring at the golf course as the sky flickered in the distance. Adam could feel the quiet struggle in her as she weighed the question.

"I won't be chased out of here by a bunch of bigots." She pushed back, turning to face them. "We need to find Borthwick. That bounder has to be somewhere on the property."

"His information would probably be in the secretary's book," Ellie offered thoughtfully. "If we found a way to lure the fellow out, we might be able to search for it."

"We don't need the book," Adam returned tiredly. "Places like this are always seething with gossip. All we need to do is talk to a few people."

"In the North Dining Room?" Constance suggested in a voice edged like a knife blade.

"No," Neil retorted sharply.

Tension snapped between them.

"That's not your decision," Constance snapped. Her tone lightened deceptively. "Besides, if we go anywhere else, it seems we'd be inviting an incident."

"Maybe I don't mind an incident," Neil returned, each word darkly clipped.

"Constance might," Ellie noted softly.

Neil's angry expression fell into something more helpless.

"I don't know," Constance mused with a spark of her usual mischief. "I could be amenable to just a bit of an incident in this place. So long as we came out on top of it."

A warm, fierce admiration rose inside of Adam, burning through the morass of guilt, anger, and worry that had been tangling up inside of him since they'd stepped up to the door.

"Still got those knives in your garters?" he asked.

Constance flashed him a white grin through the darkness. "Of course."

"Then I'm guessing we'll come out on top," Adam concluded.

SIX

A WAR RAGED IN Ellie's chest as she stepped back into the well-lit interior of the Puri Beach Club.

When she had arrived at the glittering building, she had been consumed with thoughts of Constance's easy assertion in the tonga—that the obvious solution to her and Adam's dilemma was to pretend to be married.

Constance had made it sound so simple. Nothing about it felt simple to Ellie. Not when they were talking about a man who hated to lie.

She had only half listened to what the club secretary said in his office, struggling to set thoughts of fake marriage aside to focus on their mission of locating Borthwick.

Then Adam's voice had cut through the fog.

It's fine.

It had so clearly not been fine. The tension in Adam's shoulders had made her look around to see who he was about to punch—and then she had understood.

Oh no, she had thought, distantly and terribly.

They left the veranda and stepped into the club's game room. Young men and women clustered around scattered card tables. A round of billiards was in progress, the balls clicking as they raced over pristine green baize.

Constance was composed and blazingly determined. With her fashionable gold gown and elegantly styled hair, she oozed both wealth and the natural authority of someone unshakably confident of their place in the world.

Ellie's heart tightened with admiration.

"We should split up," Constance suggested. "We'll be able to cover more of the club that way."

A low murmur of laughter sounded from one of the card tables. Scotch glasses clinked musically, mingling with the snap of the billiard balls.

Constance made a haughty assessment of the space—which was very clearly not the North Dining Room. "I'll take this one."

Neil stepped up to her. "I'll join you."

His voice carried a note of challenge, daring anyone to push back at him. Ellie had only heard that sort of thing from him when he was preparing to go to war over the proper interpretation of the Eighteenth Dynasty line of succession.

Constance looked at Neil as though considering how likely he was in his current mood to try to hit someone—and whether or not she approved of the idea.

Had her brother ever hit someone before? Ellie hadn't the foggiest idea… but she did feel oddly sure that if he had, they would have roundly deserved it.

"Fine. Stuffy's with me," Constance declared.

She strode over to one of the card tables and inserted herself among the well-dressed young people gathered there. Her introduction resounded through the room, brightly charming and unimpeachably confident.

Neil lingered beside Ellie and Adam. His shoulders were tense as he studied the reaction of the group to her arrival.

"She can handle it," Adam quietly asserted.

"Can you?" Ellie pressed, looking at her brother.

"I'll manage," Neil returned without taking his eyes off Constance.

He strode over to join her.

The diamonds at Constance's ears glittered as she casually introduced him, one of the men at the table rising to pull out a chair for her.

The club secretary had been primed to see Constance as Indian—but the people in the game room were being bombarded with her aristocratic English voice, her finishing school carriage, and her elegant dress. They wouldn't dare snub her yet—not when she might turn out to be somebody important.

Constance knew how to play that part very well.

Neil was a stiffer presence behind her, shaking his head at the fellow offering him a drink. His ready, watchful posture held the air of a guard dog.

Ellie turned back to Adam. Tension tightened his jaw as he looked across the club.

"What about you?" she asked quietly.

Adam looked startled by the comment. A deeper emotion flashed behind his blue eyes. It looked like pain. "Don't worry about me."

Ellie opened her mouth to protest.

Adam stopped her with a pleading look. "Not here, Princess."

Ellie brushed his hand with her fingers. He gave it a tight squeeze before letting her go.

"North or south?" Adam asked, looking at the doorways leading off to either side.

"Somehow I doubt we'll find out as much about Borthwick if we go north." Ellie grimaced.

"Probably not."

Constance laughed. The sound was brighter and sharper than usual, edged like a weapon. Ellie shot her a worried look.

"How many knives do you think she's wearing right now?" Adam asked.

Ellie startled at the question. "Two?"

"My money's on four."

Ellie glanced up at him with a burst of gratitude.

Adam was right. Constance could handle herself.

She threaded a hand through his arm. "South, then?"

Iron straightened Adam's spine as he faced the room, a tropical-themed lounge with rattan chairs and potted ferns. "'Sound trumpets and let our bloody colors wave,'" he muttered.

"Henry the Sixth?" Ellie commented, recognizing the phrase.

In response, Adam flashed her a hint of his usual hell-raising smile.

Ellie patted his arm, her mouth quirking wickedly. "'Cheer up your spirits. Our foes are nigh.'"

An hour later, Ellie pushed into the ladies' retiring room with a breath of desperate relief.

She despised making small talk. She was also terrible at it. How long was she supposed to natter on about horses or the weather? Whenever she tried to bring up a genuinely interesting subject—like the natural mummification properties of certain peat bogs—people responded with blank or frankly disapproving looks.

Thankfully, Adam had turned out to be adept at making people comfortable and then steering the conversation around to local authorities like Colonel Borthwick. Ellie had found it frankly shocking. She had half expected him to pin a lizard to the wall with his machete and then light up a cigar.

The Adam she had seen in the lounge had been a different person, one perfectly equipped to navigate this privileged space—but then, why wouldn't he? He'd been born to this life until he had left it to build a better one for himself.

Then Ellie had noticed the tightness in the lines that braced his smile.

He hates this, she had realized with an uncomfortable jolt. He hated every minute of it, and yet he was doing it anyway.

The ladies' room was a narrow space of floral wallpaper and polished teak. It felt like a respite after the tense exhaustion of navigating the lounge.

The night was hot and the club stuffy, even with screens open to catch the breeze from the veranda. Intermittent rumblings continued to promise some sort of storm, but the rain hadn't yet broken.

Ellie stopped at the vanity counter to press a damp towel to her face. The wet cloth was cool against her skin. She ran it over the back of her neck.

A voice spoke from behind her, bright and sharp as glass. "That tall American you're with—is he staying in Puri long?"

Ellie looked up into the mirror mounted on the wall to see a woman of perhaps twenty in a fashionably low-cut gown amply accented with cream colored lace.

"Excuse me?" Ellie prompted, struggling to catch up.

"Unless the two of you are together," the woman corrected smoothly. "I didn't see any rings and thought you might be cousins. Very… *distant* cousins."

Her smile was cold and white.

"But if I have it wrong, I wouldn't want to cut in," she continued. "That would hardly be cricket, would it?"

Ellie was left with the distinct impression that the woman did not feel the least bit inclined to bind herself to what might be considered 'cricket.' She was being toyed with, the way a bored cat might bat around a beetle it found on the floor.

The cat in the retiring room was admittedly lovely. Her pearly skin lacked any of Ellie's freckles. Her golden hair was elegantly styled. She held herself with the willowy posture of someone who had been trained in social graces.

Ellie choked as she realized that she had absolutely no idea how to answer the woman's question.

Were she and Adam together? Of course—but not in any way that a creature like this would understand.

He is mine, body and soul, Ellie burned to say. *I know the groan he makes when you touch him in the right place. I have tasted the salt of his tears on my lips. And you will keep your filthy claws off him.*

Uttering any of that wouldn't have been exactly 'cricket' either.

She and Adam weren't wearing rings. They weren't married. They weren't traveling as a couple or even the vague approximation of one. He was the friend of her stepbrother and nothing more so far as the world this woman came from was concerned.

Adam would never be tempted by a creature like the one coldly and contemptuously watching Ellie through the mirror. It didn't matter how beautiful she was.

It still bothered Ellie deeply that she had no easy way to shut the harpy down.

"He's leaving soon," she bit out instead. "We all are."

"Pity." The woman dabbed a bit of powder on her nose. Snapping her compact shut, she treated Ellie to a savage smile. "Enjoy your evening."

She drifted from the retiring room.

Ellie wondered distantly whether she ought to start carrying daggers in her own garters. She pictured what the woman's face would have looked like had Ellie thrown up her skirts to adjust her stockings and flashed a blade at her.

"Si vis pacem, para bellum," she muttered as she tugged sharply on the green fabric of her gown, meeting her own angry hazel glare through the mirror.

If you want peace, prepare for war.

Pivoting from the glass, she shoved out of the room half-blind with frustration—and ran directly into someone who was passing by.

Her human obstacle stumbled back a step as Ellie bounced off him.

"Now see here!" he spluttered... in the irritatingly familiar tones of Professor Dawson.

Who was very clearly here in Puri.

The professor brushed off his waistcoat with a red-cheeked indignation. "You might try watching where you're going, young lady!" he blustered.

Ellie stared at him. Had the man truly failed to recognize her?

Then it clicked. He hadn't bothered to *look*. She was just another female in a dress to him.

The notion filled her with a burst of annoyance. "*Really?*" Ellie snapped back.

Dawson's eyes focused—and promptly widened. "Not you!"

He tripped back with automatic fear—and then caught himself, looking around. The hall they stood in angled away from the lounge and was currently deserted.

She could see the moment the professor realized that he was facing down a single young woman, and not even a particularly big or threatening one.

The sordid notion that he might be able to get the better of her crept transparently across his features.

Ellie found herself contemplating how a physical confrontation between her and the fellow in front of her might turn out. She admittedly lacked both Constance's knives and her jiu jitsu—but then, it was *Dawson*. Even with the natural advantages of his gender, Ellie questioned whether it would really be that much of a struggle.

"And are you here all on your own, then?" Dawson prodded nastily.

"Nope," Adam replied, stepping around the corner and clamping a hand onto his shoulder.

Dawson jumped with a strangled yelp.

Adam reached around the professor to open the nearest door and shoved the man through it. Dawson fell inside, arms wheeling. Adam followed him, Ellie at his heels.

They stood in a reasonably large broom closet. Shelves along the walls were lined with towels and cleaning compounds. Mops and buckets leaned haphazardly in the corner.

"Look what you found," Adam commented to Ellie as he studied Dawson.

"I more or less tripped over him," Ellie admitted.

Dawson tugged pompously at his ill-fitting waistcoat. "I suppose I shouldn't be surprised that the pair of you would turn up here. You turn up everywhere else you aren't supposed to be. Why not India as well?"

"Having a nice vacation?" Adam asked with a wolfish grin.

"Not at all, actually," Dawson returned obliviously. "I'm quite certain I've picked up malaria. I've been feeling absolutely wretched. And the food doesn't at all agree with my constitution. It's been most unpleasant."

"How about your friends?" Adam's voice lowered dangerously.

"Friends?" Dawson echoed. "Who on earth are you—oh. Did you mean Mr. Forster-Mowbray? He hasn't come along. I gather his father isn't too pleased with him after that fiasco back in Egypt. Classic case of poor management, that, but I suppose that's what you get when you lean on relations instead of allowing more clearly qualified individuals to take charge of things. Now, if someone with a stronger university background had been assigned to lead the project—"

Ellie barely reined in her impatience. "Why are you here?"

Dawson pointed his nose in the air. "I hardly see why I need to explain myself to the likes of you."

Adam's eyes twinkled with dark mischief. "I'm not sure he's really here for anything. I think he just takes up space."

Dawson bristled. "I am a professor emeritus of the University of Saint Andrews…"

"We're probably wasting our time even talking to this guy." Adam began to steer a slightly bewildered Ellie toward the door.

"I am a critical part of this mission!" Dawson called after them indignantly.

"That right?" Adam tossed back as though only half paying attention.

"I will have you know that I was specifically requested to come lend my expertise to this endeavor," Dawson asserted defensively.

Adam raised his eyebrows in a poor imitation of being impressed. "Were you, now?"

Ellie bit her lip to keep herself from laughing out loud.

"Well, some mere colonial administrator can hardly be expected to know about the relevant ancient history and linguistic problems posed by such an expedition," Dawson elaborated self-importantly.

"Suppose not," Adam easily agreed. "Borthwick must have been real glad when you turned up."

"He is not the most effusive person, but I believe my value will become clear enough as things move along," Dawson returned, brushing at the lapel of his dinner jacket.

Ellie wondered if he realized that he had just mindlessly confirmed that he was working with the secret police chief.

"And just how long has he had to appreciate your value?" Adam dryly pressed.

Dawson frowned. "Three days?"

"Somebody wired you guys in Egypt?" Adam guessed.

"It was a telephone call, actually," Dawson returned with a conceited frown. "One can hardly trust these sorts of matters to the wires."

Ellie considered the number of operators required to connect a call from London to Cairo, all of whom would have been capable of listening in on it.

She refrained from commenting.

"Has Borthwick been a part of your order for long?" Adam casually prompted.

"What—him? He hardly knows anything about the ancient world."

"Then how'd he become interested in the Brahmastra?" Ellie cut in impatiently.

Dawson waved a dismissive hand, apparently unconcerned to learn that his enemies knew the name of the arcanum that he had been sent to India to find. "Word of it popped up in one of his intelligence networks, and the colonel could hardly leave something like that simply lying around for anyone to pick up, could he? The thing might be used to start a revolution. Thankfully, he at least knew enough about what was going on to reach out to—"

Dawson clamped his mouth shut, his eyes finally narrowing with suspicion.

"Pretty sure it was Aldbury," Adam offered helpfully.

The professor crossed his arms over his chest defiantly. "I know what you're doing. You can't make me tell you anything!"

Adam took a step toward him. The loose, lazy way he moved gave the lie to the civilized veneer of his formal dress. "Pretty sure I could," he drawled.

Ellie wondered if the room had just grown a little hotter.

Dawson scrambled back until he bumped up against a shelf of linens, arms splayed out to grip the stacks of towels.

Adam tilted his head as he contemplated the sweating academic. "What do you think, Princess?"

"I think we need to know where Borthwick has gone with the manuscript," Ellie replied—finding that she was rather enjoying this.

"Couldn't agree more." Adam had come close enough to Dawson that he now glared down at him with a looming air of obvious threat.

Ellie frowned. "Though I can't say that I approve of torture."

"What about just a little torture?" Adam tossed her a wink.

The gesture sent a shiver of wicked delight coursing down her spine.

She was fairly certain she understood Adam's strategy, and it was a perfectly good one. Dawson had the fortitude of a mayfly. Just the threat of a bit of physical coercion would surely be all they required to get him to crumble like a dry biscuit.

"I suppose I could allow just a touch of it," Ellie conceded, playing along. "If it was for a very good reason."

"I won't talk!" Dawson squawked. "You wouldn't dare!"

"I'm thinking we start with his fingers," Adam mused.

"Only the little ones," Ellie cautioned, choking back a laugh.

"Those are my favorite anyway," Adam cheerfully agreed.

Dawson made a gurgle of terror as he tried to press himself through the shelves.

The door to the broom closet swung open.

Ellie whirled to see a lean, dark figure in a plain black suit and bowler hat framed on the threshold. His coldly familiar aquiline features sent a bolt of instinctive fear through her.

Ellie greeted him levelly. "Mr. Jacobs."

Jacobs answered by pointing a pistol at her.

Adam's eyes moved from the gun to Jacobs' face. "I was wondering when you might turn up."

"I suppose it was too much to hope that I'd get through one bloody job without you two involving yourselves." Jacobs' voice dripped with irritation and disdain.

"And where have you been?!" Dawson slid toward Jacobs, pressing against the wall to stay as far from Adam as possible. "You're supposed to be on security! What use are you if you can't keep the more important members of this expedition safe?"

"Here now, aren't I?" Jacobs returned without looking at him, the pistol steady in his hand.

"Make a habit of checking the broom closets?" Adam prodded.

"I heard you from the hall." Jacobs shot a disdainful look at Dawson. "This one's loud."

Ellie had to allow that. She would certainly have been able to hear Dawson's self-important monologuing through the door if she'd been passing by.

"Bring your friends along with you?" Jacobs casually demanded.

With a jolt, Ellie realized he was talking about Constance and Neil. She opened her mouth to bluff him… and remembered with a sick jolt that she couldn't.

Because Jacobs would know.

Jacobs smiled thinly. "That's answer enough."

Ellie took a step back, her words tight. "You can't kill us."

Adam set a warning hand on her arm, but Ellie knew it was true. They had learned back in Egypt that Jacobs was only working for the Order of Albion for some obscure purpose of his own—one involving *justice.*

Whatever that meant to a man like Jacobs.

Somehow, Ellie and Adam were tied up in how he was meant to achieve it. The Smoking Mirror had shown him that—and *only* that. Jacobs had no idea what role they were meant to play.

Nor was he particularly happy about it. Ellie was painfully conscious that there were likely limits to just how far his grace would extend.

"I could still take your knees out," Jacobs snapped with exasperation.

Like that one, Ellie thought grimly.

"That'd make a hell of a mess." Adam's tone was deceptively light, but Ellie could feel the ready tension in him as he held her arm. "Lots of stained towels. Probably a whole lot of people out looking for whoever'd done the shooting."

Jacobs' jaw tightened. "Out in the hall, Professor," he ordered.

Dawson inched around Jacobs as though loath to approach the man, then scurried through the door like a startled pill bug.

"You've almost got my sympathy for being saddled with that guy," Adam commented. "*Almost.*"

Jacobs' smile was thin. "I'll say hello to Dr. Fairfax and Miss Tyrrell for you."

He stepped back and slammed the door.

Adam raced over, immediately rattling the knob. It didn't budge.

"He's locked us in?" Ellie surmised.

"Bastard," Adam cursed, thumping the door with his fist.

"Could we break it down?"

Adam's mouth curved into a smirk. "I do have a bit of a knack for kicking through doors."

Ellie's cheeks flushed as she recalled how Adam had burst into her washroom back in British Honduras, covered in muck and waving his machete. At the time, she had been only peripherally aware of just how nicely his muddy shirt had conformed to the contours of his physique, being more concerned with removing him from the premises. In memory, the incident took on a rather different tone.

Adam cheerfully shucked off his dinner jacket and tossed it aside. His bow tie and collar followed.

He opened the buttons at the top of his shirt, rolled up his sleeves, and ran a careless hand through his hair, disheveling the sun-kissed waves of it.

The changes shattered the illusion of a proper gentleman, leaving something deliciously disreputable in its place.

Ellie's skin flushed. "Do you know," she offered, carefully picking out each word. "It has only just occurred to me that there is no one else here."

Adam stilled. His look shifted over her—*all* over her—and darkened with heat.

He took a step closer. Ellie could feel the warmth of his body through the fabric of her dress.

Three weeks, she thought wildly. It had been three torturous weeks since she had last put her hands on him.

Which was far too bloody long.

He lowered his head, his breath dancing over the sensitive skin of Ellie's cheek. His hands clenched reflexively where they hovered just over her silk-wrapped hips. "He's going after Constance and Neil."

"Constance is extremely capable," Ellie reasonably pointed out.

Her fingers itched to reach for the front of his trousers.

"Ellie…" Adam groaned.

Ellie's moral compass warred with the lust raging through her veins as she gripped the front of Adam's shirt.

"I'm gonna try to bust the door," Adam declared, staring down at the curve of Ellie's décolletage.

"Yes, I suppose that would be sensible," Ellie returned.

"You're probably gonna have to let go of my shirt."

Ellie forced her hands to unclench. She faced Adam, blood pulsing hotly, breath short.

Adam forced himself to turn away with an irritated grumble. "Right."

He faced the door, readied himself, and lashed out with a furious kick.

The door didn't budge.

"Ow!" Adam bit out, hopping uncomfortably. "Ow ow ow ow…"

"What's wrong?" Ellie demanded, hurrying over to him.

"Damned thing's bolted! Who puts a deadbolt on a goddamned broom closet?"

"Are you hurt?" Ellie pressed.

"These shoes are useless for kicking things," Adam complained.

He kicked off the polished dress brogues in question, throwing his socks after them—which had the effect of making him look even more bloody enticing.

Ellie forced her attention back to the room before she gave in to the urge to pull him down onto the floor. An intriguing idea bloomed to life at the sight of the racks of cleaning supplies. "Do you know—I am quite certain that some of these compounds can be combined to create a little explosion."

"Princess…" Adam warned.

"How else do you propose we get out of here?" Ellie challenged.

Adam yanked on a cord dangling from the ceiling. A trap door fell open.

Ellie stared at the black mouth it revealed. "What's up there?"

"I'm guessing the attic."

Ellie uneasily recalled the swirling black forms they had seen by the gable outside. "Didn't it look as though there were bats roosting up there?"

"Little bats," Adam assured her. "Perfectly nice ones. Nothing like the last bunch. And if they're up there, that means there's a vent we could kick out and crawl through. You go first."

Ellie eyed the trapdoor dubiously. "Must I?"

"It's easier for me to boost you up than haul you in," Adam pointed out.

Ellie considered what having Adam boost her through the trapdoor was likely to involve. Her cheeks heated again—along with a few other places.

The pleasant promise of that fizzled against the far less enticing notion of climbing into a bat-infested attic.

Adam flipped over a bucket, setting it down as a step, and extended his palm. "M'lady?" he offered with mock gentility.

"Oh, fine," Ellie conceded, tugging up her skirts and giving him her hand.

SEVEN

*I*CE TUMBLED INTO cocktail glasses and balls bounced softly against green baize as Neil Fairfax watched Constance work her ruthless charm.

They had landed among the club's 'flash set,' elegant younger people who were avidly curious about the new arrivals. Neil couldn't help but be awed by how easily Constance disarmed them—even as he caught the odd glance snagging on the warm brown of Constance's complexion.

Let one of them mention it, Neil thought, his hands flexing at his sides. *Just one of them.*

He caught himself. What was he doing? He wasn't a fighter. That was Adam's role. Neil avoided fights. He liked things calm and predictable. So why was he daydreaming about the looks on the faces of these laughing, careless people if he flipped over their table?

Because he was wildly, ferociously angry. The notion that someone might try to hurt Constance simply because of who her grandmother happened to be unleashed a part of Neil that he hadn't known was there.

Now that the feeling was out, he was having a hard time pushing it back under control.

Since arriving in India, Neil had been overwhelmed by the noise, beauty, and color of the place. Everything was a surprise—like the fact that he had somehow ended up dancing at the festival earlier that day. To anyone watching, it would have looked as though he had known exactly what he was doing.

Neil had not known what he was doing. He remained at a loss to explain how he'd done it anyway.

Usually, Neil rooted himself in a new place through its history. He had known next to nothing about India's past when he'd learned that he was coming here. He had been frantically catching up, interspersing his study of the Ramayana with texts about the Mughal empire or the conquests of

Ashoka. The research hadn't been even close to enough, leaving him feeling as useless as a piece of excess baggage that Constance's grandmother had insisted on hauling with her.

Except for the fact that he could see through time.

Neil shied away from the thought, just as he'd done for weeks now, ever since his friend and former excavation foreman Sayyid had ruthlessly put the notion into his head. What good was it anyway? Neil didn't have the slightest notion how to use this supposed power of his. He had tried, of course, spending over an hour staring at the town of Suez to see if he could spot any sign of the ancient Greek trading settlement of Clysma hidden beneath the modern buildings.

He hadn't. Nor had he seen any echoes of the Ethiopian conquest of Socotra as they'd steamed slowly past the island on their way out into the Indian Ocean.

But he had known that the spire of the chapel at Fort George in Madras was a later addition to the structure. It had come to him with a feeling in his bones that made him want to saw the architectural feature off and toss it into the sea.

Neil's magical past-seeing abilities turned up whenever they bloody felt like it, not when he commanded them. They were just frequent enough to leave him questioning everything he thought he knew about his own academic abilities without offering a damned thing in return.

How many of Neil's insights over the years had been prompted by his supernatural powers rather than his scholarship? Could he even still call himself a historian and archaeologist?

Not that he'd shared any of this with Ellie, Adam, or Constance. What could he possibly tell them? Would they even believe him? Or would they think he'd gone completely mad?

Mad, Neil thought dully.

He forced his attention back to the game room. He couldn't afford to keep slipping into daydreams. He had a job to do, even if he didn't have the foggiest idea how to do it.

"So then he said, 'I know you are—but what about the horse?'" the posh fellow at their table announced, eliciting a screech of laughter from his companions.

What had his name been again? Frederick? Rupert?

"Jolly good one, Bunty," said the man beside him, wiping a tear from the corner of his eye.

Bunty, Neil reminded himself with a burst of rage.

The rage was out of proportion to what more or less amounted to a batch of uninteresting toffs talking about cricket. Neil had spent plenty of boring hours around people who had never heard of a funeral stela, never mind knowing how to translate one out of Middle Egyptian. He had never had to actively work to keep himself from punching them in the face before. That feeling was new, and he wasn't at all comfortable with it.

Constance pushed up from her chair. "I think I need a drink."

Bunty rose with her. "I'll fetch something for you. Champagne? Gin and tonic?"

"Aren't you a darling?" Constance tapped him playfully on the arm. "But I'd like to stretch my legs. Dr. Fairfax will escort me. We'll be back in a tick."

She slipped her hand under Neil's arm and flashed the table a glittering smile.

The others fell back into conversation as he and Constance walked away. The speculative glances and furtive tones made it perfectly clear who they were talking about.

Neil's hand clenched reflexively.

"They don't know anything about Borthwick," Constance reported under her breath as she steered him into the lounge. "I think we need to find an older set if we're going to track him down. Champagne, please."

The bartender pulled a bottle out of an ice bucket, filling her a slender glass.

Neil looked down at Constance's lovely, heart-shaped face, and the thought idly skipped through his brain. *I think I really would hit them, if any of them tried to hurt her.*

But wasn't Constance far more capable of that sort of thing than Neil? She had already bested Neil in a fight before—though admittedly at the time, Neil had lost his glasses, could barely see a thing, and was armed only with a book.

Perhaps he'd do better if he were ready for it.

Neil's brain flooded with images of his hands on Constance's arms. Her strong thigh thrusting between his legs as she tried to trip him. Neil using his greater weight to roll them, pinning her to the floor…

Neil blinked behind his spectacles, coming back to himself with an uncomfortable jolt. Where on earth had that notion come from?

Constance was an objectively lovely woman—but she was still the danger gnome, the diminutive monster that had wreaked havoc over his childhood. They were friends—just a couple of mates.

It was one thing to be mates and be aware that one of you happened to be exceptionally attractive. It was something else to vividly imagine sliding your hands up your mate's skirt while her ample breasts heaved against your chest.

"Drink, Stuffy?" Constance pressed, staring at him with a wary look that made Neil wonder how many times she had already asked.

Blood rushed to the tips of his ears.

"Beer," he blurted out automatically.

Neil hardly ever drank and had never been any good at it. At least a beer wasn't particularly strong.

The bartender handed him a glass. Neil jerked up his arm to accept it.

His first sip was appropriately bitter.

Constance grasped Neil's arm to lead him away—but they were stopped by a voice from behind them.

"Hold on. Is that Neil Fairfax?"

The plummy tones resonated with an uncomfortable familiarity. With a creeping feeling of unease, Neil turned.

A tall, thin man with ruddy hair and freckled skin sat at the bar. He wore a beard, and there were more lines at the corners of his eyes, but Neil still recognized him, memories flashing up from his years at Cambridge.

The man before him had played squash. Studied engineering. His father was a professor. Neil had bonded with him over a passing interest in botany. He'd been a decent bloke, though they'd never been particularly close. They hadn't had enough in common, besides the ferns.

"Fletcher." The name popped to Neil's lips with a vague discomfort. "Rennie Fletcher."

"It is you!" Fletcher exclaimed, rising from his stool to extend a hand.

Neil took it automatically. The smile he forced onto his face felt like glass, but must have been passable, as Fletcher answered it with a more genuine grin of his own.

Neil's question was a little more pointed than it ought to have been. "What on earth are you doing here?"

Constance cast Neil a concerned look.

"I've been in India for five years now," Fletcher cheerfully replied. "I'm practically a fixture at this point. They've got me on railroads, mostly, with a bit of bridge work here and there. But what are you doing out this way? I thought you were supposed to be in Egypt!"

I was, Neil thought distantly. *But then I abandoned my dig, betrayed the trust of my funders, and left the post in disgrace.*

His murderous idiot ex-employer had admittedly had a bit to do with it, but that was hardly the sort of thing one brought up in a chat at a bar.

Nor could Neil entirely absolve himself of responsibility for what had followed after.

"You know how these things go," Neil weakly answered.

"Do I ever!" Fletcher chuckled. "Fair warning—once you put down roots here, it's damned hard to pull them out. Mine was only supposed to be a two-year posting, and look at me now."

An uncomfortable silence lingered.

"This is Miss Tyrrell," Neil blurted out, remembering himself. "I've been traveling with her and her grandmother."

Fletcher gave a neat bow over Constance's hand. "Charmed. So are you on another dig, then? Something here in Odisha?"

Sweat started to bead on Neil's forehead. "I'm actually between excavations at the moment."

"Doing a bit of scouting, eh? Always was a little jealous of your line. Digging up ancient treasures must be a spot more interesting than studying water tables for laying track beds."

"I'm sure your work poses plenty of interesting challenges," Constance piped in charmingly.

"Challenges? Certainly." Fletcher smiled at her. "They just make for terrible dinner conversation. You should see the people I've bored over cocktails. You'd think they were all malarial."

Constance laughed brightly, which thankfully disguised Neil's half-hearted chuckle.

"Have you and Miss Tyrrell eaten yet? You'd be welcome to join me for dinner. We could do a bit more catching up."

Panic threatened to close Neil's throat at Fletcher's reasonable invitation.

"I'm afraid we're actually supposed to be meeting an acquaintance of my grandmother's," Constance cut in smoothly. "Only we can't seem to find him. His name is Borthwick."

Wary surprise tightened Fletcher's features. "You're meeting Borthwick?"

Something in the way he said the name gave Neil a chill. Fletcher was nothing if not polite, but the delicate tension in his voice spoke volumes— none of them good.

He thought of the officer he had seen across the crowd at the festival earlier that day, straight-backed with piercing eyes.

"My grandmother is, anyway," Constance dismissed lightly. "I expect we'll just be there to fill out the table. You don't happen to know where he's staying, do you?"

"He'd be in the Lal Bagh, I expect," Fletcher mused uncomfortably.

"The Lal Bagh?" Constance echoed.

"This whole property belonged to some Mughal prince who had his summer palace here," Fletcher explained. "Most of it's torn down, but they've got one of the old sixteenth-century buildings set up as a private suite. It's meant for visiting dignitaries and such, but to be honest, hardly anyone uses it anymore. The place has a reputation for being haunted."

"Does it really?" Constance brightened with gruesome interest. "By the nawab's unhappy wife? Or maybe a brother he murdered to secure his claim on the throne?"

"I haven't the foggiest idea, I'm afraid." Fletcher gave her an apologetic smile. "I think it's all nonsense myself—probably an excuse by the dignitaries to avail themselves of the more modern plumbing in the club building. Borthwick prefers the old palace building for... other reasons."

A hint of discomfort rang through Fletcher's inflection.

Charles Borthwick was the head of the Raj's secret police. Neil could think of several reasons why he might prefer a more private setting for his stay in Puri—some of them perfectly reasonable.

Others less so.

"That's ever so helpful. Thank you." Constance extended a hand. "It was lovely to meet you, Mr. Fletcher."

"You as well, Miss Tyrrell." Fletcher turned to Neil. "Do look me up if you're staying in the area. The club has all my details. I'd love to hear more about whatever you're working on."

Neil felt like a fraud. "I'll be sure to do that," he lied.

Constance steered him out onto the veranda. The night air was only marginally less thick than the atmosphere inside the club.

Neil gripped the rail, leaning over it as a maelstrom of emotion roiled through him.

"Are you all right?" Constance asked quietly.

"I ought to be asking you that," Neil returned shortly.

Constance tilted up her chin defensively. "I'm quite capable of taking care of myself."

"I know that," Neil blurted out, the wretched mess of feeling twisting tighter inside of him. "I just..."

He could hear the low murmur of laughter from the lounge, mingling with the clatter of silverware. His hands tightened on the railing.

"I don't like this place."

Constance studied him through the gloom of the veranda. The thunder of the monsoon rumbled softly again in the distance. "You have nothing to be ashamed of, you know."

Neil stiffened defensively. "Who says I'm ashamed of anything?"

Constance didn't answer. Her look was steady and understanding. In the face of it, a little of the tension in Neil's chest softly unraveled.

She glanced through the doors at the glittering people tipping back their glasses of champagne. "It takes more courage to walk outside of their circles than it does to fit into them."

The soft certainty in her words struck Neil to silence as he gazed down at her through the shadows.

A more comfortable glimmer of mischief sparked in her eyes. She pulled him along the veranda, peering into the other rooms in quick sequence until they reached the end of the walkway, where the public areas of the club gave way to guest suites. "Where are Ellie and Adam?"

"Maybe they're following another lead."

Constance mulled this over. "We'll have to go on without them," she concluded authoritatively.

"Where?"

"The Lal Bagh. Where else?"

"But we're only supposed to find out where Borthwick is staying," Neil protested. "That's what Mr. Chowdhury said."

"What if your friend Fletcher was wrong?" Constance treated him to an innocently imploring blink of her lashes. "We wouldn't want to give Mr. Chowdhury inaccurate information. We'll just pop over and take a look."

Neil groaned and let her pull him down into the garden.

The former Mughal palace building was separated from the rest of the club by a stretch of silent, manicured golf course. The elegant structure was roughly square in proportion, rising two generous stories from the broad gravel drive. The top floor boasted grand floor-to-ceiling windows that looked out over the grounds. The lower level had more of the feeling of a fortress, the windows narrow and high-set in otherwise impenetrable walls.

The door stood at the top of a modest flight of steps. It was closed.

"Do you think you could boost me into one of those lower windows?" Constance asked.

Neil considered the slender openings. Getting Constance up to one of them would require Neil to put his hands on places that made the tips of his ears turn pink. And he'd have to wade into a thick woody hedge of some flowering shrub to do it.

"I don't think so," he replied.

"Hmph." Constance frowned with dissatisfaction.

As they continued to study the building from their hiding place beside an ornamental pond, Neil found himself drawn toward lights that gleamed from the upper floor. The tall windows there had been left open to catch the night breeze from the sea, which rushed softly in the twilit gloom at the far end of the golf course.

Fuzzily, he noticed how the lower floor of the building jutted out a bit further than the second level, creating a narrow ledge below the windows. A stone balustrade lined the length of it so that someone might step outside to enjoy even more of the night air.

In fact, the Indian gentleman standing at the window seemed to be contemplating doing just that.

The man looked to be somewhere in his forties, his stomach rounded with indulgence under a silver-streaked beard. He cut an elegant figure in his richly embroidered kurta, which was tied at his waist with an ivory scarf. There was something authoritative about the way he held his head under his jewel-pinned turban.

"Maybe we can just walk in," Neil suggested thickly. "It's open to other guests."

"What makes you say that?" Constance pressed skeptically. "Your friend Fletcher didn't make it sound that way."

"Well, that Indian fellow in the window doesn't look like he'd be there with Borthwick, and he certainly isn't staff."

Constance stared at him.

"What?" Neil asked, dragging his gaze from the old palace building to look at her.

"Stuffy, there's no Indian fellow in the window."

"Of course, there…" Neil trailed off as he looked back at the Lal Bagh.

She was right.

There was no one at the window. The room behind it was still brightly lit. Neil could see that it was empty.

Not only that… but the balustrade was gone. Instead, the ledge simply dropped away—though Neil could pick out a couple of uneven places along its edge where one could see the remnants of old stonework.

Where the balustrade used to be.

He was doing it again, he realized with a sick lurch. Seeing the bloody past.

"Stuffy?" Constance prompted, her tone laced with curiosity.

Neil did not want Constance getting curious about this.

"Ha ha ha." The laugh rang false even to his own ears. He tried to make up for it by giving Constance a playful nudge with his elbow. "Nearly had you for a minute there, didn't I?"

Constance narrowed her eyes thoughtfully. "Hmm."

Neil's nerves tightened.

He felt a dart of relief as she returned her attention to the Lal Bagh.

"We need to get inside," she declared.

"Why?" Neil demanded. "Can't we just wait to see if Borthwick comes by?"

"What if he's already in there? We could be waiting all night."

Neil fought for patience. "And what are we supposed to do if we get inside?"

"Confirm Borthwick's location."

"That's all?" Neil pressed.

"Well," Constance allowed with an air of studied innocence. "We could also get a bit more of the lay of the land. Anything that might help Mr. Chowdhury's agents get their hands on the book."

Neil waited.

"And if we should happen to see a way to get hold of the manuscript ourselves…" Constance continued.

"Absolutely not," Neil retorted.

She lifted her chin stubbornly. "We don't know how long Borthwick plans to stay here or how quickly he might be able to translate Tulsidas's secret chapter. He could be gone by the time Mr. Chowdhury gets someone else inside!"

Neil groaned.

"We'll only try for it if we see a clear opening," Constance assured him.

"But Mr. Chowdhury said—"

Constance cut him off, suddenly fierce. "I am not walking out of this awful place with nothing, Neil."

He thought of the quiet cruelty of the club secretary's office. Constance had never hesitated to stand up to a bully, even if they were twice her size. It was a matter of natural instinct for her.

Neil would never wish for that to change.

"Fine," he replied. "But only so long as it's safe!"

"Of course," Constance agreed—perhaps a little too easily.

She gave him an uncomfortably measuring look, her eyes sparking with mischief. "You're a Cambridge-educated historian and archaeologist. And I'm sure you can speak fluently and intelligently about things like manuscripts and ancient languages."

"It depends on the language, time period, and region of origin," Neil returned with a note of irritation. "I might be able to rattle on about something written in hieratic, but that hardly means I can pick up a set of Shen Dynasty oracle bones and make any kind of sense of them. And even with hieratic, it varies based on whether they're using a standardized form or one with regional variations, the condition of the material, the—"

"I've made my point." Constance's mouth curved into a smile of musing satisfaction. "Doctor... Bartholomew Culpepper."

"Who's that?" Neil frowned.

"You," Constance replied. "When we knock on Borthwick's door."

"*Bartholomew Culpepper?*" Neil echoed with obvious skepticism.

"If Borthwick has heard of you at all—and that's an enormous 'if'—he'll know you as Dr. Neil Fairfax. Not Dr. Culpepper."

"What if he's seen my photograph?" Neil challenged, searching for reasons why this was clearly a terrible idea—besides the absurdity of *Bartholomew Culpepper.*

"How on earth would he have your photograph?"

"Someone from the Order might have sent it to him."

Constance stared at him. "You really don't know how that sort operates, do you?"

"What sort?"

"Yardborough has the king's ear," Constance replied. "Northcote is a banker who finances actual wars. Lady Hastings' family owns the better part of a county. They live in a different world than the one we're in."

"But aren't you..." Neil trailed off awkwardly.

"Rich?" Constance filled in bluntly. "Not that rich. My father's a baronet. Have you any notion how many baronets there are in England? I live at the edge of their class—near enough that I know how it works—but I'm not part of it. That lot... they don't just think they're better than the rest of us. We're not even part of their reality. They'd never conceive that a Cambridge scholarship student might actually be a threat to them."

Neil jolted with hurt at the old, familiar label.

He hadn't gone about Cambridge announcing that he was there on a scholarship. People had somehow always known anyway. It had put him in a different category than the men whose fathers owned half a railway or whose family pedigree went back to the Norman conquest.

"I'm not a student anymore," he snapped.

Constance rolled her eyes. "That's not how I think of you, Stuffy. But you know the sort of people I'm talking about. The sons of the realm's great men. They must have been all over Cambridge. You might have been at the same school, but they would have moved through a different level of it— one that you would never have gotten close to. The nice ones probably just ignored you. To the ones that were less nice, you were a resource for exploitation—or entertainment. And they knew that no one would ever call them to account for it."

"Bates threw a viscount into the River Cam once," Neil countered.

"He probably wasn't that important of a viscount," Constance declared. "And anyway, they couldn't have gone after Bates for that if they'd wanted to. He was one of them."

Neil stiffened with indignation. "Bates was nothing like those fellows!"

"I'm not talking about his personality," Constance returned steadily. "I'm talking about his family. They're definitely *great men*. Adam might have marched to his own drum, but at that point, he was still George Bates's son. And George Bates isn't the sort of man you cross."

Constance looked thoughtful. "Honestly, it's a miracle Adam turned out the way he did—or that he managed to get away from that world at all. But I think you can still see the scars if you look closely."

Neil reeled from the notion. *Scars?* Adam had always seemed like an immovable force, so sure of himself that it would take an avalanche to budge him.

But maybe there was more to it than that—something Neil might have caught onto if he hadn't been so busy wishing he had half of Adam's confidence.

"How do you know all this?" he asked, bewildered.

Constance looked back at the glittering lights of the club. "My mother throws every remotely viable man she finds at me. And as I'm a pretty face with a plush dowry, there are plenty of them willing to try. Most are simply bad—dull or self-obsessed, treating me like a luxurious accessory they want to dress up their drawing rooms. But the ones from the Order of Albion's world… I'm supposed to be awash with joy that they've even noticed I exist. The notion that I might not be—that I might have my own thoughts and ambitions and dreams—is beyond their power of comprehension."

Neil reeled from her revelations. Most of the powerful men at Cambridge had simply ignored him—once the bullies among them had realized that Bates would give them hell if they made Neil a target.

What Constance was describing sounded far worse. He thought of what it might feel like to have one of those *great men* take an interest in you—and wonder whether you'd be allowed to refuse.

Neil couldn't comprehend how anyone could meet Constance and believe that they could shove her into some mold of what they wanted. He had certainly never had any choice but to see her for exactly who she was, whether she was hiding his textbooks in hedgerows or leaping at him with a wooden sword while 'playing Brutus.'

'Sic semper tyrannis!' was the only Latin he'd ever heard her properly use.

"Anyone who thinks you're just a pretty face deserves to get tossed onto the floor," he grumbled.

Constance's mouth quirked into a smile. "That's very kind of you, Stuffy." She turned back to the golden gleam of the Mughal building. "At any rate, men like Northcote or Yardborough—or Lord Aldbury—aren't going to see a couple of women and a no-name archaeologist as a threat. Even Bates is invisible to them. They likely haven't made the connection. I'm sure his father isn't putting it about that his oldest son now works as a lowly colonial surveyor. The Order has no idea where Adam came from. They'd never believe any of us clever or resourceful enough to follow them all the way here to India. We could probably give them your real name at the door, and it wouldn't make any difference."

Neil warily contemplated the brightly lit windows of the old palace. "I think I'll stick with Culpepper."

"Wonderful!" Constance took his arm as her eyes sparkled with distinctly danger-gnomish energy. "Now help me steal some laundry."

"Why wouldn't we?" Neil agreed with resigned dismay.

EIGHT

Ten minutes later

EIL STOOD in front of a sixteenth-century Mughal summer palace and muttered a curse.

Evening had fallen. The thick clouds overhead were tinted a rich purple. Light from the windows spilled across the crushed gravel of the drive as a gust of rain-scented wind sent flower petals dancing over the stones.

With a crunch of footsteps, Constance joined him. Her gold dinner dress was gone, replaced by a pair of white trousers and a tunic belted at the waist by a red sash. A white turban hid the thick waves of her hair. She had stolen her new ensemble off the laundry line by the club facilities building, forcing Neil to watch the path as she shucked out of her gown and corset. His ears still rang with the sound of rustling cloth.

Neil gave Constance's disguise a careful study. The loose clothes concealed the feminine shape of her body, but he wasn't sure how anyone could look at her face and not know that she was a woman.

But then, how likely was anyone to look at her face? She was playing the part of a servant, a category of people who were invisible in a place like this.

He prayed that she could stay invisible.

A figure lurked at the bottom of the stairs. The light fell across a khaki uniform and cap, marking the man as a member of Borthwick's Indian Police detachment. The orange spark of a cigarette flared against the gloom.

"Just stick to the plan," Constance assured him in a whisper. "It'll be fine."

"Why wouldn't it be?" Neil muttered under his breath.

The constable straightened as they approached. "Yes?" he asked in heavily accented English, his eyes flicking over Neil's formal British attire.

"Dr. Bartholomew Culpepper calling for Colonel Borthwick," Neil announced.

He half expected the constable to push back about the lateness of the hour, the unscheduled visit—or the utter ridiculousness of his alias.

The man's face revealed nothing. Instead, he called up to the door, where another policeman stepped out of the shadows. The two had a brief exchange in Odia, and the second man slipped into the building.

Neil waited with the first constable, the silence growing painfully awkward. Should he try to make some kind of small talk? He quickly dismissed the idea and tried not to look too closely at the rifle slung over the man's shoulder.

The second constable returned. "The colonel will see you. Your boy?"

It took Neil a moment to realize that he was talking about Constance. He tried not to panic at the idea of either policeman undertaking a more detailed inspection of his supposed servant.

"He stays with me," Neil quickly demanded in what he hoped sounded reasonably authoritative.

The constable by the door accepted this with a shrug. "This way, sahib."

Neil stepped into a high-ceilinged hall. To his left, ornate arches framed rooms furnished with French settees and teak side tables. Only the richly patterned tiles and the distinct curves of the stonework spoke to the building's Mughal past.

A grand staircase rose to Neil's right, carpeted by a dull runner held down with brass studs.

His guide led them through the hall to a door that opened into a garden. The enclosed space was abundant with the scent of jasmine. A sprawling jacaranda tree, a month past bloom, cast deeper shadows over a patch of ferns.

Beyond the wall, violet light flickered across the distant edge of the clouds.

The man from the festival sat at a small wrought iron table. Borthwick was still in uniform, even as he sipped on a crystal glass of scotch.

"Culpepper, was it? Can't say I know the name." He pinned Neil with a cold gray stare. "Or you."

"We haven't met," Neil admitted. "I was a professor at Durham for a number of years before leaving to pursue independently funded research projects."

He clung to the story, which he'd quickly concocted on their way there.

Constance had wanted him to pretend to be an Oxford don who had fallen into disgrace after running off with the dean's daughter.

Are we trying to bluff Borthwick or write a sensational novel? Neil had pressed back.

"And how may I help you, Dr. Culpepper?" Borthwick's tone mingled the same curiosity and irritation Neil would have been feeling at an unexpected and unsociably late call.

Nothing about it signaled that the man in front of him was a threat. Neil felt a creeping sense of danger regardless. "Actually, I was sent here to help you."

"By whom?"

Neil swallowed against a dry throat. God, he was terrible at this.

"Lord Aldbury. He thought I might be able to shed some light on that little historical puzzle you're working on."

Padma had said that Borthwick was an associate of Aldbury's but had been short on the details of their relationship. Neil hoped he was making a reasonable leap of deduction—and not stumbling over a cliff.

The garden was shadowed with gloom. Neil found it hard to read the nuances of Borthwick's expression as the colonel absorbed his story.

Did Neil need to brazen this out—or grab Constance and throw them both over the garden wall before someone got off a shot?

He thought of what Constance had said while he waited for her by the laundry line.

We know far more than we ought to about who they are and what they're doing here. We can use that.

"It's a late hour for a call," Borthwick noted neutrally.

"Aldbury made it out to be rather urgent," Neil replied. "I came directly from the train—just stopped at the club for dinner. I can't think straight when I'm hungry."

He was nattering on like an idiot. He needed to get out of here. He had done what they had come here for. Borthwick was in the building. Wasn't that all they needed to know?

Constance's words floated back to him.

I am not walking out of this awful place with nothing.

A low roll of thunder sounded in the distance. The wind set a few small dry leaves dancing around Neil's polished shoes.

"I could take a look at it now, if you like," Neil offered.

His heart pounded in the wake of his own words. This was insane.

Borthwick silently studied him. Neil couldn't even begin to read what was going on in the man's mind.

"Why not?" the colonel abruptly concluded.

Without further ceremony, he rose and strode into the house.

"Follow him!" Constance hissed.

Hell, Neil thought inwardly, fighting the urge to panic.

He forced his feet to move, hurrying back into the ornate Mughal hall after the spymaster.

"Have you been in India long, Dr. Culpepper?" Borthwick asked without looking back at him.

"Just a day or so." Neil swallowed thickly, studying Borthwick from behind. The man had a whip hanging from his belt. The coil of dark, braided leather was held in place by a brass snap.

Neil didn't know much about military equipment, but it seemed like a very odd accessory for a secret policeman.

It was even odder that the man would have been wearing it while sipping scotch on his patio.

"Where were you before?" Borthwick casually demanded.

"Egypt."

Borthwick stopped.

Neil froze, conscious of Constance's presence at his back. The hall was lit by only a single lamp, but it glared like a spotlight after the gloom of the garden.

"Egypt," Borthwick echoed thoughtfully. "Interesting. What were you doing there?"

Neil reached for a response that was as close to the truth as he could get without stumbling into something Borthwick might actually have heard about. "Excavating an Old Kingdom funerary chapel in the Giza necropolis."

Borthwick absorbed Neil's answer. Nothing in his expression gave any clue as to what he thought about it.

The colonel turned away to climb the stairs. "What brought you to India, then? Presumably, it wasn't Lord Aldbury. You would hardly have had time to get here from Egypt on his word."

Neil had half anticipated the question and quickly rattled off his story. "I'm researching a paper on Gupta-era architecture. I've a theory that the Persians actually brought Late Period Egyptian influences with them when the Achaemenid Empire invaded, which carried over into later municipal building styles."

"Hmm," Borthwick commented neutrally.

Was he bored? Neil hoped the man was bored. Bored was much safer than interested.

They reached the top of the stairs, Neil's nerves jangling with his sense of how far they had come into the palace—and how far they were to an escape should they need one.

His attention dropped once more to the whip at Borthwick's belt.

"That's not standard issue, is it?" he blurted out.

Borthwick's eyes glittered with a spark of amusement. "No. Surprisingly useful piece of equipment, though."

Useful. Neil wondered what that meant—and felt even more deeply uncomfortable.

Borthwick led him into one of the rooms that faced the drive. The space was set up as a library. A heavy oak desk in the center held a stack of blank paper and little else.

One wall was lined with bookshelves, though Neil could tell that the volumes were merely decorative. A few landscape paintings hung on the walls, just as dull as the ones in the clubhouse.

A plinth by the window held a marble statue of a robust Englishman in Georgian dress and a wig. Neil could just make out the name on a plaque beneath it.

CLIVE

Borthwick swung back one of the paintings to reveal a safe set into the wall. He twisted the dial for the lock, and the door popped open.

The colonel took a carved wooden box from inside and set it down on the desk without any ceremony. "There you are."

Without waiting for Neil to respond, he moved to the window to study the incoming storm. The opening reached from just above the floor to nearly the height of the ceiling, some twelve feet overhead. The narrow glass had been swung aside to admit the evening breeze.

Neil risked a quick glance at Constance. She had positioned herself in the corner of the room and answered his look with a glare. He could readily interpret the meaning of it.

What are you standing around for?

He moved to the desk.

The box was a work of art. Relief carvings ornamented every inch of its surface, shimmering with inlaid details in mother-of-pearl.

Neil opened it. Inside lay a stack of almond-hued pages covered in age-browned script.

Bark paper, he automatically cataloged. It wouldn't be an uncommon material for sixteenth-century works from this region.

He peeked up at the door to the library, wondering whether he ought to snatch the bark pages out of the box and make a run for the stairs.

The constable from outside stepped into view beyond the threshold. He leaned against the rail of the stairwell in a manner that indicated he intended to stay there, rifle slung casually over his shoulder.

Neil chanced another look at Constance. She mouthed a word at him with barely concealed irritation.

Stall.

Pulse pounding, Neil sat down in the chair and lifted the manuscript from the box.

The bark panels were held together with a ribbon, its color paled with time. Neil loosened it with a delicate tug and began to flip through the pages, moving with painstaking care.

The bulk of the manuscript was written in Devanagari, the most common writing system on the Indian subcontinent. The script was used for a range of Indian languages, which meant the text could be anything from Sanskrit to Bhojpuri.

Nerves taut, Neil chanced a look at Borthwick.

The colonel was still gazing out the window.

Fingers shaking at the risk, he flipped to the final page.

He could immediately see that the script was not Devanagari. The lines of the characters were straight rather than rounded, each glyph set off distinctly. It reminded him a bit of how Middle Egyptian differed from Demotic.

Brahmi, he thought with a shivering sense of interest.

He turned back another page and saw more Devanagari. Only the final bark panel had been inscribed in the once-forgotten script of ancient India.

Neil couldn't possibly hope to make sense of it. He knew that Brahmi had been deciphered decades before, but it wasn't a subject he'd ever directly studied.

If he was going to buy them more time for whatever Constance might be planning, he needed to look busy—but how could he do that when he was actually hopelessly lost?

The obvious answer popped into his mind—Neil had, after all, been a student for most of his life.

"Is it all right if I take a few notes?" he asked.

"Be my guest," Borthwick replied.

Neil took a pen from his pocket with shaking fingers and pulled a sheet of blank paper from the pile on the desk.

"What do you make of India so far?" Borthwick asked.

Neil stiffened in the chair, but the colonel was still staring out the window at the still, humid night.

"It… seems very lovely," Neil replied lamely.

Constance rolled her eyes at his pathetic response.

"I assume you're speaking about the geography," Borthwick replied evenly.

Neil latched on to the excuse. "That's all I've really had a chance to see so far."

Borthwick didn't answer.

With a pang of relief, Neil returned his attention to the manuscript. As he hadn't the foggiest idea what else to write, he decided to simply transcribe it, copying the Brahmi lines onto the notepaper.

"Most scholars I've met argue that India is complicated." Borthwick spoke as though he and Neil were already halfway into a conversation. "They point to the proliferation of princely states. The diversity of languages, faiths, and ritual practices. I've heard one scholar say that India shouldn't be considered a country at all—that Kashmir has as much in common with Tamil Nadu as France does with Serbia."

Neil was conscious of Constance standing in the corner behind him, all but invisible as far as Borthwick was concerned. With a burst of indignation, he set down his pen. "Surely there are overarching elements of culture and identity that bring the people of the different provinces together."

Borthwick turned to look at him, his mouth curving into a narrowly amused smile. "Like what?"

Neil could see Constance's glare in the corner of his eye, warning him to keep his mouth shut—but he couldn't. His own anger was still too close to the surface, primed by what he'd witnessed back at the club. "The Ramayana, for instance."

"The Ramayana," Borthwick echoed thoughtfully. "A prince in exile loses his wife to a demon king. Sets out on a heroic journey to retrieve her. But that's only a devotional story for the Hindu portion of the population."

"It's not a religious text for Indian Muslims, but they might still value it as part of their history," Neil retorted.

At Borthwick's thoughtful look, Neil's throat tightened. He forced his attention back to the manuscript, scribbling a few English words over the Brahmi characters he had painstakingly inscribed. *Coveted… godly… Nominative case?*

The annotations were all nonsense, but at least if Borthwick came over to look, it would seem as though Neil was doing what he ought to be.

Possible reference to the Laws of Manu, he wrote between another copied line of text, recalling a tidbit from his Sanskrit class.

"I'll tell you what I think keeps India together," Borthwick continued after a moment, startling Neil into scraping his pen against the paper. "More than any fairy tale."

Neil paused, looking up.

Borthwick's steel gaze bored into him. "*We do.* It's the British Empire that stops India from devolving into a chaos of warring factions. Of course, it will take more than a few rail lines and telegraph wires to truly modernize the country—and the irony is that so many Indians are determined to thwart the influence of civilization every way they can."

Neil's grip on the pen tightened.

"The princely states are hardly any better," Borthwick continued as though Neil were still participating in the conversation. "They present themselves as a bridge between the old orders and the modernity and prosperity of the empire, but most of them are secretly funding the revolutionaries among the hill tribes. Oh, they're clever enough about it—they know perfectly well that if they're ever caught, it would mean the confiscation of their estates and the loss of even the shallow illusion of independence they currently maintain. But it isn't that hard to see, once you know where to look for it."

Neil found himself thinking of the moment of tension between Constance's Uncle Vijay and his solicitor earlier that morning.

One does not survive as an autonomous state in a land ruled by a British imperial viceroy without constant vigilance.

"What do you make of it, then?"

Borthwick's voice came from far closer by. Neil startled as he realized that the colonel now stood right in front of the desk.

"Sorry?" Neil started to sweat.

"The manuscript," Borthwick elaborated smoothly.

Neil scrambled, words spilling out of his mouth. "It's written on pressed birch bark—I believe the local term for it is bhojpatra. I would estimate that it dates to the late sixteenth century. The text is in Devanagari, except for this final page, which looks to be in Brahmi."

Borthwick's interest sharpened. "You figured that out faster than the other one."

The other one.

The words echoed threateningly through Neil's brain.

He could feel the potential before him for a leap of intuition—one that would either help him secure Borthwick's trust or completely bollocks things up.

We know far more than we ought to.

"Do you mean Professor Dawson?" Neil asked carefully.

"Is there someone else I should have been expecting?" Borthwick returned dryly.

"No," Neil hurriedly replied. "I just… wasn't certain that he was here."

His throat was dry. Borthwick was still studying him. The silent weight of his attention was a vise compelling Neil to keep talking.

Neil was certain that if he did, he was going to blow the game. All Borthwick had to do was continue giving him that waiting, expectant look, and Neil would spill it all.

He grasped for something he could say instead—something other than *I am trying to steal your manuscript.*

"The man's an idiot," he burst out.

Dark amusement flashed through Borthwick's pale eyes. "That aligns with my own assessment."

Relief washed over Neil. He forced a stretched, awkward smile before bowing back over the manuscript, copying out another line of the Brahmi.

How many people could actually read Brahmi?

Certainly not Dawson.

And then Neil's overtaxed brain finally spat out another obvious and deeply unsettling deduction.

If Borthwick knew Dawson, that meant that Dawson was *here*.

And Dawson would certainly know that Neil was not Dr. Bartholomew Culpepper.

Neil forced himself to keep writing. It gave him a reason to avoid meeting Borthwick's eyes. "Is the professor here, then?"

"No," Borthwick scoffed.

Neil felt a rush of relief.

"He's at the club," Borthwick elaborated—and Neil's relief evaporated.

Constance shot him another warning glare.

Neil shut his mouth. *Clearly Vedic,* he scribbled between another pair of lines on his transcription. *City… treasure… army…*

He hoped the sound of his pen scratching against the paper sounded convincingly scholarly.

The bust of Clive by the window seemed to eye him with disdain for his awful performance.

Borthwick moved to the bookshelf. Sweat ran down the back of Neil's neck, tracing along his spine. Why wouldn't the man bloody leave?

"I'm afraid this sort of work does require time."

Borthwick adjusted the line of the meaningless volumes on the shelf, leaving them a bit straighter than they were before. "Take as long as you need."

Neil risked a more direct look at Constance. She continued to be ignored by both Borthwick and his constable—just another servant lingering in the corner.

Her hand drifted to her pocket… where Neil knew she had hidden at least one of her daggers.

He shook his head urgently.

Constance frowned at him.

He frantically wrote out another line of the script. He had nearly reached the end of the Brahmi text—which begged the question of what he would do then. Go back and start over at the beginning?

The constable lingered just outside the door, looking bored.

Neil's nerves jarred at the soft scuff of Borthwick's boot on the floor.

"And that is ultimately why any effort at increasing Indian representation in the administration is doomed to failure," Borthwick commented.

"What's that?" Neil's mind struggled to connect the man's words to the earlier thread of their conversation.

Borthwick ignored him. "Some of the more liberal-minded among the civil service might claim to be working toward the goal of an independent India," he continued casually. "But India is no more capable of ruling herself than dogs are of organizing a kennel."

Neil's fingers clenched around the pen.

Constance was hearing all of this as she stood behind him, invisible and silent. Neil's own silence made him feel complicit. Every cell of his body rebelled against it—until he realized with a shiver of fear that Borthwick wasn't just putting noise into the room. The secret police chief was casually sharing his abominable thoughts on India for a deliberate and specific reason.

Coming here was a mistake. They should have gone to find Ellie and Bates. They should have asked Constance's uncle to loan them an army. A maharaja must have some sort of army, mustn't he?

Another thought tugged at the back of Neil's mind, fighting to be heard over the racket of his rising fear… something about Dawson's proximity that Neil ought to have remembered. Something important…

Neil had copied the last line of the Brahmi. He blinked down at a page filled with characters he didn't understand.

Now what?

Purple light sizzled across the night, accompanied by a tearing boom. The sky ripped open with a thick, drenching downpour that pounded against the narrow ledge outside the window. Neil blanked with momentary awe at the sheer, furious force of the storm.

Borthwick was still talking. "What the liberals fail to understand is that it has always been a matter of war here, however much it might currently wear the veneer of civil cooperation. The British presence in India has been and always will be a matter of conquest."

A door slammed open below.

Constance went still.

The constable called down over the railing. "Ki-e achhi?"

The reply was inaudible.

"Let him up this time," Borthwick snapped with a note of irritation.

Let him up. Had Dawson come back to work on the manuscript? Neil could certainly imagine the professor inspiring that tone of bare tolerance.

He shot a frantic look at Constance—but she didn't return it. Her focus moved from the door to the open window as her expression firmed with grim determination.

Footsteps sounded on the stairs, and Neil pushed to his feet.

Borthwick turned at the scrape of the chair legs on the floor, pinning Neil with a watchful, curious look.

Neil needed a reason for standing.

Clearly, he wanted to stretch his legs for a bit.

How would Dr. Bartholomew Culpepper do that?

He could pick up the manuscript.

As soon as he thought of it, Neil was suffused with the knowledge that it would be a very bad idea.

Neil snatched up the sheet of notepaper instead. He held it out in front of him as though reading it while he paced.

Run, his instincts screamed. *Run now.*

But where could he go? There was only one bloody door.

Neil forced himself to breathe. This was Dawson he was worried about. Dawson was an idiot. Maybe Neil really could bluff his way through this. Perhaps he could paint the professor as a dissatisfied academic rival. Translate a word or two of the Brahmi to show off his skills.

The footsteps reached the top of the stairs. Neil froze by the window as reality snapped into place.

He wasn't going to translate any of the Brahmi.

The newcomer stepped into the room—and at the sight of his face, fear solidified in Neil's gut like a shard of ice.

Not Dawson, he thought with cool, blinding panic as he stared at the only man who had ever actively threatened to torture him.

A man it was impossible to bluff.

A man who would kill him without being put off his tea.

Mr. Jacobs wore his usual black suit and bowler hat. Rain dripped from the brim.

"Ah," he said in a dry, even voice as he met Neil's panicked stare. "I was wondering when you'd turn up."

"Blast," Constance bit out in a very English and female voice.

Everyone's heads snapped around as though seeing her for the first time.

She bolted for the desk—and the manuscript.

Borthwick's whip fell into his hand. The coiled leather lashed out toward Constance's reaching hand with a crack like a gunshot.

She dodged away with barely a breath of space to spare.

Neil reacted on instinct. He shoved the page into his pocket, grabbed the bewigged statue of Mr. Clive from the plinth, and chucked it at Borthwick and Jacobs.

Jacobs ducked, momentarily prevented from aiming the pistol he had just torn from his coat. The statue crashed against the wall, forcing Borthwick to flinch back from the shards of stone.

Constance was still running.

She hit Neil in the chest and shoved him backwards through the open window.

He fell into a curtain of pounding rain. Borthwick shouted. A pistol cracked, and Neil felt a burn against his flank.

Terror jolted him wildly at the notion that he was about to plummet headfirst to the ground—until his back slammed against a solid surface.

The ledge, Neil blankly recalled. He had landed on the narrow band of stone that circled the upper floor of the building.

A rifle blast thundered, and chips of stone peppered down onto Neil's spectacles.

Constance's solid weight came down on top of him. Gripping the lapels of his jacket, she rolled—and they tumbled over the side.

Neil crashed into the thick, woody hedge that framed the building.

Branches tore at his face, the smell of flowers choking him. He spilled out of the shrubbery onto the gravel drive, soaked, battered, and dizzy.

Constance grabbed his sleeve, hauling him up.

"Run, Stuffy!" she shouted, and yanked him into the blinding wash of the rain as the rifle fire behind them mingled with the crack of thunder.

NINE

*E*LLIE ABSORBED THE expression of blank surprise on Mr. Chowdhury's face as he stood in the doorway to the hotel suite. She decided that it was fully justified.

Her evening dress was torn at the shoulder and smeared with bat guano, her hair half falling from its pins. Adam was covered in guano as well, stripped to his shirtsleeves and waistcoat. His feet were bare and muddy. He currently held a sixty-pound dog like a baby as it quivered with relief at being reunited with him.

That was still better than Constance, who had lost her entire dinner ensemble. She was dressed like an Indian servant—one who'd had an intimate encounter with a shrubbery. Pieces of bush were still stuck in her cockeyed turban.

Neil's face was scratched. The side of his jacket was torn. His spectacles were bent.

All of them were soaking wet.

Mr. Chowdhury took it all in with an astonishing degree of aplomb.

"I take it things did not go entirely according to plan?" he commented mildly.

They had not, Ellie acknowledged, gone entirely according to plan.

She and Adam had crawled into the attic above the broom closet, which had indeed been infested with bats. They had been perfectly normal bats, but even bats that were not flesh-eating monsters were problematic when unexpectedly disturbed.

Adam had finally managed to kick through the vent in one of the clubhouse gables. They had descended a vigorous wisteria vine to the golf course, where they had been doused by an abrupt downpour—and then nearly barreled over by an openly fleeing Neil and Constance.

With all the shouts of alarm and searching lanterns behind them, any opportunity to compare notes on the evening's activities had been cut short.

Mr. Chowdhury swung open the door, allowing them inside.

The hotel suite consisted of a parlor with two attached bedrooms and a private washroom. It was clean, comfortable, and discreet—which was good, as they had hardly been very discreet themselves when they had paraded through the lobby.

"We ran into a couple of old friends." Adam set down the dog and collapsed into an armchair, sprawling across it without any mind to the havoc he wreaked on the upholstery.

Kalb immediately crawled back up into his lap, where Adam absentmindedly scratched his ears.

Ellie could see where Mr. Chowdhury had been sitting before they came in, the place distinguished by a peaceful cup of tea and a few newspapers. The tall, distinguished solicitor returned there to pluck a throw blanket from the back of the chair.

"Professor Dawson and his handler, I presume?" he filled in as he held the blanket out to Ellie.

Ellie accepted it, wrapping the cloth around her drenched, guano-stained gown. She dropped onto the settee. "You presume correctly."

"Well, Stuffy and I succeeded in tracking down Colonel Borthwick and bluffing our way into his stronghold." Constance unwound her turban, shaking out the length of cloth to allow more pieces of shrubbery to tumble onto the carpet. "Everything was going swimmingly until Mr. Jacobs turned up there as well."

"If by 'swimmingly' you mean that Borthwick was obviously suspicious and refused to leave us alone with the manuscript for so much as a minute." Neil peeled off his dinner jacket with a wince.

A crimson stain lined a tear in her brother's shirt at the side of his stomach. Ellie stiffened at the sight, still clutching the throw blanket. "Are you bleeding!?"

"Why on earth would I be… oh!" Neil glanced down at his side and went over a bit green.

"Looks like somebody winged you," Adam commented casually.

"Has Neil been shot?" Constance excitedly pulled at the torn edges of Neil's shirt. "Let me see!"

"I have not been shot!" Neil protested as he tried to pivot his torso away from Constance. "I fell into a hedge! It's just a scratch!"

As though to prove the point, Neil yanked the shirt from his trousers and lifted it, exposing a pale sliver of his flank—which was marred by a distinct red welt.

Ellie shuffled over in her throw blanket to examine the wound. "I'm afraid that does look rather familiar."

"Familiar?!" Neil echoed in alarm. "Why would it look familiar?!"

"She's seen this sort of thing before," Adam cheerfully asserted, scratching Kalb's ears. "Haven't you, Princess?"

He punctuated the remark by giving Ellie a wink.

Ellie blushed at the memory of examining Adam's close encounter with a bullet in a dark, watery cenote—very shortly before he had kissed her senseless.

"But there isn't any hole!" Neil squirmed to try to get a better look at his own side. "How can it be from a bullet if it didn't make a hole?"

"When it just sorta skims you," Adam replied authoritatively.

"How do you know I didn't do it when I fell into the hedge?" Neil challenged.

"Well…" Ellie prodded lightly at the injury. "You can see where the heat from the bullet has slightly cauterized the outer edges of the… er…"

She trailed off as she took in Neil's alarming pallor.

"We can wrap it up nicely for you," Ellie assured him instead.

"Not until I've had a better look at it," Constance cut in crossly. "I've never seen an actual gunshot wound before—even one that hasn't made a hole."

Neil clamped a hand over the injury—wincing at the contact—then treated her to a forbidding glare. "No."

Constance slumped down onto the settee with a pout.

Giving up on trying to contort himself into the right angle for a look, Neil turned to a small mirror mounted on the wall. He shifted until the raw, blood-smeared welt slashing across the side of his abdomen was framed in the glass.

"Eurrrgh," he gurgled queasily.

"Throw a little petroleum jelly on there, and you'll be good as new in a day or two," Adam helpfully instructed him.

"Were you able to confirm Colonel Borthwick's location while you were entirely ignoring my instructions and getting yourselves shot?" Mr. Chowdhury mildly inquired as he sat back down in his chair, legs elegantly crossed.

"We did better than that." Constance perked up excitedly. "We know exactly where he's keeping the book. If I'm able to return to the building with a bag of sawdust, twenty or so yards of rope, and a live rooster, I feel quite certain—"

"There's also this." Neil pulled a piece of crumpled paper from his pocket. It looked only slightly damp, unlike the rest of him. He offered it to Mr. Chowdhury.

"*The nominative case?*" Mr. Chowdhury skeptically read from the page.

"Ignore all that," Neil instructed with an embarrassed flush. "It's the rest of it that might help—the Brahmi."

Ellie hurried over to Mr. Chowdhury, tripping slightly over the throw blanket that she still wore. "What Brahmi?"

"The Brahmi from the manuscript," Neil elaborated. "Or at least the last page of it. I managed to copy it down before Borthwick, er…"

"Became aware of our espionage and shot Neil," Constance filled in cheerfully.

"I have not been shot," Neil protested again, still looking green.

"Just grazed a little," Adam helpfully elaborated.

Ellie leaned further over Mr. Chowdhury's shoulder for a better angle, consumed by scholarly curiosity about the transcription.

Mr. Chowdhury cocked his eyebrow in a manner that perfectly combined a hint of amusement with mild disapproval.

"Er… sorry," Ellie began awkwardly. "It's only that I have a tremendous interest in ancient Indo-Aryan languages…"

He handed her the paper, rising from his chair.

Ellie snatched it, dropped into his seat, and eagerly scanned Neil's copied lines. "Oh, but this is wonderful! Do you know, I think I can see some similarities to Phoenician in some of the character styles."

"Are there really?" Neil perked up, forgetting his injury for a moment to come peer over Ellie's shoulder.

"Do we need the book if we've got a copy of the important stuff?" Adam asked.

Mr. Chowdhury moved to the doors that opened onto the suite's narrow balcony. He studied the rooftops, which still glistened from the recent downpour. "Trying to get the manuscript from Borthwick involves risk— which is why I very clearly instructed you not to try to do it."

"We weren't *trying*, exactly," Constance protested. "We just… fell into it."

"Fell into the colonel's study," the solicitor returned dryly. He frowned, his mind working. "It will take Borthwick time to track down someone who can translate the text. If we can beat him to it and reach the astra first, it might be possible to avoid a confrontation entirely."

"Which I'm guessing would be a safer option than sending your own people in—and risking Borthwick finding out where they came from,"

Adam added.

"Rather," Mr. Chowdhury agreed.

"I'm afraid this is my first encounter with Brahmi," Ellie admitted, waving the page with Neil's transcription. "I'd need access to an extensive library to make any sense of it."

"You don't need to make any sense of it," Mr. Chowdhury corrected her. "His Highness will do that."

"Uncle Vijay?" Constance piped in with a spark of delighted interest.

"He has made an extensive study of Sanskrit and ancient Indian literature. The royal library at Nandapur will have whatever else he requires," Mr. Chowdhury explained.

"Royal library?" Ellie's thoughts leaped excitedly to what she might find in the official collection of a kingdom that had been founded before the reign of Edward I.

Adam's eyes twinkled knowingly. "Don't let your fingers get too itchy, Princess. As best I can figure, it's a solid two-day trip to Nandapur." He looked to Mr. Chowdhury. "Can we afford that kind of time?"

"Nandapur is also a secure base for planning whatever operations are required next." Mr. Chowdhury tapped his fingers thoughtfully against the table. "And it is where our resources are focused. That may prove critical."

That 'our' seemed oddly intimate for a man who otherwise uniformly referred to Constance's royal relative as 'His Highness.'

Mr. Chowdhury's fingers stopped tapping. "We'll go. But we'll travel separately. It's best no one associates you with the royal party, especially after tonight's... *complications*. I'll arrange a compartment for you on the eight-thirty train."

He straightened. "You had all best clean up and get some sleep in the meantime. You'll find your trunks in your rooms. I took the liberty of having dinner sent up in case you didn't have a chance to eat."

"Are we to be left to our own devices for the evening, then?" Constance asked the question with an air of studied innocence.

A wicked spark of hope flared at the thought. Might they finally have a night where they weren't being thoroughly chaperoned? Ellie would very much like to act on some of the impulses she had been robbed of in the broom closet.

Of course, her brother was unlikely to approve of being made an accessory to Ellie and Adam's intimacies—even if Ellie could have brought herself to ask him. The very notion of that made her want to pull the throw blanket over her head.

Constance, however, was nothing if not a trusty companion in subterfuge. Surely she could find a way to distract Neil and give Ellie and Adam a chance to spend a private hour together.

Maybe two hours, Ellie corrected as her gaze roamed over to Adam's sprawled, half-dressed figure.

"Not exactly," Mr. Chowdhury replied.

A knock sounded at the door. Neil automatically pulled it open to reveal the tall, frowning figure of Mr. Mahjoud.

The dragoman was exceptionally tailored, as always. He carried a slender overnight bag as he crushed all of Ellie's nascent sensual hopes.

"His Highness the Maharaja of Nandapur is looking for you," Mr. Mahjoud reported tiredly.

"I'm sure that he is," Mr. Chowdhury returned with an indulgent quirk of his lip. "I'll leave you to it, then."

Mr. Mahjoud took in the scene—Neil's bloody shirt, Ellie's guano-stained blanket, Constance's servant's uniform, and Adam's bare toes.

Still sprawled on Adam's lap, Kalb lifted his head hopefully.

"Are we planning to wash up at some point this evening?" Mr. Mahjoud demanded with an air of resigned disdain. "Or do we harbor ambitions of ruining all of the hotel furniture?"

TEN

$\mathscr{A}$N HOUR AND a much-needed bath later, Ellie shrugged into her dressing gown. She stepped into the parlor to find Mr. Mahjoud clad in a set of elegant silk pajamas, staring down at the blanket and pillow laid out on the settee—which was at least a foot shorter than Mr. Mahjoud himself.

Mr. Mahoud gave a long-suffering sigh that spoke to the burden of being assigned to mind a batch of messy adults who really ought to be able to handle themselves.

Ellie could hear Constance belting out a music hall tune to the accompaniment of splashing water from the washroom down the hall.

There was no sign of Adam, but light shone from the room he shared with Neil. Ellie gave the door a little rap. It swung open at her touch, revealing her brother standing by one of the two beds, staring down into his opened travel trunk. He had changed into a clean undershirt, the bandage over the bullet graze just visible through the fabric. His feet were bare beneath the cuffs of his trousers.

Neil didn't seem to have heard her come in. He was uncomfortably engrossed in whatever he was looking at.

On Adam's bed, Kalb sprawled across the blanket, completely passed out. His legs twitched as he dreamed of chasing lizards. Ellie wondered whether Adam would bother to move him.

Probably not.

She peered over her brother's shoulder to see what he was staring at so fixedly inside the trunk. A long, slender bundle wrapped in an old towel rested on top of his things, a hilt of age-yellowed bone protruding from the top.

It was Dyrnwyn, the mythical sword of Rydderch Hael.

A few weeks ago, the arcanum had been a family heirloom of Julian

Forster-Mowbray. Now it was Neil's. Constance had bestowed it upon him on a desert ridge in Egypt after Julian was sent bolting back to the Nile.

Not that Neil wanted anything to do with the sword. He was stuck with it regardless until they could think of a place to put it where it wouldn't just end up back in Lord Aldbury's attic.

At least now, Ellie understood why Neil had been so adamant about Vijay's servants not opening his luggage. Dyrnwyn had a habit of bursting into wild blue flames when handled by someone it deemed well-born or worthy—which included Neil. The sword might also decide that one of the hotel staff fit the bill, which could result in the room getting scorched.

Ellie pulled her attention from the arcanum to her brother. His shoulders were slumped with exhaustion and dismay. His soft brown hair fell over the top of his spectacles much like it had nearly two decades before, when he had burst into her life and very quickly gone from stranger to family.

The thought sparked a burst of love and affection.

"How are you, really?" Ellie prompted.

Neil startled, dropping the lid of the trunk. "What? Oh. I'm fine."

Ellie sat on the bed beside the trunk. "It would be quite understandable if you weren't, you know."

Neil dropped down to sit on the other side of the trunk, wincing slightly as the movement irritated his wounded side. He took the glasses off, pulled a handkerchief from his pocket, and tried to clean them.

"The last few weeks haven't exactly been ideal. Losing my job. Being kidnapped by my murderous boss. And now—you know. Possibly being shot. Not that any of it could really be helped."

Ellie felt a little dart of guilt, as she had been the one responsible for throwing Neil from his comfortable life into a maelstrom of unpredictability and danger.

He looked forlornly at the spectacles in his hand. "I'm just not at all certain that I'm cut out for this."

"I think you've been handling all of it splendidly... for the most part," Ellie hedged.

Neil winced at the reminder, clearly intuiting that 'for the most part' referred to the idiotic apology letter he had written to the man who had later kidnapped and tried to kill him, along with his sister and friends.

"You've always been braver than I am. All of you—Bates and Connie too."

Ellie's heart twisted at the quiet resignation in his words. "There's more than one sort of courage, Neil."

He slipped the spectacles back on. Ellie could feel the weight of his lingering skepticism.

"Have you thought about what you're going to do with it?" she asked, deliberately changing the subject. "The sword, I mean."

Neil stared down at the lid of the trunk as though he could see through it to the arcanum inside. "Not really."

Ellie studied her brother for a moment—pale and bespectacled, stripped to his undershirt with a minor gunshot wound on his side. "Have you considered possibly... using it?"

Neil blinked at her with surprise. "What on earth would I use it *for?*"

Ellie didn't have an answer. She couldn't picture her brother swinging the blade about like a medieval warrior.

"Maybe it wouldn't have to be for fighting," she offered instead.

Neil's expression of low-grade horror fell away into something more uncertain.

The door flew open as Constance kicked it. Her generously curved figure, framed in the opening, was swathed in an embroidered silk dressing gown. Dark hair spilled over her shoulders in wet, glorious waves.

"Tub's open, Stuffy," she announced cheerfully.

Neil stared at her.

Constance shamelessly eyed his bare forearms before flouncing away. "I'm off to go air dry."

Her words from earlier that afternoon rang through Ellie's mind.

It's time to consider more extreme measures...

Would Constance actually do it? Entering into a fake engagement seemed excessive, even for Ellie's danger-magnet friend. Neil would also have to agree to the arrangement—and he patently disliked anything that hinted of scandal and danger.

But then, he was also afflicted with a distinct chivalrous streak.

Ellie wondered if she ought to warn him. It would be the sisterly thing to do, she supposed... but the notion of actually pushing the words out of her lips turned her throat dry with mortification.

I think Constance might be planning to fake engage you.

Neil ran an exhausted hand over his drawn features, unsettling his spectacles again. "I'd best go wash up."

He staggered for the bath.

Well, there would be time to consider the matter again later, Ellie supposed... and then tried not to feel too guilty about the relief that washed over her at avoiding the situation for now.

Mr. Mahjoud sat on the sofa in his elegant silk pajamas, reading a book.

Ellie took a nosy peek at the title before she caught the dragoman glaring at her over the top of the pages.

She gave him an awkwardly apologetic smile.

A tell-tale orange glow flared beyond the doors to the balcony. Intuiting its significance, Ellie slipped outside, eager to escape the tired weight of Mr. Mahjoud's perpetual disapproval.

The air was fresh and cool in the aftermath of the rain. Adam leaned against the rail, a cigar held casually between his fingers—but he seemed to have forgotten it, his attention focused on the object in his other hand.

Ellie caught a flash of gold framing an ivory face where a needle pointed north. It was Adam's compass—the one his father had once given him.

The finish was scratched and dented. Rust stained the hinges.

Ellie recalled the engraving from inside the lid.

May you always know your path. -GB

Adam clicked it shut as he looked up, slipping it into his pocket. His mouth curved into a wry smile as he wiggled the cigar. "I know. It's a terrible habit."

Ellie's thoughts were momentarily stalled by the enticing sight of his well-muscled figure. "Mr. Mahjoud is reading the rail timetable," she reported awkwardly.

"How much you wanna bet he's hiding a romantic novel in there?" Adam suggested mischievously.

Ellie frowned skeptically. "Machiavelli, perhaps."

"My money's on Jane Austen."

The night was soft with gloom. Adam was gently illuminated by the light filtering through the balcony doors and the glow of his cigar. Windows glinted with warmth in the surrounding buildings, filtered through colorful curtains.

Adam's gaze dropped to Ellie's robe—and warmed. "I remember this one."

"I suppose you would."

Ellie had been wearing the same garment when Adam had kicked through a washroom door into her life. The length of blue silk was far less practical than Ellie's usual wardrobe—but Constance had packed it, and there hadn't been much time for shopping over the last few whirlwind weeks.

Adam traced his fingers softly along the collar—and then lower, to where the curve of her breast pressed against the fabric.

The gesture wasn't strictly appropriate—but then, the balcony was dark. Ellie wasn't sure how much Mr. Mahjoud could see if he looked outside.

Perhaps he found the rail timetables particularly engrossing… though Ellie doubted they were engrossing enough for the dragoman to fail to notice if she grabbed the front of Adam's shirt and dragged him down to her for a kiss.

Never mind that kissing was rarely where such things ended these days.

"Wanna tell me about what happened during the parade today?" Adam asked.

Engrossed in her wicked thoughts, Ellie was momentarily thrown by the question.

"When you stopped by that play," Adam clarified.

Ellie recalled standing amid the shifting crowd of happy devotees at the Jagannath festival as the air danced with the scents of sweat, incense, and fried pastries. Painted actors in elaborate costumes and masks had stepped out onto their makeshift stage, garlanded with flowers and singing stylized recitations... and Ellie had been picked up and thrown somewhere else.

Somewhere older.

Costumes lined with the feathers of tropical birds. Drums and rattles sounding in the shadow of a towering white temple.

A spray of blood. A cheer. The moon rising over the ceiba trees.

"It reminded me of Tulan," Ellie admitted.

The answer was true... but not entirely honest. Ellie found herself compelled to share more.

"'Reminded' isn't precisely the right word," she confessed. "It felt more like someone ripped me out of where I was and threw me back there again."

Adam watched her patiently through the gloom. "Thought it might've been something like that."

Ellie had told him before about what had happened when she had made contact with the Smoking Mirror—how in that impossible conversation with a scarred, gold-eyed ghost, the knowledge of an entire civilization had been poured into her brain.

You want to know who we were.

In that moment, Ellie had wanted it with all the compulsion of a lifelong student of history confronted with a place that had been lost to the mists of time.

The mirror had fulfilled that desire in a manner that still made her feel queasy and breathless when she thought about it. The knowledge now haunted her mind like a ghost itself. Ellie couldn't call it up at will. If she tried, it only slipped away from her, teasing along the edge of her conscious-ness.

The memories came to her on their own terms. Something would spark that distant sense of recognition, and suddenly Tulan would flood her awareness, thrusting her back into a place that had disappeared over two hundred years before she was born.

Once it passed, only fragments remained—a melody on a flute carved from bone. The way the wind moved through the feathers on a headdress. The glitter of jade and gold.

The words burst out of her on a wave of guilt and frustration. "It's like it's all right there inside my mind, only I can't *do* anything about it. I am the last living repository of the knowledge of an entire world, and I can't bloody remember it!"

"What would you do if you could remember it?" Adam pressed softly.

Ellie threw up her hands. "I don't know! It isn't as though anyone would believe me if I ever did manage to write it all down. But I feel like I ought to be doing *something* to try to preserve it. I must owe the people of that place at least that much."

Owe her *that much,* Ellie silently corrected, thinking of the scarred, solemn face of the woman who still occasionally haunted her dreams.

Adam's hand clasped her shoulder. "You'll figure it out."

The steady faith in his voice warmed her—but doubt lingered. "Will I? It's not as though there's a guidebook for this sort of thing. I just feel so *useless.*"

"The last thing you are is 'useless,'" Adam firmly corrected.

The words comforted her, even if the guilt still lingered.

"At the club tonight," she said carefully. "You suspected what it might be like for Constance, didn't you? Before we'd gone inside."

"I should've thought of it sooner than that."

"I don't think it would have stopped her," Ellie pointed out.

"No," he agreed tiredly.

"I suppose I should've thought of it as well," she confessed uncomfortably. "I know this isn't England—not that England is entirely free from such attitudes."

"It's not like here," Adam replied shortly.

Ellie studied the tight expression on his face. "Or like America?"

Adam gazed out over the rooftops. "America's… bad."

"Is that why you left?"

Adam laughed. The sound was dark and uncharacteristically edged. "I left for a whole lot of reasons, Princess."

"I'm sorry."

"For what?" Adam demanded.

"You don't like to talk about it—your life in San Francisco, I mean."

Adam gripped the rail, still holding the cigar between his fingers. The familiar lines of his face were brushed by the faint light coming through the doors. "It was a different world. Not a very nice one."

Ellie felt a tug in her chest. "I can't see you ever fitting in someplace like that."

"I didn't," Adam returned shortly. "That's why I kept finding ways to run away from it—not that I knew that was what I was doing at the time."

"What did you think you were doing?"

Adam turned to lean against the rail, the lines of his body projecting a deliberate insolence as he crossed his arms over his broad chest. "Screwing up."

She thought of the golden compass in his pocket. "You're talking about your father."

Adam didn't respond… which was answer enough.

Ellie didn't know very much about Adam's relationship with George Bates, but what she did know made her dislike the man immensely.

Adam had never been good enough for his father. Ellie knew that Adam blamed himself for that, at least partly.

Ellie blamed George Bates.

She wondered what it would feel like for home to become a place where you not only didn't belong, but were no longer even welcome to *try*.

Where the doors were only open if you pretended to be someone entirely contrary to who you really were.

She imagined going back to Canonbury and telling her parents that she was involved with a man in a manner that would never end with marriage.

Her stepmother, Florence, would be hysterical. Ellie could already envision the tears and dramatics, just like she could picture the startled worry on her father's face.

What she could *not* imagine was the pair of them ordering her out of the house and telling her never to come back.

Adam had suffered that, fundamentally betrayed by the people who should have loved and supported him most.

The thought made Ellie burn with a hot, protective rage. "It takes a great deal of courage and integrity to see past the world you've been given and realize that there is more out there—and then leave everything you know behind to go and find it."

Adam uncrossed his arms, gazing down at her. "You did that too."

"What on earth do you mean?"

"Going to university. Applying to the civil service." Adam's mouth quirked into a hint of a roguish smile. "Stealing a map to an ancient lost city."

"I didn't *mean* to steal it," Ellie cut in defensively, blushing.

"Not getting married," Adam finished firmly.

Ellie remembered her conversation with Constance in the tonga and felt a guilty pang. How much integrity could there be in pretending to go along with an institution she opposed? But what other choice did she have if she and Adam wanted to be together?

She didn't have an answer to either of those questions.

Adam brushed his knuckles gently over her cheek. "You've got more integrity in your little finger than anyone else I've ever known."

"I'm not so sure about that," Ellie grumbled guiltily.

"I am. And it still never ceases to amaze me that out of all the guys in the world, you've settled for me."

"You have a great deal to recommend you!"

"Unemployment?" Adam suggested wryly.

"How about bravery? Principle. Compassion. Strength. Intelligence." She punctuated each remark with a poke at his solid chest.

"Now you're just buttering me up," Adam protested.

"I am listing objective facts."

"Not gonna put anything in there about my manly physique?" Adam's mouth quirked wickedly.

"I think you are quite aware of my opinion of your physique."

Adam took a step closer—which brought them into a very intimate proximity. "Doesn't hurt to have a reminder every now and then."

Ellie's mind bloomed with all the things she might do to appreciate Adam's physique, were Mr. Mahjoud not reading the rail timetables on the other side of the glass doors. "I think rather than a reminder, I might prefer an uninterrupted hour in a broom closet," she grumbled.

Adam laughed.

"Don't tell me you weren't thinking of it as well," Ellie accused.

The night burst with noise and color as chrysanthemums of pink, orange, yellow, and purple bloomed to life against the night sky. A triumphant roar rose from the distant festival.

Adam's body was etched in dancing hues of blue and gold. His scent filled her senses, salt and forest and animal heat mingling with the tang of cordite from the display overhead.

"You don't wanna know what I was thinking, Princess," Adam warned darkly.

Ellie's desire warred with her common sense. "Why not?"

Adam leaned in close, the heat of his breath brushing against the skin of her cheek as the colors continued to crack and shimmer overhead. "Because we're on a balcony."

"What's wrong with balconies?" Ellie's hands twitched at her sides with the urge to reach up and tear open the buttons of his shirt.

Adam's hand glided over the small of her back, the callouses on his fingers catching lightly against the delicate silk. "Gravity."

"Who needs gravity anyway?" Ellie protested breathlessly, tilting up her face. Adam was so close to her now that the gesture made the subtle roughness of his cheek glide against her jaw.

Adam's hand flexed against her back with barely contained power. "Can't say I care to mind it much at the moment," he muttered, eyes darkening with wicked determination.

The French doors flew open. Constance plowed through them in her dressing gown, arms spread wide and happily toward the sky. "Fireworks!"

Adam stepped back. Ellie whirled to grip the railing, forcibly trying to steady her breath.

Constance shouted loudly back into the parlor. "*Stuffy! Come see!*"

Neil popped into view in his worn blue robe and gray striped pajamas, toweling his hair. "What's that?"

"Lord Jagannath must have made it to his aunt's house. They're putting on a show!" Constance grabbed him by the arm and hauled him out onto the balcony—which had grown rather crowded.

With a whistle and a bang, more color burst to life in overhead, orange and red joining shimmering falls of green and yellow. Constance's heart-shaped face was lit with the dancing hues, her eyes wide with childlike joy.

Neil stared up at the show from behind her—and worry twisted through Ellie's gut. He knew that Ellie and Adam were involved with each other... but she hadn't exactly advertised what the two of them had gotten up to during those stolen nights in Cairo.

Knowing Ellie had romantic feelings for his best friend was one thing. Learning that they had done debauched things together while deliberately remaining unmarried was something else entirely.

For a moment, Ellie wondered what it would feel like to lose her brother over that. What if by letting him see who she really was—and what truly mattered to her—she risked having him shut her out of his life forever?

Neil wasn't just her family. He was her friend. Her colleague. The first person in the world who had shared and understood her scholarly passions and her boundless curiosity. Their relationship hadn't always been easy, punctuated by periods of hurt and confusion… but through all of that, there had always been an immense and unmistakable bounty of love.

The notion of having all of that torn from her was *wrenching*.

Emotion roiled through her with the power of a storm, threatening tears.

Neil's mouth tightened with concern. Ellie could read the question in the angry look he shot at Adam.

Has he hurt you?

She had to choke back a wild laugh at his assumption—and at his quick instinct to protect her.

She shook her head, reassuring him. Neil warily accepted it.

With the memory of that terrible fear still twisting through her, Ellie reached out her hand.

Neil blinked down at the gesture—and pulled her gently to his side.

Ellie found herself securely wrapped in her brother's arm. She let her head fall to his shoulder, soaking up his steady warmth.

The shocking impulse toward tears flooded up in her again, but different now. The tide was warmer and richer, woven through with gilded threads of affection.

Ellie felt the truth in her bones. She wouldn't lose Neil over the question of who she needed to be. Some of her choices might be harder for him to understand, or could drive him to worry… but he would *never* walk away from her.

She tightened her grip on his waist as though her arms could communicate what words would never be big enough to hold.

Ow, Neil mouthed softly, wincing at the pressure on his wounded side.

Sorry, Ellie mouthed back with a wince.

He shook his head ruefully—and subtly tightened his warm hold on her shoulder.

Ellie leaned against him as he gazed up at the fireworks through his spectacles.

Like a compass needle returning to the north, her eyes moved to where Adam stood by the rail.

He was watching her and Neil, smiling with a warm understanding that only Adam Bates would have so quickly, intuitively grasped.

He punctuated it with a casual fist to Neil's shoulder.

Neil startled—and then smiled at him as well, the expression more tentative but unmistakably genuine.

"Beautiful," Constance breathed in front of them, absorbed by the colors blooming across the sky—prayers made light and shot into the stars. "It's beautiful."

ELEVEN

Two days later

CONSTANCE JABBED HER elbow into Ellie's ribs. "Wake up, Eleanora! You're missing Nandapur!"

She returned her attention to the window of the carriage, soaking up the view with a hungry sense of wonder as Ellie blearily lifted her head.

Constance shared the conveyance with Ellie, Neil, Mr. Mahjoud... and Adam's dog. Kalb had been unceremoniously tossed in with them a few hours before. They had completed the two-day journey from Puri at a breakneck pace. As they moved deeper into the Odishian countryside, muddy rice paddies had given way to rolling green hills speckled with wildflowers.

All of their travel had been expertly arranged, from the first-class tickets waiting for them at the train station to the well-sprung carriage they had transferred to after completing the rail leg of their journey.

The carriage only seated four—plus the dog. Adam had quickly volunteered to ride on horseback instead, along with a trio of Uncle Vijay's guards, who had forgone their vivid livery for less conspicuous attire.

Ellie rubbed her eyes. Kalb thumped his tail hopefully. Mr. Mahjoud looked bored.

Neil had stuck his nose into a book all day. He pulled it out at Constance's exclamation, blinking through his spectacles at the window as though just realizing there was still a world outside.

They passed down a broad street lined by charming buildings painted in bright colors. Rolling hills rose up behind the structures, richly green with the abundant rains of the monsoon. The town was busy with shoppers and pedestrians. Vendors showed off their wares under bright awnings.

Constance spotted the confectionery layers of a temple rising to the east behind a market that covered most of a tree-lined plaza.

It was all she could do not to jump from the moving carriage to explore.

Ellie leaned over to share the window, her curiosity awakening with the rest of her.

A twenty-foot wall loomed ahead of them, punctuated by two gleaming white towers. The enormous wooden doors between them were carved with a scene of warriors on horseback marching in triumph under a gleaming sun.

"Is that the palace?" Ellie pressed wonderingly.

"No," Constance corrected her with a grin. "That's just the front gate."

The doors swung open, pulled by servants in Vijay's familiar purple and gold livery. The carriage rolled past them into a broad courtyard. They had barely stopped before Constance wrenched open the door and spilled out into the afternoon sunlight.

The royal palace of Nandapur sprawled before her. The main building, set across from the gate, rose five generous stories with wings on both sides topped by soaring spires and elegant domes.

Constance had seen it before, but only in faded photographs in her grandmother's albums. Those images didn't even start to do justice to the splendor before her.

Pale stone walls gleamed gold in the afternoon sunlight. Beyond the roofline, rolling green hills were accented by the sparkling silver ribbon of a distant waterfall.

This magnificent place belonged to her, in a way. Constance wasn't here as a guest. She was coming *home*.

"Fiddlesticks!" Ellie breathed out beside her, staring at the sight.

Adam swung down from his horse with easy grace. The animal nosed him affectionately as he paused to rub its neck. His lanky yellow dog leaped out of the carriage and shook itself vigorously—then launched across the courtyard like a golden comet, scattering a cluster of alarmed doves.

"Nice place," Adam commented, ignoring the dog as he raised an eyebrow at the building.

Neil joined them, staring up at the palace with shock. Constance caught his book as he started to drop it. She pressed it back into his chest.

He clung to the volume like a life preserver. "You can see the Mughal influence in the window arches," he mumbled helplessly.

Constance repressed the urge to smirk at him. "I believe the oldest parts of the complex date to the time of the Gajapatis."

Neil pinned her with a hungry look. "Do you know where they are?"

Constance found herself wondering distractedly what else might provoke that darkly intense interest besides historical architecture.

The entrance to the palace sat at the top of a low, broad stairwell. A pair of servants in purple and gold waited there with an air of stoic gravity.

A skinny child slid out onto the landing between them. The girl was perhaps twelve, all elbows and knees with a big white grin. She wore a pair of salwar trousers and a kameez tunic that would have been quite nice if it hadn't been smeared with dust. Silver studs sparkled on either side of her nose.

She bounded down the steps with an energy that reminded Constance of Adam's hyperactive dog.

"You are the English visitors!" she called out excitedly, the words warmly accented.

"I'm American, actually," Adam cheerfully corrected her.

The girl craned her neck back, taking in his sun-kissed hair and blue eyes. "An *actual* American?"

Adam grinned. "All the way to my boots."

"But have you chased a stampede?" the girl demanded. "Gambled with cards? Involved yourself in a gunfight?"

"Yes, yes, and…" Adam cast a sheepish look at Ellie. "Why would I do something as crazy as get into a gunfight?"

Ellie paled at the obvious lie.

Constance made an internal note to pry that story out of Adam later.

"What's your name, kid?" Adam asked.

"Vanika."

"And have you read a great many dime novels?" Constance cannily guessed.

"I have read loads of books. They help me with my English." The girl shifted her focus back to Adam with obvious fascination. "America sounds *very* exciting."

Adam forced his face into a stern expression. "Just steer clear of those gunfights. All right?"

"I like swords." Vanika eyed Adam's belt with a spark of interest. "Are you wearing a sword?"

"Kinda. Wanna see it?"

Ellie went even paler.

Before Adam could show off his enormous knife, his dog cannoned into their group, having given up on chasing the birds. Kalb immediately jumped up on the child, lathing her face with his tongue.

Vanika giggled, giving the animal an enthusiastic hug as she let out a stream of affectionate remarks in a language Constance didn't recognize.

"Is this an American dog?" the girl pressed.

"He's Egyptian, actually," Ellie replied.

Selukis, the breed of dogs kept by the nomadic Arabs, were rumored to have descended from the dogs of the pharaohs. Ellie had once reluctantly admitted to Constance that Kalb bore a distinct resemblance to canines depicted in ancient Egyptian bas-relief carvings.

Though I don't recall seeing any New Kingdom artwork depicting pharaonic dogs stealing drumsticks off the table or trying to sleep on the furniture, Ellie had grumbled.

Vanika finally disentangled herself from the dog—after giving him another squeeze and receiving a thorough licking of her ear. "But come! I will show you to the family."

The girl raced for the stairs, Kalb scrambling after her. She exchanged a few quick words with the waiting servants, this time in Odia.

Constance followed her into an elegantly appointed hall where a fountain splashed softly into a shallow pool. The space was framed by ornate stone arches leading into other areas of the palace. "Are you one of my cousins?"

Vanika snorted as she led them past walls completely covered with inlaid silver mirrors. "No. But here is the old armory! As you can see, there is a very nice collection of both swords *and* guns."

Constance peered into the room. The walls were covered in displays of antique weaponry, from bows and arrows to daggers, maces, and ancient muskets. A beautifully ornate cannon sat in the center of the room, framed by cases holding elaborately decorated scabbards.

She stepped inside, stopping at a display of jeweled daggers and mentally comparing them to the ones strapped to her garters. "I could have fun in here."

Mr. Mahjoud followed her. He paused at a case of swords, giving the blades a bland study.

Constance studied him in turn. Was there a telling gleam of familiarity in Mr. Mahjoud's eyes as he looked over the weapons?

She had not given up on her theory that beneath his fussy waistcoats, Mr. Mahjoud was actually a deadly Sudanese warrior.

"Hmm," Mr. Mahjoud commented, apparently unimpressed.

Constance decided that this response clearly supported her hypothesis.

"But if this is the old armory, does that mean there's a new armory?" Ellie wondered with a frown.

Vanika whistled a suspiciously casual tune, ignoring the question.

"You've got all kinds of fun stuff in here. But what's with the big outfit?" Adam nodded to an enormous blanket of thin metal scales that hung over a wooden scaffold roughly twice his own height.

"That is for the elephants," Vanika authoritatively informed him. "From when the maharaja's herd was actually used for war."

Adam looked intrigued. "You're saying 'herd' like there's still one kicking around."

"Why wouldn't there be?" Vanika returned dismissively. "Now come on!"

She dashed from the armory, leaving the rest of them to hurry after her through a twisting maze of hallways. The girl named rooms with a wave of her hand as they raced by.

"That's the Rani Salon, and that's the Courtyard of the Winds. They call that one the Peacock Room—because the walls are decorated with peacocks," she added with a roll of her eyes.

Ellie quickened her pace to catch up with the child. "I believe I heard something about a library."

"Oh, that. It's enormous," Vanika commented distractedly.

"But is it nearby?" Ellie pleaded hopefully.

"Not at all," Vanika replied and dashed onward.

She led them through soaring audience chambers and jewel-like gardens. Constance drank it all in, tying the places she passed to the stories in her head. There was the stone bridge where one of her great-great-grandfathers had declared his allegiance to the Sultan of Golconda. The tower with the blue roof was where a long-dead maharaja had imprisoned his mad brother.

All of it was real, and she was *here*.

A high, clear voice called out to them from the top of a stairwell as they entered a more modern wing of the palace.

"What are *you* doing down there?"

The speaker was a boy of nine who glared down at them with his hands on his hips, elegantly dressed in a shimmering jacquard sherwani. Unlike their guide, he was completely free of dust.

Vanika skidded to a stop at the foot of the stairs. "Who said it was any of your business?"

"You're supposed to be in school," the boy accused.

"I thought you didn't *want* me to be in school with you," Vanika shot back saucily.

"I don't want you there! But you're still *supposed* to." The boy studied Constance and the others with undisguised curiosity. "Lady scholar. English archaeologist. Yankee surveyor. And that one must be my cousin." His finger stopped on Constance.

"It's rude to point!" Vanika cried out triumphantly, jabbing a finger at the boy.

"It's rude to miss school!" the boy retorted.

"So *you're* one of my cousins, then," Constance pressed.

The boy straightened with an air of dignity. "I am Arjuna Krishna Devi, son of Balaram Hari Devi and nephew to His Highness Maharaja Vijayrama Chandra Devi."

Constance could see a slight resemblance to her uncle in his high cheekbones and the firm set of his chin. The boy was clearly a self-important monster. She was delighted regardless. He was *her* self-important monster—a newly discovered part of her family.

Arjuna regally inclined his head, the bow just low enough to be polite without compromising his superior status. "Welcome to the Palace of Nandapur."

"I already welcomed them," Vanika retorted.

The boy's dignity flew out the window. His eyes narrowed as he rattled off a stream of surly Odia.

"I'll tell your uncle you said that," Vanika shot back wickedly. She pointed, calling over her shoulder to Constance and the others. "The royal ladies are waiting for you in there! Have a nice day!"

Her skinny legs took the stairs two at a time. She dashed past Arjuna.

"Where do you think you're going?" he protested.

"To school! You're going to be late!"

"I'll pinch your cheek so hard, it will turn red!" Arjuna shouted after her.

"I'll push you so hard, you'll land on the moon!" Vanika called back.

"Great kid," Adam declared authoritatively as he watched the children chase each other around the corner.

"Did that girl just say there was more than one royal lady?" Neil sounded intimidated by the prospect.

Constance felt a quick thrum of excitement.

They passed into the room that Vanika had indicated, an expansive parlor furnished with soft cushions and thick carpets under walls of soft sea green. A barrier of elaborately carved stonework provided a filtered view over a garden punctuated by more elegant fountains.

Constance's grandmother sat on the divan beside a lovely Indian lady in her forties with softly rounded cheeks. A red bindi accented the space between the stranger's brows. She wore a rose-hued sari, gold sparkling at her wrists and ankles.

The round-cheeked woman rose from her seat, extending her hands. "You must be Constance! I'm your Auntie Parvati—your Uncle Balaram's wife."

"Uncle Balaram?" Constance echoed helplessly.

"Vijay's younger brother," Padma filled in from her regal perch on the cushions.

Constance stared at the lovely woman currently clasping her hands and smiling at her with generous affection. Giving in to the impulse, she pulled her into a hug. "I'm so terribly pleased to meet you!"

Parvati hugged her back with an easy laugh. "And we are so happy you are finally here with us!"

Her newly discovered aunt's arms were soft and warm. She smelled like orange blossoms.

Constance quickly brushed a few tears from her face as she pulled back. "Goodness, look at me!"

Parvati cupped Constance's cheek, her eyes warm with affection. "But someone should have told us that you were here! I meant to meet you at the door."

"Don't worry about it." Adam yanked back on Kalb's collar as the dog sniffed suspiciously at a plate of pastries on the table. "That cute kid showed us how to get here."

"Who is Vanika, anyway?" Constance asked.

Her grandmother and her new aunt exchanged a look.

"She is an unofficial ward of His Highness's." Parvati's succinct reply implied that there was more to the story.

Mr. Chowdhury strode into the room with an air of efficiency and purpose that Constance realized must be routine for him. "Ah—here you all are."

Parvati warmly clasped his hands in greeting. "Nawaz! When did you and Vijay arrive?"

"Three hours ago," Mr. Chowdhury replied. "But His Highness had to proceed directly to a meeting."

Constance's aunt hadn't greeted Mr. Chowdhury like a solicitor. The comfortable familiarity with which she'd spoken his forename felt more like the way one would welcome family.

Vijay swept into the room, dressed in purple trousers and a gold-embroidered white kurta. His turban was held in place by a jeweled pin, making him look very much the part of a royal prince. "Hello, everyone! What a journey, eh? Glad we all made it. Thankfully, it's no easier for the Raj to get here, which generally keeps them out of our hair. I don't think any of us mind that too dearly—do we, Nawaz? And as for you four..."

He clapped a hand on Neil's shoulder. Neil jumped at the impact, tearing his attention from the ornamental stonework.

"I hear you had quite an adventure at the club," Vijay teased. "I can't tell you how grateful I am that you acquired that transcription. It's exactly what we needed. Very well done, the lot of you."

Neil's ears turned pink at the unexpected praise. He made an instinctive adjustment to his spectacles, clearing his throat awkwardly. "Yes, well… It was nothing really. Just a bit of luck."

Vijay met Neil's gaze significantly. "I think it might have been a bit more than that."

Constance recalled how Neil had withstood the subtle threat of Borthwick's interrogation in the study of the Lal Bagh. He must have been terrified, but he'd managed to parry Borthwick's thrusts and make his transcription of Tulsidas's secret chapter right under the colonel's nose.

It had *been rather well done*, she thought with a warm tingle in her chest.

Vijay shifted his attention to the table. "Is that coconut pitha?"

He plucked a pastry from the tray between his aunt and sister-in-law, then threw himself down on the sofa, popping the treat into his mouth.

Kalb watched with dangerously fixed attention.

Vijay turned to Parvati, his eyes twinkling. "Well, Bhauni—now that you've finally met our English cousin, what do you think of her?"

"I think she is far more lovely than her photographs give her credit for." Parvati smiled at Constance with warm affection. "We are going to have to hide her away, or all of the princes of Odisha and Andhra Pradesh will be battering at our gates for the chance to court her!"

"Maybe we should let them come. She might fall in love with one of them, and then we could keep her here with us in India." Vijay gave Constance a wink.

"As I recall, the Maharaja of Sonepur has a very eligible young nephew," Padma added smoothly.

There was nothing teasing in her grandmother's tone. Alarm rang through Constance's brain.

"Oh yes—Chandrabhanu Naru!" Parvati exclaimed brightly. "He is quite dashing. But what about Narayan Goinda of Mayurbhanj? He is second in line for the throne after his brother and was recently widowed. He has established no less than three schools for girls, and I believe he also writes poetry."

"You are throwing a birthday party for Arjuna in four days. Why don't you invite them both to attend?" Padma's expression was bland as she sipped her tea.

Constance stared at her.

Invite them both.

Her Aai wasn't just prodding her about being overly picky with her suitors. Now she was inviting them over.

There was no more room for uncertainty about the matter. Aai had chosen sides in the debate over Constance's marriage prospects… which meant that Constance was in trouble.

She could feel the trap closing over her. She had to find a way out of it—and quickly.

"Don't these stone carvings remind you of Cairo's Fatimid architecture?" Neil exclaimed excitedly as he studied the ornamental wall.

"Splendid idea!" Vijay asserted happily.

"Fiddlesticks," Ellie muttered under her breath.

Vijay turned his attention back to his sister-in-law. "Bhauni, will you see Constance and her friends settled in? I'd best get right on this translation. Feel free to explore the palace in the meantime—it is entirely at your disposal. Nawaz, you'll join me?"

"Of course, Your Highness," Mr. Chowdhury replied with a decorous nod.

"*Your Highness.*" Vijay rolled his eyes. "He knows I hate it when he does that while we're at home."

Even through her lingering shock, Constance registered the oddity of Vijay's words. *While* we're *at home…*

Did her uncle's solicitor live in the palace?

"Well, then," Parvati offered cheerfully. "Shall we get you settled in?"

TWELVE

$\mathcal{E}$LLIE WAS QUITE CERTAIN that she was lost. The royal palace of Nandapur was enormous. Buildings dating from multiple centuries sprawled across the property, connected by lush gardens or covered walkways. Ellie wandered through them in a daze, assaulted by gorgeous wonders at every turn.

Constance's Aunt Parvati had shown Ellie to her airy, high-ceilinged guest room to change and wash up—tasks that Ellie had managed in about ten minutes. She supposed the rest of the household must be resting before dinner, but Ellie had dozed through most of the ride to Nandapur. She wasn't feeling remotely tired—nor could she have nodded off when she was so busy worrying about Constance.

Ellie hadn't missed the significance of Padma's suggestion that a few princes be invited to the upcoming birthday party for the gloriously arrogant nine-year-old they had met on the stairs. Constance had to be worrying about what it all meant—but when Ellie had gone to find her, her room had been empty.

With Constance unavailable, Ellie had decided to see if she could locate the maharaja's enticing royal library.

She didn't appear to be on the track of any books at the moment. The wing she had wandered into belonged to an older part of the palace that was clearly under renovation. The rooms that lined the hall were empty of everything but stacks of tile, lumber scraps, and tools. A doorway nearby was in the process of being framed out. In another chamber, a beautiful mosaic had been partially restored.

At some point, she supposed she must run across another servant who could steer her to her destination—or at least point her back toward the family quarters of the palace.

Not that she had seen anyone for a while.

Ellie rounded another corner and found herself in a cool, shady passage-way, lined on one side with pillars that framed a view of a secluded courtyard. The space was shaded by thick, sprawling fig trees. Flowers spilled from stone beds around the bluish-green square of an artificial pool. Deep, wide steps led down to the cool water, which was fed by a working fountain.

Illustrations from past readings popped helpfully up into Ellie's mind. It resembled a Maratha bath. She was impressed to see that it was still func-tional.

The water looked inviting, even though the afternoon was more richly sultry than oppressive. She had dressed simply in a light blouse and skirt, and the gray clouds overhead moderated the intensity of the summer heat, promising more rain.

She was thinking of the additional research she would like to do on Maratha plumbing technology when she rounded another corner—and realized someone stood in the passageway in front of her.

It was Adam. He was wet.

His sun-gilded hair was tousled and damp. He hadn't shaved, his jaw shadowed by two days' growth of beard. Moisture still clung to his skin—which Ellie could see quite well, as he wasn't wearing a shirt.

The shirt was in his hand, along with his shoes.

A heat that had nothing to do with the weather flooded through her at the sight of the broad, tanned expanse of his chest.

"You're here," she pointed out densely.

"Sure am." Adam's gaze was warm.

Ellie's appreciation of the view was only slightly handicapped by an itching sense that something was missing. "Where's the dog?"

"He's around here somewhere," Adam said, clearly unconcerned about the notion of his unruly animal running loose in a four-hundred-year-old royal palace.

"Probably a good thing," he added. "I don't know how I would've kept him out while I was in the pool."

Ellie imagined a soaking wet Kalb leaping onto the maharaja's furniture… but even that horrifying notion slipped from her mind as the rest of Adam's words penetrated her brain.

"You were in the pool?" she asked stupidly, her eyes locked onto the moisture still glistening on his broad shoulders.

He closed the rest of the distance between them, his body painted with the soft shadows of the passageway. "Thought I could use a rinse."

She glanced down at Adam's legs. "Your trousers are dry."

Adam kept his face suspiciously straight. "Well, I wouldn't want to track water all over this nice palace, now would I?"

The image blazed across her mind of Adam falling into the cool turquoise embrace of the pool, then standing to let the water sluice down his skin.

She thought of how the drops would follow the hard angles and planes of his abdomen… his hips…

Ellie's throat went dry.

"I was looking for the library," she blurted out.

Adam braced an arm against the pillar, leaning over her. "Were you, now?"

"But it appears this wing is being renovated."

The door to the room beside them was propped open. A canvas drop cloth covered the floor, held down at the corner by a bucket of paint.

"Haven't seen any renovators," Adam commented.

A drop of water curved down his neck, sliding onto his bare, tanned collarbone.

"Guessing they have the day off," he added.

He was less than a step away. As though of its own accord, Ellie's hand rose to his chest. She pressed her palm against the place where the squared muscles of his pectorals gave way to the taut washboard of his abdomen.

He was still damp.

"You know, I don't believe anyone is expecting us until dinner." She shared the information casually, as she might note the possible provenance of a Grecian vase.

Her hand moved lower. It glided over the firm ridges of muscle until it reached the waistband of Adam's trousers.

She closed her fingers around the brass buckle of his battered leather belt. The flesh of his stomach pressed against the back of her knuckles with the pull of his breath.

"When's dinner?" Adam asked in a voice like gravel.

"Seven," she replied weakly. "And… what time is it now?"

"Five."

Ellie swallowed thickly against a dry throat. "Perhaps we should find a way to… pass the time."

Adam's eyes shaded to a darker cobalt. "How about I take you into that room right there, lay you out on the floor, and put my mouth on you?"

Ellie wondered how exactly her knees were still working.

"That sound all right?" Adam finished evenly.

Her mind, usually so full of words, offered her only one in response.

"*Please.*"

Adam swung her up into his arms and carried her inside.

An hour later, Ellie lay across the rumpled canvas, lightly sweating as she stared up at the aged plaster of the ceiling and listened to the rain pound down outside the window.

Her bones felt like butter. Every nerve sang with satisfaction.

She was very glad that the maharaja had given his renovators a holiday. Otherwise, they would most certainly have heard her shouting, even over the rumble of the afternoon storm.

Adam sprawled beside her in a delicious expanse of tanned skin and muscle.

"That was…" Ellie began.

"Damned overdue," Adam finished for her.

Ellie's response was an incoherent gurgle.

Adam chuckled warmly, rolling onto his side to face her. He threaded his fingers into her hair, pushing it gently back from her face. "What do you think of Connie's family so far?"

Her brain was still buzzing with the sated aftermath of their activities. "I think Padma is going to pressure her to marry," she mumbled.

"Picked up on that too, did you?"

Ellie's focus sharpened. "You noticed?"

"I might avoid social machinations like the plague, but I can still tell when they're happening right in front of me."

The dark note in his voice reminded Ellie of Adam's own troubled history in high society.

"Any idea what Connie plans to do about it?" Adam prompted.

A warning thrill chased over Ellie's skin. "What makes you so sure she has a plan?"

"It's Constance," Adam returned dryly. "The question's less whether she's got a plan and more how crazy it is."

Ellie clamped her mouth shut as she considered Constance's plan.

Adam read the look. "That crazy, huh? Do I even want to know?"

"I'm really not sure that you do," Ellie warned him.

"Fair enough," he returned easily. "But you'll tell me if I can help her—right?"

Ellie warmed in a manner that had nothing to do with the humidity. She touched her hand to Adam's face—rugged, strong, and unquestioningly loyal. "I promise."

She let her hand drop as she mulled over Adam's earlier question. "The family are all lovely." She hesitated, then added the rest. "Mr. Chowdhury seems very close to them."

Adam traced a finger along the line of her collarbone. "I've been wondering if he might be a bit more than just a 'close personal adviser.'"

"Like what?" Ellie frowned, half her attention consumed by the softly ridged texture of his touch.

Adam answered her with a cocked eyebrow.

Ellie sat up. "You mean… He and the maharaja. You're suggesting they might be…"

She blushed rather than complete the sentence.

Ellie was aware that there were gentlemen who formed a more particular sort of attachment to each other. She'd known several women who had done the same, calling themselves roommates while being devoted in a way that had nothing to do with platonic ideals of feminine affection. It was a fairly open topic of conversation among the more radical ladies in the suffrage movement.

She considered Mr. Chowdhury's careful formality, which he maintained strictly even though he and the maharaja were obviously very old and dear companions.

The solicitor's obvious concern about Vijay's safety and discretion.

The easy, familial warmth in Parvati's greeting.

The way the two men seemed to be able to communicate with a look.

"That would explain a few things." Ellie frowned thoughtfully. "I'm not sure how the Hindu faith treats such relationships."

"I don't think Mr. Chowdhury is Hindu," Adam countered. "Nawaz is a Muslim name."

"I suppose that complicates the matter."

"And I'm guessing the British administration here wouldn't tolerate it any more than they do back in London."

"But isn't Nandapur a royal state?"

"It's a British tributary," Adam corrected her. "Constance's uncle has the power to run a lot of things his way, but the Raj would jump at any excuse to depose the family and annex Nandapur outright… like finding out that the maharaja is romantically involved with his lawyer."

Ellie felt a flare of quick anger. "How desperately unfair!"

"You think so?"

"Don't you?" Ellie pushed back angrily.

"As it happens, yeah. But that's not an opinion everybody shares."

"I have never much cared whether my opinions were popular or not," Ellie grumbled.

Adam chuckled warmly. "No, you sure haven't."

Sympathy tugged at her. "It must be terribly hard constantly having to hide what the person you love really means to you."

Ellie's mind caught up to the words that had just come out of her mouth—and connected them to the man lying beside her with a lurch of guilt. "But then, you'd know all about that, wouldn't you?"

Adam gently pushed her back down onto the floor, bracing himself over her. "Pretty sure I've made my opinion about that clear."

Ellie's corset was hanging from a shelf on the wall. Her chemise and drawers lay in opposite corners of the room.

His trousers were draped over a paint bucket.

"You might have," she allowed—a mite breathlessly.

"Then one of these days, you're going to have to stop apologizing for it."

An enticing sense of threat darkened the words. Adam's skin brushed against her own like silk every time she inhaled. The sated feeling of the moment before was rapidly evaporating, replaced by a rising swarm of very appealing possibilities.

"What are your feelings about preventatives?" Ellie blurted out.

Adam's expression blanked with surprise. "Say what?" he demanded, half choking on the words.

"You know." Ellie's cheeks flushed. "Devices designed to interrupt the natural consequences of the act of…"

"I know what they are, Princess." Adam's eyes twinkled. "Curious where you heard about them, though."

"The Cairo book bazaar," Ellie informed him. "You remember when we paid it a visit before we left for India? I might have accidentally purchased a very informative volume by Mr. Richard Carlile on the prudent regulation of the principle of love."

"That the one you were gonna use to teach Connie Latin?"

"Er… no," Ellie awkwardly corrected. "That was a different volume of very great—er—*scholarly interest* which sadly escaped our possession."

Adam's mouth twitched with suppressed humor. "I see."

He moved off her. The change did make it easier for Ellie to concentrate—even if she somewhat regretted it. He propped himself up on an elbow at her side instead, gazing down at her.

"It's only that as creative and enjoyable as your *improvisations* have been," Ellie offered tactfully, "it seems to me that there's another area of activity we might explore if we had a reliable method of preventing the potential complications of conception."

She gave in to the impulse to raise her hand to Adam's arm, exploring the smooth, taut texture of his skin.

The hungry, appreciative look he gave her in response sent a shiver over her skin despite the languid heat of the afternoon.

"Unless you think we're not really missing out on much," she added diplomatically.

"That's not exactly what I'm thinking right now."

"I see," Ellie replied, feeling the room get warmer.

"You would if you looked down," Adam returned with a smirk.

Ellie gave him an admonishing shove. Adam obliged her by rolling onto his back.

She took this as an invitation to prop herself up on his chest. "But I'm serious! Do you think something like that could work for us? Could we even find what we required if we wanted to?"

Adam drew her head down to rest against his shoulder, Ellie's arm draped across his chest. His fingers stroked through the tangled waves of her hair.

Her pins were scattered all over the floor.

"I can probably track something down if I ask the right people," he mused. "Not sure whether it'd be legal, though."

Ellie lifted her head with alarm. "I don't want you to be arrested for purchasing contraband materials in a foreign country."

Adam's mouth curved into a wicked smile. "It'd be worth it."

"Adam..." Ellie began.

He pushed a tangle of hair away from her face. "Don't worry about it. I've got a fair amount of experience with not getting arrested." His expression grew more serious. "But none of this stuff is completely foolproof."

Ellie felt a burst of irritation. "One would think that the scientific world would put a bit more effort into such matters—perhaps by developing a safe and reliable means of pharmacologically adjusting a woman's chemistry to prevent one or more of the necessary components for conception."

"I'll write to my senator about it," Adam quipped. "But in the meantime— if we do this, we'd need to do it with an understanding that it's still possible you'd end up pregnant."

"How possible?" Ellie pushed back uneasily.

"If we use it right? Pretty unlikely," Adam allowed. "But you'd need to consider how you'd feel about it if something did go awry."

Ellie sat up. The conversation had become too serious to have while lying on the floor. "How would *you* feel about it?"

"Over the moon?" Adam replied where he still laid beside her.

Ellie blinked down at him with shock. "What?"

Adam sat up, running his hand through his hair as he gave a helpless chuckle. "This isn't quite the conversation I thought we'd be having when I dragged you in here."

"You hardly dragged me. As I recall it, I'm the one who had hold of your belt buckle. And I didn't think we'd be talking about anything at all."

Adam gave her a self-satisfied smirk. "Kept your mouth pretty busy for a while, anyway."

Ellie blushed at the memory.

He sobered. "Getting back to what you were asking… I don't want you to get me wrong. The idea of being responsible for something as helpless as a baby scares me more than an army of carnivorous ants."

He raised his hand to her face, brushing his thumb tenderly along the curve of her cheek. "But I'd do it with you. In a heartbeat."

The room began to spin.

Ellie stepped away from him. She plucked her combinations from the floor, pulling them back on.

"But we're not married!" she burst out desperately.

Adam came to his feet as well. He tugged on his trousers and fastened his belt with a casual yank. He gently took hold of her shoulders. "I am aware of that. But I'm pretty sure I made it clear that I'm in this for the long haul."

Ellie melted into him, her arms circling his waist. "You have," she admitted—and then pulled back to look at him worriedly. "But what if I never *want* to have any children?"

"You don't. You already told me that."

Ellie released him to pace across the canvas. "I find them deeply off-putting. Like little monsters who are utterly incapable of articulating their needs but punish you for failing to meet them regardless."

Adam regarded her warily, as though he had found himself in the room with a cornered hyena. "Have you actually been around many kids?"

"I generally avoid them."

"I mean, not that your description's entirely inaccurate, but—"

"They are tiny bundles of inescapable obligation that tie a woman even deeper into the virtual slavery of the patriarchy."

"Ooookay," Adam returned carefully. "That's one way of looking at them…"

Fear snapped through her like a shot of ice in her chest.

"I don't know if I can ever bring myself to do that," she blurted out, holding her arms close to her chest.

Adam gazed down at her softly. "Why's that a problem?"

"Because it means if you stay with me, you'd be giving up your chance to become a father," Ellie pushed back, the fear still clawing at her.

Adam cupped her cheek. "I'm all right with that."

The fear pushed harder. "But what if—"

Adam set a finger to her lips. "I picked you. I'm going to keep on picking you. That's how this works."

Ellie's fear broke, shivering away like falling petals. She fell into Adam, leaning against the warm, bare skin of his shoulder as his arms came around her back. "You say the most unforgivably romantic things sometimes. Do you know that?"

"Maybe I'm trying to get you into bed." His voice danced with humor.

"You just had me in bed."

"That was the floor," Adam reasonably countered.

She raised her hand to trace the delicate lines at the corners of his eyes—the ones that always looked to her like joy.

"I love you, you know," she said softly. "Rather desperately."

Adam dropped his lips to the top of her hair with aching tenderness. His chest pushed against the circle of her arms as he drew in a deep, uneven breath. "Me too, Princess. Me too."

THIRTEEN

*A*DAM BATES WAS feeling pretty damned fine. His body hummed with the after-effects of his time with Ellie. Finding her in the hall after his cool immersion in the pool had been a gift—and Adam had made good use of it.

He was already hungry for more.

Laying his woman out on the floor and giving her everything he had until she was groaning with pleasure had rapidly become one of Adam's favorite hobbies. He'd had far too few opportunities to enjoy it.

He wasn't sure he'd ever get enough—not unless he somehow stole Ellie away to a cabin in the woods for a month.

Or two.

Maybe three, Adam thought, his mind bursting with ideas for how the pair of them could use that time—especially if he got hold of that contraband she'd asked him about.

Granted, these weren't the sort of things Adam ought to be thinking about while sitting at a maharaja's dinner table.

Vijay had opted to make the evening meal a casual family gathering… which was good, as Adam had left his only dinner jacket in a broom closet at the Puri Beach Club. Kalb hadn't been invited to join them, because while Adam had been giving Ellie a thorough re-education in the arts of mutual pleasure, the dog had been rolling around in a swampy puddle at the bottom of a broken fountain. He was being thoroughly scrubbed down by the palace staff.

Adam wondered what it'd be like if he and Ellie got muddy together. He supposed he could haul her into that pool he'd found earlier to rinse off. Watch the water slide over every one of those fantastic curves…

"More pilau, Mr. Bates?" Constance's auntie asked the question in a tone that implied she'd done it once or twice before.

"Huh?" Adam returned blankly.

"She means the rice." Constance elaborated wryly. "Or did you want something more spicy?"

"Rice," Adam blurted out. "Rice is great."

"I'll take the spicy stuff," Neil cut in cheerfully.

Adam froze with the spoon of rice suspended in midair.

"The Andhra chutney?" Parvati offered helpfully. "Or the chili dosa?"

"Both?" Neil asked hopefully.

Parvati loaded the pancakes and crimson peppers onto his plate. Neil dug in with obvious relish.

Constance shifted a surprised and questioning look to Adam.

Adam shoved the rice into his mouth—which kept him from needing to say a damned word.

After dinner, Parvati and Balaram took their leave for the evening, and the rest of the party retreated to Vijay's study. Kalb was delivered back to Adam, thoroughly groomed and clearly miserable about it. The dog immediately plunged behind Adam's legs and hid there as though Adam's shins were capable of concealing sixty pounds of quivering Seluki.

The generously sized room was hung with antique tapestries and paintings that even Adam could tell were worth a small fortune. Bookshelves showed off an assortment of objects that looked to have been chosen out of personal interest rather than value. Musical instruments accompanied well-tended orchids, and tattered novels were stacked beside a wind-up bird that glittered with jewels.

To the left of the bird sat a rock. As someone who'd once had a particular attachment to a rock, Adam strolled over to check it out while the others settled in.

"Look, Princess," Adam said as Ellie came into the room. "The maharaja's got a lucky rock."

The rock was less ordinary on closer inspection. One side of it had been sheared off to form a flat surface that was covered in lines of carved text. The glyphs reminded Adam of Neil's transcription of the Tulsidas manuscript. He leaned in to read aloud the small type on the card next to the stone, where a translation of the script was written in both English and Odia. "*Two and a half years have passed since I became openly a Sakya…*"

Ellie's focus sharpened with rabid interest. "That's one of the edicts of Ashoka—the earliest evidence for the existence of the Buddhist faith *in the world.*"

"Definitely lucky then," Adam concluded.

Her eyes narrowed suspiciously. "Don't even think about stealing it to replace the one you lost."

"I didn't lose it," Adam reminded her. "You threw it in a river. And anyway, I don't need to. I've got Kalb."

"The dog?" Ellie looked down at the animal with obvious skepticism.

Kalb wagged his tail hopefully in response.

"He's lucky, too. Aren't you, buddy?" Adam gave the Seluki a vigorous rub between his ears. Kalb panted blissfully as he absorbed the attention.

"That one's from a ruined stupa at Deomali." Vijay sprawled across one of the chairs in a manner that perfectly balanced comfort with regal elegance.

The way Ellie fixed her attention on him reminded Adam of how Kalb looked when he spotted a pigeon. "Were you able to date the site?"

"There were other engravings with references to the Kalinga War."

"The Kalinga War?" Ellie's eyes glittered avidly.

She was cute when she was excited. Adam fought back a smile.

"Not that I was able to take a very good look at them," Vijay added. "The whole place is infested with pit vipers."

"Pit vipers?" Constance moved closer to her uncle, delighted by the idea of her dashing relative stumbling across a colony of deadly snakes.

Vijay leaned in. "There I was with a boy from the village and a trained mongoose named Tipu Sultan—"

Mr. Chowdhury cut in smoothly from where he stood behind Vijay's chair. "Perhaps we should discuss the translation?"

Vijay flashed him a boyish and thoroughly unrepentant grin.

Yeah, Adam thought distractedly. There was definitely more going on between those two than legal advice, even if the solicitor did play it safe with his formal demeanor.

He wished them well of it. Adam had never had much tolerance for the rabid wolves who salivated at the chance to grind someone else down because they happened to be different.

That had gotten him into trouble once or twice.

Well—maybe more than twice.

Padma took the other chair, settling into it with regal grace. Mr. Mahjoud stood in attendance behind her, wearing a freshly pressed suit and a dapper fez. Ellie positioned herself on the settee, her back straight with the posture of an attentive student.

Adam left the seats to the others, leaning against the bookcase. Kalb collapsed into a pile of lanky golden limbs by his boots, worn out from the day's exertions.

Neil wandered into the study and immediately pivoted toward the rock. "Hold on—is this Ashokan?"

"It's the maharaja's lucky rock," Adam informed him.

Neil blinked at him through his spectacles.

"How well do you four know the story of the Ramayana?" Mr. Chowdhury asked, reining in the conversation with a practiced air of authority.

Neil reluctantly tore his attention from the rock.

"My brother and I have both read Mr. Dutt's English translation," Ellie replied.

"I didn't need to read it," Constance asserted, plopping down on the sofa beside her. "I've only been hearing about Lord Rama all my life, thanks to Aai."

Mr. Chowdhury shifted a questioning gaze to Adam.

"I figured I'd let them do the reading," Adam filled in.

"How much do you recall about Lord Rama's exile?" Vijay pressed.

Neil adjusted his spectacles, falling easily into the mode of an oral report. "It came about as a result of the treachery of Rama's stepmother, Kaikeyi. She leveraged a past oath the king had made to her and used it to force him to banish Rama to the forest of Dandakaranya, which was known as the abode of the rakshasas—demons with great powers. Rama's loyal brother Lakshmana went with him, as did his wife, Sita."

"For all the good she did," Constance grumbled.

Adam cocked a brow at her dry tone.

Padma's eyes glinted dangerously. "Do you disapprove of Lady Sita, Kondi?"

"She follows her husband into the forest, gets herself kidnapped, and then sits around waiting for a rescue," Constance rattled off. "Why would anyone be impressed by that?"

"Had she not been kidnapped, Sri Rama might never have gone to war against Ravana and stopped his tyranny," Vijay countered reasonably.

"That doesn't make Sita any less useless," Constance stubbornly retorted.

"She certainly isn't treated very fairly by her husband," Ellie added with a disapproving frown. "Even after she's rescued, Rama forces her to walk through a fire to prove that she was faithful to him while in captivity—as though her virtue was more important than the fact that she'd managed to stay alive!"

Constance waved a hand at Ellie. "See?"

"And what do you know about the astras?" Mr. Chowdhury pressed with a note of mild exasperation at the digression.

Neil answered from where he hovered by the bookshelves. "Divine weapons. They were gifted by the gods to those they deemed worthy."

"But the astras aren't physical objects," Ellie clarified. "They're *invocations*. Once someone has been granted the sacred mantra by the gods, they can summon the power of the astra into any vessel they choose. A spear, a stone, a blade of grass…"

"Or an arrow, obviously," Constance piped in. "Lord Rama was an archer."

"Each invocation of the weapon can be used precisely once," Ellie noted. "After which the astra must be summoned into a new object to be wielded again."

"And the Brahmastra?" Vijay prompted with uncharacteristic solemnity.

Neil shifted uncomfortably. "I was left with the impression that the Brahmastra could kill anyone that it was directed at."

"It can do a great deal more than that," Padma corrected him. "When Sri Rama invoked it against the god of the sea and was then deterred from killing him, he shot his arrow into the wilderness instead and created the Thar Desert."

Neil adjusted his spectacles. "How big is the Thar Desert?"

Mr. Chowdhury met his gaze from across the room. "It covers a significant portion of Rajasthan."

Adam had always had a knack for geography, which meant he had a pretty good sense of the scale of destruction they were talking about—a wave of power that leveled entire forests and scorched hundreds of miles of grassland. Lakes dried up like pots left too long on the stove.

Anyone unfortunate enough to be there burned to ash.

Part of him wanted to shield himself from the notion by mustering up a comfortable skepticism—but he couldn't. He'd seen too damned much of what other arcana could do to doubt the stories about this one.

Then Mr. Chowdhury made it worse. "There are also indications that the astra could potentially be directed at a more… *dispersed* target."

Adam crossed his arms. Kalb sensed the tension in the movement, glancing up at him curiously. "What's that mean, exactly?"

Ellie stiffened. "You're talking about Lakshmana and Indrajit."

"Who?" Constance frowned with confusion.

Vijay replied from his throne-like seat. "Miss Mallory refers to a lesser known incident from the Ramayana narrative. Indrajit was the eldest son of the demon king Ravana. Rama's brother Lakshmana became so enraged with Indrajit that he called the Brahmastra not just to kill Ravana's son, but with the intention of slaying every demon on the earth."

"Only Rama stopped him, because not all the demons were part of Ravana's army," Ellie added uneasily.

Neil stepped forward. "Hold on—are you saying that this weapon is capable of wiping out an entire category of people? All of them, regardless of where in the world they happened to be? Just like that?"

Padma answered him in a voice as dry as gravel. "That is our understanding."

"Hell," Adam muttered feelingly.

Padma set down her tea. "And now perhaps you see why we have reason for concern."

Concern. The word was a gross understatement when talking about a weapon that could wipe out an entire people.

Grim determination settled over Adam. "I can't say I'm fond of the notion of a weapon like that falling into the hands of a guy like Borthwick."

"An object infused with the power of the astra cannot be banished or undone," Vijay elaborated. "It may only be destroyed by being used. We believe that Tulsidas's text refers to an instance of the Brahmastra that was created but never launched against a target."

Ellie's fingers tapped thoughtfully against the arm of the sofa, her mind working. "Like the one Lakshmana summoned against Indrajit and the rakshasas."

"But that means if even Borthwick found it, he could only use it once," Neil deduced hopefully.

"I'm not sure it needs to be more than that to be a real bad idea," Adam pointed out.

Mr. Chowdhury exchanged a knowing look with his prince. "That is our thinking as well."

"So how do we find it?" Adam demanded. "Did you get anything useful out of that transcription?"

"Dr. Fairfax copied the glyphs with reasonable accuracy," Mr. Chowdhury replied.

Neil slumped with relief. "Oh, thank God!"

Vijay pulled a notebook from his pocket. He scanned the room, ensuring that he had everyone's rapt attention, and then read. *"To seek the lost astra, keep your father's oath and follow Lord Rama's footsteps across the River of Wisdom."*

"That could refer to keeping the path of proper dharma," Ellie mused.

"Or that we're going into the woods," Adam countered. "Isn't that where your prince was exiled in order to *keep his father's oath?* A haunted forest?"

"The Dandakaranya," Mr. Chowdhury confirmed.

"That happen to be a real place, by any chance?" Adam pressed.

"The wilderness at the western border of Odisha has long been associated with Lord Rama's exile," Vijay replied.

"There a river around there?"

Padma answered. "A tributary of the Godavari known locally as the Jnananadi."

"Which is Sanskrit for *River of Wisdom,*" Vijay explained with a hint of mischief.

"Tulsidas wasn't beating around the bush," Adam noted dryly.

"Apparently not," Ellie agreed. "But is there more?"

Constance popped up from the couch, leaning over her uncle's chair as she read excitedly from his notebook. *"Join the Lord of the Dance on the ridge that points to the dawn of the longest day. Let his shadow lead you to the ruins of the most loyal kingdom."*

She looked wonderingly to Ellie, Neil, and Adam as she finished. *"Seek the path to the Astra of the Creator by the Waters of the Son of the Wind, where nobility of spirit is never untouchable."*

"But what does all that mean?" Neil demanded helplessly.

Vijay's reply carried a dangerous note of challenge. "I suppose the answer to that question lies on the other side of the Jnananadi."

At his words, emotion chased through Ellie's eyes like the quickly turning pages of another book.

Excitement at the prospect of chasing down another mystery from the past.

Fear of what failing to find it might mean.

Adam looked to the maharaja and his companion. "I'm guessing you don't have a map with a handy 'X' right over these Waters of the Son of the Wind."

"No," Vijay admitted. "In fact, the region we're speaking of has been only loosely mapped at all. It isn't generally considered very *salubrious* territory for casual explorers."

"Why's that?" Adam demanded.

"Pythons," Vijay replied. "Tigers."

"Tribal revolutionaries," Padma added.

Vijay picked innocently at the cuff of his tunic. "I can't say I know anything about that."

Mr. Chowdhury glanced up at the ceiling as though searching for patience, muttering under his breath.

Adam checked to see if Mr. Mahjoud showed any sign of recognition at the solicitor's words, because he was fairly certain the man had just recited a d'ua for patience against adversity.

"The Adrija Khond are a lovely people," Vijay insisted.

"If one dismisses the rumors that they formerly engaged in human sacrifice," Padma blithely countered.

Neil blanched with discomfort. "What's that?"

Ellie lifted her chin stoutly. "I was under the impression that accounts of human sacrifice in India were greatly exaggerated by colonial agents as an excuse to dispossess less privileged castes and lay claim to their natural resources."

"I'm sure you're right," Vijay returned lightly.

Mr. Chowdhury shot him a dry look before elaborating. "The Adrija are one of the clans that populate the remote hill villages. They speak a different language from the Odia people here in the plains and have their own faith and cultural practices. They are sometimes… *wary* of outsiders."

Adam had the distinct impression that Mr. Chowdhury was choosing his words with great tact.

Vijay crossed his legs, waving a regally dismissive hand. "But the royal family of Nandapur has a relationship with the clan going back generations. There's a quaint tradition where whenever a new member of the family takes the throne, the Adrija engage in a ritual kidnapping and carry him off to the forest. They pretend to mull over whether to sacrifice him or a water buffalo for a little while, and then opt for the buffalo."

Ellie perked up. "What a fascinating bit of ethnography! It clearly implies a ritual assertion that the Adrija are not obligated to accept the rule of the Nandapur kings but only choose to do so of their own free will."

"I doubt the Adrija would do much of what I asked them to if they didn't want to," Vijay agreed. "They're terribly independent-minded. But they have also historically made up a significant portion of the royal army—not that we have one of those anymore."

Vijay punctuated the remark with a sly look at Mr. Chowdhury.

"Of course not," Mr. Chowdhury replied tiredly. "Because maintaining your own army would be considered grounds for the Raj to declare war upon you."

"If anyone can tell us where the rest of the landmarks from this text are located in the forest, it will be the Adrija Khond," Vijay asserted. "I would love to bring you to the village and introduce you to the local leaders there myself, but one of Nawaz's sources has informed us that Colonel Borthwick is headed to Nandapur."

Adam was starting to get a headache. "I'm guessing that means he found somebody to read that manuscript."

"And deduced the most likely place to start the journey," Vijay confirmed. "But they'll have a difficult time finding a guide. There aren't many people outside of the hill tribes who are willing to go into that forest."

"On account of the tigers," Adam filled in.

"Don't forget the demons." Vijay's eyes twinkled mischievously before he once more assumed a regal air. "I will do what I can to delay Borthwick here."

"*Carefully*," Mr. Chowdhury added pointedly.

"When am I not careful?" Vijay complained.

"Far more often than I would like," Mr. Chowdhury drolly returned.

"The colonial authorities are always hunting for an excuse to annex the territory of the remaining princes," Vijay elaborated dismissively.

The solicitor's reply was weighed with a concern that had nothing to do with the law. "The rest of the princes are not *you*."

An answering feeling flashed in Vijay's eyes before both men swept the look under their respective veils again—one of regal authority, and the other of intellectual control.

"Borthwick already suspects you're up to more than you ought to be," Padma warned.

Constance brightened with avid fascination. "Are you?"

Vijay flashed her a grin, and Mr. Chowdhury gave a long-suffering sigh.

Padma's authoritative tones cut through the room. "You will have to send them alone."

Vijay frowned, displeased by his aunt's assertion. "We have ample resources here that we can put at their disposal."

"None of which can be seen to be associated with any effort to thwart Borthwick." Padma shifted a merciless glare to Mr. Chowdhury. "Or am I wrong, Nawaz?"

Mr. Chowdhury's jaw was tight. "No."

"One of your sources," Adam echoed significantly. "That's who told you Borthwick was coming. Not your local administrator?"

Vijay gave Adam a thoughtful look. "That's right."

"And is that usually how you find out high-ranking Raj officials are going to be in the neighborhood?"

"It is not," Mr. Chowdhury replied significantly.

"The man's on a secret mission to retrieve a priceless Indian artifact," Vijay dismissed. "That's not the sort of thing one formally announces one is doing."

"Perhaps he's trying to sneak past you," Constance theorized.

"Or catch you getting involved," Adam countered.

Adam felt the full royal weight of the maharaja's disapproving glare, but refused to back down.

"And what happens if Borthwick does find out you're part of this?" he pressed.

Mr. Chowdhury answered. "He loses Nandapur."

The words had weight.

Vijay turned an imperious glare on his solicitor. Mr. Chowdhury faced it steadily, his expression soft with unveiled sympathy.

"Damn you," Vijay cursed—but Adam could already see that he had given in.

"Utilizing Nandapur's resources must be a last resort." Padma's words had the air of a final ruling.

Ellie lifted her chin stoutly. "The four of us were already planning to see this through to the end."

"I should like to see you try to leave me out of it," Constance challenged.

Neil straightened. "Of course, I'll help—not that I know what use I'll really be."

"You were plenty of use last time," Adam pointed out.

Neil glanced over at him with an expression of quiet surprise.

"They will need a guide to the Adrija village—and an introduction," Padma declared. "The Adrija will be especially cautious of strangers if Borthwick is involved."

Adam's hackles instinctively rose. "Why's Borthwick a threat to this village?"

"The Criminal Tribes Act," Mr. Chowdhury replied. "It empowers Borthwick, as head of the Thuggee and Dacoity Department, to declare any tribal community unlawful."

"Unlawful," Ellie echoed tensely. "And what does that mean, exactly?"

Mr. Chowdhury's eyes flashed with an anger that belied his habitually cool manner. "It means that the movements of every man, woman, and child in the community can be proscribed. The whole group might be forcibly relocated and kept under police guard. No one can go anywhere without a pass. Sometimes the male children are removed from their families and sent to reformatory camps."

Ellie's knuckles whitened where she gripped the arm of the sofa. "How is that legal?"

The solicitor answered her tiredly. "The assumption is that criminality is a heritable trait. If one determines that a particular village includes a number of lawbreakers, one can reasonably prevent further crime by declaring the entire group criminals in advance."

"*Reasonably,*" Ellie echoed tautly.

Adam shared the feeling he could hear in her voice, a low hum of anger rising at Mr. Chowdhury's description. "And how many villages has Borthwick declared criminal?"

Mr. Chowdhury met his gaze. "Forty-three."

"My God," Neil said softly, his face drawn.

Adam's fist clenched.

Forty-three communities condemned on the word of a single administrator, from grandparents to infants. Told where they could live. Separated from their families. Subject to untold other discrimination—because who would protect the people of a group that had been branded with such a stamp of disgrace?

The situation promised suffering that would resonate down generations… and all on one man's word.

Ellie stiffened with furious indignation. "No one should have that kind of power."

"Especially not Borthwick," Neil added shakily, likely recalling his time with the man while he had made his illicit copy of the manuscript.

"Is it a good idea to involve these Adrija with that much at stake?" Adam demanded.

"They won't want Borthwick wandering around their territory, either," Vijay returned. "And they know how to be discreet."

"Who will guide them to the village?" Padma demanded.

Vijay glanced significantly at his companion.

Mr. Chowdhury blanched. "Are you quite sure that's a good idea?"

"They would only need to be led as far as the village," Vijay countered.

Mr. Chowdhury rubbed a tired hand over his angular features. "Fine."

Padma rose from her chair in a regal dismissal. "Then it's settled. They will leave in the morning."

Vijay treated Adam and the others to a final royal glare as he paused by the door. "If any of you should find yourselves facing the slightest *hint* of danger—"

"We'll lay low and call for help," Adam promised—and tried to ignore the itch of worry at the back of his skull.

Mr. Chowdhury spoke authoritatively from the maharaja's side. "I'll see to all the arrangements. You should be ready for departure immediately after breakfast."

"Any questions?" Padma prompted casually.

Ellie bit her lip with everything she obviously wanted to ask. Neil looked a bit ashen.

Constance bounced on the settee with excitement. "None, Aai!"

"Then go to bed," Padma ordered.

"Ma'am," Adam acknowledged—and herded his friends out the door.

FOURTEEN

$\mathcal{N}$EIL FAIRFAX'S MIND raced as he walked through the twilit shadows under the ancient, sprawling trees. He was facing yet another plunge into danger, this time in the form of an expedition to a legendary forest in the company of a band of revolutionaries. All of that would have been quite enough to keep him from sleep, but a different worry had carried him outside.

He had found his way to one of the maharaja's many gardens, the quiet pathways swathed with the gloom of evening. Here and there, light filtered through the leaves from the softly glowing windows of the palace wings that framed the secluded space.

The lamp Neil carried spilled a golden pool of illumination over the walkway in front of him. In his other hand, he held a long bundle wrapped in an old towel.

The air smelled of frangipani. Artificial waterfalls splashed softly into trickling streams that fed the abundant flowerbeds. The many trunks of an enormous banyan tree whispered with the quick movements of night birds while smaller animals scurried through the ground cover.

Neil froze at the sound of a strange, nasal squawk—then breathed a sigh of relief as a peacock waddled onto the path in front of him.

Kalb burst from a wall of fragrant lantana, treating the bird to an excited bark. The peacock startled with a raucous squawk, tail feathers flaring out in a threatening display.

Kalb scrabbled back with a whine.

The peacock charged at the dog, which whirled into a retreat. Both animals plunged back into the lantana in an explosion of pink petals.

Neil watched them pass with a blink of surprise. The garden settled back into quiet chirps and rustles.

Those ordinary sounds of the night mingled with something unexpected as Neil continued along the path. He was arrested by the twang of a sitar, the delicate flow of notes cascading through the air in a melody edged with longing.

Unaccountably stirred, Neil looked for the source of the sound—only for it to suddenly stop.

He found himself gazing out over a broad, square pool of water illuminated by a sliver of moonlight. A structure stood in the center of the pond, cleverly built to appear as though it floated on the mirror-still surface. It was anchored to the shore by a slender walkway. The walls were made of delicate wooden screens that had seen better days. Two sides had fallen in, which afforded Neil a view of the interior.

The building was abandoned, and the music had gone. Neil wondered if perhaps the notes had traveled to him from somewhere else, like one of the distant palace windows he glimpsed now and then through the interlacing branches of the jackfruit trees.

A soft, uncanny chill shivered down his spine. Neil shook it off and moved on.

Beyond another bend in the path stood a small pavilion. The domed roof was held up by airy columns linked by waist-high balustrades. Marigolds clustered around the foundation. Another frangipani stood to one side of the building, bursting with pale white blooms.

Slivers of light from another section of the palace were just barely visible through the leaves, marking the place as sufficiently secluded for Neil's purposes.

His boots were silent on the thick, soft grass as he stepped off the path. Climbing the low steps, he set the slender bundle he'd been carrying down on one of the stone rails. The folds of the cloth fell aside, revealing what lay within.

Neil stared down at the sword Dyrnwyn as though it were a snake poised to rise up and strike him.

He hadn't really handled the arcanum since Constance had shoved it at him after his near-death encounter with Julian Forster-Mowbray on a ridge beyond the Amarna plain. He knew that it was ridiculous for him to keep lugging it around the world wrapped in an old towel in his trunk—but a substantial part of him would have been perfectly content to keep doing exactly that.

The other part, both uneasy and impossible to dismiss, had been driven out to the garden by the echo of his sister's words.

Have you considered possibly using it?

Neil had not. He wasn't sure that he wanted to. But he knew he owed the sword more than he'd been giving it.

He gave the arcanum a closer inspection where it lay on the rail, mentally cataloging its features. The sword was both humble and beautiful. The blade was iron with a naturally duller hue than modern steel would have. In the light of Neil's lantern, subtle variegations rippled through the metal in elegant waves. The shapes were evidence of the twist-welding technique that some ancient Anglo-Saxon blacksmith had used to craft the weapon.

The hilt was carved bone wrapped in gold filigree. Neil wasn't certain what type of bone. That thought occurred to him frequently and uncomfortably when he had cause to touch it. The material was softly yellowed with age and smooth from centuries of handling, ending at the crossed iron bar of the hand guard.

They were all the same features that he had cataloged the last time he'd studied Dyrnwyn, back in Egypt.

Which left only the least comfortable part of his examination to complete.

Drawing in a deep, uneasy breath, Neil lifted the sword from the railing.

Silent tongues of pale flame whirled up the dark gray length of the blade.

Neil stared at the uncanny fire with dismay. Dyrnwyn was only supposed to react magically when held by someone 'well born or worthy.' Admittedly, it had burst alight once before when Neil had snatched it up to defend himself and Constance from his murderous ex-employer—but part of him had dared to hope that might have just been the sword reacting to the extremity of his circumstances. Surely Dyrnwyn didn't think him *routinely* worth its magic.

The softly flickering light in his hand begged otherwise.

"Bugger," Neil cursed aloud.

A voice called from beyond the curve of the path. "Is that you, Stuffy?"

Footsteps crunched along the gravel. Neil fumbled his grip on the sword, then quickly slammed it down onto the balustrade and released the hilt.

The flames snuffed out with a soft *whoosh*.

He threw the old towel over the mythical weapon, then whirled as Constance poked her head around the trunk of the frangipani.

"I thought I heard you just then," she commented cheerfully.

Neil didn't answer. He was too busy staring at her.

Constance had changed since dinner. Gone was her fashionable skirt and striped blouse. Instead, she was draped in elegant folds of purple and gold. The featherlight silk wrapped around her waist, crossing her shoulder to fall down her back. A closely-fitted choli with cropped sleeves left the soft curves of her arms exposed.

Constance preened, doing a turn. "Do you like it? It's Auntie Parvati's. She said this was the Santali drape. I must admit, it's a sight more comfortable in this heat than buttoning into a waistcoat."

The soft glow of the lamp cast notes of gold over the thick black length of her hair, loosely braided and tossed over her shoulder. The pale flowers of the frangipani shone like stars behind her.

Neil's voice came out in a croak. "It's… nice."

Constance set her hands on her hips, unimpressed. "Nice?"

"Very nice," Neil quickly corrected himself.

He was glad that in the gloom of the garden, Constance couldn't see the tips of his ears turning pink—because he could feel them burning.

His response obviously fell somewhat short of her expectations. He struggled for something better. "It suits you."

Constance twisted as though trying to get a better look at herself. "Do you really think so? I still don't know that I feel entirely Indian."

"But you aren't entirely Indian," Neil replied a little stupidly.

Constance cocked an eyebrow at him.

Neil swallowed thickly. "I mean that you're both. British and Indian." He suppressed the urge to wince. "Which is nice."

"I suppose I'll take that as a compliment. What are you doing out here, anyway?"

Neil was uncomfortably conscious of what was hidden under the old towel on the railing behind him. "Just needed a little air?" he offered weakly.

Constance climbed the steps to join him inside the pavilion. She gave the space a thoughtful study. "This garden's meant to be haunted, you know. Supposedly a princess here had to be married off to an evil Mughal lord, but she was in love with someone else and used to sneak away to meet him in the Floating Hall."

"Floating Hall?" Neil echoed.

Constance studied the high arch of the dome. "That building on the lake. Her lover was an itinerant musician who had stolen her heart with his playing."

Neil's thoughts tumbled back to the delicate notes that he had heard as he passed the ruined structure earlier. "Sitar," he burst out.

Constance looked surprised. "Did someone already tell you the story?"

Neil felt dizzy. "I'm sure I… read it somewhere."

He hadn't read it somewhere. It had been his bloody power acting up again—right when he didn't need it to, just like always.

Those inconvenient outbursts seemed to be happening more often. Perhaps Sayyid had flung open a door in Neil's mind when he had mercilessly thrust the uncomfortable truth about Neil's leaps of historical intuition into his awareness.

Or maybe it was just India. He *was* traveling through a land with an exceptionally rich history. But then, London was rich with history too, and Neil didn't run about seeing men with togas wandering the streets.

Well—there had been that one time in Colchester. But those toga-clad fellows outside the market had clearly been fraternity pledges.

Except that Neil didn't know of any fraternities in Colchester.

The blood drained from his head. They might not have been fraternity pledges. Just like the fellow in Renaissance dress drinking a mug of ale in a smoke-stained Blackfriars pub might not have been a rogue actor.

Maybe Neil wasn't tumbling into the past more often. Maybe he'd been doing it all along—and was only now figuring that out.

For all the bloody good it did him. What had Sayyid called him back in Egypt? A wali—the Islamic term for someone gifted by God, like a saint.

If Neil were a saint, he was an utterly useless one.

With all this musing, Neil had gone conspicuously quiet. Thankfully, Constance didn't seem to notice. She seemed a mite preoccupied herself.

She hopped up to sit on one of the rails, her legs dangling over the floor. She wore a pair of delicate leather sandals, her toes peeking out from under the hem of her sari.

They were very nice toes, Neil noted distractedly.

"It's funny, isn't it?" Constance mused, swinging her perfect toes. "Ten years ago, you were Ellie's stick-in-the-mud older brother, and I was a pest setting beetles loose in your sock drawer. And now here we are."

"Here we are?" Neil echoed confusedly.

"Friends," Constance pressed back impatiently. "Aren't we?"

Neil wondered absently at her question. Were they friends?

Constance had grown from the danger gnome into an exceptional woman bursting with intelligence, courage, and principle. Neil had become remarkably fond of her in the relatively short time since they had become reacquainted. In fact, she fit into his life so naturally that he found it hard to imagine how he had gone through so many years without her.

Of course, they were friends… even if Neil's brain occasionally spat up random, awkward thoughts about how pretty she was.

Like now, as the gilded threads of her sari shimmered where they framed the curve of her hips.

Neil yanked his attention from Constance's hips. "Obviously. Yes."

The words were a bit lacking after all the extra time it had taken him to answer, so Neil pushed them a bit further. "You know I'm here for you, Connie."

The response was solidly friendly.

Constance's eyes narrowed thoughtfully. "It's funny that you should say that, Stuffy… because as it happens, I need to ask you for a somewhat unusual favor."

A thrill of warning danced along Neil's spine. "A favor?"

"Nothing too dramatic, I promise," Constance quickly assured him.

Neil did not feel very assured—but it would hardly have been friendly of him to admit that. "I'm happy to help. What do you need?"

His attention hitched once more on Constance's elegant toes. He could glimpse the perfect turn of her ankle above the strap of her sandal.

"Just for us to become engaged for a little while," Constance replied lightly.

Neil's thoughts stuck on how Constance's ankle must necessarily lead to the firm, strong curve of her calf. "What's that?" he asked blankly.

Then his mind caught up, and the columns of the pavilion tilted dangerously.

Just for us to become engaged.

Constance hopped down from the rail. "Not for real, of course. We'd only be pretending—but at least that would stop my family from throwing suitors at me. They are determined that I must marry before my next birthday, which is only four months away, as you know perfectly well."

"November twelfth," Neil blurted out automatically. His head was still spinning as he struggled to absorb Constance's words.

A pretend engagement. Between him and Constance.

The spinning burned away in a rush of righteous indignation. "Hold on—*determined* that you will marry? What does that mean, exactly?"

Constance didn't seem to hear him. "And now it appears that Aai has decided to take sides in the matter. You know how Aai gets when she has set her mind to something. She is terrifyingly effective. But if I'm able to convince the family that I'm already getting married, it would give me time to think of a more permanent way to diffuse the situation."

"But what are they threatening to do?" Neil's voice rose. "Marry you off to the next bounder who comes along?"

Constance arched a brow at the blazing heat in his tone. "I don't believe that's precisely what they have in mind."

"Then what the devil *do* they have in mind?" Neil stormed across the pavilion. "What else does it mean, exactly, to compel someone to become married?"

Constance looked wryly amused as he paced the ground in front of her. "I believe the intention is to push me to stop being quite so particular and agree to select one of the available gentlemen for myself."

"Because that's a bad thing? Being particular about who you're planning to spend the rest of your life with?" Neil whirled on her. "Back in Puri, you said the men who courted you acted like you were some prize they wanted to mount on the wall like a bloody hunting trophy."

Constance watched him with barely concealed curiosity. "A good few of them, certainly."

Neil's voice echoed off the dome of the pavilion with considerable force. "How can your parents think it's acceptable to pressure you into marrying someone who's going to treat you like that?"

"I suppose they think I'm being overly picky."

He jabbed a finger at her. "But *are* you opposed to marriage?"

"Not on principle."

Neil threw up his arms. "Then why would they assume you aren't reasonably and intelligently assessing the merits of the potential candidates that you've been introduced to?"

Constance's eyes danced with humor. "They likely think I'm too young to know any better."

"So you're too young to know any better, but old enough to be compelled into precipitously binding yourself to a person who would have an inordinate amount of power over you for the rest of your life."

Constance's mouth twitched with a barely suppressed smile. "You realize you sound like Ellie right now."

"She's my sister," Neil retorted. "It's not as though I've never listened to her."

"I had no idea you were such a liberal thinker."

"It's not liberal to state obvious facts!"

Constance patted his arm soothingly. "Of course, it isn't. So—what do you think?"

"About what?" Neil frowned, momentarily confused.

"Pretending to be engaged with me," Constance replied. "Just for a little while! As soon as I've figured out a better strategy for escaping their scheme, we'll find a way out of it."

Neil's righteous anger crashed into a muddle of worry. "How does one find a way out of an engagement?"

"You just break it off," Constance airily assured him.

"But… what do we tell everyone?"

"That we changed our minds."

Neil's thoughts moved through cake batter. "Have you ever known of someone who called off an engagement before? Was it really that simple?"

Constance shifted uncomfortably. "Not exactly."

Neil felt a low thrill of alarm. "What does that mean?"

"Well, Albert Harper ran off with his fiancée's cousin."

"I see."

"And then there was Richard Lattimore," Constance continued. "He turned out to have a load of gambling debts."

"Right," Neil returned, unease creeping up his spine.

"Nobody ever gave a reason for why Mr. Lang broke things off with Miss Caffrey—but everyone simply assumed that he found someone with more money."

Neil stiffened with indignation. "That fellow sounds like a rotter."

Constance's face fell with dismay. "They *all* ended up sounding like rotters." She shook her head. "I take it all back. We can't have a fake engagement."

"Hold on—I didn't say that," Neil pushed back. "I just think we need to consider all the possible—"

"No." Constance took up his place pacing across the pavilion floor. "Don't you see? Even if we made it clear that it was a love match, and not that you had seduced me to get your hands on my fortune—"

"That I *what?*" Neil burst out with a lurch of mortification.

"Don't worry about it. I'm sure we could have convinced them," Constance assured him with a dismissive wave of her hand.

Her words sparked a wicked curiosity. "How would we have done that, exactly?"

"But it doesn't matter," Constance pressed on, ignoring his question. "I'll have to find another stratagem for escaping Aai's marital machinations. I won't be responsible for branding you a rascal and ruining your future marriage prospects."

"*My* marriage prospects?" Neil stared at her, his mind struggling to keep up. "I am an unemployed archaeologist from a family nobody has ever heard of."

Constance set her hands on her hips. "Don't be silly. You have a great deal to offer a potential wife."

"Like what, exactly?" Neil asked, bewildered.

"All sorts of things!" Constance studied him with frank curiosity. "Haven't you any interest in being married?"

Neil adjusted his collar. It suddenly felt a bit tight, even though he had left his bow tie back in his room. "I suppose I've always assumed that I would marry, once I met the right person."

"What would the right person look like?" Constance pressed with a note of avid interest.

Neil's mind blanked of everything but hair like polished ebony, enormous brown eyes, and a gorgeously curved body with knives strapped to it.

"No idea," he blurted out.

Constance was clearly dissatisfied with his response. "But what's in your 'wife space?'"

"My 'wife space?'"

"You know." Constance waved an impatient hand. "The place in your life that a wife would fit into. What do you imagine she would do all day while you're off being scholarly? Make you dinner? Paint watercolors? Manage your household?"

"What household? In Canonbury, there's just Sylvia who does the cooking and a girl who comes in three times a week to clean. But neither of them requires much managing. Sylvia knows what she's doing better than Mum does."

Constance gave an exasperated huff. "Then what do you expect your wife to do all day?"

"Whatever she wants to?" Neil returned uncertainly.

Constance considered him thoughtfully. "You have really given no thought at all to what role a woman might play in your life?"

Neil's mind was abruptly flooded with thoughts of one role he had most certainly imagined a woman playing in his life.

Very *vividly* imagined.

Not that anyone had played that role for him as of yet.

Of course, he knew perfectly well what would be involved. One could hardly study Greek pottery for two semesters without learning a thing or two about the arts of love.

A few less scholarly reference volumes had fallen into his hands as they circulated around Cambridge. The fervor with which Neil had devoured them had been far from strictly academic.

At Constance's inquiry, he remembered those illicit readings once again… only it was Constance's face he saw hovering above him as she pinned his hands to the headboard.

Constance who was staring at him right now, puzzled by Neil's conspicuously ongoing silence.

He jolted with panic. "Obviously," he burst out.

Neil realized that might not have been an appropriate answer.

Had she even asked him a question?

He couldn't remember.

"I mean—nothing," he amended.

The pavilion spun gently around him. Neil wondered if he would feel like this if he were ever run over by a stampede.

Constance's brow furrowed with concern. "Are you quite all right?"

He drew in a careful breath, wrestling to regain his self-control. This was Constance. She was his friend—practically a sister. Certainly not someone he was going to haul against his body as he ran his hands over her…

"Fine," Neil coughed out desperately. "Excellent."

Constance eyed him skeptically. "You're not having some sort of mild seizure?"

Neil gritted his teeth. "I am not having a seizure."

"Well, that's good," Constance concluded. "As for the rest—pretend I never brought it up."

Worry still roiled through Neil's chest, mingling with the lingering after-effects of his wretched burst of lust. "But what will you do?"

Constance waved dismissively. "I'll think of something."

"If you're sure…" Neil returned uneasily.

Constance crossed her arms over her chest. "You are *not* pretending to marry me, Stuffy."

"Right," Neil agreed awkwardly.

"Honestly, you're a dear for even considering it." After a moment of thoughtful hesitation, Constance punctuated her words by popping up onto her toes and planting a kiss on his cheek.

Her lips were a soft pressure against Neil's skin. His hand twitched with the urge to reach for her silk-clad hip.

Danger gnome, he reminded himself urgently.

"See you in the morning," Constance promised, and hopped down from the pavilion.

Neil watched her go, unease settling inside of him like a lump of stone.

He tried to reason the feeling away. Everything would be fine. Constance was a master at dreaming up ways to get herself out of trouble—or into it.

Mostly the latter, he admitted uncomfortably.

She would find her way out of this particular trouble, he was sure of it.

Refraining from entering into a false engagement over the matter was clearly the more sensible course of action.

Everything was going to be fine.

Swallowing a lingering thread of unease, he turned back to the problem that had brought him out into the garden in the first place.

The sword was still hidden under the folds of the old towel where it sat on the balustrade. Neil didn't particularly feel like facing that dilemma again that evening. He bundled the mythical weapon in the cloth as he scooped it up.

Dyrnwyn slipped free of the fabric.

With a flailing instinct, Neil lurched for the hilt. His fingers closed around bone—and the blade *whooshed* with flame.

The towel caught fire.

Neil frantically shook the cloth loose from the fiery arcanum, then stomped on it to extinguish the smoldering edges. He held the sword out awkwardly in the air at his side as he prayed he wasn't about to set something else alight.

The weight of the weapon pulled his arm back. Neil fumblingly righted his grip just as the blade swung against one of the pavilion's mossy pillars.

It seemed to snag against the stone. With a twist of his wrist, Neil pulled it loose.

He clasped the flaming sword with both hands, holding it still and steady in front of him as he caught his breath. Carefully, he shifted Dyrnwyn to his left hand, then used the right to pull a handkerchief from his pocket. He yanked the scrap of fabric around the hilt, and the blade finally snuffed out.

Shoulders sagging with relief, Neil finally wrapped the weapon in the slightly charred towel. Holding it to his chest, he indulged in a moment of feeling wretchedly sorry for himself.

How had he ended up with this thing? What the devil was he going to do with it?

He resigned himself to completely failing to find an answer to either of those questions tonight.

Picking up the lantern, he turned to go—then hesitated as something caught his eye on the surface of the nearby pillar. He brought the lamp closer, where the glow fell across a straight, dark cut that marred the stone.

The line was very regular for a natural fault in the rock. Strangely, it looked as though the moss that grew over the surface was neatly severed as well.

That's odd, he thought with an uneasy itch of discomfort.

He backed away from it—both the railing and the feeling—and hurried from the pavilion.

FIFTEEN

$\mathscr{E}$LLIE FELT FRESH and rested as she stepped into the breakfast room the next morning. The space was bright and airy with a Morris print paper on the walls and thick Persian carpets on the floor. The buffet table was loaded with platters of unfamiliar dishes that all smelled delicious. She headed for the teapot first, pouring out a cup of strong, milky brew.

Neil trailed into the room. He wore a green canvas shooting jacket over a brown waistcoat. Elle was momentarily thrown by the sight of him in something other than tweed, but he must have already dressed for their excursion.

His eyes were ringed with shadows behind the frames of his spectacles.

"You look a bit rough," Ellie pointed out.

"Thank you," Neil replied tiredly.

"Was it the heat? Or was the bed too soft?"

"Connie asked me to marry her," Neil replied distractedly as he poured himself a cup.

Ellie froze with the sugar spoon suspended over her tea.

"I mean to pretend to be marrying her," Neil quickly corrected himself. "To be engaged. Pretending… to be engaged."

"Drat," Ellie blurted out. "I wondered whether she really planned to go through with that."

Neil fumbled his tea, nearly spilling it. "You *knew* about it?"

Ellie squirmed. "It's possible that she might have briefly mentioned that the notion had occurred to her…"

"And you didn't think to tell me?"

"I didn't know she was serious!"

"When is she not serious?" Neil protested, only barely keeping a hold on his cup. "She was serious about starting an ant farm in the scullery!"

"But what did you, er…" Ellie started uncomfortably.

"I didn't," Neil returned bluntly. "She withdrew the request."

Ellie frowned with surprise. "She did?"

"She was worried about what it would do to my reputation."

Ellie absorbed his response. "I'll admit I'm relieved. I mean, it had occurred to me that Constance's parents might escalate the issue by threatening to arrange a match…"

Neil choked on his tea. "Hold on—what?"

"Well, it is fairly common practice in India," Ellie reasoned. "I don't believe Auntie Padma would actually force Constance into anything, but I wouldn't put it past her to wave the threat around. The woman is entirely—"

Neil frantically spun Ellie around as Padma stepped into the breakfast room, Mr. Mahjoud looming at her back.

"Good morning. Lovely weather," Neil sputtered. "Excellent… tea."

Padma studied them mercilessly. "Jhia. Dr. Fairfax. I hope you are both feeling ready for your expedition?"

"Entirely ready," Ellie confirmed, plastering a smile on her face.

"Yes," Neil agreed, nodding his head excessively.

Padma drifted past them to the settee. One of the household staff followed her there, carrying a personal tea service.

Constance's Aunt Parvati came into the room alongside her husband, Balaram. "Good morning, everyone!" she said brightly.

"Yes. Morning," Balaram added more stiffly.

He planted himself in a chair and immediately put the newspaper up in front of his nose.

Parvati joined Padma on the settee, greeting her with a kiss on the cheek.

Neil hauled Ellie over to the window at the far end of the room, nearly causing her to drop her tea.

"But are you absolutely *certain* Aai wouldn't compel Connie into something?" he whispered fiercely.

"She would have to get Sir Robert's permission, and he's English," Ellie reminded him.

"Aren't he and Lady Tyrrell the ones threatening her in the first place?"

Ellie frowned at the reminder. "But the maharaja must have a say as well, and he seems very modern. Surely he wouldn't go in for that sort of thing."

"We have only known him for three days!" Neil's voice tightened. "How can you know how modern he is?!"

Ellie eyed the clammy cast to his complexion. "Are you sure you're all right? You've gone over a bit peaked."

Constance strolled into the room. Her thick black hair was coiffed with careless elegance. She wore a very smart skirt in hues of emerald and cream with a matching jacket and a dashing scarf. Her stride was militant as she crossed to them.

"Good morning," she announced stoutly.

Adam followed her inside, his hair still damp from a wash. His shirt was open at the throat under his battered summer jacket, while his trousers were tucked into calf-height riding boots. Kalb trotted at his heels.

He headed straight for the food table. "These look like doughnuts."

"That's dahibara aloodam," Constance explained. "You put that potato curry on them and some of those crunchy things."

Intrigued, Adam began loading up his plate.

Neil faced Constance awkwardly. "So, then. Did you manage any more—er—planning? About… things?"

"I am still working on ideas," Constance replied. "But don't you worry about it."

Neil looked worried.

"Worry about what?" Adam said, joining them with a bowl full of curry-drenched pastries.

Across the room, Padma gracefully lifted her tea. "Have the invitations gone out for Arjuna's party yet?"

"I was planning to mail them later this morning," Parvati returned cheerfully.

Padma waved a hand to Mr. Mahjoud, who pulled a piece of paper from his valise. "I took the liberty of making a little list of some additional guests it might be nice to have."

A worried frown creased the space between Constance's elegant brows.

Neil's grip tightened on his teacup.

"And what about those arrangements we spoke of?" Padma pressed lightly.

"Arrangements?" Neil blurted out quickly.

Parvati cast him a reassuring smile from across the room. "The gardens are very abundant at the moment," she promised.

Padma smiled serenely. "You are so very skilled at bringing things together."

Neil seemed to go even more pale—if such a thing were possible.

"Are you sure you're all right?" Ellie demanded.

Over by the tea table, Parvati studied the list. "You wish to invite the Rani of Sonepur?"

"Of course," Padma replied, casually stirring her spoon. "It can be ever so helpful to connect with other mothers in these situations."

Neil stared into his cup, and then abruptly set it down. His hand was shaking.

"And Prince Shahir of Talabad!" Parvati exclaimed, still reviewing the paper. "I have heard that he has the most enormous—"

"Constance and I are getting married!" Neil burst out.

The room went silent.

Adam's eyebrows rose.

Constance froze.

Ellie forced herself to swallow her mouthful of tea—after barely keeping from spitting it onto the Persian carpet.

Padma's gaze glittered like ice from across the room. "What surprising news. And when was this happy decision made?"

Clammy sweat broke out along the line of Neil's forehead. "We… I… It's…"

He appeared to be choking on the words.

Constance recovered from her obvious shock. She grasped his hand, tugging him to her side as she turned to face her grandmother. "We have actually known since Egypt. We were simply waiting for the perfect time to tell everyone. Isn't that right, darling?

Darling? Ellie thought, reeling.

"Time," Neil rasped weakly. "Yes."

"And the perfect time was over breakfast on a Wednesday." Padma's tone was bone-dry.

Constance pushed on with breezy aplomb. "It must certainly be reassuring to know that I'll be venturing out to the edge of the wilderness under the protection of my fiancé!" She patted Neil's arm. "Really, Dr. Fairfax was just being thoughtful of everyone's sensibilities."

"How very considerate," Padma returned smoothly.

Beside Ellie, Adam's spoon continued to hover over his bowl. "I think I missed something."

"Later," Ellie pleaded under her breath.

Parvati rose from her chair, her round cheeks glowing. "Oh, but this is absolutely splendid! I am so very happy for both of you!" She turned to her husband, who still had his nose pressed to the financial section. "Su-ṇu-chha, Pati!" she exclaimed, batting him on the shoulder as she gesticulated at Constance and Neil, rattling on to him in Odia.

A liveried messenger hurried into the room, making a low bow to Padma.

"Pardon the interruption, ma'am, but His Highness requests your presence for a moment."

Padma pinned Neil and Constance with a look. "Do be sure not to run off while I'm away. We clearly have a great deal to talk about."

She glided from the room.

Neil whirled to Ellie and her companions. "What did I just do?" he wheezed desperately.

"Sounded an awful lot like you announced that you were marrying Constance," Adam offered.

Neil's breath came quickly, his pallor deepening. "It all happened so fast. The maharajkumari started talking about arrangements, and then before I really knew what was happening, the words were coming out of my mouth—"

Constance's eyes flashed dangerously. "Are you telling me that you just fake engaged me because of the *florals?*"

"Fake?" Adam echoed.

"Florals?" Neil said, blinking.

"Fiddlesticks," Ellie cursed.

Parvati hauled Balaram from his chair and dragged him with her as she crossed over to them.

"Smile!" Constance ordered in a hiss as she whirled Neil to face her relatives.

Balaram had his newspaper tucked under his arm. "My congratulations to you both."

He extended his free hand. Neil stared at it.

Constance subtly elbowed him.

Neil took Balaram's hand and rapidly shook it. "Yes. Thank you. Sir."

"This is the loveliest news!" Parvati enthused with genuine excitement. "And Dr. Fairfax, let me be the first to officially welcome you into the family. We are so very glad to have you."

Neil stared down at where Parvati clasped his hands, clearly both moved and mortified.

"But you shall have to tell me all of the details!" Parvati continued as Balaram sidled away to return to his paper. "How did the proposal happen? Was it terribly romantic?"

"Oh, yes!" Constance hurriedly assured her aunt. "Stuffy does love to put on a good show."

"Stuffy?" Parvati echoed, confused.

Neil coughed, pounding his chest as his breath turned to a wheeze.

Ellie stepped in. "Excuse us for a moment. I haven't yet had a chance to congratulate my brother myself."

She grasped Neil and Constance by their arms and hauled them to the window.

Neil looked panicked. "I just lied to your aunt!"

"*That's* what you're worried about?" Constance seethed.

"She's nice!" Neil retorted.

Ellie shot Adam an uneasy look. "I should probably try to explain…"

"It's a hell of a goddamned picture, but I think I'm getting it," Adam replied.

"It's my grandmother that you should be worried about!" Constance hissed to Neil.

"Oh God!" he wailed.

"I'm sure we could tell them it was all a slight misunderstanding…" Ellie hedged.

"No," Constance cut back grimly. "We're in it now. There's no way out but through. We'll simply have to discuss the rest later."

The words sounded like a threat.

"Princess alert," Adam muttered as Padma returned to the breakfast room.

"I see we are all still celebrating the happy news?" Padma observed blandly.

"Yes," Ellie replied awkwardly. "It's very… celebratory."

Constance snuggled into Neil's side. "Of course, Neil and I have known about it for a while."

"Indeed," Padma agreed wryly. "Kondi, I wonder if I could part you from your intended for an hour to accompany me on an errand in town. Miss Mallory, I thought you might like to join us."

"Me?" Ellie protested helplessly.

Constance snagged her arm, hauling Ellie to her other side. "Ellie is ever so fond of joining things. Aren't you?"

"I am," Ellie quickly agreed.

Adam clamped a hand on Neil's shoulder. "I'll just take care of my good buddy here. Make sure he doesn't hyperventilate. From happiness."

"It has been known to happen," Ellie helpfully added.

Neil forced a weak smile.

Padma's mouth curved with a hint of threat. "How very wonderful. Shall we?"

Constance steered Ellie toward the door, pausing to call back over her shoulder at Neil. "Don't miss me too much, Sugar Plum!"

"What?" Neil blinked with confusion.

Ellie turned the corner on Constance's arm, and her friend leaned in for a darkly conspiratorial mutter. "I do hope your brother's subterfuge skills can be improved quickly."

"I wouldn't count on it," Ellie warned grimly as they hurried after the princess.

SIXTEEN

CONSTANCE WASN'T SURE whether she ought to feel grateful or murderous. She had thought that the question of a fake engagement had been firmly settled the prior evening. What had Stuffy been thinking when he blurted it out over breakfast?

Constance and I are getting married.

He might at least have warned her that he had still been thinking about it—though to be fair, based on the look on his face as the words had come out of his mouth, Constance wasn't sure how much actual thought had been involved.

Still, it was done now. She would just have to find a way for them to extricate themselves from the fiction once it was no longer convenient. She would not have this little stratagem put Neil's reputation or their friendship at risk. However precipitously he'd done it, he'd done it for *her*, and she was hardly going to repay that by letting him be thought a cad.

At least she would have plenty of time to think of a solution to that problem—and to the ongoing pressure from her family to wed—thanks to Neil.

She would let him know what she thought about the particulars of his method once she had another moment alone with him.

After navigating a maze of elegant hallways, Padma led Constance and Ellie through an unobtrusive door. Constance squinted at the change in light as she found herself standing outside the looming palace wall. Looking back, she could barely see the opening they had utilized, its lines disguised by the texture of the stonework.

"Is this a secret exit?" she demanded. "How long has it been here? Who else knows about it? Does Uncle Vijay use it?"

Padma ignored her questions, striding purposefully up the alley, her pink and blue sari flowing elegantly around her ankles. Mr. Mahjoud fell into step behind them as Constance hurried after her.

"Your announcement this morning was very interesting, Kondi," Padma commented smoothly. "I must admit, I was a little surprised that after all the suitors you rejected, you would pick Dr. Fairfax to marry. Not that he isn't a very nice young man, but he isn't nearly as well-established as the others that you have turned down. He is not particularly wealthy. He has no title. One cannot even say that he is a rising political star, which might at least gain you a future as a cabinet minister's wife."

Constance felt a mingled dart of panic and outrage. "Julian Forster-Mowbray was wealthy. I suppose I ought to have picked him instead, and never mind the minor complication that both he and his father were part of a secret society of merciless magical artifact thieves."

Padma faced Constance with an uncharacteristically frank expression. "I was not aware of Lord Aldbury's involvement with the Order of Albion until the recent events in Egypt. He was a mistake, as was his son."

Constance thought back to her tea with Lord Aldbury. To be perfectly honest, she hadn't been paying him a very great deal of attention. Knowing that a person was only speaking to her in order to size her up as breeding fodder was a guaranteed way to make her lose interest in a conversation.

She recalled a tall man, attractive for his age. His hair was dark, shot through with streaks of silver, and his easy, charming manner was touched by the natural arrogance one expected from a man of his station.

None of it was out of the ordinary, and yet she remembered him now with a whispering sense of unease. It seemed to her that there was something uncomfortably familiar about his eyes—not in the color, which matched that of his son, Julian, but in the measuring glint as he had watched her from across the table.

She wondered where she had seen that look before.

Padma's dangerously musing tone cut into Constance's thoughts. "Of course, the princes your Auntie Parvati would introduce you to have been known to the family for many years. They are responsible, charming, influential, *and* wealthy. Perhaps you have made your decision a little hastily. I do find myself wondering what exactly Dr. Fairfax has to offer you to compare with all of that—with no offense intended toward your brother, Jhia," she added with a nod to Ellie.

Ellie kept her mouth firmly closed as though she was afraid of what might spill out if she opened it.

Constance fought a quick burst of nervousness. Had her Aai seen through the ruse?

No. The argument was exactly the sort of objection she ought to have anticipated her grandmother would make. Oddly, what she felt in response was less fear and more a quick, unexpected burst of anger. What right did Aai have to criticize Neil like that? Even if everything she said was technically true, it was both rude and inaccurate to reduce Neil's value to how much money he had or how important his family was. Neil was a great deal more than either of those things, and anyone with eyes in their head ought to be able to see it.

Constance burned with the urge to set her grandmother straight, and for once, she had no interest in doing it by way of a creative falsehood. She didn't need to pretend that Neil was the secret heir of a marquis in order to justify her desire to marry him—however fictional their engagement might happen to be.

"No, Neil isn't a noble," Constance retorted. "Or rich, or influential. But he's brave—and not because he chases after lions for fun. Because doing dangerous things deeply intimidates him, and yet he does them anyway, if he knows it's the right thing to do. He's fearfully intelligent, but instead of being full of himself, he actually listens when you're talking to him. He's patient, thoughtful, and terribly sweet. Most astonishingly of all, he actually admits when he's been wrong—and then he tries to change, even if it's hard. I'd have trouble naming any other man I've met who's willing to do that."

Padma was watching her with a close, unreadable expression, but the words were coming readily now. Constance let them spill out of her boldly.

"Maybe Neil isn't rich, but I don't need a rich husband. I have plenty of money. I need a husband who isn't going to try to turn me into something I'm not. And Neil would *never* do that."

She raised her chin, fixing her grandmother with a challenging glare. "If I have all of that, then I have everything I could possibly need. Neil and I will sort out the rest. It's not like the man can't find another job. He's a brilliant scholar with a Cambridge doctorate, for goodness' sake."

Padma's eyes glinted cannily behind her serene expression. "My apologies, Kondi. This changes everything. I did not realize that you were in love with him."

Constance reeled from the quick shock of her grandmother's assertion—but forced herself to recover. "Of course, I'm in love with him," she replied breezily. "Why else would we be getting married?"

"Why else, indeed?" Padma returned blithely.

Constance let out a low breath of relief as Padma turned to lead them down the busy street.

She had done it—convinced her grandmother that her affections for Neil were genuine. And all she'd had to do was rattle off a load of things that she actually thought about him.

They were all very nice things, Constance allowed. It was true that Neil didn't have money, or a title, or a powerful family—but he was decent, kind, and principled. He had made mistakes, certainly, but he wasn't afraid to own up to them and try to do better.

Constance hadn't been lying when she'd said she had never found that trait before in a man who'd vied for her hand.

She had absolutely no doubt that Dr. Neil Fairfax would distinguish himself in life, given a little time. The trouble in Egypt had admittedly set back his career, but only temporarily. Neil really was exceptionally clever. Recalling the way he could rattle off translations of hieroglyphs without even thinking about it made Constance feel oddly tingly.

Any woman ought to be proud to have him as her husband, no matter his background—and surely someone would, Constance realized with a jolt. Neil was hardly going to remain a bachelor forever. One day, someone was going to realize what a diamond in the rough he was.

Not that the man was all that 'in the rough.' He was easy enough to look at.

Constance recalled what it had been like to dance with him during the Jagannath festival—the exhilaration of their impossible ability to follow the unfamiliar steps mingling with something a little hotter as Neil had hauled her up against his chest while the tabla pulsed with a tantalizing rhythm.

Neil had a very nice chest. Constance had made a reasonable study of it when they'd sheltered overnight in a rock cut tomb after escaping from Julian's dahabeeyah. He was terribly pale but also elegantly well-defined—all that lean muscle promising unexpected strength.

Not that she'd had any intention of doing more than looking. She'd been justifiably furious with him at the time. Still, there was no harm in acknowledging that the fellow was shockingly well put together for a scholar.

His future wife would undoubtedly appreciate all of that, along with his long-fingered hands, the hints of green in his eyes, and the way his hair felt like silk when you ran your fingers through it.

Hold on—when would Constance have ever run her fingers through Neil's hair? Had she just imagined how it would feel? That was silly. Why on earth would she do a thing like that? She had probably just picked a bug out of it once in the past... or, more likely, put a bug into it.

That sounded right.

Her grandmother was still talking. Constance snapped back to herself, struggling to catch up.

"…planning it all, of course, as soon as you are back from your mission," Padma finished.

"Planning?" Constance echoed carefully.

Padma shot her a dry look. "Yes, Kondi. Weddings do take a great deal of planning."

Panic iced through her. "Surely, there's no need to rush."

"No?" Padma returned. "Are you not so eager, then, to start your married life with Dr. Fairfax?"

Constance sensed a trap. "Oh—I'm desperately eager," she quickly countered. "You have no idea how eager I am. I'm practically burning up with eagerness."

Ellie stumbled beside her.

"It's only that—you know—one hardly wants to rush these things," Constance continued hurriedly. "The anticipation is half the fun, isn't it?"

A strangled sound gurgled at the back of Ellie's throat. The noise gave Constance a spark of helpful inspiration. "Besides, Neil would want his parents to be able to attend, and Ellie's father gets terribly seasick. Why, he can barely handle anything longer than a channel crossing! They would have to complete the journey to India overland. Or we can simply plan the ceremony in England. Really, that makes the most sense. I'm sure Neil and I can contain ourselves until then."

"Can you?" Padma returned with deceptive ease.

Constance schooled her features into an expression of solemn determination. "With great fortitude."

"How lucky that you are such a model of self-control," Padma returned, straight-faced. "But ah—here we are."

They stood before a small building of roughly the same dimensions as the neighboring storefronts. The bricks of the facade were painted in bright hues of blue, green, purple, and gold. A small tower rose over the back half of the structure in cake-like layers that tapered to a rounded peak at the top.

"It's a temple!" Constance exclaimed, recognizing the distinctive shape of the shikhara that crowned the sanctuary.

"Of course, it is." Padma took a basket from Mr. Mahjoud. "Now come inside, and don't forget to take off your shoes."

Constance followed her grandmother into the colorful building, buzzing with excitement about her first visit to a Hindu temple. She had watched Padma perform puja to the murtis on her household altar before, so the concept of Hindu prayer wasn't completely foreign to her. However, both of her parents were Church of England, and Constance still attended services with them when Sir Robert and Lady Sabita insisted on it.

It was easy enough to sneak a novel into the hymnal and catch up on a little reading during the sermon.

She remained deeply curious about her grandmother's faith, soaking up all of Padma's stories about her beliefs and practice.

"Who are we coming to see, then?" Constance asked excitedly as she freed herself of her boots, setting them on the rack for shoes that stood by the temple steps.

Padma answered her with a secretive smile.

They stepped from the covered porch into a modest hall. The temple was a place of neighborhood worship rather than a sprawling institution like Lord Jagannath's home in Puri. The tile floor was swept clean while the paint on the walls was slightly cracked with age.

A young priest stepped forward to greet them, dressed in dhotis with a saffron scarf over his chest. After a brief and polite exchange in Odia with her grandmother, he led them into the temple's inner sanctuary, where a single goddess in painted stone and plaster awaited them, standing on a raised platform.

The blue-skinned woman with four arms waved a bloody sword in one hand. Another held up a severed head. A necklace of carved skulls ringed her neck while severed arms, daubed with red paint, served as her kilt. The accessories were admittedly gruesome, but the figure was still surprisingly lovely. Her eyes were large and luminous under arched brows accented by a red bindi. Her sky-hued complexion was smoothly polished. The vermilion dart of her tongue extended from between bow-shaped lips while marigolds garlanded her chest.

A beautiful man lay on the ground at her feet, bare-chested and prone with a serene expression on his face. The goddess's uplifted right foot was just coming down to rest against his flawless skin.

Constance recognized it all with a buzz of excitement. "Is this Kali?"

"Dakshinakali," Padma mildly corrected her. "But you may call her Maa Kali if you like."

Padma rang a brass bell that hung by Kali's shrine. The clear, low tone echoed through the close space of the sanctuary. As the sound faded, Padma gracefully dropped to her knees and pressed her forehead to the floor in front of the goddess.

Constance had been through this before when she had watched Padma perform puja at home. She pressed her palms together and gave the goddess a respectful bow, nudging Ellie to do the same. After all, even if one wasn't strictly speaking a Hindu, one could certainly be polite.

"Isn't Kali a goddess of death?" Ellie asked.

Padma removed items from her basket, handing them to the priest—a garland of red hibiscus blooms, a bag of rice, a box of sweets. "Maa Kali is many things."

The priest set Padma's offerings out at the feet of the goddess. The figure's two open palms were painted crimson and held out in gestures of blessing. Constance vaguely recognized the position of her upper hand—raised to the shoulder with the palm facing out—as the mudra for fearlessness. "Who's the fellow under her foot meant to be, again?"

"Lord Shiva," Padma replied. "He is her husband, when Kali is Parvati."

Constance decided to offer Ellie a little help. Her friend was already frowning with confusion. "The Hindu gods are always turning into each other. Don't worry too much about it. But why is Kali stepping on her husband, Aai?"

The priest began to pray over the offerings, his voice low and even.

Padma gazed steadily at the goddess. "Kali's rage is the rage of a mother—rage against the evil of the world that would exploit the powerless. There is no force like Kali when her thirst for vengeance has been unleashed. She grinds the most powerful demons into dust and feasts on their blood. Then she dances with a violent joy that would tear the world to pieces if she were not stopped."

The priest finished his prayer. He lifted a flickering oil lamp from the altar and brought it to Padma.

"That is why Shiva lays himself down in her path," Padma continued. "It is only when Kali feels his flesh beneath her foot that she remembers herself and reins in her rage. Now shush."

Padma brushed her fingers over the fire, gracefully bringing them to her forehead. The priest brought the lamp to Constance, who did the same, imitating her grandmother's gestures.

The heat of the flame danced against her palms under Kali's steady gaze.

Constance looked helpfully at Ellie. "You can do it, too, if you want to."

"Even if I'm not Hindu?" Ellie pressed uncertainly.

"Our gods are not jealous," Padma informed her warmly.

Ellie considered her words, then tentatively offered her hands to the priest. He brought forward the lamp, and she moved her fingers from the fire to her brow. The gesture was more awkward than Padma's had been, but the temple attendant didn't seem to mind.

"Sit," Padma ordered, lowering herself to her knees in front of the goddess.

Constance studied Kali's fiercely lovely aspect. She was less familiar with this deity, as Kali wasn't among the murtis that sat on her grandmother's altar at home. Still, she had to appreciate a divine lady who wasn't shy about carrying her own weapons around.

She wondered what Ellie thought of all this. Participating in a temple puja was perfectly thrilling to Constance, but Ellie didn't have a Hindu grandmother.

Ellie studied Kali with frank curiosity and wonder. She certainly didn't appear to find any of this strange or savage. Constance could practically hear the questions whirring around in her friend's brain. She was sure they would all come spilling out as soon as Ellie sensed it was an appropriate time to ask them.

The thought triggered a warm burst of affection.

Constance had no qualms about asking questions. She could hardly imagine Kali was going to mind. She looked like the sort of woman who appreciated a forthright nature. "This is all very lovely, Aai, but is there any particular reason why we're here?"

"You girls have both said that you find Lady Sita, Lord Rama's wife, to be weak," Padma returned frankly.

"That's because she spends most of the story sitting around waiting to be rescued," Constance pointed out.

"Not every story," Padma corrected her.

"Do you mean that there's another one?" Ellie pressed, curious.

The priest took a seat at the edge of the room, waiting with comfortable patience.

"They call it the Adbhuta Ramayana," Padma replied. "It records the sage Valmiki's words when he was asked whether Lord Rama's story contained any wisdom that had been hidden from those who were not ready to understand. In response, Valmiki told of another battle—one that had not been mentioned in the original text. A battle against the demon king Ravana's older and more powerful brother, Thousand-Headed Ravana."

"Thousand-Headed Ravana?" Constance returned dryly.

"Do you want to hear the story or not?" Padma treated Constance to a withering glare.

Constance schooled her features. "Yes, Aai."

"Lord Rama was not powerful enough to defeat Thousand-Headed Ravana," Padma continued. "He fell in the battle. Seeing him wounded, Sita's rage was kindled, and she rose against the demon herself... as Kali."

Constance studied the fierce, blue-skinned goddess with her bloody sword and garland of skulls, comparing the image to the lithographs of Rama's pretty, placid wife. "You're saying Sita turned into Kali," she elaborated skeptically.

"I am saying," Padma returned patiently, "that Sita was Kali all along."

"I thought Sita was supposed to be an avatar of Lakshmi, Vishnu's consort," Ellie cut in.

"She is that, too," Padma easily agreed.

"She can be both?" Ellie pressed, confused.

Padma dismissed Ellie's concern with a wave of her hand. "Kali slays Thousand-Headed Ravana—not with an astra, but with her own hands, tearing the heads from his body. She slaughters every one of his demon followers as well, and then she dances in their blood."

"But that doesn't make any sense," Constance protested. "If Sita could be Kali any time she wanted, why didn't she just kill the first Ravana herself after he kidnapped her? Why sit there pretending to be helpless until her husband came to rescue her?"

"Sita knew her role in the story," Padma countered. "It was Lord Rama who was meant to strike Ravana's death blow."

"You're saying she chose not to save herself because she was following... fate?" Ellie filled in awkwardly.

Padma pinned both Constance and Ellie with an uncomfortably penetrating look. "I am saying that Sita is both more powerful and more complicated than you give her credit for."

A chill shivered over Constance's arms.

She considered what her grandmother was suggesting—that Sita had kept her own power concealed in order to let Rama's story play out the way it had been meant to.

Rama's tale was certainly influential. It was woven into the fabric of India, as much a part of the country as the distinctive flavors of its food, its famous Mughal palaces, or the rains of the monsoon.

If Sita had simply obliterated Ravana, there would hardly have been any story at all.

Constance thought of the pieces of Rama's tale that were ingrained in her consciousness—the stringing of Shiva's bow and the sacrifice of the giant vulture Jatayu. The monkey king Sugriva's duel with his usurper brother. The loyal Hanuman discovering his own divine nature as he carried a mountain to the dying Lakshmana.

The epic was woven from gleaming threads of faith and devotion, friendship and sacrifice. Of what it meant to be a king and a warrior—to stand up for justice and bring people together.

How might India be different if that story had never happened?

"And is that why she let Rama send her away at the end of the story?" Ellie pressed crossly. "Because of fate?"

Constance had nearly forgotten that part of the tale—how Rama had fought long and fiercely to save Sita from the demon king, only to exile her to Valmiki's ashram after they finally made it home. It seemed like another example of Sita's placid acceptance of the most rank injustice.

A soft breeze, scented with the monsoon, whispered through the humble sanctuary. It stirred the delicate petals of the flowers that garlanded Kali's throat and flickered the flame of the lamp.

Padma replied in a voice like the tolling of a low bell. "Every woman has secrets."

The words sank through Constance's skin, and she thought of her own secrets. There was obviously the lie she had told that very morning... but Constance hid more than just a fake engagement. There were knives in her garters and a thirst for adventure in her heart. Even her Indian self was a secret, not that she deliberately hid it... but she had sometimes allowed it to be overlooked, glazed over as inconsequential. Her grandmother's murtis concealed behind English oak doors.

The world didn't make room for everything that Constance truly was, a creature of hunger and dreams, hope and determination.

And what of her grandmother's secrets? Constance still didn't know why Aai had chosen a kind-hearted English civil servant over the princes that must have been lined up at her feet.

Then there was Ellie, struggling even now with the question of how much she needed to conceal her principles, her passions—and her love.

We are all hiding, Constance thought with a shiver of surprise. It was what the world demanded of women in order to protect their hearts. Fight their battles.

Survive.

Perhaps that was the lesson woven through Sita's placid smile—the secret of what had to be kept safe until the time was right to unleash it upon the world.

None of their stories were true when one only read what was written on the surface.

Padma spoke again, her voice edged like iron. "Charles Reginald Borthwick has harmed more innocent people than I could hope to count. He will go on harming them, unless he is stopped. He is just another demon, dressed up in a uniform with the power of an empire at his back. Should he gain the Brahmastra, he could unleash exponentially more destruction. I brought you here for Kali's blessing because that is what she does—bring down demons."

Constance gazed up at the beautiful, dangerous goddess on the altar. "Then I'm glad we came."

Her grandmother's hand brushed Constance's cheek, dry as paper and softly warm. Her eyes shone with a quiet, steady pride.

They rose together. The priest stirred, offering Padma a bowl of bright red paste. She swiped a bit of it up with her thumb and marked her forehead with a practiced gesture—a simple dot beneath a crimson crescent.

She turned to Constance.

Constance lowered her head and felt the warm pressure of her grandmother's thumb on her brow. The paste tugged against her skin as it softly dried.

"Don't forget to take your leave," Padma chided gently.

Constance gave the goddess another bow, her palms pressed together over her breast. *If you are in there,* Constance thought, projecting the words from her quick-beating heart to the figure in front of her, *help us beat this rotter.*

The flame of the puja lamp danced in a wind that Constance couldn't feel.

As she turned to go, the priest held out an offering wrapped in silver paper.

"What's this?" Ellie asked in a whisper.

Constance peeked into the wrapping. "They're treats!"

"It's prashaada. Kali's blessing," Padma corrected her wryly.

Constance popped the prashaada into her mouth, letting the sweet flavor dance across her tongue. Did it make her feel blessed?

She felt… *ready*, and let that warm, steady conviction carry her back out into the clear light of the morning.

SEVENTEEN

Neil raised a hand to shield his eyes from the sun that gleamed off the pale stone as he stepped out of the palace. The forecourt was framed by high walls, save for a patch of vibrant green that marked the entrance to the garden where Constance had made—and then withdrawn—her request that Neil pretend to be her fiancé.

Not that the withdrawal had mattered. Neil had gone and put his foot in it over tea and curried doughnuts, panicking at the notion that Constance's lovely and well-meaning family might try to marry her off to some wealthy, handsome Indian prince.

Well, now they were all convinced she was marrying herself off to an unemployed archaeologist.

Neil hadn't enjoyed lying to Constance's relatives, but he couldn't entirely regret his rash words. What did his own reputation matter, anyway? He hadn't any left worth speaking of.

The lingering nervousness he felt about his fake engagement centered on the bigger question of how he and Constance would manage to break it off and still remain friends.

Neil admittedly didn't have much experience with such matters, but he couldn't think of a single acquaintance who still chummed around with their ex-fiancée.

Constance's friendship mattered to him. The idea of sacrificing it—even to save her from a charming Indian prince—left Neil feeling bereft.

Surely, they would find some solution to that problem… even if Neil hadn't the foggiest notion what it might be.

He shook off the swirling mess of worries and crossed to where Adam stood beside a quartet of horses. His strapping American friend wore a rifle across his back in a way that looked entirely natural while he offered the animals treats from his pockets and rubbed down their necks. One of the mares, a gleaming chestnut, had taken a liking to him, huffing and nibbling at his hair.

His leggy dog bolted across the paving stones after a cat that slept placidly on a bench. The cat waited until the dog was a breath away before suddenly bristling with teeth and claws.

Kalb scrambled back, whining with terror. He hid behind Adam's legs, quivering.

Adam eyed Neil warily. "Doing all right, Fairfax?"

Neil opened his mouth to give him a comfortably reassuring answer—and lost the words as Ellie descended the palace steps.

"What's wrong with your legs?" he blurted out instead.

Ellie glanced down at the loose khaki trousers she wore with her blouse and light jacket. "What on earth do you mean?"

"I think he's talking about your pants, Princess," Adam replied, scratching the chestnut mare behind her ears.

"Oh, these!" Ellie's face broke out into a happy smile. "I picked them up at a secondhand shop in Cairo once I knew we were coming to India—and I'm quite glad I did. It's much easier to travel through the wilderness in trousers than a skirt. Really—one would think that women's dress had been explicitly designed to make it difficult to do anything other than lie around the house!"

Adam made an appreciative assessment of the lower half of Ellie's ensemble. "They look good."

"But everyone can see them!" Neil waved a helpless hand at his sister's legs.

"Like who?" Ellie retorted. "Do you think the Adrija Khond are going to care whether or not I'm wearing a skirt?"

"Maybe?" Neil pushed back hopefully.

Ellie's eyes shifted to the weapon on Adam's shoulder. "What's that?"

Adam's grin was unapologetic. "It's a Winchester lever-action repeater."

"Of course, it is," Ellie returned with an exasperated sigh. "But where on earth did you find it?"

"The armory."

Neil frowned, recalling the room they had seen on their whirlwind introduction to the palace. Had that really just been the previous afternoon? "But all the rifles in the armory were old."

"Not *that* armory," Adam corrected him. "The one we're not supposed to know about."

"How do *you* know about it?" Neil protested.

Adam answered him with a wink.

Constance's voice rang out from the palace steps. "Good morning, everyone!"

Neil glanced over at her—and froze as he realized that she, too, was wearing trousers.

Constance's attire was not secondhand. The garment was in a rich shade of plum that perfectly matched her fashionable jacket and had been expertly tailored to glide mercilessly over every curve of her legs.

The ensemble was topped by a matching hat with a dashingly turned-up brim.

Adam tipped back his own battered fedora. "Well, don't you look ready for an adventure?"

"I do, don't I?" Constance pivoted proudly to show off. "Oh, Ellie! You're in trousers too! Isn't this fun?"

Neil's gaze locked helplessly on the taut line of Constance's thighs. "But wouldn't you be better off in something a little less…"

Mind-numbingly attractive, Neil's brain finished for him.

Constance rolled her eyes. "Do get over it, Stuffy. Lady pirates have been wearing these for centuries."

"You're not a pirate," Neil reasonably pointed out.

"Not *yet*," Constance corrected him. "Oh! I have something for you."

She pushed a thin leather bundle into his hands.

"It's a scabbard," she explained as Neil examined the object with surprise. "The style is a bit unusual, as it's meant to be worn on one's back instead of around the hips, but I thought you might be more comfortable with that. It's not like you're planning to go into battle with that old thing."

The *old thing* in question was Dyrnwyn, wrapped up in the bedroll that hung from the side of the mule carrying his luggage.

He hadn't wanted to bring the blasted sword with him, but he could hardly risk leaving it in his room. What if one of Parvati and Balaram's children had decided to go snooping? They were as well-born as it got, so of course, the stupid arcanum would light up for them. They might burn down the entire bloody palace.

The leather straps of the scabbard were worn but supple. More leather wrapped the wooden core of the sheath. To Neil's admittedly inexpert eye, the size looked like a decent match for Dyrnwyn's length.

There was only one way for him to be sure of that. Pulling a handkerchief from his pocket, Neil wrapped it around his palm and drew the sword from the bedroll with a grimace.

He tried the sheath. The blade slid home as though made for it.

Ellie perked up. "Is that a Mughal design?"

"I didn't bother reading the label," Constance replied dismissively.

Ellie frowned with disapproval. "Does that mean you stole this from one of the cases in the armory?"

"The *old* armory," Adam helpfully elaborated with a hint of mischief.

"No one was using it," Constance easily dismissed. "Now—the strap goes over your shoulder, like this."

She swung the leather over Neil's shooting jacket, the unexpected contact shocking him into compliance.

Constance yanked tight a buckle—and then reached around Neil's waist.

He froze. His nose was in her hair. It smelled lovely.

They were standing far closer together than they ought to be.

Except that we're technically engaged now, his brain unhelpfully reminded him.

"And this buckles around your waist," Constance finished.

Neil was agonizingly aware of the tickling brush of her fingers against his waistcoat as she fiddled with the fastener.

"If I can just… get it to… There we are," Constance declared with a final tug.

She stepped back to admire her handiwork.

Adam studied Neil thoughtfully. The dog appeared to do the same, sitting by Adam's boots.

"It fits well enough," Ellie commented.

"I think it suits him." Constance set her hands on her more-visible-than-they-ought-to-be hips. "You know, Uncle Vijay told me that in the Hindu stories, flaming swords represent the triumph of knowledge over ignorance. The final incarnation of Vishnu is supposed to wield one when he comes to end the Kaliyuga."

A weapon of knowledge. Neil found the notion oddly comforting.

Not that he loved the idea of wearing the sword at all. He would certainly have tried to get out of it, if Constance had given him any warning. Still, the weight of it on his back and the worn leather hugging his waist felt oddly… right.

"Thank you," he said, surprised to find that he meant it.

Constance beamed at him.

A trumpeting call echoed over the courtyard.

"What on earth was that?" Ellie wondered.

"Think it might've been an elephant," Adam mused.

"An elephant?!" Ellie's eyes went wide.

"The kid mentioned something about a herd yesterday when she was showing us around the palace," Adam reminded her.

"Then why didn't we hear them before?" Ellie protested.

"Because they are only just returned from the southern grazing lands," a clear voice announced authoritatively from the steps.

Neil looked up to see Vanika, the skinny twelve-year-old from the previous afternoon, bound down to the courtyard with lanky enthusiasm.

She skidded to a stop beside them. "They range in the royal preserve as much as possible, but they're brought back when anyone reports poachers in the area. Or they need a wash."

"How many elephants does His Highness have?" Ellie pressed with obvious interest.

"Seven." Vanika braced her hands on her hips. "They are brought out for festivals and state appearances."

"Which does not in the least justify the cost of their upkeep," Vijay added as he strolled out of the palace with Mr. Chowdhury.

The maharaja was simply and elegantly dressed in a white suit with a purple waistcoat. He hopped down the steps with an energy similar to that of the twelve-year-old girl, Mr. Chowdhury following behind him at a more sedate pace.

"You wouldn't believe the tab for their fodder," Vijay continued lightly. "But Nawaz insists we keep a royal herd."

"Because if you do not, you undermine your legal arguments for preventing the Raj from capturing bulls on Nandapur's land," Mr. Chowdhury elaborated with the air of a well-worn debate.

"Yes, yes," Vijay agreed dismissively. "Can't have them all done in for ivory or used to haul artillery through the jungle. Your guide wouldn't stand for that, now would she?" He gave Vanika's hair an affectionate ruffle. "Vanika's father is my mahout—the elephant handler."

Neil stared down at the skinny child. "Guide?"

Vanika crossed her arms imperiously. "I should like to see you try to reach Ranyapali on your own. Nobody finds the Adrija Khond if we do not want them to."

Adam watched the girl with an air of warm amusement, his arm slung around the chestnut mare. "You're Adrija?"

Kalb greeted the girl by jumping up to cover her face with kisses. She hugged the dog back. "Of course, I am," she retorted.

"She's part of the Kōnja clan," Vijay elaborated. "Her grandfather was the abbaya—the local leader."

"Is that why you're attending school with the princes?" Ellie asked.

Vijay laughed. "She wasn't *supposed* to be—but she kept sneaking in, and she proved better with her mathematics and her Sanskrit than any of the boys. So I told her to stay."

Neil regarded the lanky girl with a twist of worry. "But will it be safe?"

Vanika frowned at him. "Safe for me to go back to my own village?"

He thought of Borthwick's cold gray eyes measuring him from across the room and how readily the whip had fallen into the man's hand—and why a whip at all?

Because it would hurt more, Neil realized with a chill.

"She won't be going beyond the village," Mr. Chowdhury declared.

Vanika peeled herself away from Kalb, who dropped to her feet and gazed up at her with unbridled adoration. She glared mutinously at the solicitor.

Vijay came to Mr. Chowdhury's side. "Agreed. You're to bring Connie and the others to your grandmother's house and no further. Is that clear?"

"Fiiiiine," Vanika promised with eloquent resignation.

"But I'm forgetting myself!" Vijay exclaimed with a clap of his hands. "It seems I owe two of you a hearty congratulations!"

With a guilty lurch in his guts, Neil realized the maharaja was referring to his fake engagement.

The guilt evaporated into an even less comfortable sensation as Constance hooked a hand through Neil's arm and plastered herself to his side.

He could feel the curve of her hip brushing against his leg.

Don't think of trousers, he pleaded with himself desperately.

"That's very kind of you, Uncle Vijay," Constance asserted, treating her royal relative to a blinding smile.

"Kind!?" Vijay exclaimed. "Let me tell you how cross I was at learning that the two of you had kept such a delicious secret from me! I might just forgive you for it—if you promise to bring our Connie back to India to visit us every few years."

Neil felt an unexpected burst of indignation. "Why wouldn't I?"

Constance's eyebrow cocked with surprise.

"It's a long trip," Vijay challenged.

"This is Connie's other home," Neil retorted. "It doesn't matter how far it is."

Vijay's eyes twinkled as he addressed Mr. Chowdhury. "I told you I liked him."

Neil went over a bit dizzy.

"Are we going, then?" Vanika cut in impatiently. "Or are we planning to stand around chatting in the drive all day?"

Neil rode over wide green meadows dotted with wildflowers. The clear morning light had given way to high gray clouds pierced here and there by golden rays. He was grateful for the cover overhead, as it somewhat softened the thick heat of the afternoon.

Sweat beaded on his skin. He had stripped to his shirt and waistcoat but kept the scabbard. The weight across his back was starting to feel familiar.

There was no road, only a dry track of packed earth that wended between shivering grasslands and sprawling, ancient trees. Their twelve-year-old guide navigated the trails with ease despite a complete lack of signs or other markers of direction.

They passed clusters of tall mango trees. Trumpetbushes burst with yellow next to small farmhouses. Cows grazed in unfenced fields accompanied by wandering chickens.

Adam and Ellie rode ahead, alongside Vanika. It had taken Adam some coaxing to get Ellie into the saddle. Neither she nor Neil had ever had much cause to ride when they had lived at home. Neil had made up for it since, especially once he had gone to Egypt, and was now fairly comfortable with the whole process—unlike Ellie, who had looked at the horse as though she suspected it might bite her.

"I don't see what's wrong with walking," Ellie had grumbled.

When Kalb wasn't sprinting after some small animal, he trotted happily alongside while Adam and Vanika kept up a running line of easy chatter. The girl was clearly taken with Neil's friend, her head stuffed with stories about dashing American gunslingers.

Neil rode several paces behind them… with his fake fiancée.

Not that Constance would be engaged to him for long. Their mad arrangement would most likely be over in a month or so.

Wouldn't it?

He tried to imagine pretending to be marrying Constance for more than a month. A trickle of sweat ran down his back.

They passed a tumbled pile of ruined houses set under the leaning branches of an almond tree. The thatch on the roofs had mostly rotted away.

"There seem to be a lot of empty villages around here," Neil noted.

"I think those are from the famine," Constance replied with uncharacteristic solemnity.

"What famine?"

She watched the path as it twisted across the landscape under the looming clouds. "It was thirty years ago. A third of the people died."

"Here?" Neil studied the landscape around them, which did seem to be very sparsely populated.

Constance's eyes were sad. "In Odisha."

"A third of *Odisha?* But that must have been…"

"Over a million people," Constance filled in.

Neil reeled as he tried to absorb the sheer scale of what she described. He thought of other empty buildings that he had seen as they had traveled from Puri to Nandapur. He hadn't paid them much mind at the time, but now those collapsing walls and broken fences took on a terrible significance. "But… *how?*"

"There was a drought. The authorities didn't have enough reserves to feed everyone."

Her words caught in Neil's ear. He remembered a radical classmate of his at Cambridge who had railed about the impact of British policy on the horrific famine in Ireland during the middle of the century. "Didn't have enough—or couldn't be bothered redistributing what they had?"

Constance watched the ruined homes recede behind them. "Aai told me that my grandfather believed very firmly that the administration could have done more than they did."

"Your grandfather was English, wasn't he?" Neil asked.

"He was the Agent for Nandapur—that's the chief local administrative officer, representing the Raj to the royal court. It was all very scandalous. Indian Civil Service members weren't supposed to marry natives—even royal natives. I think he nearly lost his post over it."

"When was this?" Neil asked.

"Just after the mutiny. I still don't know exactly how it came to happen—if Aai pursued my grandfather because she thought an alliance with an Englishman would protect the family or because she wanted to escape from some other match that her father had arranged for her. Or maybe she just fell for him. One can't always account for love."

Neil gazed at Constance's elegant profile. "I suppose not."

"After the famine, my grandfather told Aai that he couldn't do it anymore—serve as Agent and see all this suffering but not really be able to change anything about it. He asked her if she would go back to England with him. She agreed. She thought there would be more opportunities for my mother and her sisters there."

"Your mother has sisters?"

Constance shot him a wry look. "She has three of them."

"And they all live in England?"

"Well, all except Auntie Hannah. She moved to Canada."

"I didn't realize you had aunts." Neil felt a touch ashamed at the admission.

"I would hardly have expected you to investigate my family tree while I was painting glue onto the seat of your chair," Constance cheerfully replied.

"I had forgotten about that one," Neil grumbled.

Constance's eyes sparkled wickedly. "How could you forget that one? You had to crawl out of your own trousers to escape."

Neil ran a hand over his face. "Yes, well. I suppose it just got lost in between all the other ways you attempted to torment me."

He wondered how much else he had overlooked about Constance during those early years. He might have grown up with her, but he'd hardly been quizzing her about her hopes and dreams between rescuing his scorched term papers and shaking moles out of his boots. In the brief few weeks since they had become reacquainted, he was constantly stumbling across new discoveries, all of them adding to his respect and admiration for the woman who rode beside him—astride, in her damnably well-fitting trousers.

Neil forced his attention from the curve of her thigh back to the road.

"*A million people*," he said, unable to shake the thought from his mind. "How could anyone let something like that happen? If a famine had threatened to take out a third of the population of Essex, I should imagine a great deal more would've been done about it! Did this one not matter as much because they were Indians?"

Constance studied the achingly green landscape, painted here and there with sunlight where it broke through the clouds. "I doubt the English did as much for Odisha as we might have done for our own people." She caught herself. "Their own people? I'm not really sure which side I'm supposed to be on in all of this."

His chest tugged with an ache of admiration and sympathy. "I'm afraid I'm woefully unqualified to help you answer that question."

Constance reached over to pat him consolingly on the knee as they rode. "You still have your uses."

"Do I?" Neil wondered skeptically.

"Certainly," Constance assured him, eyes still twinkling. "And I'll be sure to let you know all about them—just as soon as I figure out what they are."

Neil struggled to hide a smile. "Why do I find myself recalling that time you put pepper in my tea?"

Constance snorted.

A rumble of soft, distant thunder echoed across the fields.

"Should we find a place to stop?" Neil pressed. "It looks like it might rain."

"It's the monsoon," Constance countered. "If we insist on avoiding the rain, we won't get anywhere until October. Come on!"

EIGHTEEN

$\mathcal{E}$LLIE'S MUSCLES BALKED at the unaccustomed effort of the ride as the day drifted toward afternoon. Sitting on top of an animal that did all the walking for you really oughtn't be so strenuous—or unsettling. Ellie was uncomfortably conscious of just how far the ground was and how easily she might land there if the horse grew irritated with her.

She glanced back at Constance and Neil. They had fallen a little behind, out of earshot but still comfortably within view.

"Worrying about your brother?" Adam asked.

He was perfectly at ease riding beside her, his borrowed Winchester slung over his shoulder. Unsurprisingly, he had shucked out of his jacket the moment they'd left the palace. It was slung across the back of his saddle, where he would likely be perfectly happy to lose it forever. The sleeves of his shirt were pushed up to expose his tanned forearms.

Vanika bounced ahead of them on her mule, Kalb trotting happily at her side.

"There are so many ways this pretend engagement of theirs could go wrong," Ellie admitted.

Adam shot her a thoughtful look. "You haven't wondered…"

"Wondered what?" Ellie pressed when he trailed off.

"Whether there might actually be something going on between those two."

"Neil and Constance?" Ellie echoed uncomfortably. "My stick-in-the-mud brother and the girl who spent most of our childhood finding creative ways to torment him?"

"She's not a kid anymore," Adam pointed out.

Ellie raised her brows.

His blue gaze sparked with warm humor. "Don't worry, Princess. I've only got eyes for one set of trousers around here."

Her cheeks flushed.

"So?" he prompted.

"Don't be silly," Ellie quickly answered.

"You saying that because you're sure? Or because the idea gives you the willies?"

Ellie shot him a glare. "Constance and Neil are two grown adults perfectly capable of making their own decisions in life. Why should I have the 'willies' about whatever they choose to do with each other?"

"No idea," Adam replied innocently.

"Not that they have chosen anything of the sort," Ellie continued. "They have both made it quite clear this engagement is nothing but another of Constance's mad schemes. Why, Neil spent most of breakfast looking as though he was about to lose his tea. That's hardly what one would expect from someone harboring a secret tendre."

Adam's mouth quirked with mischief. "Wanna bet?"

"Bet?" Ellie echoed indignantly.

"Wager," Adam elaborated. "Gamble."

"I know what a bet is."

"You win, and I won't smoke anything for the rest of the month," Adam vowed.

"The rest of the month?" Ellie pressed back dryly.

He shifted uncomfortably in the saddle. "The year?"

Ellie considered this narrowly. "It's July."

"That's still five months."

"It's not that I disapprove on moral or hygienic grounds," she quickly went on. "I don't even mind the smell, really."

Adam grinned at her wickedly. "How about the taste?"

Ellie had admittedly become quite familiar with the flavor of tobacco when Adam's tongue had explored her mouth.

"I should say that depends upon the particular blend," she answered carefully, conscious of the twelve-year-old girl riding a short distance ahead of them.

Adam laughed, deep and rollicking. Vanika twisted in her saddle to look back at them.

"It's only that some physicians have suggested there might be a link between tobacco use and certain ailments of the lungs," Ellie continued, lowering her voice.

"I only do it every once in a while."

"We don't know what frequency might expose you to risk!"

Adam brushed his knuckles along the line of her cheek. "Interested in keeping me around, huh?"

Ellie tilted up her chin. "I should think that I have made that rather clear by now."

Adam's attention drifted lazily to where her trouser-clad legs hugged the saddle. "I can think of a few ways you've gotten the point across."

The heat seemed to rise—which ought to have been impossible as it was already sweltering.

"A full year," Adam declared. "July to July."

"A full year?" Ellie tried to disguise her interest. "With no tobacco whatso-ever?"

"Or any of the other stuff they smoke around here," Adam solemnly promised.

Ellie's curiosity sparked. "Are there other things they smoke in India?"

"Your turn," Adam ordered instead of answering.

Behind them, Constance was cheerfully rattling on at Ellie's brother, who looked hot and tired. All of that was perfectly normal... except that her brother was actually *listening*. Ten years ago, he would have been exasperatedly waiting for Constance to leave him alone or reeling with bewilderment at her flood of commentary on something he couldn't begin to understand because it didn't involve ancient history or dead languages.

Neil and Constance were adults now. Why wouldn't he listen to her? That was what friends did—and they were friends, weren't they?

It was all perfectly friendly.

Neil loosened the button at his collar, searching for relief from the heat.

Constance's attention dropped to the hollow at the base of his throat—and held there for a long moment.

A nagging unease darted through Ellie.

"So? What are you going to wager?" Adam prompted.

"Nothing," Ellie blurted out.

Adam cocked an eyebrow.

"I mean—I'm not a gambler," Ellie quickly corrected. "I haven't the foggiest idea."

"You could let him get another dog!" Vanika sang out—incidentally proving that she could hear them perfectly well.

At her side, Kalb barked loudly at a passing crow. The dog jumped as though trying to snatch it out of the air... not that the beast would have any notion of what to do with the bird if he succeeded.

Ellie felt her face drain. "Absolutely not."

"What? Don't think you'll win?" Adam challenged.

"That is not what I am saying at all. I mean only that gambling is a terrible habit that we should certainly not encourage around impressionable young people."

"She does not think she will win," Vanika translated cheerfully. "I do not blame her. When the lady came outside, Dr. Fairfax spent far too much time looking at her trousers."

"He was only surprised that she was wearing them!" Ellie countered stoutly.

"Oh? I am sure that is all it was, then," Vanika conceded breezily.

The girl turned around again, whistling a cheerful tune.

The electric green fields gave way to steep, rolling hills where low scrub grew over red earth. Thickets of brush framed the trail, chirping and buzzing with birds and insects. The afternoon was high, and the heat thickened despite the steady gray cover overhead. Ellie gripped the pommel of her horse as she rode up a sharply inclined path.

They crested the hill—and the forest sprawled out before them. The thick green blanket covered a landscape of verdant mountain peaks dazzled here and there with rays of sun that broke through the gaps in the monsoon.

Ellie was stunned with wonder. This was the Dandakaranya, the mythical wilderness of Rama's exile.

Where the dry red earth gave way to the shadowed beauty of the legendary forest, great black birds wheeled over the view like dark slashes against the gray sky. Ellie recognized them as vultures.

There had been vultures in the Ramayana. Their king had sacrificed himself to try to save Sita from being kidnapped by Ravana.

The ones circling through the sky in front of them felt like guardians of a barrier she was poised to cross.

The feeling shattered into alarm as four men slipped from the rocks to either side and leveled muskets at their party.

The weapons qualified as antiques but were oiled and well cared for—which left Ellie with no doubt as to their ability to fire. Even if a musket could take only a single shot before reloading, that was four shots too many for their current circumstances.

Adam made a similar calculation. He slowly raised his hands, leaving the Winchester untouched on his back. Neil did the same—then grabbed at the reins as his horse shied beneath him.

The men on the other side of the weapons wore homespun shirts and dhotis. Their feet were bare, and their expressions were watchful.

An older gentleman stepped out to join them. A white lungi circled his waist like a kilt, and his chest was bare. The cropped, curling hair of his head and beard were richly streaked with silver.

He held a bow and arrow with casual readiness in his wiry arms, his amber eyes steady—until they dropped to Kalb as the dog plopped down at his feet.

Kalb panted up at the warrior as though hoping for a treat. *And why wouldn't he*, Ellie thought irritably.

"Jignesh!" Vanika shouted happily.

The girl leaped off her mule and ran up to the older man, throwing her arms around his chest. She let off a quick stream of words in an unfamiliar language. Ellie assumed it was Kuvi, based on the very limited reading she had done about the Khond.

Vanika's tone turned from affectionate to chiding as she waved her hands from the armed men to Ellie and the rest of her party.

"Hao, hao!" the older warrior protested, separating his arrow from his bow and holding them up with an air of tired conciliation.

Vanika turned back with a smug air, casually scratching Kalb between his ears. "I told Jignesh that he can't shoot any of you."

Neil looked quietly alarmed. "Would he have shot us if she hadn't told him not to?" he asked under his breath.

Adam regarded the men thoughtfully. "I'm guessing these folks have good reason to want to know who's coming to visit."

Vanika led them forward, Kalb trotting at her heels. Jignesh dismissed his men and joined them, his long legs easily keeping up with the tranquil pace of the horses.

The hill descended into a lightly forested valley sheltered by the surrounding slopes. The Adrija village sat at the base of it, framed by tidy fields of turmeric and other crops. Thirty houses lined the single dirt road. The buildings were simple, with a single story and a thatched roof, but their craftsmanship was apparent in the elegant carvings around the door frames and the painted murals on some of the walls.

Flowering bushes in hues of gold and crimson brightened the landscape. Jasmine vines twined up the pillars that supported covered front porches, while bushy neem trees provided oases of shade.

A weathered post stood in one of the fields beside the village. The wooden column was roughly twice Ellie's height, the top half bifurcated into a pair of tapering points like the horns of a cow. The monument felt vaguely ritual, piquing Ellie's anthropological interests.

Jignesh split off with the horses, leading them away for rest and food, while Vanika led Ellie and her companions into the village. Women watched curiously as they passed. Silver rings thickly decorated their ears and noses, while tattoos ornamented their cheekbones, chins, and foreheads in geometric arrangements of dots and lines.

Vanika stopped at a larger house shaded by another fragrant neem and dashed inside. A quick burst of Kuvi reached Ellie's ears before the girl popped back out onto the covered porch alongside a diminutive woman with age-silvered hair. The older lady regarded Ellie and the others with an expression of mild surprise on her tattooed features.

"Attuburhi, evasi Bates Sahib, Mallory Memsahib, Tyrrell Memsahib, Fairfax Sahib. Oh—and Kalb." Vanika punctuated her last introduction by scrubbing the dog's ears. He soaked up the attention with panting adoration. "This is my grandmother, Nirjara. Everyone here respects her because she's the kuttakaru."

"Kuttakaru?" Ellie echoed the unfamiliar word.

"It means she speaks with the gods and the dead," Vanika replied.

"Like a priest, you mean?" Ellie pressed curiously.

"Do your priests actually speak to the gods?" Vanika retorted with an air of challenge.

"Not usually," Ellie admitted.

Vanika smirked. "Then they are not like my grandmother."

A group of children raced up to the house in a hurried mass. One of the oldest among them, a boy of around ten, grabbed Vanika's arm and tugged, rattling off a quick stream of chatter as he pointed toward the hills, imparting some childishly exciting news.

"Hao, wai!" Vanika answered quickly.

She hopped down from the porch, calling back over her shoulder. "You can all wait here! My attuburhi will take care of you until my cousin arrives."

Constance regarded the child with mingled humor and irritation. "And where are you going?"

"Nowhere important!" Vanika asserted unconvincingly, then bolted off, trailed by a wave of other children.

Nirjara smiled warmly, motioning them to the stools scattered about her porch. "Aas, bas e-thi," she offered in careful Odia.

Ellie dropped onto one of the low seats, a thousand questions burning on the tip of her tongue—not that she could ask any of them. It appeared that any conversation with the older woman faced a substantial language barrier, and their translator had just skipped away into the village.

Neil sat down beside Ellie. Adam crossed to the end of the porch, leaning against the pillar as he studied the village.

Kalb flopped down by Ellie's feet, huffing a tired breath over her boots.

Constance poked her head into the house. "This is splendid!"

Their hostess took out a set of small cups, filling them from a jar by her feet.

"Thank you," Neil said as he accepted one. He took a sip and immediately coughed.

The vessels were full of some sort of alcohol. Ellie had been able to tell that with a sniff. It burned at her nose like Adam's occasional pours of whiskey.

The smoky, floral scent tickled strangely at the back of her mind.

Constance smirked at Neil and then tossed back a stiff slug of the liquor with no apparent impact.

Nirjara made an encouraging gesture at Ellie, nodding at her cup. Not wanting to offend her host, Ellie lifted it to her mouth.

Flowers danced over her tongue with a tantalizing burn… and the world around her snapped away, replaced by somewhere else.

A circle of women laughed under the full moon, dressed in embroidered robes accented with jade and gold. A white stone pyramid rose in the distance, painted silver by the night through the dancing leaves of the ceiba trees.

A priestess clapped for attention with an indulgent smile.

The clay cup at her lips. The burn against her throat—honey and fire, petals and sunlight.

"Stone Flower Water," Ellie blurted out loud, clutching the cup between her hands.

She wasn't under the moon. She sat on the porch in the heart of the Adrija village.

Constance cast her a curious look. Neil didn't seem to have noticed, engrossed in trying a more tentative sip of the liquor.

Adam set a gentle hand on her shoulder, glancing down at her with a flicker of understanding. The touch was an anchor linking her more solidly to the hot Indian afternoon—and not a place a thousand miles away and centuries in the past.

Ellie was afraid to take another sip. She glanced at Vanika's *kuttakaru* grandmother to try to discern how that might be received and was surprised to find the woman watching her with a look that felt oddly *knowing*.

Nirjara turned away to raise a hand in greeting to someone coming down the road.

While their hostess's attention was diverted, Adam plucked Ellie's cup from her hand, swapping it with his own—which he had already drained.

Ellie flashed him a grateful smile.

In answer to Nirjara's wave, a young man hopped onto the porch. He did not look very happy to be there.

The fellow was objectively dashing, with wavy black hair and the build of a natural athlete under his loose cotton shirt and casual trousers. He appeared to be a few years shy of Ellie's own age but carried himself with a straight-backed air of natural authority.

Constance frankly assessed the newcomer.

"Guests from the maharaja, is it?" the young man summarized tersely. "I'm Subhas Kōnja. Mind if I ask why you've come?"

Nirjara scolded him. "We'ima, Na'tya."

"Hao, Attubuṛhi," Subhas replied with a note of exasperation. He sat down on one of the stools. "My grandmother has requested that I hear you out," he reported obediently—if not particularly enthusiastically.

"Your English is excellent," Constance commented. "Are there many people here who speak it?"

"No," Subhas returned shortly. "I'm at Ravenshaw, the university in Cuttack."

Nirjara tsked lightly, her eyes sparking with humor.

Subhas suppressed a sigh. "I am there studying law on a scholarship program funded by His Highness the Maharaja of Nandapur, for which I am eternally and deeply obliged to him," he rattled off with a clear note of sarcasm.

Constance's brow arched.

"What?" Subhas pushed back, challenging. "Am I supposed to celebrate that the means of determining who has the opportunity to better themselves lies with an unelected hereditary ruler who grows fat on the tax revenues of the working people?"

"We're hoping to find a guide into the forest," Adam cut in tactfully.

"Why?" Subhas demanded flatly.

"Familiar with a guy by the name of Borthwick?"

Subhas's expression darkened with recognition. "I know who he is."

Ellie recalled the information that Mr. Chowdhury had shared about the Criminal Tribes Act. A firebrand law student from a place like Ranyapali likely knew far more than she did about the impact of such laws—and what a man like Borthwick could do with them.

"He's headed this way," Adam explained. "Looking to get his hands on a historical curiosity he believes is hidden somewhere in your woods."

Subhas's eyes flashed with defiance. "Best of luck to him finding it."

Ellie's temper flared. "*Join the Lord of the Dance on the ridge that points to the dawn of the longest day,*" she recited tersely.

Subhas's mouth tightened.

"I take it something about that description sounds familiar?" Adam drawled.

"Borthwick has the clues as well," Ellie pointed out.

The look Subhas fixed on them was impressively intimidating for a man barely over twenty. "And the General Superintendent of the Thuggee and Dacoity Department is following these directions to what, exactly?"

Ellie answered a bit more uneasily. "A surviving invocation of the Brahmastra."

Subhas crossed his arms. "You are aware that you're talking about a load of mythological nonsense."

"Ina vestenju," Nirjara ordered.

Subhas translated for her, rattling off a stream of Kuvi. Nirjara eyed the four of them thoughtfully as she responded.

The younger man's mouth firmed unhappily at her words.

"What'd she say?" Adam prompted.

"That I have spent too much time at the university and too long away from the forest." Subhas paced to the end of the porch, staring out at the thick clouds that loomed over the village. "I don't know anything about astras— but I know about the British using any excuse they can muster in order to scout our territory for natural resources to exploit. Lumber. Tin. Coal."

He turned to face them with his arms crossed over his chest. "Why you?"

Adam met Ellie's look, and a shiver of uncomfortable understanding passed between them before he answered. "Borthwick's traveling with some old friends of ours. We've got some idea what we're walking into."

"You have no idea what you're walking into," Subhas cut back. "This is the Jāṛa Kṛa'ni in the monsoon season. You'd be lucky if you weren't swept away in a landslide."

"Jāṛa Kṛa'ni?" Neil echoed.

Subhas glared at him. "The Forest of Tigers."

Ellie raised her chin with an air of challenge. "What about Dandakaranya?"

Nirjara gave a throaty laugh at the sound of the name.

Subhas shrugged. "That's what the Odias call it. They think Rama passed through here."

"Are you not a Hindu yourself?" Constance pressed.

Subhas scoffed as though at a mild insult. "No."

He was quiet for a moment. Ellie could see the quick gears of his mind whirring. He straightened as he reached his conclusion. "We'll take care of it."

Neil shifted uncomfortably. Constance frowned.

Ellie felt a quick pulse of fear. "We want to help."

Subhas assessed them frankly. Ellie and Constance were quickly dismissed. He hitched slightly on the sword at Neil's back before taking in the rest of Neil and looking unimpressed.

He halted a breath longer on Adam, eyes moving from the machete at his belt to the breadth of his shoulders before his expression closed. "I fail to see what help you would be."

"We have done this sort of thing before," Ellie pushed back.

"Not here, you haven't."

Ellie climbed to her feet to face him. "We know the people you're dealing with."

Subhas glared back at her. "I know Borthwick. And Borthwick's the one that matters."

"But…" Ellie began.

Subhas stepped closer, something dangerous coming into his expression that belied his cultured accent and relative youth. "It's *my* forest."

He turned to leave.

Ellie scrambled for a way to call him back. She wanted to find an argument that would convince Subhas to let them help—but she couldn't. It *was* his forest, after all.

Constance had no such qualms. She shot to her feet, hands braced on her hips. "Oh no, you don't! You aren't pushing us out of this so easily."

"And what are you going to do? Scold Borthwick into submission?" Subhas stubbornly retorted.

A cold fury slipped over Constance's features.

Subhas moved to the steps. "We're done here."

He stopped as a dagger embedded itself into the post beside his head.

His grandmother chuckled with wheezing amusement.

Subhas turned with slow disbelief.

Constance plucked a second blade from her trouser pocket—which she had apparently cut open in order to more easily access her garters. "You were saying?" she prompted sweetly.

Subhas's eyes blazed, leaving Ellie with no doubt that he had plenty indeed to say on the subject, once the shock of having a dagger thrown at him by a scion of the local royal household had worn off.

He didn't get the chance, as a familiar nine-year-old boy sprinted up to the porch, spilling out a monologue with breathless urgency.

Ellie understood only a single word of it—one that sent a chill shivering over her arms.

Vanika.

Adam's focus sharpened. "What happened?"

Subhas translated as the boy kept talking. "The children took Vanika to see a party of soldiers they found marching on the edge of the Adrija lands."

Ellie's stomach sank with sudden worry. "Soldiers?"

Subhas barked a rebuke at the boy, clearly unhappy that this was the first he was hearing of the intruders.

"Ninge, Abbaya!" the boy pleaded apologetically.

"What about Vanika?" Adam demanded.

Subhas met his demand with a coiled fury. "Do you honestly care?"

Adam's jaw firmed stubbornly. "She's a good kid."

Subhas measured the reply and begrudgingly accepted it. He returned his attention to the boy.

The child rattled off the rest of his account, and Subhas's mouth tightened into a tense line. "He says Vanika went to talk to the soldiers, then sent the other children back with a message."

"What message?" Ellie pressed.

Subhas's dark eyes snapped with threat—and worry. "That she found Borthwick… and has the situation under control."

"Hell," Adam cursed feelingly.

NINETEEN

SUBHAS LEAPED DOWN from the porch, stalking through the village. Adam followed him.

Ellie hurried after, still cold with shock. "Borthwick is *here*? How is that possible? He was going to Nandapur! How could he have made it here so quickly if he hadn't even arrived by the time we left?"

"Because he never went to Nandapur," Adam bit out. "I'm guessing he never meant to… which means he planted that rumor specifically to keep Connie's family pinned down."

Ellie felt the blood drain from her face. "He suspects they're involved in this."

Adam caught up to Subhas. "You're sure those kids saw soldiers? Not police?"

"They know the difference," Subhas retorted.

"Why does that matter?" Ellie pressed with a twist of unease.

"Bigger guns. Better training." Adam glanced at Subhas. "And I'm guessing the Indian Army doesn't hand out detachments for just any damned reason."

"No," Subhas returned shortly.

"How on earth does a twelve-year-old girl think she has that situation *under control?*" Ellie demanded.

"Bhanja said he recognized two of the English words she spoke to the soldiers," Subhas replied.

"What words?" Adam pressed.

Subhas met his gaze. "'Help'—and 'money.'"

Adam closed his eyes. "The damned kid's trying to bluff Borthwick into thinking he can bribe her as a guide."

Ellie recalled Vanika's brash confidence and found Adam's theory all too plausible.

A new and terrible thought snapped through her. "Was there another white man with the soldiers? Lean and pale with dark hair and eyes? He wouldn't have been in uniform."

Subhas frowned with irritation at the question, but he called out to Vanika's young messenger, who was now on the porch of one of the nearby houses with his mother.

The boy answered. Even without knowing Kuvi, Ellie could tell it was an affirmative.

Jignesh called Subhas from across the village. Ellie grasped Adam's arm as Subhas stepped away to join him.

"Jacobs is there. And he'll know she was lying."

"Yeah," Adam agreed grimly.

"Then why would he let her come with them?"

"Because he wants to find out why an English-speaking village girl would suddenly show up offering to help them along."

Fear tightened Ellie's throat. "She has no idea how much danger she's in."

Worry darkened Adam's eyes. "I know."

Subhas gave Jignesh another order, and the old Adrija warrior broke away to hurry to the other houses in the village. Jignesh had been the one to lead the party that had easily ambushed Ellie and the others on their way to Ranyapali, but he clearly deferred to the younger man—the one Vanika's friend had called 'abbaya,' the term Vijay had given for the local clan leader.

Ellie was starting to suspect that Subhas Kōnja was capable of handling himself in places far more dangerous than a classroom.

Adam strode back over to Subhas. "Where are they?"

Subhas made a mental calculation. "I know the trail they're following. If the detachment is marching at a regular pace, they should now be about two and a half miles to the northwest."

Adam glanced unerringly to a point between the distant peaks beyond the village. He didn't have to check the compass in his pocket to know where they needed to go.

Families crowded onto their porches, children held close as they watched Subhas with tight concern. Jignesh waved to some of the men as he stalked past. They slung quickly assembled packs over their shoulders as they hopped into the road to join him.

Ellie startled as Kalb pressed himself to the back of her legs, nearly knocking her over. He whimpered as though sensing that something was wrong.

Adam stepped closer to Subhas. "We have to get her out of there."

Subhas assessed the gathering Adrija. "My men and I will ambush Borthwick's line."

Ellie stiffened with alarm. "You're talking about a battle! People will get hurt!"

"My people," Subhas returned dangerously, "are more than capable of a fight."

"*Vanika* could get hurt!" She looked frantically to Adam. "There must be a better way!"

Grim understanding tightened Adam's mouth. "There is—if you and I go get her."

Shock momentarily blanked her thoughts as Adam's logic became clear.

She and Adam could go after Vanika—because they had an advantage against Borthwick that no one else in the village could replicate.

"Fiddlesticks," Ellie breathed out uneasily.

Constance and Neil joined them, Nirjara following more sedately in their wake.

"And why should I believe that the pair of you can do what my men and I can't—in *our* forest?" Subhas's voice dripped with skepticism.

Ellie reeled as she answered him. "Because the pale man with Borthwick needs Adam and me alive."

Subhas's eyes narrowed skeptically. "For what?"

A single word echoed through Ellie's brain, crackling with anger and disdain across a windswept desert night.

Justice.

"Long story," Adam cut back, visibly mustering patience. "Look, best-case scenario, we track Borthwick's expedition, sneak in after dark, and get the kid out before anybody notices we were there. She's not a prisoner—*yet*—so it shouldn't be that complicated. But if it gets complicated, Ellie and I won't get shot over it. Jacobs would have to stop anyone who tried."

"You realize this sounds insane," Subhas noted.

"Sure does," Adam agreed tiredly. "But so do magic mirrors and deserts that turn into waves, and I've seen both over the last few weeks. You going to tell me nothing has ever happened to you that you couldn't explain?"

Subhas cast a frowning, uneasy look at his grandmother.

The village kuttakaru smiled back at him serenely.

Adam pleaded with them. "Ellie and I have an advantage in this situation that might keep people from getting killed. Let us use it. *Please.*"

The women and children hovering outside their houses continued to watch worriedly. Jignesh's men scattered to gather supplies, the old warrior deftly supervising the preparations.

Nirjara prodded her grandson with a finger, asking him a question. Subhas answered with obvious reluctance.

The older woman's serene smile carried a hint of mischief. "Tari Penu hāḍa. Ēvari haladu."

"What did she say?" Ellie asked.

Subhas rubbed an exasperated hand over his features. "That Tari Penu says you should go."

"Tari Penu?"

"Our god," he replied dryly.

Ellie thought of the carved pillar that stood sentinel on the far side of the village.

"Though how much of it is Tari Penu and how much is Attubuṛhi meddling, I couldn't say." Subhas faced Adam with an air of frank challenge. "Do you have any idea how to track a body of men in the forest without being seen?"

"Yes," Adam returned flatly.

Subhas absorbed the unquestioning confidence in his response.

Adam adjusted the fall of the Winchester across his back. "Two and a half miles to the northwest."

The younger man came to a decision. He looked far from happy about it.

"Borthwick will have to find a way to cross the river," he begrudgingly filled in. "You can't use the same route. He'll watch his flank… but we have our own crossings. Take the game trail that branches to the north a mile up the valley. Follow the level ridge to the west until you see a dry streambed on the southern slope. You'll find what you need there." Subhas's eyes glinted with challenge. "Do you have all that?"

"I got it," Adam replied, meeting his gaze.

He whistled, and Kalb—who had been starting to creep after a chicken—darted to his side.

"At the river, watch out for the bodh," Subhas added with deceptive ease.

"What's a bodh?" Adam asked.

"It's a rather large catfish."

"Am I watching for it in case I get hungry?" Adam quipped.

Subhas ignored the question, authority coming into the line of his shoulders. "My men and I will go after your astra—not because I think there is a magical weapon hidden in the forest," he emphasized with a glare. "But if there's anything out there important enough to catch Borthwick's attention, I don't want him to have it."

Adam's thumb hooked around the strap of his rifle. "Sounds like a plan."

Neil straightened with determination, stepping forward. "I'm coming with you."

"You come," Adam pushed back mercilessly, "and you'll be handing Jacobs exactly the leverage he needs over the two of us—because he'll have no problem hurting you."

Neil's eyes sparked with frustration. "Am I just supposed to sit around and wait to see whether you come back?"

"No one is sitting around," Constance cut in. "We're going with Mr. Kōnja."

Subhas looked frankly horrified at the idea. "Absolutely not."

Constance narrowed her eyes. "Do I need to remind you what I can do with my daggers?"

Subhas stepped closer. "I don't need daggers if I have guns."

"I'm also trained in the Japanese art of jiu jitsu." Constance flashed him a dangerous smile. "I could show you, if you like."

"I'll pass," Subhas retorted.

Frustrated, Constance jabbed an angry finger at Neil. "What if he can see ghosts?"

"What?!" Neil blurted out, horrified.

Adam cocked a questioning eyebrow. Ellie frowned.

Was this some gambit Constance had cooked up to try to get herself onto Subhas's expedition? If it was, it seemed quite far-fetched.

Except that Neil had suddenly gone very, very still.

A dart of unease shivered up Ellie's spine.

Constance was defiant. "You heard the sitar player in the garden at Nandapur—don't even try to pretend that you didn't! And you saw a Moghul prince in the window of the Lal Bagh in Puri."

Neil forced out an unconvincing chuckle. "But that's… I mean, that was obviously just…"

Constance crossed her arms, waiting.

"I was imagining things!" Neil protested.

"Imagining things that actually happened?" Constance pushed back relentlessly.

Neil pressed his fingers to his temples. "No! It wasn't like that."

"I was right there, Stuffy. I don't know why you're even trying to deny it. I'm almost certain you did it in Egypt as well with that Eighth Nome official in the rock cut tomb."

Adam shot a questioning look at Ellie, but she was just as bewildered by the exchange as he was.

"That's not what happened!" Neil's voice held a note of panic.

"Are you calling me a liar?" Constance challenged.

"Of course not!"

"Well, if I'm not a liar…" Constance began.

"It's not ghosts!" Neil burst out.

"What else could it be, Stuffy?!"

"Time!" Neil blurted—and then clamped his mouth shut as though horrified by what had just come out of it.

He spun on his heel and walked away from them.

Constance stared after him, wide-eyed. Subhas watched with an air of bewildered amusement.

Neil dropped down to sit on the porch of one of the houses, putting his head in his hands.

Ellie walked over to join him.

"Time?" she asked carefully.

Neil drew in a slow, uneven breath. "Sometimes… occasionally… I seem to be able to… see through time."

He raised his head with a look of desperation. "It's not like it happens constantly. In fact, mostly it's not really *seeing* anything at all. It's just an… an instinct. You know—like when it's obvious that someone's mucked up their analysis of Punic orthography."

"I don't actually know when someone is doing that," Ellie replied in a deliberately reasonable tone. "Because no one has figured out how to decipher Punic yet."

Neil looked queasy.

Ellie couldn't blame him. She was feeling a little queasy herself.

Her brother had been *seeing through time?* How could that be possible?

But then, she was also acquainted—however unpleasantly—with a man who always knew when someone was lying, which was just as impossible.

Was Neil like Jacobs? What did that even mean?

Ellie didn't know.

"How long has this been happening?" she demanded.

"I don't know." Fear and discomfort tightened Neil's words. "I didn't realize I was doing it at all until Sayyid brought the whole thing up, and then made me—"

Neil clamped his mouth shut.

Adam knelt down beside him, his voice calm. "Made you what, buddy?"

Neil pressed his fingers to his eyes behind his spectacles. "Find the Staff of Moses in a cubit box."

Ellie's head began to spin.

"But I thought Sayyid found the staff," Constance protested as she joined them.

Neil stiffened with a flash of indignation. "Sayyid isn't the only one who can find things, you know!"

"Apparently not," Ellie agreed numbly. Very gently, she reached out and took one of her brother's hands. "Why didn't you say anything?"

"It… It just seemed so…" Neil forced himself to meet her eyes, his expression desperately unhappy. "I'm sorry, Peanut."

Ellie clasped his hand a little tighter, at a loss for how else to respond.

What could she say? Her brother had supernatural powers—*Neil*, of all people! The most unmagical person in the world!

"This is *fascinating*," Constance asserted with obvious relish.

"And we're gonna have to shelve the topic for later." Adam pushed to his feet. "We need to move."

Subhas had been reluctantly translating for his grandmother. At her response, he looked up at the sky as though striving for patience.

"Tari Penu is full of opinions today." He lowered his glare to Neil and Constance. "Fine. You two can join us."

Constance bounced to her feet. "Excellent! Come on, Stuffy!"

She hauled Neil upright.

Adam's attention shifted worriedly to the northwest.

Ellie was worried too. She was far from certain how far Jacobs' forced indulgence would extend. She could still remember the moment on the cliffs behind Tell al-Amarna when his sheer fury at her and Adam's constant interventions had threatened to tip the scales of whatever dark calculation had otherwise stayed his hand.

The weight of how suddenly the stakes had shifted settled over her like lead. She and Adam had to find a way to bring Vanika home—while letting go of the purpose that had brought them out here in the first place. It would be up to Subhas to save the Brahmastra now, but Ellie could see that he was a natural leader who clearly had the trust and support of his people. Constance and Neil would be there as well, with whatever help they could offer.

And as for Neil… Ellie hadn't even begun to wrap her head around the revelation of the secret power he had been hiding from her for who knew how long.

"You ready?" Adam asked her.

Worries whirled through her mind like frightened birds. Ellie drew in a breath of air scented with both flowers and the electricity of a coming storm.

She lifted her chin with determination. "Yes."

"Then let's go," Adam concluded, taking her hand.

TWENTY

$\mathcal{A}$DAM STALKED ACROSS the ruddy hills northwest of Ranyapali, his thoughts locked worriedly on the skinny twelve-year-old girl he needed to rescue.

He liked Vanika. He had liked her from the moment she had bounded down the steps of the palace to greet them when they arrived in Nandapur. He liked that she read cowboy books, traded insults with princes, and eyed his machete like she wanted to try it on for size. She was a great kid, and Adam had let her walk into the worst kind of trouble while he sat around drinking flower booze with her grandma.

He knew that Vanika had put herself in that dangerous position—hell, she'd been ordered by a damned maharaja not to go any further than the village—but she was a kid. It should have been Adam's job to make sure she actually listened, and he had screwed that up.

He hadn't been lying about the advantage he and Ellie had when it came to dealing with Jacobs—but the truth was, Adam would've gone after Vanika regardless.

As Adam followed the route Subhas had given him, red earth and scrub gave way to stands of tall, graceful trees clustered around streams that carried the waters of the monsoon into the valley. Here and there, gaps between the hills revealed glimpses of the deeper forest, thickly green and dancing with shadows.

Ellie hiked at Adam's heels. Kalb trotted ahead of them, frequently glancing back as though urging them to move faster. Adam could almost imagine that the dog had some idea of who they were trying to find and wanted to help. Maybe he even could. Adam hadn't had much time to try training Kalb, but he was a hunting breed, and hunting breeds usually had great noses. Certainly, he'd proved himself more than capable of finding things like hidden cats or an abandoned plate of cookies.

"But why didn't he tell us?" Ellie burst out behind him.

Adam cocked an eyebrow at her in an unspoken reminder that whatever conversation she had been having in her head, she was only just now letting him in on it.

"Neil," Ellie grumblingly elaborated.

"Your brother was never going to be comfortable with having magical past-seeing abilities," Adam pointed out.

He had been thinking about Neil's revelation as well. After the initial shock, Adam had found himself less surprised than he might have been about the whole business. In a mad sort of way, it fit. It had always been a bit uncanny how Neil knew stuff about the past. He couldn't always say where he'd picked up a particular piece of information. He'd just dismiss it as 'obvious' or say that he must have read it in a book.

But some of the stuff Neil came out with had been things even their professors hadn't known—and they were the guys who wrote the books.

If Neil had some kind of supernatural gift for sensing what was true about history, it would certainly explain a few things. Adam could hardly dismiss the notion out of hand. He'd seen far too much weird stuff over the last few months for that.

"I know he wouldn't be comfortable with it." Words spilled out of Ellie now as she hiked in Adam's wake. "But he still might have told *me*."

"Have you told him you're carrying Tulan around in your head?"

"No," Ellie admitted tightly, and then rushed to explain. "It isn't that I don't trust him. I just hardly understand what's happening myself. How can I strike up a conversation—one where he's sure to have a hundred questions—about a subject that's still an infuriating mystery to me?"

"You and your brother have a lot in common," Adam commented softly and significantly.

Ellie let out a frustrated sigh. "You're right. It's wrong of me to take it personally. But... we might've *helped* each other."

"You still can. You *will*, once we get through all this."

"But that's three of us now who can do things that ought to be impossible. Does that mean the whole world is full of... of..." Ellie pressed a hand to her temple. "I don't even know what word to use for it! I don't know if there *is* a word."

Adam frowned thoughtfully. "Someone's gotta know."

Ellie's focus sharpened. "What do you mean?"

"All this stuff isn't coming out of nowhere. These magic trinkets we've been stumbling across are all talked about in the old myths and stories. It just turns out they weren't as made up as we thought they were."

He took a step closer to her, reading the frustration, worry, and hope roiling behind her hazel eyes. "Those old stories were full of people who could do crazy stuff as well. Maybe that part wasn't all made up, either. And if that's true—if this has been going on the whole time—you can't be the first person to have figured that out."

Ellie looked dizzy. "You mean… someone might've written a book about it?"

Adam laughed. "Hell, I don't know, Princess. Maybe? Or maybe they're still out there working on it. I just can't think how you'd be the only one."

Ellie paced along the path. Adam could practically see her mind whirling. "But why do some people have these abilities and not others? Are they always there, or do they pop up somewhere along the way during one's lifetime? Of course, there must be a difference between how someone like Jacobs or Neil came to do what they do, and me, with it all starting from touching the Smoking Mirror… and what *about* the mirror? How does a power like that come to exist? How on earth does one *manufacture* a flaming sword? Where did all these arcana *come* from?"

"I can't even begin to tell you." Adam repressed the urge to smile.

"But you think somebody can."

Adam shrugged. "Feels like a reasonable assumption."

"But how would we ever *find* them?"

Adam could see how much the question meant to her. He pushed a loose curl of hair back from her cheek—and waited, because he knew there was more she still needed to say.

She drew in a deep, unsteady breath. "I don't know what I'm supposed to do with this… this *place* that's living inside me."

"Then we'll find out," Adam vowed to her. "You and me. Together. Whatever that means. Got that?"

Her eyes were wide with feeling as she nodded.

Adam couldn't help himself. He leaned down for a kiss, soft and gentle like the seal of a promise.

"Now let's go get that damned kid," he declared.

Adam smelled the river before he saw it, the distinct aroma of wet stone and mud carrying through the thick heat of the afternoon. Sound came next in a soft rush of moving water.

Kalb stiffened, quivering. Adam quickly snatched hold of his collar as a new noise emerged from the low susurration of the water—a number of men calling back and forth to each other from a short distance away.

Adam crouched down in the thick ferns that grew between the slender trees. He gave Kalb's ears a scratch. "Good boy. Now stay here."

"That dog has absolutely no idea how to stay," Ellie warned him.

Kalb sat, panting at them with a blankly waiting expression.

"See?" Adam murmured back.

He crept forward through the underbrush, keeping low. A few yards further, the land dropped steeply away in a muddy cliff. Adam lowered himself to his belly and snaked forward until he could see over the edge of it—which thankfully wasn't terribly high off the ground.

The river lay before him, a softly curving band of gray water roughly twenty yards across. The surface was smooth, but Adam could tell that the water was running fast, fueled by the rains. In places, it already flooded over the banks.

There would have been no swimming it safely even if there hadn't been an Indian Army platoon working just below.

The detachment numbered around thirty, which was more than enough to mean trouble. They all wore turbans, which were standard issue for Indian Army sepoys. The beards on all their faces weren't, signaling to Adam that he was probably looking at a Sikh company.

The men were building a pontoon bridge using lumber from the riverbank. Two sections already extended out into the water. A third would get them the rest of the way across.

With a hissing rush, a tree collapsed below Adam's perch. A handful of the soldiers efficiently attacked it with axes and saws.

Ellie wriggled into place beside him, a streak of mud marring the freckles on her nose. "Do you see Borthwick?"

"Not yet."

"What about Jacobs? Or Vanika?"

Adam made another scan of the band of men—and suppressed a sigh. "Found her… with another old friend."

Vanika stood near the back of the operation, her arms crossed over her chest with an air of forceful confidence. Beside her, Professor Dawson fanned himself with his pith helmet, his skin ruddy with heat over his ginger beard.

Adam could hear his distinctive whining complaints from all the way up on the hill.

He made a quick assessment of the rest of the uniformed bodies working below. "We can't get to the kid in the middle of all this. We'll need to follow them until they set up camp for the night."

"That means getting over the river. Any chance we could sneak across their bridge?"

Adam thought of what he knew of Colonel Charles Borthwick—and of Jacobs. "Doubt it."

"Subhas mentioned that the Adrija had a crossing."

"Then let's go see what we're dealing with."

Adam guided Ellie back from the drop. Kalb still waited, quivering with the effort it took to remain sitting. At the sight of them, the dog let out a groaning, eloquent whine.

"Good boy," Adam said, rubbing his ears.

Kalb leaped up to trot after them.

Adam studied the landscape, his mind automatically mapping the way they'd come against the directions Subhas had given him back in the village. *Game trail... level ridge... dry streambed...*

He led Ellie and the dog up the river, then picked their way down another slope, pushing past a stand of wild sugarcane to bring the water back into view.

The forest loomed on the opposite bank. It wasn't the thick tropical growth of British Honduras, where palms had mingled with plantains under the sweeping arms of mahogany trees. This wilderness was quieter and older, towering teaks rustling softly over ground papered with ferns and wildflowers.

The mythic name for the place echoed through Adam's mind. *Dandakaranya.*

He didn't pretend to know what he would be getting himself into over there. A new forest meant new resources—and new threats—but that wasn't what set the hairs itching at the back of Adam's neck as he studied the whispering green depth of the shadows under the canopy.

"Ugh," Ellie complained behind him. "Why does he have to do that?"

Adam glanced over to see her shove Kalb back from her face, which he'd been lapping with his tongue.

"Because he loves you." Adam nodded across the river. "There's our ferry."

Subhas's crossing was a rope. The far end was tied around a thick-trunked tree. The woven length of hemp was green with age, dipping down into the water, which had already risen to cover the tree's roots. The river rippled subtly where it passed over the barely submerged line.

Adam crept closer, pushing through another stand of brush. His side of the bank was flooded as well. He had to peer through the shimmering water to see where the near end of the rope was tied off around a fig tree.

From where he stood, his view of Borthwick's work site was blocked by a broad curve in the current. "We ought to be out of sight of the bridge here. It should be safe to cross."

Ellie's skeptical look communicated that she possessed a different interpretation of what constituted *safe*. "Won't we have to leave the dog behind?" she asked hopefully.

"He can swim it. Can't you, buddy?" Adam patted Kalb as the Seluki panted up at him adoringly.

"But he was raised in a desert."

"With a great big river running through it. He'll be fine."

Without waiting for further debate, Adam slipped into the water. It lapped around his shins, slightly cooler than the sultry heat of the afternoon.

The rope had obviously been there for a while, but it felt solid, if a bit slippery with algae.

"I want you to go first." Adam raised a hand as Ellie opened her mouth to protest. "If you're behind me, I might not know you're in trouble until I'm on the other side."

Ellie grimaced, unhappy with Adam's logic but unable to counter it. She joined him in the water, her boots splashing softly. "What do I do? Just grab on and drag myself across?"

"That's it." Adam adjusted the straps on his pack. They'd traveled light, and it wouldn't be the first time their gear had ended up under water. He was mostly worried about the Winchester. Guns didn't like getting wet. Adam would lose the rounds in the stock, but the bulk of the ammunition was in an oilskin pouch in the pack.

He could clean the rest. Adam didn't mind stripping and oiling a Winchester. The gun went back together like butter.

Leaning over to grab the rope, Ellie took a step forward—and plunged into the river as the bank disappeared under her feet. She clung to the line, sputtering.

Adam couldn't resist cracking a grin. "How's the water?"

"Why don't you come in and find out?" Ellie threatened.

Her shirt had gone translucent, clinging to her skin. Adam could clearly make out the lines of her no-nonsense corset.

Adam liked that corset. He appreciated how easily it came off.

Ellie noticed the lower angle of his attention. "This is hardly the time."

"You asked me about preventatives," Adam helpfully reminded her.

Suppressing a smile, Ellie threw a handful of water at him, then pulled herself along the rope.

Adam slipped in after her. He could feel the tug of the current as the cool depth enveloped him. The river was moving fast, but the rope held, thick and sturdy.

A louder splash sounded as Kalb leaped in after them. The dog angled away from the rope, aiming for an oblivious duck.

At least he was generally going in the right direction.

Ellie had made it roughly halfway across the water. Adam glanced downriver, but Borthwick's project was still safely out of view.

He started to relax. They would be spending the rest of the day wet, but it looked like rain anyway, and it was certainly warm enough.

A flicker of movement caught his eye as a dark shadow shifted across the gray water just ahead of where Ellie gripped the rope. Adam focused on it with a frown.

Whatever it had been, it was gone. All he could see was the softly rippling gray of the river.

Adam dismissed it. The movement had probably just been a reflection of the clouds shifting overhead. He kicked his boots to help propel himself along the rope.

Water pulsed oddly against his legs as if something had just pushed back against the current.

That was weird.

The shadow returned, sweeping past him as a dark shimmer under the surface.

Must be Subhas's bodh, he thought automatically.

Something less comfortable tugged at the back of Adam's mind—something about *scale*.

Subhas's words echoed through Adam's mind.

It's a rather large catfish.

The duck suddenly took flight—even though Kalb was still nowhere near it.

Adam's nascent unease flared into full-blown alarm—and eight feet of slick black body broke the surface of the water, arrowing for Ellie.

"Move!" Adam shouted, hauling toward her. "Ellie, get out of the—"

Ellie went taut on the rope as the black shape pulled at the lower half of her leg.

Adam didn't stop to think.

He launched himself at the fish, snagging a hand around its dorsal fin just as Ellie lost her grip on the rope.

Quick water swept them downriver.

The bodh was huge. A distant part of Adam's brain clocked it at roughly thirteen feet. The rest of him focused on trying to wrap his legs around it for a better grip.

Ellie cried out with pain—and then choked as the river swamped over her face.

The sound was like a siren screaming through Adam's brain.

Catfish liked to drag their prey under to drown.

The bodh whipped beneath him, furious at having acquired a two-hundred-pound anchor when it had been aiming for an easy lunch.

Adam released half of his grip on the fin, freeing a hand. He yanked his machete from its sheath and drove it into the creature's flank.

The catfish thrashed with pain and outrage. Ellie compounded the problem by smashing her boot into its face.

Between the pain up front and eighteen inches of steel in its side, the damned thing finally let go.

Ellie surfaced with a gasp as the river pushed them past a massive boulder that split the stream. Her mouth twisted with pain, she flailed for some of the weeds trailing out behind the rock.

She managed to grasp them, halting her flight down the river.

Beneath Adam, the catfish pivoted back for her.

Adam fought to keep hold of the thing, gripping both the slippery fin and the handle of his knife. The damned fish was easily strong enough to push against the current, even with Adam clinging to its back. It quickly gained on Ellie as she worked to keep her hold on the slimy fronds.

A machete in the side ought to have been a deterrent. The bodh was more stubborn than Kalb going after a sausage.

That didn't leave Adam with a whole lot of options.

He found himself with even fewer as the catfish dove.

Adam had only a moment to haul in a breath before he was under the water, the fish writhing furiously in his grip. He forced himself to open his eyes despite the burn.

He would have been happy to let the monster go, but he could see Ellie's legs kicking frantically above him as she tried to keep her tenuous grip on the weeds.

Adam couldn't risk the bodh going after her again. Ellie wasn't that strong a swimmer. If the catfish got hold of her, it'd haul her under the river before

Adam knew what the hell was happening.

Lungs screaming, Adam hauled against the machete, using the leverage to pull himself further up the catfish's body. He snagged his left arm around the pectoral fins, putting the bodh in a chokehold—not that chokeholds mattered to something with goddamned gills.

The fish lurched for the surface, dragging Adam with it.

They broke through the water, and Adam hauled in a desperate breath. Biting out a curse, he yanked the machete free and slammed it into the soft spot behind the bodh's skull.

The monster convulsed in Adam's grip—just as the current slammed him against a slick, solid surface hard enough to drive the wind from his chest.

The twitching body of the fish pinned him there. Adam shoved it back, fighting the frothing pressure of the water, and bought himself just enough space to roll up onto whatever the hell he had just run into.

He brought the machete with him, yanking it from the catfish's head with a jerk of his arm.

The hell was he going to lose his knife to that thing.

Flopping onto his back with the bloody blade in his hand, Adam stared up at the heavy gray sky as he gasped for breath.

"Ellie…" he croaked out.

The word was both a reminder and a prayer.

Adam forced himself to roll over, hands pressed against a slick platform of rope-lashed logs—which jarred under his knees at another impact. With a muffled gasp, Ellie hooked her arms over the edge of the wood.

Adam tossed aside the machete to grab her. He hauled her onto the platform, quickly checking for damage.

"I'm all right," she assured him with a breathless wince.

Adam had already shoved up the torn leg of her trousers. Sharp little wounds circled her calf, streaming blood mingling with a wash of muddy water. The sight sparked both fury and relief—because it could have been much worse.

Ellie's hand tapped his shoulder, the gesture off-target as she stared at something behind him.

"Er, Adam…?"

He turned to find himself facing a line of extremely surprised Indian Army sepoys.

Because he had landed on their bridge.

Hell, Adam thought as he slowly raised his hands.

Borthwick's men had moved the last platform into place. The bridge now stretched across the river, expertly anchored to the banks. The detachment had been in the process of bringing over their supplies when Adam had landed in front of them.

The monstrous catfish floated limply alongside the logs, gore and blood streaming from the machete wounds in its head and side.

The cluster of astonished soldiers parted for someone coming up from behind them.

Jacobs stepped to the front of the line. His eyes moved from Adam, kneeling on the platform and splattered with fish blood, to Ellie, sprawled beside him in trousers with blood streaming down her calf.

He stopped at the corpse of the thirteen-foot catfish softly bumping against the bridge.

Jacobs began to laugh.

The sound was helplessly involuntary—an irresistible hysteria at finding himself facing his two least favorite people and a dead monster in the middle of the wilderness.

A trim, silver-haired figure with sun-weathered skin joined him at the front of the soldiers. Adam recognized the man's wiry build, neatly trimmed mustache, and cold gray eyes from the crowd at the Jagannath festival.

He was looking at Colonel Charles Borthwick.

"Well," Borthwick commented mildly. "This is unexpected."

TWENTY-ONE

Six RIFLES LEVELED at Adam's head with a series of rapid clicks. Adam froze on his knees, hands still raised, his heart thudding as the moment balanced on a wire.

Borthwick's expression read of mild surprise and curiosity. Ellie and Adam hadn't been the ones who invaded his suite back in Puri, nor had he seen them during the festival. Everything in his reaction now depended on the other man who stood before the line of soldiers.

Jacobs.

Borthwick opened his mouth to speak—and a muddy missile launched itself onto the bridge. Kalb skidded across the logs with an uncharacteristic grace, panting happily as he dripped muck and river water onto the logs.

"Aw hell," Adam blurted out, knowing exactly what was coming next.

The dog went into an exceptionally vigorous shake, spraying everyone within a twelve-foot radius.

Standing at the front of the line of soldiers, Borthwick took the worst of it. Muddy water splashed across the front of his uniform.

The colonel flinched back, his eyes flashing with quick fury. He wiped a hand over his khaki jacket—just above the stock whip coiled at his belt.

None of this was good.

"Do you know these people?" Borthwick demanded.

He was speaking to Jacobs, the question prompted by the pale man's involuntary response to Ellie and Adam's unorthodox entrance.

Not that Jacobs was laughing anymore. The shock of their bizarre appearance on the bridge had faded. In its place, a frustrated and angry calculation shifted across his angular features.

Time crawled as Adam waited for his answer.

"As it happens," Jacobs evenly replied.

Adam scrambled furiously for an escape. He could grab Ellie and roll them off the bridge. Keep her under the river for as long as he could and hope the current carried them out of range.

Except that the rifles pointed at his head were Martini-Henry MK IVs. They had a firing range of four hundred yards.

He and Ellie weren't going to make it four hundred yards—assuming they weren't shot before they hit the water.

"This is Mr. Adam Bates," Jacobs announced. "And his wife."

Adam stilled at the unexpected word. *Wife?* Why the hell was Jacobs calling Ellie his wife?

Borthwick eyed Adam with closer interest. "Not one of the San Francisco Bateses?"

Adam's chest tightened.

The San Francisco Bateses.

Was it possible that a high-ranking Indian colonial administrator had heard of his family?

A colonial administrator who was friendly with the likes of Lord Aldbury.

Yeah, Adam thought with a lurch of dismay. It was possible. After all, it wasn't as though George Bates kept a low profile.

"He is indeed," Jacobs replied—fixing Adam with a look that he could read as clearly as paint slapped onto a wall.

Play. Along.

Adam had never stopped to discuss his family history with Jacobs in between trying not to get killed by the man—but Jacobs wasn't the kind of guy who left things to chance. Adam couldn't really be surprised that his enemy might have taken the time to figure out exactly where he'd come from.

Not that any of that mattered right now. Jacobs was obviously setting him up, and Adam could think of only one reason for him to do that.

Because it would keep him and Ellie alive.

"Which of them do you belong to, then?" Borthwick pressed.

Knowing that it was probably the best way to keep himself free of bullet holes for the next ten minutes, Adam forced himself to answer—even though he hated every syllable.

"George Bates," he ground out. "I'm George Bates's son."

Adam could feel Ellie's astonished gaze on his back as Borthwick coldly assessed him. The colonel was weighing the plausibility of a son of George Bates turning up on a river in the backwoods of India, slaughtering oversized catfish with a machete.

To anyone who knew anything about Adam's father, it would sound pretty damned far-fetched.

Borthwick's gray study halted on Adam's face. "You look like him," he commented.

The words felt like a punch in Adam's gut.

Borthwick hadn't just heard of his family. He *knew* George Bates... because he was right.

Adam was taller than his father. His dad had a beard, his blond hair gone to silver. But they had the same sky-blue eyes... and more or less the same damned face.

Being reminded of the resemblance made Adam want to hit something.

He was kneeling on the ground with six rifles pointed at his head. The woman he loved was still bleeding.

Shock and helplessness coiled around him like a snake, tightening his breath.

A shout of protest went up from behind the sepoys, and a moment later, Vanika pushed to the front of the line. Her gaze shot to Adam and narrowed into a ferociously disapproving glare.

Adam could read her meaning clearly enough. Vanika was furious at his intervention.

To be fair, she probably had been slightly better off before Adam had thrown himself at Borthwick's feet in a spray of fish blood.

A gratingly familiar voice sounded from down the bridge.

"Excuse me! Pardon me! I really must be..."

Dawson stumbled past the soldiers, who glared at the intrusion. At the sight of Ellie and Adam, his eyes widened with shocked recognition.

He opened his mouth to speak—and Jacobs snapped an elbow into his gut.

Dawson wheezed, doubling over.

Borthwick glanced back at the two men with a frown.

"The professor's feeling a bit off," Jacobs filled in.

That counted as the second time in the last five minutes that Jacobs had saved Adam's neck. It probably wouldn't be the last, based on how quickly all of this was going to hell.

Adam wondered when Jacobs would get tired of it.

Focus, he reminded himself fiercely. He couldn't afford to let his thoughts scatter. Only one thing mattered right now—more than Dawson or the tangled threads of Adam's past that had suddenly whipped up to ensnare him.

Stay alive. Save the kid.

He drew in a deep breath, keeping his eyes on Borthwick. He forced his voice to steady.

Adam had no reason to be afraid. He was George Bates's son.

"Are your men carrying a medical kit?" he asked. "I need to see to my wife."

Borthwick briefly assessed the wounds on Ellie's leg. "Subedar Singh Rao!"

An officer stepped forward. The stars on his collar and shoulders called out his higher rank. In the Indian Army, a subedar was roughly equivalent to a lieutenant.

"Sir," Singh Rao said, coming to attention. He cut a striking figure, tall and broad-shouldered with graceful features over a glossy black beard.

"Have two of the men carry Mrs. Bates across." Borthwick waved a dismissive hand at Ellie's prone figure.

Adam quickly stepped in front of her. "I'll take care of it."

The words came out sharper than he had intended. Singh Rao paused in the process of giving an order to two of the riflemen, flashing Adam a thoughtful look.

"Come on, Princess," he said, levering Ellie to her feet and scooping her into his arms.

Her leg was slick with blood where he held it. Eyes bored into the back of his head—Borthwick's quietly measuring. Vanika's fierce with irritation.

Jacobs' flat with warning.

With the weight of all of that bearing down on him, Adam crossed the bridge.

Adam barely noticed that he had entered the Dandakaranya. As the forest loomed around him on the far bank of the river, blooming with strange flowers and softly whispering trees, all his attention was on Ellie's leg.

They sat on a tarp spread near the quietly rushing water. Kalb lay nearby, still wet and panting blissfully.

The noble-looking subedar, Singh Rao, had given Adam back his machete, passing it to him with an air of unimpeachable professionalism. Adam had cleaned the blade off with a swish in the river.

He'd lost the Winchester. Borthwick had relieved him of the gun and passed it off to one of the sepoys, ostensibly to have it cleaned.

Adam doubted he'd be getting it back anytime soon. Borthwick didn't seem to be treating him as an enemy, but he clearly wasn't about to let an unknown quantity wander around his camp with a well-oiled repeater.

There had been another close call with Dawson once they'd crossed the bridge. The professor had stomped over, opening up his mouth to protest, only for Jacobs to clamp a hand down on his shoulder.

"Why don't we take a little walk?" Jacobs had silkily suggested before steering Dawson aside.

Jacobs would find a way to keep Dawson quiet. He was intimidating as hell even when he wasn't trying all that hard—and Dawson had never had much of a spine. Still, it was yet another move Jacobs had been forced to make to protect them. Adam was under no illusions that the man was happy to be doing it. He undoubtedly saw their arrival as a deliberate attempt to get in his way again, testing just how far he was willing to go to protect whatever precious *justice* was somehow tangled up with their fates.

Jacobs would have a limit. Adam had no desire to find out what it looked like.

"We're on damned thin ice," he noted under his breath.

"It's certainly further than we'd planned to push him," Ellie quietly agreed as she watched Jacobs walk away with the professor.

"Which is why we'd better make sure you've got two working legs." Adam picked up Ellie's ankle and set it on his knee.

"You're going to bloody your trousers," Ellie protested.

Adam glanced at the catfish guts that still stained his pants, then cocked a skeptical eyebrow.

"Oh, fine," Ellie huffed.

He studied her injuries. The wounds didn't quite circle her leg. The sides of her calf were fine. The punctures on the back were the worst, but thankfully her trousers were made of sturdy twill, which had helped blunt the impact of the bodh's teeth.

Three of the holes were a bit larger than the others. "Those are going to need stitches," Adam determined.

Ellie looked queasy at the idea. "I'm sure they're not *that* bad…"

"This is gonna be easier if you roll over," Adam replied unrelentingly.

"Blast it anyway," Ellie muttered.

She lay on her stomach on the tarp, resting her chin on her hands. Kalb immediately squirmed over to her, lapping at her ear.

"Absolutely not!" Ellie flailed awkwardly at the dog.

"She knows you care, buddy," Adam translated.

Kalb settled for lying down at Ellie's side, huffing an adoring breath that stirred the loose hair at her forehead.

Ellie glared back at him warningly.

Kalb hopefully wagged his tail.

Borthwick's first aid kit filled a well-supplied trunk. Adam pulled out a bottle of rubbing alcohol and twisted it open.

Ellie winced.

"I haven't done anything yet." Adam's mouth twitched with amusement. "I'm cleaning my hands."

"Just get on with it," Ellie ordered with grim impatience. "Turnabout is fair play, after all."

Adam fought back a smile at the not-so-distant memory of how Ellie had stitched up his hand with a flask of cask strength hooch and a scavenged needle. At least this stuff was all sterile—and he was actually capable of stitching in a straight line.

He flexed his hand, smiling at the crooked scar on his palm. "Good point," he agreed and doused her leg with alcohol.

Ellie hissed between her teeth.

Threading his needle, Adam gave the first wound a careful study. He set the point against her flesh.

A low, angry voice snapped from behind him. "You're messing everything up!"

Adam glanced over his shoulder. Vanika leaned against one of the trees behind him, her skinny arms crossed over her chest.

"Look away!" she hissed.

Adam turned back to meet Ellie's surprised stare.

Borthwick's soldiers were clustered several yards away, taking a tea break. None of them paid Adam any mind. Jacobs and Dawson were still gone.

Borthwick was nowhere to be seen.

Vanika's voice was tight with irritation. "I have a *plan*. I am going to lead the colonel into the forest and leave him where it will take him at least a week to find his way out again."

"You're in over your head, kid." It took effort for Adam not to turn around and punctuate the remark with a stern glare.

"This is my forest!" Vanika snapped back. "You are the one who is in over your head. You nearly got yourself eaten by a bodh!"

Adam had to give her that one.

"I have the situation under control," Vanika asserted.

"Jacobs knows you're lying," Adam warned her tightly.

"How can you be sure of that?"

Adam put all the certainty into his words that he could muster. "*I know.*"

Vanika went quiet. He hated that he couldn't look at her—but the kid was right. The sepoys were bound to notice if their unexpected guest suddenly started chatting with the twelve-year-old villager who had attached herself to their party.

"I don't need to be rescued," Vanika spat out. "Stay out of my way."

Footsteps crunched as she stalked away.

Adam's grip on the needle tensed with worry and frustration.

She was just a kid.

"That could have gone better," Ellie commented in a low voice.

"Yeah," Adam agreed through gritted teeth.

Her leg still bled sluggishly. He needed to focus on taking care of her—but he also had to warn her about another pit looming before them, one that made his stomach tie into knots.

"Borthwick knows my father."

Ellie's brow furrowed with mild confusion. "I think that's what's keeping us alive at the moment."

"That's not what I mean." Desperation roughened Adam's voice. He fought for the words that would make her understand what that entailed— what he would need to do in order to keep them all alive.

The notion left him feeling queasier than a ride in a hot air balloon.

"My father never wanted *me*."

Ellie's face softened with sympathy. "Adam…"

"No," he cut in sharply. "Listen to me. Things are going to be different. I have to be—"

Kalb jumped to his feet with a bark.

Borthwick walked up to them, his gray eyes placid in a face weathered by years in the sun. "Are you sure you wouldn't like my medic to see to that?"

"I've got it," Adam managed.

"Don't let me interrupt." Borthwick punctuated the remark with a permis- sive wave of his hand.

He wanted Adam to keep going… while he watched.

Ellie's calf tensed at the colonel's words. She didn't like the idea either.

Adam was pretty sure their opinions didn't matter.

"Try to relax your leg," he pleaded.

Ellie drew in a breath, and the muscle under his hand softened.

Adam drove the needle through her skin, smooth and precise. He knew what he was doing. He'd set stitches before.

Mostly on himself.

Ellie pressed her face into her arms, muffling a curse. She should have been shouting them at Adam, but she wouldn't want the enemy looming over them to see it as a weakness.

Nothing about Ellie was weak. Adam bit back the urge to say as much, sliding the catgut through her calf.

"I'm curious what George Bates's son is doing in the wilds of Odisha," Borthwick mused.

"Chhattisgarh," Adam bit back automatically.

Borthwick's silence had weight. Adam refused to cow to it, keeping his attention on Ellie's leg.

"The river marks the border," he elaborated shortly. "We're in Chhattisgarh now. And I came to survey a mining operation my father is thinking of investing in."

Adam had known Borthwick's question must be coming. He had started working up an answer as soon as they'd crossed the bridge.

"Your father does engage in some... *unusual* investments."

"My father," Adam retorted tightly, "knows how to make his money work for him."

Nothing about that was a lie. Adam just left out all the pain the man caused in the process.

Not that George Bates cared much about any of that.

He pulled the catgut taut. He had to keep going. It wasn't fair to Ellie to leave her waiting for the rest of the pain while Borthwick talked... which was likely intentional, Adam realized with a burst of helpless fury. The colonel had chosen this moment, when Ellie was vulnerable and Adam clearly needed to focus, to strike with his interrogation.

Borthwick probably knew quite a lot about interrogations—including the value of pressing your subject while they were distracted.

He could feel the cold weight of the man's attention and knew Borthwick was studying every nuance of Adam's responses.

"How do you know him?" Adam asked.

The question had been burning through his mind ever since Borthwick had made his casual comment about Adam's appearance.

"We met through a conference on security issues for Asian trade routes," Borthwick replied.

The explanation made sense. Adam's father had built his empire on insuring trans-Pacific shipping.

It had substantially expanded from there.

"Odd line for a man of your background—surveying," Borthwick observed.

"Never said it was my line," Adam returned bluntly.

Ellie lifted her head to glance back at him with a flash of confusion.

Stay quiet, Adam willed at her. *Please, Princess.*

"You knew we were in Chhattisgarh," Borthwick pointed out.

"I can read a map," Adam snapped back—dread slipping out in the form of a flash of temper. "And I know how to find what I'm looking for."

"Useful skills." Borthwick's steel eyes were unrelentingly focused. "Though I must say I find it odd that a man would bring his wife on such an excursion."

Adam's jaw tensed with instinctive rage. Borthwick talked over Ellie like she wasn't even there.

But then, wasn't he doing the same thing?

Not that he had a choice.

He grasped for a response, even though he knew it was a weak one. "We're newlyweds. It's kind of a… honeymoon."

"In India," Borthwick clarified skeptically.

You're George Bates's son, Adam told himself desperately.

His father's voice echoed through his mind, clear and harsh.

A Bates doesn't apologize to anyone.

Adam fixed Borthwick with a glare. "She likes history."

The words came out as a threat.

Borthwick's response took longer to come than it should have. Adam couldn't help feeling the pause was deliberate.

"Well, there's plenty of that about the place, I suppose," the colonel finally replied, his posture easing.

Adam reeled from the change. Did it mean that he had just passed Borthwick's test?

No, he thought with a tight thrill of fear. Every instinct told him that Borthwick's tests were never really over.

He realized that he was tying off the last stitch. He'd finished the job without even knowing, Ellie's three deeper wounds now sporting tidy, even rows of catgut.

Borthwick dismissively assessed Ellie's calf. "You won't want your wife walking on that leg. We can put her on one of our animals, but I don't have men to spare to escort you back to civilization."

"I don't need an escort," Adam ground out.

"Nonsense. This area is crawling with violent tribal thugs. I couldn't conscience sending you off with a wounded woman hobbling you. You'll join us on our route until she's capable. There's plenty of territory to explore out here. I'm sure you'll find something useful. Was it silver that you were after?"

The question was casual. Adam smelled another test in it.

They weren't going to stop, he thought grimly. Borthwick didn't trust him. Adam wasn't sure a man like Borthwick ever trusted anybody.

"Tin," he retorted shortly. "There's no silver in Chhattisgarh."

Adam didn't know if that was true—but he had plenty of experience calling a bluff.

"Indeed." A note of approval flashed behind Borthwick's expression before his tone shifted to one of impatient command. "Jacobs!"

Adam startled. He had never heard anyone use Jacobs' name like that before—the way you would summon a servant. It seemed like a risky way to call a man who oozed competence and menace.

Jacobs had returned to the clearing a moment before, steering Dawson with him. At Borthwick's call, the professor skittered away like a beetle from an overturned rock.

A flicker of irritation briefly tightened Jacobs' jaw. "Colonel?"

"Clear one of the mules for Mrs. Bates," Borthwick ordered, frowning down at his pocket watch. "Take on whatever you can of the displaced gear. Sort out the rest among the other men."

"Certainly," Jacobs replied with unimpeachable smoothness.

He turned to go.

Borthwick snapped shut the watch. "*Mind your place.*"

The words were sharpened by an unmistakable thread of steel. Jacobs' back stiffened as though someone had just struck him.

Adam found himself distantly wondering if Borthwick was about to get a knife thrown into his throat.

He knew firsthand that Jacobs had an immense degree of self-control. The fact that Adam was sitting here and not lying on top of a cliff in Egypt riddled with bullets was ample evidence of that—but Adam was also damned certain that Jacobs was not a man who tolerated being disrespected.

Rage flickered through Jacobs' eyes like a passing ghost, but his hand didn't go to his pocket, or his sleeve… or the myriad other places where he probably had some weapons stashed.

"Certainly, *sir*," Jacobs corrected instead, coldly emphasizing the word.

Borthwick dismissed him with a wave of his hand, turning to Adam with a note of weary endurance. "One does have to stay on top of these things with the lower orders."

Adam's temper flared. He recognized the irony of feeling compelled to defend Jacobs, of all people.

Not that he could do it.

Borthwick's remark required a response… but it wasn't Adam who had to give it. It was someone else—someone he had given up everything *not* to become.

Feeling as though he took a step over the edge of a brutal precipice, Adam gave Borthwick the answer he was waiting for.

"Tell me about it."

He felt Ellie still with surprise as he wrapped a bandage around her leg. Kalb lifted his head as though confused.

"Join me at the front of the line," Borthwick said.

The words were phrased like an invitation—but Adam knew better. Panic pushed a response from his lips before he could think better of it.

"I should stay close to my wife."

Borthwick frowned with an air of mild disapproval. "Nonsense. My subedar will see that she has everything she requires. Singh Rao!"

The officer from the bridge stepped away from the other men at Borthwick's summons. "Sir."

"Assign Mrs. Bates an escort, would you?"

"Yes, sir," Singh Rao replied with clipped professionalism.

Adam reached down for Ellie's hand, gently levering her upright. He held her for a moment longer than he should, achingly conscious that Borthwick was still measuring him.

He hadn't been able to warn her.

Ellie searched his face, looking for some hint of reassurance.

Adam couldn't give it to her. Things were already bad—and they were only going to get worse.

Borthwick hovered in front of him with an air of mild impatience. "Shall we?"

Every instinct in Adam's body raged against what he was about to do.

"Don't worry, sweetheart," he said, the words distant and lightly patronizing. "You'll be just fine."

Shock and confusion swept through Ellie's features—but nothing more. Because after that, Adam turned and walked away from her without looking back.

TWENTY-TWO

$\mathcal{E}$LLIE STARED AFTER Adam and felt as though she had just been slapped.

Her leg sang with pain. Her wet clothes clung uncomfortably to her skin. She had been tired, sore, and worried since they had crossed the river—but now she was something else as well.

Scared.

Adam's last words had been so shockingly out of character, her mind struggled to absorb them. His casual dismissal had reminded her of the way a man might speak to a nervous dog.

Don't worry, sweetheart.

Blast it, Adam didn't even talk to his *actual* dog that way. What the devil was going on?

Kalb, for his part, remained at Ellie's side, even though he quivered as he watched Adam leave, whining at the back of his throat.

Deserting Ellie with such condescension hadn't been the only bizarre thing Adam had done. She had also been thrown by his easy agreement with Borthwick's vile remarks about the 'lower orders.'

Ellie was hardly going to be the first one to rise to Jacobs' defense—the man had, after all, once threatened to flay her alive—but Adam had never given a damn about the circumstances of a person's birth. It was antithetical to everything Ellie knew about him.

He had tried to warn her about something before Borthwick had interrupted them.

Things are going to be different.

Adam's bizarre behavior was obviously some sort of act, but it had the air of a performance that he had rehearsed before. How was that possible when all of it was so contrary to the man Ellie had come to know—and to care about very deeply?

The question made her think of the words that had torn from Adam's throat just before Borthwick's arrival, which had struck her at the time as a strange non sequitur.

My father never wanted me.

The lid to the medical kit dropped shut with a snap. Ellie jolted at the sound, which sent a zing of protest through her new stitches. Singh Rao, the tall, self-composed officer who had been left to deal with her, motioned crisply to one of his sepoys, who collected the trunk and carried it away.

"Mrs. Bates?" Singh Rao prompted with brisk courtesy.

She would have to put her worries about Adam on hold for now. There would be time to address them later—once they had made it through the afternoon without rousing any more of Borthwick's suspicions.

"Yes. Of course," Ellie agreed and let the bearded subedar lead her to the patiently waiting mule.

The sun kissed the horizon as they stopped for the day, the pale glimmer barely visible through the endlessly marching trees.

The forest whispered. Birds flitted through the canopy, chirping softly. The ground was thick with grass and wildflowers.

Shadows painted the space between the trees, lengthening with the coming evening. The impatient voices of the sepoys and the crunch of their boots felt like an intrusion that the Dandakaranya did not welcome.

The men set up camp with practiced efficiency. Ellie had quickly determined that she was unlikely to find allies among them here as she had in British Honduras. These weren't hired hands simply along for a paycheck. They were rigorously disciplined professional soldiers trained to follow Borthwick's orders.

Only Singh Rao was fluent in English. The sepoys conversed in Punjabi, a language Ellie could barely recognize, never mind speak.

To her surprise, Kalb had stayed by her side all day. As she sat on a rock by the edge of the camp, he stood sentinel by her knee, occasionally letting out a mournful sigh. She might almost think that the animal felt responsible for protecting Ellie while Adam was away.

Ellie gave in and rubbed him between his ears. The dog panted happily at the attention—then stiffened, going still.

She slowly turned her head to see Jacobs standing beside her.

He wore his usual plain black suit and waistcoat, despite the lingering heat of the afternoon. Ellie couldn't see even a gleam of sweat on his skin—

unlike Dawson, whom she could hear complaining about the climate from across the camp. She wondered if Jacobs could compel his pores to behave by sheer force of will.

"I assume the day hasn't gone quite the way you planned," Jacobs commented mildly, keeping his eyes on the sepoys.

The fact that he remained standing while Ellie sat on the rock left her feeling uncomfortably vulnerable. She supposed that was deliberate. This wasn't a casual chat. Jacobs had come for a reason—which made this conversation dangerous.

"You might say that," Ellie returned carefully.

"I do hope you're not expecting me to stand by while you sabotage this expedition."

Ellie's mind spun as she absorbed the significance of his words. Clearly, Jacobs assumed that she and Adam had come intending to get in Borthwick's way. That conclusion was perfectly logical... if Jacobs had no idea about their connection to Vanika.

And he didn't, Ellie realized with an unsteady wash of relief. He wouldn't have seen Vanika with them. So far as he knew, she was just a girl from the village who had gotten herself in over her head.

If he figured out she was more than that, everything would change. Jacobs wouldn't hesitate to use the child as leverage to force Ellie and Adam to get out of his way.

Ellie had to keep their interest in Vanika a secret... and she was talking with a man who would know the minute she lied.

The threat of that settled over her. Ellie swallowed thickly and forced herself to go on. "You helped us on the bridge."

"Don't mistake that for anything more than it was."

"And what was it?"

"I kept you free of bullets—for the moment. If you'd like to stay that way, you'd best figure out how to extricate yourselves from this situation."

"I'll take that into consideration," Ellie coolly replied.

Jacobs gave a dark, tired chuckle. "Sure, you will."

Ellie took a chance, keeping her voice even. "What about the girl? What's she doing here?"

"She's our guide." Jacobs' voice dripped with irony.

"You don't sound convinced of that."

"Why should I be? She's lying."

Ellie's pulse thudded dangerously. "Then why hasn't Borthwick gotten rid of her?"

Jacobs' expression iced with a brief flash of anger. "The colonel does not share my assessment of the situation."

Surprise pushed the words from Ellie's lips before she could think better of them. "You mean he doesn't know what you can do."

Jacobs was no longer pretending to watch the soldiers as they set up the tents. "I'm not sure I know what you mean."

Ellie recognized the words as a warning—and ignored it. She was too caught up in the implication of what he had just inadvertently revealed.

Dawson had known all along that Jacobs could discern a lie. Ellie had simply assumed that Jacobs' employers were aware of his uncanny talent as well. After all, that astonishing asset might easily have explained how Jacobs could rise from his checkered background to become the tool of some of the most powerful people in the empire.

But if the Order of Albion knew of Jacobs' power, why wouldn't they have told Borthwick about it?

The answer spilled out of her as her thoughts continued to spin. "They don't know either, do they? The Order. You haven't told any of them. But why wouldn't you? Unless…"

More pieces snapped into place, driven by Ellie's knowledge of the man who loomed over her—which went far deeper than she would ever have wanted. Opposing him had brought them into an unwelcome sort of intimacy.

"You want to keep using it against them," she burst out, reeling. "You don't want the Order to know that you can detect a lie because you want to be able to catch them if they're lying to you."

Worlds moved through Jacobs' midnight eyes. Ellie read surprise there, along with anger, wariness… and a knife-thin, grudging respect.

"You don't trust them," Ellie accused.

A dark, quick laugh caught at the back of his throat. "Why would I ever *trust* them?"

Ellie shook her head. "Then why do you do this? Why are you here? I saw the way Borthwick treats you—like you're nothing. Julian was hardly better, except that he was too frightened of you to say any of it. Is it like that with all of them?"

But Ellie already knew the answer. Of course, it would be like that. The names Julian had given them were some of the most powerful people in the realm—individuals born to a sense of their own elevated place in the world.

Jacobs wasn't one of them. Ellie knew it from more than just the hint of the East End that threaded through his speech. He carried himself like a man who had once battled for every scrap of bread. He would have had to claw for each bitterly won step up the ladder of power, knowing that all that stood between him and death was the question of just how much violence he could wreak on whoever tried to take advantage of him.

"You aren't a man who'd tolerate being treated like that," Ellie declared firmly. "Not without a *reason*. And it's not money. You could find another job if you wanted. You're too bloody clever not to. It must be something else—something only the Order can give you."

Jacobs' tone was rich with threat. "Careful, Miss Mallory."

Ellie couldn't be careful—not as the last piece of the puzzle clicked into place in her brain. The shock of the picture it created drove her to her feet, even as her wounded calf issued a fiery protest at the movement.

Standing brought her to Jacobs' level—far closer than she had realized that she would be. Astonishment pushed the words from her lips in spite of her unease. "But there's only ever been one reason for you—the same one that keeps you from shooting Adam and me on sight. The Order must be tangled up in it as well—your *justice*."

Ellie had an unsettlingly intimate view of the impact the word had on him. Furious determination wrenched under the surface of his implacable rage.

An unexpected impulse rose inside of her. Ellie gave it voice in spite of all the very good reasons why she shouldn't.

"But we could help you. If that's really what this is—if it's really a matter of justice. Maybe that's why you saw us in the mirror."

Jacobs reeled with uncharacteristically bald disgust. "I bloody hope not," he snarled.

He stepped closer, using his slight advantage in height to force Ellie's head back, his eyes blazing like black coals. "I won't save you from your own stupidity—not if it costs me this mission. And don't underestimate Borthwick. He's a bigger monster than the one that tried to eat you this afternoon."

Ellie clung to defiance against the storm of his anger. "That's rich, coming from a man who once threatened to flay me alive."

"I threatened to flay you because I needed to get a job done. Borthwick will do it because he wants to hear you scream."

The assertion cracked out of him like a whip, leaving Ellie speechless.

Jacobs leaned in, his lithe form coiled with threat. "*Stay out of my way.*"

Then he was gone, stalking across the camp as the sepoys moved aside with wary looks.

Ellie's hands shook as though she had opened up a basket to find a cobra waiting inside of it, escaping peril by the merest breath of fortune.

Warmth pressed against the side of her leg as Kalb leaned into her side, gazing up at her with concern.

"Oh, fine," she conceded, dropping back onto the rock and drawing the dog's head into her lap.

TWENTY-THREE

$\mathcal{F}$OR POSSIBLY THE first time in Adam's life, the forest felt like a threat. He had always been aware of the dangers that lurked in any wilderness, from mudslides to parades of carnivorous ants, but going into the woods had still been like coming home. Which was funny, as he'd barely seen a real forest while growing up in San Francisco. The epic redwoods that had once stood across the bay in Marin had been stripped away years before he was born, their lumber used to feed the insatiable hunger of the gold rush.

The Dandakaranya was deeply, wildly beautiful. Tall, graceful trees whispered softly in the light breath of a breeze. Muntjacs darted through the undergrowth while parakeets soared among the branches. Insects chirped and buzzed while the sweet scent of flowers danced through the air. Green life teemed around Adam, fueled by the rich rains of the monsoon.

There would be snakes here. A rogue bull elephant could be a hell of a problem if you crossed it in the wrong mood. Malaria was a risk, along with flooding triggered by heavy downpours.

Adam wasn't afraid of any of that. It was the forest itself that felt off, despite its undeniable beauty, like a familiar tune sung in the wrong key.

Or maybe it was Adam who was off-key.

The soldiers in Borthwick's detachment weren't amateurs. They kept up a hard march through the afternoon, covering miles of terrain—and all the while, Borthwick asked Adam questions.

Where he'd gone to school. What his father thought about tariffs. How his mother was doing. Was she involved in any charity work? Borthwick had a cousin who was friendly with her. Apparently, they went to shows together.

He wanted to know about Adam's younger brother. What was Ethan's role in the family business? How often did the two of them get to see each other?

Adam lied about all of it. He lied and lied, and every lie was like tearing the stitch out of an old wound.

That life was closed to him. He'd been booted out of it when he finally made it clear to his father that he could never pretend to be the man George Bates had wanted him to be.

Most of it, Adam had been glad to leave behind.

Some of it had hurt.

Borthwick talked about India. He complained about 'rebellious tribes.' Called the Thuggee—the murderous cult that was ostensibly the reason for the existence of his department—a 'useful exaggeration.'

"The liberals back home haven't a clue what it's really like out here. If we need to color things up a bit for them to stomach giving us the tools we need, I won't lose any sleep over it."

Adam had agreed that this was an entirely sensible approach.

"After all," Borthwick went on, "we all know what we're really after in this godforsaken place. Don't we?"

Money, Adam heard George Bates reply inside his mind.

The seemingly casual comments were a test that Adam had to pass over and over and over again. He only succeeded because the situation demanded he play precisely the role that he had refused for twenty years of his life.

Refused—or abjectly failed at.

And every time he had failed, his father would tell him why.

Nobody cares what you really think.

Why can't you take something seriously for once in your life?

Adam knew the script. He had always understood the expectations. He had just fought, blood and bone, for a way to be the kind of man his father could be proud of without losing some sense of his own heart.

It had never worked.

Adam made it work now by setting his heart firmly aside as he answered Borthwick's questions and nodded along with his casual bigotry.

I'm doing this for a reason, Adam reminded himself. *And soon—God, let it be soon—I'll be able to stop.*

Tents sprang up around him like mushrooms. As Borthwick was pulled into the logistics of establishing camp for the night, Adam managed to slip away in the hive-like business.

He burned with the urge to find Ellie. He needed to make sure she was all right—and that she knew he hadn't meant any of the things he'd said while he was stitching up her leg. That he hadn't wanted to walk away and leave her there. He had to make sure she understood that none of it was *real.*

But she'd already know that. This was Ellie. She'd understand that something was off, even if she didn't yet know why—and she would keep trusting Adam in spite of all of it.

Even if part of him didn't feel like he deserved it.

Maybe his need to see Ellie was less about reassuring her and more about reminding himself of who he really was—climbing back out of the skin of lies before it strangled him.

Adam found Ellie at the edge of the camp, staring through the tents as though lost in troubled thoughts. Kalb had laid his head in her lap. Ellie's hand absently stroked his ears.

Adam's instincts flared. "What's wrong?"

Ellie looked up at him in surprise. "Nothing. I…" She shook her head as though to clear it. "I just had an unexpected chat with Mr. Jacobs."

A clean, familiar anger snapped through Adam. He embraced it. "Did he threaten you?"

Ellie removed Kalb's head from her knee and stood up to join him. She winced at the movement, and Adam reached out instinctively to catch her. Placing his hand on her arm was hardly an intimate gesture, but at that slight contact, Adam's need for her hit him like he'd been wading through a storm and Ellie was a spit of dry land.

Habit demanded that he let go. Adam had barely let himself touch her when other people were around, carefully maintaining the illusion that their relationship was nothing more than friendly.

With a start, he realized that he didn't have to do that here. Thanks to Jacobs' lie on the bridge, the soldiers around them—who were barely paying any attention anyway—all thought that Ellie was his wife.

Adam let his grip slide down to her palm and gripped it. The warmth of her skin was a balm.

Ellie squeezed his hand comfortingly. "Jacobs didn't threaten me. Well—not any more than usual. But he is going to do everything he can to drive us away from here," she warned.

Urgency snapped through Adam. He needed to use this moment before it was stolen from him. "Ellie… about earlier, when I left you. I…"

With a rustle of leaves, Dawson stumbled out of the forest. The professor drew up short at the sight of Ellie and Adam. "Oh—it's you," he noted with a distinct lack of enthusiasm.

Adam's words died in his throat. He faced the man like an untrustworthy bridge. Dawson could easily out them both to Borthwick—which would likely get them shot no matter what Jacobs had to say about it.

The professor brushed at his bush jacket. The garment looked worse for wear since British Honduras. The man's face was red and sweating under his pith helmet.

With horrified irony, Adam absorbed that his life might actually depend on this moron.

Dawson eyed Adam skeptically. "Mr. Jacobs tells me that you've realized your interests and ours are aligned when it comes to this particular mission."

Adam's brain scrambled to catch up with the professor's words.

Jacobs had apparently dealt with the problem that Dawson posed by telling him a story only a full-blown idiot would have failed to see through.

But then, Dawson *was* a full-blown idiot.

"He… let you know that, did he?" Adam carefully offered back.

Dawson straightened self-importantly. "If you'll recall, I did come up with that suggestion myself back when we first traveled together in British Honduras. I do tend to be quite prescient about these things."

"Uh-huh," Adam returned vaguely.

"I asked him what changed your mind, and he said I ought to just ask you about it."

Dawson stared at Adam expectantly.

Adam cursed Jacobs. He'd bet good money the bastard had done that deliberately.

Ellie had warned him that Jacobs planned to make their lives uncomfortable. Nobody had ever accused him of being bad at his job.

"I must've just… thought a bit more about what you said," Adam offered awkwardly.

"As well you should," Dawson easily agreed. "I know we've had our little troubles in the past, but it's nothing we can't put behind us, being reasonable and well-educated gentlemen. Mr. Jacobs isn't exactly scholarly in his inclinations, as you well know, and the colonel is always busy. It will be nice to know that there's one person in this camp with whom I can engage in civilized conversation about scientific and historical matters."

Standing right next to Adam, Ellie's eyes narrowed dangerously.

"Right. Yeah." Adam hooked a hand through Ellie's arm—in case she was considering trying to stab Dawson with a stick. "Sounds great."

"Speaking of which," Dawson continued, brightening. "I've been working on a very interesting theory about the influence of hermit crabs on Indian temple architecture—"

"Mr. Bates?"

Adam turned to find Borthwick's lieutenant, Singh Rao, waiting behind him.

"The colonel would like to see you, sir," the stoic officer reported.

Adam almost felt relieved at being summoned by Borthwick… but then, maybe navigating a web of lies was still preferable to hearing Dawson talk about hermit crabs.

"You go on," Dawson gracefully allowed. "I'm sure we'll have plenty of time to catch up later."

Adam forced a smile through gritted teeth. "I'll be looking forward to it."

Dawson strolled off, whistling tunelessly.

"That man…" Ellie began dangerously, glaring after him.

"…is a jackass," Adam filled in.

Singh Rao gave a cough that sounded suspiciously like a barely suppressed laugh.

Adam glanced back at him, but the subedar had straightened, pulling his face back into its usual sober mien.

"If you would?" Singh Rao gestured him forward.

Adam squeezed Ellie's hand, willing his grip to communicate the words he couldn't say.

Ellie squeezed back, her gaze steady as Adam let her go.

Singh Rao led him across the camp to another tent, smaller than the structures being used as barracks for the men but bigger than the two-man canvas that had been loaned to Adam and Ellie. The interior was simply furnished with a bedroll, lantern, and folding camp desk.

Borthwick waved Adam over to the desk as they arrived. "You said you're handy with a map, Mr. Bates. Where would you say we are at the moment?"

Adam studied the inked lines on the unrolled paper. Much of the territory had been only loosely surveyed, perhaps by way of a ridge expedition mapping the various peaks. Everything between would be a guess.

With the ease of years of experience, Adam fitted the undulating lines of the hills into his brain. Even before he'd gone to British Honduras, he'd been good at matching a landscape to paper.

He instinctively picked out the Adrija village by the distinct curves in the topography and was relieved to find the location unmarked. His study moved to the river, and beyond that through the loosely mapped region of the forest.

He set down a finger. "Here."

Borthwick exchanged a significant look with Singh Rao. "Quite on the nose of what we'd calculated," he said with a note of approval. "And the subedar was actively tracking our progress. You weren't bragging about your surveying skills."

Adam wanted to shrug off the compliment. His father would've scolded him for that.

He kept his shoulders stiff.

"Now, why don't we see where we're going next?" Borthwick mused.

He gestured to one of the two sepoys at the door of the tent. Adam heard a quick order in Punjabi, and a moment later, another soldier stepped inside, marching Vanika with him.

Vanika's eyes flicked to Adam and narrowed to a glare.

At least he wouldn't have to worry about Borthwick thinking that he and the kid were on the same side.

Borthwick paced around the table as he regarded the girl. "Tell me, then—where is the next leg of our route?"

Vanika raised her chin confidently as she answered him. "We follow the base of the ridge for half a day's walk. Then turn to the west, between the two streams."

As lies went, it wasn't bad. Vanika's gaze never wavered. Adam might've even have bought the bluff himself—if he hadn't caught the subtle hint of gloating behind her expression.

"What do you think, Mr. Bates?" Borthwick asked without looking away from the kid. "Will the girl's directions take us where we need to go?"

Singh Rao studied the map. The subedar's expression was unreadable, sheathed in the unimpeachable professionalism the man wore like another part of his uniform.

The ground seemed to shift under Adam's boots, turning treacherous. "I don't know what you're looking for."

"Join the Lord of the Dance on the ridge that points to the dawn of the longest day," Borthwick recited.

"Uh-huh." Adam kept his tone neutral.

"You won't find it marked on the map," Borthwick continued, "but I would still be interested in your general impressions."

Vanika didn't so much as glance at Adam. She didn't need to. She was perfectly confident that Adam would confirm her route.

Why wouldn't he? She had led him out from Nandapur expressly to help stop Borthwick.

She had no reason to suspect that Adam would do anything else.

Singh Rao stepped back from the map, making more room for Adam at the desk.

Adam's guts twisted. *Hell.*

Without wanting to, his brain instinctively mapped Vanika's directions against the contours of the landscape. They led to a real place… but not one that matched anything in the clue from Tulsidas's manuscript.

The kid was deliberately guiding the colonel and his soldiers astray.

Borthwick and Singh Rao might not have put it together. If Adam confirmed Vanika's route, they could follow it, putting them miles out of the way—and clearing a path for Subhas and his team to get to the Brahmastra first.

But there was also a damned good possibility that Singh Rao had seen the same thing Adam had in the map—and that all of this was just another test.

Adam had gambled for some high stakes before. Hell, he'd even sought them out—but not like this.

His heart clenched as he made the call.

"She's taking you the wrong way."

He could see the moment Vanika's confidence shattered, along with her trust. Stark betrayal twisted across her face, followed by a wrench of fear. She might've been punching above her weight, but she was still a *child*—a twelve-year-old kid who stood in a room full of people who wouldn't hesitate to kill her.

And her bluff had just been called by the one person she'd thought was on her side.

I'm going to get you out of here. Adam willed the thought at her, but how could she possibly understand it? He couldn't let any of it show on his face.

As far as Vanika was concerned, Adam was no better than the man he was pretending to be. The line between that awful fiction and reality grayed inside of him, and Adam felt sick.

"He's lying!" Vanika protested.

"Why don't we see who's lying?" Borthwick casually replied.

With a flick of his thumb, he loosened the whip at his belt.

Adam's throat closed.

He knew what a stock whip could do. When he was seventeen, he had spent some time at a ranch in Marin—one of his father's many investments. He had never been happier in his life than when he was riding with the herders across the hills. The men had all carried whips in case of a stampede because the crack of the poppers could help direct fear-mad cattle away from danger.

Adam had once seen an overzealous rider use his whip to strike an angry bull. The flail had ripped open the beast's hide like a surgeon's blade.

The man had been let go, but Adam had never forgotten what that injury had looked like.

And a bull had a damned thick hide.

Borthwick unfurled the leather coil.

Singh Rao's eyes dropped to where the braided length slapped the ground, and for just a moment, a flash of disapproval cracked through the man's cool facade.

The subedar pulled the feeling back behind his mask, directing his gaze forward.

Singh Rao wore a sidearm on his belt next to a sheathed dagger. The two soldiers at the door both held rifles.

Borthwick had the whip.

Four men, all armed, stood against Adam and one skinny twelve-year-old girl. Even with his machete, he would be shot as soon as he moved, and it still wouldn't save the kid—but he couldn't stand there and watch Vanika get flayed. *He couldn't.*

Borthwick used the handle of the whip to push up Vanika's chin, forcing her to look at him. "Do you know what this is?"

Angry, frightened tears streaked down Vanika's cheeks. She nodded.

"*Answer me,*" Borthwick ordered.

"Yes," Vanika replied, her voice shaking.

Adam's hands clenched on the frame of the desk.

"You're going to tell us where we need to go." Borthwick continued smoothly. "Because I'm going to show you what happens when you try to get the better of me."

Fear and anger knotted tighter as Adam's sense of desperation rose.

Paper crinkled under his grip.

The map.

There was one way Adam could stop Borthwick's sadistic lesson—besides throwing his body into the path of it, which would only delay the inevitable.

He could make it unnecessary.

Subhas Kōnja had known where the clue from the manuscript pointed, but Adam hadn't bothered to press him for directions, focusing on his own mission. He inwardly cursed himself for that now as he traced the blue curves of the topography, urgency pounding through his skull.

The ridge that points to the dawn of the longest day.

Sunrise on the summer solstice… here in the Northern Hemisphere, that meant the sun's furthest northern point of rise before shifting back east with the shortening of the days.

Odisha and Chhattisgarh sat at a similar latitude to British Honduras, so Adam knew pretty damned well where the sun would rise on a sultry late

June morning.

The change in the topography of the mountains was subtle, just a slight variation in the contour at the top of one of the low, rambling peaks. A little jut of land pointed like an arrow ten degrees north of due east… right where Adam needed it to.

Borthwick ran his hand along the length of the whip, his eyes on the girl. "Shall we, then?"

He made it sound like an invitation to dance.

Adam couldn't worry about all the problems he was causing for himself. He would deal with that later.

Right now, all he could do was act.

"It's here," Adam announced loudly, setting his finger on the paper. "The ridge that points to the dawn of the longest day."

Borthwick glanced back at Adam with mild surprise.

Singh Rao stepped forward to study the map.

Shock widened Vanika's eyes. With an uncomfortable lurch, Adam realized that she stood in exactly the same spot. She hadn't tried to run or hide from Borthwick's threatened violence. It would have been futile to try—but thinking of the courage it must have taken to face Borthwick with defiance and dignity instead made Adam's chest hurt.

Singh Rao gave Borthwick a nod.

The colonel's steel gaze shifted to Adam. "Useful skills indeed, Mr. Bates."

Adam forced himself to bury his rage, fear, and guilt behind a facade of bored indifference. "You might still need the girl after you get there. And she'll be easier to transport if she's uninjured."

"I suppose you're right," Borthwick mildly agreed. "So long as we've made our point clear."

With a flick of his wrist, the whip snapped out.

Adam took an instinctive, desperate step forward—even as he realized it would be futile. He could never reach her in time.

The flail snapped a breath away from Vanika's face, cracking like a gunshot through the claustrophobic space of the tent.

Vanika flinched at the sound—and choked out a brief, heart-wrenching sob.

Borthwick assessed her reaction coldly. "It would seem that we have."

Singh Rao's gaze fell to Adam's right foot—which lay one betraying pace ahead of the other.

Adam's pulse ratcheted up. It had to be patently obvious that he'd been on the verge of intervening.

He waited for Singh Rao to call it out. Whatever personal dislike the subedar might have for the notion of whipping a child, he was still an officer—someone who'd been trained and sworn to strict notions of duty.

With an unreadable expression, Singh Rao looked away. "We can be on the ridge Mr. Bates indicated by early tomorrow afternoon."

Borthwick's icy gray stare still pinned Vanika in place. "Make it noon."

"Yes, sir," Singh Rao acknowledged briskly.

With an easy twist of his wrist, Borthwick coiled back up the whip. He gestured dismissively to the sepoys at the door. "Take her out of here. See that she's watched."

Singh Rao repeated the order in Punjabi. The men dragged Vanika from the tent. The girl didn't resist—except to throw one last terrible look back at Adam, tears tracking down her cheeks.

Adam barely realized that he had started to follow, drawn after Vanika as his heart ached with the need to try to fix what he'd just broken.

Borthwick's voice stopped him.

"Mr. Bates."

Adam tore his eyes from the slight figure dwarfed by the soldiers at her sides. He forced himself to turn to where the colonel waited within the tent.

"Join me for dinner," Borthwick invited.

Every cell in Adam's body rebelled against the idea. A thousand responses flooded his brain, from thin excuses to shouts of outrage.

He couldn't say any of them.

Because he was George Bates's son.

"Sounds great," Adam replied instead.

Something shriveled up inside of him like a dying leaf, and Adam walked back inside.

TWENTY-FOUR

ANCIENT TREES SOARED over ground thick with ferns, flowers, and twisting vines as Neil hiked through a legend.

This was the Dandakaranya, the demon-haunted forest of Lord Rama's exile. It felt like a place that had fallen out of time, where at any moment Neil might stumble across someone from a hundred years in the future—or two thousand years in the past.

More than he usually did, anyway.

It hadn't yet rained, but it would. The sky was heavy and gray where it was visible through the canopy. Sweat ran down the line of Neil's back under his shirt and waistcoat, even with a pair of buttons loosened at his collar.

There were twelve men in their party besides Subhas, Neil, and Constance. They ranged in age from the silver-haired Jignesh to a pair of teenagers. All of them were armed. Several carried bows and arrows. A few hung wicked-looking axes from their belts. Most held Enfield muskets like the ones used to threaten Neil on his approach to the village. The guns were antiques, probably dating back to the time of the mutiny, but they were all in working order. The men carried the weapons in a way that signaled they knew perfectly well how to use them.

Subhas was clearly the leader, despite being younger than many of the others. Even Jignesh, the oldest, deferred to his orders, though the two men often talked things through before coming to a decision.

Constance walked ahead of Neil, easily keeping up with Subhas's merciless pace. She had cheerfully slipped out of her jacket as soon as they'd crossed the river, stashing it in the small pack she carried on her shoulders as she took in everything around her with a wide-eyed air of wonder.

Neil caught himself staring at the way her thighs flexed against the well-tailored fabric of her trousers as she hauled herself up another step.

He pushed to catch up to her so that he would stop staring at her derrière.

"Water?" he offered, slipping the canteen off his shoulder and holding it out to her.

Liquid spilled over the column of her throat as she downed a hearty gulp. She wiped a hand across her mouth before handing the canteen back.

It took Neil a moment to remember to accept it.

"How's it work, then?" Constance demanded.

"The canteen?" Neil echoed, his mind still fuzzy from the way the damp glistened on her neck.

"Not the canteen, Stuffy. Your magical past-seeing powers!"

Neil choked on his own sip of water.

He thought of the look on Ellie's face when he had blurted out his secret. It had read of shock and disbelief—and then a flash of betrayal.

Which was understandable. It hadn't been fair for him to hide the truth from everyone for so long. He owed his sister an explanation for why he had kept it to himself… which shouldn't be hard to provide, as Neil knew exactly why he'd done it.

He was ashamed.

Respected academics weren't supposed to have supernatural powers. Magically seeing into the past was the most unscientific thing Neil could imagine, right up there with talking about faeries and hunting for ghosts. If any of his old Cambridge colleagues had found out about it, they would have laughed him out of the room—or stopped talking to him altogether.

Neil's strange ability was a danger to everything he had built over the course of his education and career… though admittedly less so now that he'd blown his professional reputation to bits by sabotaging his own excavation back in Egypt.

Constance waited for him to answer.

Neil slung the canteen over his shoulder alongside the scabbard for his equally impossible sword. He started walking. "I don't know. It just… happens."

"But what's it *like?*" Constance pressed, hurrying alongside him.

Neil fought an unfair sense of irritation. "It's different every time."

Constance studied him cannily as he used a skinny tree to haul himself up a steeper section of the path. "Have you ever done it when I was there?"

Neil stilled halfway up the slope. "Yes."

"When?"

He forced himself to look back at her. "Tell al-Amarna."

Constance's eyes widened with recognition. "You called it beautiful, only we were standing in a dusty field with a bit of rubble. Not that I'd put it past you to find a field full of rubble lovely," she added dryly. "But that's not what you were seeing, was it?"

Neil braced his feet on the rocks, swallowing thickly. "I was looking at Akhetaten, Akhenaten's capital. Not… as rubble."

He closed his eyes, and he was there again—the palaces and temples rising up from the sand. Curtains billowed from windows, fruit trees shaded secluded gardens, and women laughed over the lilt of music.

"Engadu!" one of the Adrija men complained, waving for them to stop blocking the path.

Neil ripped himself from the memory and scrambled up the rest of the incline.

Constance gripped the tree below him. She frowned at where to go next, her reach not being quite as long as Neil's.

He extended his hand. Constance clasped it, and Neil hauled her up, instinctively catching her as she reached the top.

She fell against him, soft curves palpable through her blouse and trousers.

Fiancée, Neil thought numbly.

Fake fiancée.

He let her go and quickly hurried after the rest of the men.

"How did you do it then?" Constance pressed impatiently.

"How did I do what?"

"Akhetaten!"

Neil's jaw tightened. "I didn't do anything. It just happened."

"How long has it been 'just happening?'"

"A few years?" Neil mumbled back.

"Two? Five?"

Neil turned on her. "I don't know exactly! I told you. It doesn't always happen the same way. Maybe I've been doing it forever, and I just…"

He bit back the rest, pushing angrily through an innocent stand of waist-high grass.

Constance clamped a hand around his arm and hauled him out of the path.

The men behind them chuckled as they passed, sharing knowing looks.

"Stuffy, I am not going to think any differently of you just because you can do a bit of magic," Constance huffed.

Neil stilled with surprise at her words.

He hadn't even known the fear existed until Constance voiced it—but there it was. And why wouldn't it be? How couldn't his impossible, unscientific ability change the way people thought about him?

They would assume he was crazy. Or worse, they would expect him to be some kind of magician—which he wasn't.

"You won't?" he pushed back tentatively.

Constance let out an exasperated huff. "You're my friend! I just want to know what this means to you."

Neil was touched.

Constance spilled out the rest. "I'm also desperately curious, and it's entirely unfair of you to leave me in suspense."

Neil suppressed a helpless groan, acknowledging that Constance wouldn't leave him alone until she had the whole story.

"What it means is that I'm now questioning whether I can actually consider myself a scholar when everything I thought I'd accomplished as a historian and academic might just be some mad parlor trick," Neil confessed miserably.

He had been tormented by that doubt ever since Sayyid had mercilessly forced the epiphany about his power onto him back in Egypt. What did it mean that Neil could magically see the past? Was everything he'd accomplished during his career now a lie? And what about the future? Using a supernatural power in one's scholarly endeavors without actually realizing it was one thing, but what were the ethics of going forward with his studies now that he knew what he was doing?

Neil loved his work. He wanted to do more of it—to painstakingly unearth the relics of history and puzzle through their subtle details, teasing out the secrets of lives hundreds or thousands of years in the past. But how could he keep at it now that he knew the real source of his 'leaps of intuition?'

"Don't be silly," Constance retorted.

Her blunt answer threw him. "Silly?"

"You are one of the cleverest people I've ever met!" Constance hooked a hand through his arm and dragged him back onto the path. "You read journals in German and letters in Ancient Egyptian…"

"It's not 'Ancient Egyptian,'" Neil grumped. "There's Classical Egyptian and Late Egyptian, and they each have distinct and important variants—"

"My point exactly," Constance cut in. "There is simply no way you would be able to rattle on about the Roman invasion of Britain, Norse trade routes, and the historicity of Troy the way you do if it were all just magical powers."

She was right. Not *everything* Neil had ever learned was in doubt. There were piles of knowledge in his brain that had come from books—because he remembered reading them, spending late nights at Cambridge poring over excavation reports.

They continued to climb the steep, thickly wooded slope. The trees thinned out further up the rise, where more of the gold-gray light of afternoon filtered through the rich green leaves.

"It's very kind of you to say that, but it's hard to imagine how I can possibly be both of these things," Neil replied. "A scholar and…"

"Magical?" Constance looked thoughtful. "I suppose I'm having trouble figuring out how to be British and Indian, but I *am* both of those things—more so now than I was even a week ago. And I wouldn't wish myself to be anything other than what I am—if wishing could make any sort of difference. So I suppose I'll have to figure it out."

Neil stopped. "You're right."

Constance was clearly pleased. "Am I?"

"I am… both," he admitted, even as part of him twisted queasily at the words. "There's no point in wishing it were any different. But I haven't the foggiest idea how to go about it!"

Constance studied him as Neil ducked under a branch heavily laden with flowers. "But you've already been going about it, haven't you? I mean—I've always been myself, and I've gotten along well enough at that, I think. I'm just seeing it all differently now than I did before. Encountering circumstances that make being both Indian and British more… complicated."

Neil's heart tightened at her words. He glanced back at her as he held up the branch.

"There is absolutely no doubt in my mind that you are going to do it splendidly," he burst out feelingly. "Britain and India are both lucky to have you."

Constance's grin was like a beam of sunshine breaking through the monsoon. "Do you really think so? I mean—I agree with you, but it's still nice to hear someone else say it."

An answering smile tugged irresistibly at Neil's lips. "I'll say it as often and as loudly as you like," he vowed—and found to his surprise that he meant it.

Her eyes narrowed playfully. "Do you need me to tell you that you can be both a scholar and a little magical?"

Neil grimaced as a wave of familiar discomfort washed over him. "I'm not sure I'm ready to hear that yet. I still wish the whole thing had never come up back in the village. It's only going to make everyone think I can do something that I can't. I don't really *do* it at all. It just… happens."

"Well, if it's happening at all, it sounds to me like you're halfway there,"

Constance concluded authoritatively.

A low rumble of thunder echoed through the trees. Jignesh leaned over the path above them, his amber eyes bright in his weathered face. "Up! Quick!"

Neil offered Constance a hand and helped her scramble up the last of the climb.

They emerged at the top of the ridge, where the forest gave way to a flat, rocky plateau accented by tufts of grass and scrubby bushes. At the end of it, a natural arrow of land jutted from the peak, pointing slightly northeast.

The point was topped by a stubby column of stone roughly Neil's height. The surface of the monument was round at the top and smoothly polished.

Subhas stood beside it. The law student had pulled off his shirt, tucking it into the back of his trousers. The strap for his Enfield crossed over the objectively well-defined musculature of his torso.

"Hmm," Constance mused.

"What's that?" Neil asked.

"Just admiring the scenery," she returned blandly. "But isn't this a Shiva stone?"

"Of course, it is!" Neil exclaimed, scholarly fervor kicking into gear. "It's a lingam, one of Shiva's sacred symbols. Shiva is known as the Supreme Lord and Destroyer—but also Nataraja, the Lord of the Dance. *Join the Lord of the Dance!*"

Neil punctuated the remarks with eager jabs at the smooth, polished pillar—and then caught himself at Subhas's dry look. "But you must have already known that."

"Where are we supposed to go next?" Subhas asked.

"Let his shadow lead you to the ruins of the most loyal kingdom," Constance recited.

Subhas's haughty expression flickered with uncomfortable emotion—and he glanced to the south.

Neil followed the look to where a pale stone needle pierced the canopy. It emerged from the trees like a finger of bone, hugged by the ridge that circled the cupped hand of a broad, forested depression.

His blood thrummed with rising excitement. "That pillar must be at least forty feet tall to break through the canopy. Carved from a single piece of stone, I should expect, or it wouldn't have remained intact without regular maintenance." He whirled back to face Constance and Subhas. "Don't you realize what this means? A monument like that wouldn't be isolated in the middle of the wilderness. There would need to be access to quarries.

Engineers. Laborers. Ritual or civic centers that justified an immense architectural undertaking."

"It's a city," Subhas returned flatly.

The words sparked an overwhelming sense of wonder.

An entire city hidden in the deep forest, untouched for centuries. It would be rife with knowledge about India's past, just waiting to be painstakingly uncovered.

Neil was unable to keep the eagerness from his voice. "You've been to it?"

Subhas's expression hardened. "No."

"Why not?"

"We don't go down there."

The assertion was so surprising, Neil found it hard to absorb. "But don't you want to know what's there?"

Subhas's voice snapped with anger. "And what good do you think that would do us? Should the Adrija submit a paper on it to the Royal Geographical Society?"

His voice dripped with sarcasm. Neil's billowing excitement about the promise of the pillar abruptly popped, leaving behind an unexpected uncertainty.

"I…" Neil started. "That's not what I was…"

"Do you know what I *want*?"

Subhas stepped closer to him. They were roughly even in height, but Neil felt smaller in the face of Subhas's ferocity.

"I want to know that my village isn't going to be labeled 'criminal' and forced from our homes on some Englishman's whim. I want to know that we won't be shut out of the forest that feeds our children." Subhas waved a hand over the dark, secret sprawl of the wilderness around them. "That all this isn't going to be torn up for some mining contract granted by men who've never so much as seen it. Do you know what I've learned about the law after three years at university? I've learned that it exists to protect your interests over ours."

"Mine?" Neil echoed, thrown.

"The English." Subhas bit out the word like a curse. "And it is not enough to steal our present and our future. You steal our past, too." He jabbed an accusing finger at the pale tower that tantalizingly pierced the canopy below. "What do you think would happen if word about this got back to Madras? How quickly do you think some English expedition would be out here to cut it all down and carry it away to one of your museums—for *safe-keeping?*"

The words whipped with sarcasm, cutting like blades.

Shame burned through Neil as Sayyid's voice echoed in his memory.

No matter that it is our history the world is digging up. Our language on the walls. Our ancestors in the sarcophagi. I could only—ever—be the help.

Neil's chest ached with guilt. "You're right. Of course, you're right."

"I don't even care," Subhas retorted. "It's not the ruins that concern me. It's that your people would happily eradicate my own if you thought we were in the way of claiming them."

His eyes were like embers, flaring with a terrible and bitter heat. "Tell me I'm wrong."

Neil wanted to. Two months ago, he would have, flush with faith in his profession and the institutions that shaped it.

That faith had died in the echoing silence of an Old Kingdom quarry, witnessed by the endless columns of chiseled stone—and the heartbroken gaze of the friend he'd let down.

"I can't," Neil admitted helplessly.

Constance watched them silently, her eyes wide with surprise at how quickly the dynamic had turned.

"You're here because my grandmother wants you here, and I respect her wishes," Subhas bit out. "But I don't trust you, and I won't let you get in our way."

Neil felt the words like blows. He wasn't sure that he didn't deserve them.

Subhas turned toward his men, who watched the exchange from the other end of the peak like they might eye a tiger mauling its prey. "We can be there in a half-day's walk tomorrow, but we're stopping here for the night. It's going to rain."

As though to punctuate his remark, another roll of thunder rumbled across the sky.

He walked away.

Neil remained rooted to the spot like a statue, his mind and heart reeling.

"Neil?" Constance asked softly.

"It's all right," Neil blurted out. "It's… He's… I'm…"

The words failed him.

Constance looked quietly sympathetic, but she said nothing to reassure him. How could she?

Subhas wasn't wrong.

Neil had spent so much time over the last few weeks tormenting himself over the question of how to reconcile his impossible powers with his identity as a scholar. He had nearly forgotten the other lesson he had learned in Egypt—the one Sayyid had so painfully taught him.

If he was ever going to do this work again—work that he truly, passion-ately loved—he had to find a way to do it differently. To do it right.

Neil stared out at the uneasy promise of the slender stone that pierced through the shadowy trees.

"We should go help," he concluded numbly, and turned away from it.

TWENTY-FIVE

RAIN WASHED AGAINST Ellie's tent in a rasping patter. The downpour had started an hour before, but inside the canvas shelter, she remained dry—drowning only in her own worry.

A single paraffin lantern illuminated the two bedrolls. Kalb lay on the ground beside the blankets, his eyes mournfully fixed on the entrance as though he could will Adam to appear there. Every now and then, the dog let out an eloquent huff of longing.

Ellie thought of Adam's casual theory that Kalb was his new lucky rock. He would have to revisit that hypothesis, as nothing had gone right for them since they had left the palace.

She was exhausted. Her leg hurt. She itched with the need to know how Adam was doing, but going out to look for him would only raise Borthwick's suspicions higher than they were already—if she even made it that far. Regular patrols circled past her tent, the men set to guard the camp through the night. Jacobs would also be attuned to anything she or Adam might do that could cause him trouble.

As much as she hated it, for the moment all she could do was wait.

Ellie pulled a cigar tube from the pocket of her trousers. Unscrewing the lid, she slid a slender carved bone into her palm and traced her thumb over the rough texture of the Glagolitic characters carved into its smooth surface. They spelled out the word *světŭ*... for light.

Instinct tickled. Ellie looked up to see a figure lingering in the rain-soaked gloom beyond the open flap of the tent.

A woman stared solemnly at Ellie through the downpour, wrapped in the pale folds of a drenched sari.

Black hair streamed over her shoulders. Her eyes glinted through the darkness like flecks of obsidian.

A whisper hissed through the monsoon that battered the tent.

Listen.

Kalb jumped to his feet, barking wildly at the entrance. Ellie jerked, startled by the sound.

The woman was gone. It was Adam who stood in the rain.

The water slicked his shirt to his skin. His gaze was hollow. For a moment, Ellie wondered if he was just another product of her tired, wandering mind, but then Kalb wagged his tail in frantic greeting, dancing at the threshold.

Ellie pocketed the firebird bone as she stood, joining the dog just shy of where the rain crashed down. Adam met her there, lingering in the downpour.

"Adam?" Ellie prompted, instinct softening the word.

"I'll get everything wet."

Adam spoke as though answering a question Ellie hadn't asked. The helpless despair in his voice cut her like a blade.

She reached out through the rain to take his hand and draw him into the tent.

In the dim light of the lamp, his golden hair was darkened to bronze, plastered to his head with the damp. Water streaked down his jaw.

Kalb jumped at him, whining.

"Down, buddy." Adam's gentle rebuke was duller than usual, but he gave the dog a token rub between the ears.

He pulled his soaked shirt over his head and stuck it outside, wringing it out with an angry, powerful twist of his arms—and then lingered there, stalled on the threshold as though lost.

Kalb sat down at Adam's feet and huffed up at him worriedly.

Ellie took the shirt from his hands, hanging it from one of the poles to dry. She drew him from the flap, pulling it closed, and then turned to face him, worry quickening her pulse. "What happened?"

"Vanika's under guard," Adam reported in a clipped, flat voice.

"Why?"

Adam closed his eyes as though her question was a blow. "Because I told Borthwick she was lying."

Shock jolted through her. "Why would you do that?"

"She was trying to lead him off track. Borthwick asked me to validate her route. I told him it was wrong."

He threw the words down like stones, sharp and harsh.

"He was testing you," Ellie deduced.

"Of course, he was testing me. But she doesn't know that. She's twelve years old. She thinks I betrayed her. I *did* betray her."

Worry rose at the acid in his words. "Adam—" Ellie began to protest.

Adam cut her off, his voice raw with guilt. "He was going to hit her with that goddamned whip, and I said nothing. I stood there and watched while he threatened that kid with something that could rip the skin off her back."

Ellie's heart skipped uneasily. "You wouldn't have let him do it."

"There were four armed men in the room."

"*You wouldn't have let him do it*," she cut back with fierce certainty.

Adam was bleak with despair. "Vanika doesn't know that. Not anymore."

Ellie gripped his bare shoulders and spoke with all the conviction that she could muster. "*She will.* When we get her out of here."

Self-loathing snapped through his tone. "That's going to be a lot harder for us to do now because of me."

"You didn't have any choice."

"You sure about that?" Adam pushed back bitterly.

Ellie felt the coiled strength in his arms as she forced him to face her. "*Yes.*"

Adam's cold expression crumbled, exhaustion and fear showing through. "I gave him the damned directions, Ellie. I told him right where he needs to go. It was the only way I could think of to stop him from hurting her."

Ellie pressed her palm to the stubble on his jaw. "I understand."

Adam pulled away from her. His hands clenched as his body went rigid with the force of his emotions. "And then I spent the rest of the night pretending I was fine with that. That I could have a friendly dinner with a man who'd flay a child because she's poor and Indian and that means she doesn't count."

"It was just an act, Adam."

He looked haunted. "It's not an act. It's who I'm supposed to be."

The words chilled her. "What on earth are you talking about?"

"*That's the man I was supposed to be*," Adam repeated in a snarl. "That's the son George Bates would've been proud of."

His strange protest from earlier that day rang through Ellie's mind.

My father never wanted me.

A low hum of shock numbed her thoughts. "That's what you were trying to tell me after we crossed the river."

Anger mingled with a terrible shame in Adam's eyes. "I have to go along with all of it. The bile Borthwick spits about this place. The way he talks down to everyone around him as if they're worthless. I have to pretend that all of it is fine, because that's what my father would have expected. That's the man he wouldn't have cut off." His voice caught, the words becoming uneven. "Ellie, the look on that kid's face…"

Ellie gripped his arm. "That isn't you."

"It has to be until we get Vanika out of here—however long that takes. I just…" Misery tightened his features. "I could never be what my dad expected, even when I *wanted* to. And Christ, Ellie—there was a time when I wanted it more than anything in the world. It's taken me my whole life to get away from that. I lost my home over it. My little brother."

His voice broke on the word.

Brother.

"Putting it all back on again now, like this, it's…" He trailed off bleakly.

Ellie's mind spun. She had known Adam's relationship with his father had a dark history ever since that night on the Sibun River when he had casually told her how he'd been disowned after quitting college. She had glimpsed more of it in the way he'd tormented himself about the nature of their relationship back in Egypt, where George Bates had echoed through the words that fell from Adam's lips.

That he was irresponsible. Careless. Impulsive.

This felt deeper, and Ellie began to wonder whether she really knew just what sort of monster Adam's father had been.

What sort of monster he *was*.

She took Adam's hands. "No matter what this requires of you, there will always be one person in this camp who knows the real Adam Bates."

Relief softened the taut lines of his face. He had needed to hear that, Ellie realized—even as an odd thought tumbled into place behind it.

"Well… I suppose there are two of us, really," she allowed.

"Two?" Adam echoed.

"Myself… and Jacobs."

Adam's brow quirked with a flicker of his usual insouciance. "I'm not sure I find that comforting."

"Neither am I," Ellie admitted.

A little spark of humor crept back into Adam's eyes. "What about Dawson?"

"I don't think Dawson pays enough attention to anyone outside himself to know another person. He's probably barely noticed that you're American."

"Oh, I think he's got that part figured out well enough," Adam drawled back.

Ellie frowned thoughtfully. "I've been wondering about him."

"Dawson?" Adam filled in skeptically.

"No," Ellie returned dryly, and then sobered. "Jacobs."

Adam waited with wary curiosity as she elaborated.

"In my experience, most people who hurt others do it because it makes them feel powerful—in control. Wouldn't you say that's true?"

"Yeah. I'd say that's right."

Adam's flat reply made Ellie think—uncomfortably—of someone who spoke from experience.

Ellie mentally filed through every threat she had experienced from the man they spoke of—every leveled gun or brandished blade. "But that's not why Jacobs does it. Hurting us doesn't make him feel bigger. He does it because it's his job, and his job gets him closer to what he wants."

"There are a whole lot of people out there with jobs who still draw the line at torture and murder," Adam pointed out coldly.

"They do," Ellie agreed. "But that just leaves me wondering why Jacobs is different. I've read of men who were incapable of remembering faces the way the rest of us can. There are people who lack the ability to see certain colors. What if Jacobs was born without... I don't know. A moral code?"

"He has a code. It's just not one that makes a hell of a lot of sense to the rest of us."

"Maybe... empathy, then," Ellie filled in. "The ability to care about how his actions impact other people. But if that's true, would it make him more evil? Or less?"

"Why's it matter?"

"Perhaps it just occurred to me that there might be a way all of this plays out where we find ourselves on the same side," Ellie admitted uneasily. "And I suppose I'm trying to figure out how I would feel about that. If Jacobs wasn't on this quest of his any longer—this search for justice—do you think he would still be dangerous?"

"I'm sure he'd be just fine... until someone got in his way again."

Ellie put a hand to her head as her temple throbbed. "You're right."

Adam gazed down at her steadily. "I'm never going to trust the man, Ellie. He's tried to hurt you, and as far as I'm concerned, that's a line nobody gets to cross."

"I would never ask you to trust him," Ellie assured him.

The words rang oddly in her ears.

Adam's tone shifted to one of quiet concern. "What about you? I'm not the only one here pretending to be someone I'm not... *Mrs. Bates.*"

Ellie was thrown by the question. "Oh! But that's not the same thing at all."

"Isn't it? You never wanted to be married. You've got some pretty damned good reasons for that. And now you're stuck masquerading as my wife."

Ellie opened her mouth to respond—and the words died in her throat.

You're going to have to become fake married.

She hadn't yet found an opportunity to bring Constance's breezy suggestion up to Adam. This seemed like an absolutely wretched time to try, when he'd just bared his soul to her about how much it was hurting him to have to pretend to be someone else with Borthwick.

But if she didn't, would that mean she was only biding her time for a moment where Adam might be more willing to agree to live a lie with her?

No—that was precisely why she had to do it now. If she hid the notion from him when she was still seriously contemplating it herself, then she was lying to him—or even worse, hoping he'd change the part of himself that inconvenienced her.

Never, Ellie vowed fiercely.

Steeling herself, she sat down on the bedroll and drew up her knees. "While we're on the subject…"

Adam looked from the blankets to his damp trousers.

"You could take them off," Ellie suggested.

"Slept in worse." Adam kicked off his boots and dropped beside her.

Kalb flopped down at his side, gazing up hopefully. With a sigh, Adam rubbed his belly. The dog melted into the gesture.

Weariness was written in the slump of Adam's shoulders. "On the subject…?" he prompted.

Ellie drew in a breath and got to it. "Constance has suggested that perhaps utilizing a fiction of sorts around our actual marital status might be a valid way of navigating our rather unique situation."

"You lost me," Adam informed her bluntly.

"She thinks we should pretend to be married," Ellie blurted out.

Adam's brows arched with surprise. "But you'd hate that."

"I would?"

"Pretending to be married?"

"To *you*," Ellie emphasized. "I know it would look like I was going along with an institution that I fervently oppose, but we wouldn't be—not really— and we would both know that. We'd just be… choosing who we decided to share that with."

Adam looked thoughtful.

Ellie hurried on, her stomach lurching with worry. "I'm sorry—I shouldn't have even brought it up. I'd be asking you to do exactly what you just told me has been so dreadfully bad for you—living a lie."

He shook his head. "It's not the same thing at all."

"It isn't?"

His brow rose. "Pretending I want to marry you? That's not a lie, Ellie. I already told you, I would've asked you weeks ago if I thought you'd be open to the idea. It's not lying to pretend to do something I would've happily done all along. Hell—in a way it'd be more honest than what we *have* been doing."

Hope fluttered up in Ellie's chest, light and fragile. "It would be?"

"What do you think's more real? Pretending I'm just your brother's friend, and then sneaking off to fool around with each other when no one's looking?" He traced his fingers along the line of her jaw. "Or telling the world that we're crazy about each other?"

Hope welled up in Ellie, turning real.

Adam drew her down to the bedroll, wrapping his arm around her back. Ellie tucked herself against his side, her head resting on his bare shoulder.

She traced her fingers over the familiar contours of his chest. "I have been thinking of what Zeinab said back in Egypt—that we don't have to fight tyranny by banging on the door. And we don't. It's none of their business how we've chosen to love each other. Or what we do to protect that love in the face of a world that refuses to understand it."

His face darkened with worry again. "I just don't want to let you down."

"Who's voice is that?" Ellie chided him softly.

"This time? Mine."

Understanding snapped into place with a wrench. "Pretending to be that other Adam is hurting you."

"And keeping us all alive," Adam countered.

"*For now*. But don't you dare forget who you really are underneath it all. That's the man I chose—and I was quite certain I would never choose any man at all, given how insufferable most of them are. That ought to tell you how truly extraordinary you are."

Adam traced his hand along the side of her face. "What I'm mostly feeling right now is lucky."

Kalb perked up, his tail whacking happily against the ground.

"Luck had nothing to do with it," Ellie countered quickly.

"With you landing on me in British Honduras?"

"Well—maybe that, a little. But not everything that came after."

"I dunno, Princess." Adam's lip quirked with a hint of mischief. "I think we've had more than a few good turns."

"Those are entirely down to my studies and your extensive repertoire of skills."

"Extensive, huh?"

Ellie blushed. His comment gave her ideas, as it had been meant to. Not that she could act on them in the middle of an enemy camp with soldiers patrolling outside. "You know perfectly well what I mean."

Adam gentled with an aching tenderness. "I guess I do."

Tears pricked at the corners of Ellie's eyes. She dropped her head back to his chest again, holding him as worry, fear, and love mingled inside of her. "I'm going to get you out of here—you, and Vanika, and even your terrible dog."

"He's a good boy," Adam protested tiredly.

Kalb dropped down against Ellie's back with a sleepy huff and a soft warmth.

"He is… tolerable," Ellie allowed.

"He's gonna grow on you. Just wait." Adam yawned, exhaustion apparent in every line of his frame. "And I'm supposed to be the one getting you out."

"We will both leverage our respective skills, I'm sure."

Quiet settled in around them.

"Adam?"

"Hmm?" he returned, a little dull with sleep.

She lifted her head to look down at him. "There's a reason it feels awful—what you're doing with Borthwick."

He opened his eyes, watching her.

"It's because that man—the one your father tried to turn you into—isn't who you are. And it never would have been. Not in any imaginable universe."

She saw the impact of the words—and was glad that she had said them.

"Get some sleep, Princess," Adam finally said.

Sandwiched between the warmth of the man she loved and his blasted dog, Ellie let the night claim her.

TWENTY-SIX

SHELTERED UNDER A rock outcropping, Neil watched the drizzle patter steadily against the leaves as Subhas's men dozed around him. They had camped a short distance from the top of the ridge in a shallow cavern framed by close-growing trees. A pair of men sat at the edge of the overhang, talking softly to each other as they kept watch by a small, smoldering fire.

Sleep evaded him. It wasn't because of the rustic conditions. Neil had camped in rougher spots over the years at various excavations. He had learned that if he worked hard enough during the day, his body didn't much mind where he put it down for the night. He worried about the girl, Vanika. He worried about what it might mean for that horrible man, Borthwick, to acquire the power of the most powerful weapon in India's history.

He worried about Ellie and Adam. Were they safe? What had they thought of his supernatural revelations earlier that afternoon?

And he worried over his argument with Subhas by the Shiva lingam. If Neil followed his passion to learn and discover, would he inevitably end up harming people?

I am one giant knot of worry, he thought absently as the rain shimmered down through the night.

Constance slept deeply on her bedroll beside him. Her features were soft, her dark hair curling against her neck. She was the one person Neil wasn't worried about—even though he was sure she would do something reckless before this adventure was through.

She would be reckless, but she'd find a way to pull it off. Neil was oddly certain of that.

Tomorrow, they would reach the ruins. Would Neil be expected to magic his way into knowing what that place had been and where to find what they were looking for in it?

He had no idea how to do that, which left him already feeling the weight of how he would end up disappointing everyone.

It seemed like Neil had been doing a lot of that lately.

He pictured Sayyid's warm eyes drawn with pain as his friend revealed how Neil had hurt him, over and over again, by failing to acknowledge the differences between the two worlds they lived in—English and Egyptian.

How do I fix it? Neil had pleaded.

Join the revolution? Sayyid had wryly returned.

Neil wasn't sure what use he'd be in a revolution, but he had to find some way to work against the terrible old patterns that shaped the field that he loved. Labeling himself hopeless and giving up was the coward's way out—no better, really, than ignoring that the injustice existed.

Subhas's words from the ridge echoed through his mind. *It is not enough to steal our present and our future. You steal our past, too.*

All of that had stung… because it was true.

The Adrija leader was also awake, firelight flickering over his skin on the far side of the cavern. Subhas's shoulders were bowed with the weight of all the troubles he carried.

With an uncomfortable determination, Neil picked his way through the sleeping bodies to join him. He frowned at the rain as he struggled to figure out what he wanted to say.

Subhas spoke without looking at him. "I apologize for this afternoon."

Neil startled. "You don't need to do that."

"Just because you're English doesn't mean you're one of them. If I paint you with that brush before I've given you a chance to show me who you are, I'm no better than they are."

Neil rested his arms on his knees, gazing back out at the forest. "I came over here to apologize to you."

Rain glittered beyond the overhang, tapping out a steady rhythm against the trees. Subhas shrugged.

"How bad is it?" Neil carefully pressed.

"All the hill tribes have ever wanted is to be left alone—but we're a problem. This forest…" Subhas nodded at the shadowy wilderness that lay beyond the low red firelight. "It's full of wealth. Lumber. Minerals. We're in the way of that. The Raj will either move us or lean their weight against us until there's no other option but war. And that would give them the excuse to kill us."

Neil tried to imagine what it would feel like to know that the most powerful empire in the world wanted you and the people you loved out of its way.

He couldn't.

There were scars on Subhas's chest. The man was built like a warrior and held his rifle in a way that made it very clear that he knew how to use it. Yet Neil had no doubt he would be a pure terror in a university classroom as well—or a courtroom. "Is that why you're studying law?"

Subhas scowled. "That's what His Highness Vijayrama Devi would tell you. But I haven't found a law yet that the English can be bound by."

"Would it be better if India were governed by Indians?"

Subhas's fierce expression fell into uncertainty and exhaustion. "I honestly don't know. Most of the nationalists think India's future depends on industrialization—joining the rest of the great economies of the world. That means resources, and as they're almost all higher-caste Hindus or wealthy Muslims, I cannot hold out much faith that they will put the welfare of a few hundred poor hill folk over the needs of a new nation."

"Then what's the answer?" Neil demanded.

"So far?" Subhas's eyes glinted in the near darkness. "Making ourselves hard to kill."

Neil thought of how easily the men around him had snatched up their weapons to come out here. How silently they could move through the forest.

Was that the answer? Would it always come down to war?

"I'm no good at fighting," Neil confessed uncomfortably. "Connie's better at it than I am."

Subhas nodded at Constance's sleeping figure. "Your wife?"

Neil realized that they had never bothered to clarify the nature of their relationship to Subhas. It hadn't seemed important. It wasn't, really.

There were so many answers he could give—that they were engaged. That they were friends.

That Constance was the girl who had tormented him for fun as a child.

The woman who haunted his heated, guilty dreams.

"I don't know what we are," Neil admitted.

Subhas's mouth quirked with a hint of mirth. "Don't you?"

Neil blinked, thrown by his response.

Across the cavern, one of the sentries hissed for Subhas's attention. Subhas rose to his feet in a breath, drawing his Enfield up with him, his eyes locked on the slowly shifting shadows under the trees through the shimmering rain.

Instinct lowered Neil's words to a whisper. "What is it?"

Subhas held the musket steady. "Tiger."

A silent message moved swiftly through the cavern. Men woke, gathering weapons and shifting to their feet.

Constance sat up, her hair tumbling loose around her shoulders. She frowned across the cavern at Neil and Subhas.

"Might it just go on its way?" Neil suggested hopefully.

"It might."

Subhas's tone did not inspire confidence.

Out in the forest, a glimmering shadow darted between a pair of thick-trunked trees.

Jignesh was poised on the far side of the cavern with his bow in his hand. He clicked his tongue warningly, gesturing at Subhas's Enfield.

Subhas muttered a curse and lowered the weapon.

"What's wrong?" Neil pressed in a whisper.

"We can't use the guns," Subhas bit out. "We don't know where Borthwick is. The sound could lead him right to us."

Constance watched their exchange from her bedroll with furious curiosity. She stood, clearly intending to cross the camp to Neil and Subhas.

Jignesh stopped her, dropping his hand from the bow just long enough to tug her back against the wall of the cavern behind the row of focused archers.

Constance's eyes flashed with irritation, but she stayed in place. Neil felt a pang of fervent relief.

He pulled his attention back to Subhas. "What about the fire? Aren't tigers supposed to be afraid of flames?"

"It isn't big enough."

"Could we build it up?"

"The wind is blowing the wrong way. We'd smoke ourselves out."

The implication sank in. "You mean that if it comes for us, you have to try to kill it."

"Yes," Subhas replied shortly.

Neil's throat tightened. "Can someone do that with a single arrow?"

Subhas's jaw flexed with tension. "It will likely take more than one."

Neil pictured an infuriated tiger with an arrow in its flank tearing into the camp—or stuck full of darts like a pin cushion, falling down to bleed out on the rain-soaked ground.

One image filled him with fear—the other with a terrible sense of grief.

The tiger emerged from the shadowy trees with a shiver of silent movement. Muscle rippled under striped fur turned pale with contrast in the gloom of the night and the low, smoldering flicker of the campfire. Power gleamed in every sleek, graceful movement. The step of a massive paw. The shift of a shaggy head, golden eyes glinting through the darkness. The careless flick of a sinuous tail.

The animal was beautiful… and Neil had absolutely no doubt that it was fully capable of slaughtering him.

The tiger shook itself, raindrops flying from its coat in a sparkling shower—then stared into the cavern.

The air around Neil went taut, pulled between the men with their arrows and the elegant beast in the rain-glittering night.

Across the cavern, Jignesh held his bow in wiry, weathered arms. His eyes flicked to Subhas, the question in them clear without speaking a word.

Should we shoot?

Constance saw it as well. Her face twisted with dismay at the idea of all that graceful strength falling into the mud in a mess of torn fur and blood.

Neil's own sense of helplessness choked him—until it abruptly shattered.

Afraid of flames…

The solution burst across his mind like a blow to the head, as obvious as it was patently lunatic.

Neil fought the urge to burst into hysterics.

The tiger shifted, coiling with readiness. Subhas's mouth drew down with worry and determination. Jignesh's bowstring tightened.

Constance's expression hollowed with grief.

"*Don't,*" Neil burst out lowly, the word as fierce as a prayer.

Subhas shot him a furious glare.

Neil ignored it—and sprinted for his blanket.

This is madness, he thought as he snatched up the leather scabbard.

I'm about to get myself mauled by a tiger, he reasonably deduced as he stumbled out into the rain.

Jignesh made a quick, disbelieving outburst. Neil sensed the arrows trained on his back—because he had just put himself between them and their target.

The tiger swiveled its head, fixing him with an unblinking golden stare— even as the world turned to a mosaic through the rain-spattered glass of his spectacles.

"I'm an idiot," Neil acknowledged aloud.

He whipped out his sword.

Blue-gold flames whirled up Dyrnwyn's length, their intensity glaring after the gloom of the cavern. Neil clung to the sword desperately, holding it out before him almost as though he had some bloody notion what the devil to do with it.

The tiger stilled.

Everything stilled, as though Neil had stepped into a painting. Pale light painted stone and leaf, tree and flesh. Men hovered at the edge of the cavern with their arrows notched.

Subhas's brows rose with surprise. Constance's eyes widened as though Neil had just fallen out of the sky.

Rain sang against the leaves, plastering Neil's shirt to his shoulders.

Dyrnwyn glowed like a star.

Neil filtered everything out—the branches hanging low over the mouth of the overhang. The damp soaking his clothes. The fact that he could barely see, the world a speckled wash of green, black, and gold, fractured by the water on his lenses.

Only the tiger mattered.

He knew when the animal began to shift, sensing it in the crunch of a paw on dead leaves and the orange shimmer through the dancing kaleidoscope of his spectacles.

Neil swung his blade to the left.

The tiger stilled—and a branch crashed to the ground at Neil's feet.

He fought the instinct to jump back, keeping his eyes on the cat. He couldn't risk looking at what had just happened, even as part of his brain wondered wildly why a limb would have fallen when it was still covered in sturdy green growth and he hadn't felt Dyrnwyn so much as brush against an obstacle.

Neil shoved it all aside. He could worry about it later—once he'd managed to stay alive.

The tiger froze again, its yellow gaze fixed on Neil with unblinking intensity. The sword's weight tugged at his shoulders as the moment stretched.

He wondered what he would do when the tiger inevitably decided to attack. Could he possibly manage to direct the sword into some sort of defensive thrust?

Neil very much doubted it.

The tiger studied him as though measuring Neil's worth as a threat… or as a meal. It was planning something—but what? Would it use all that sleek, coiled power to try to dart around Neil? Or bat his sword away with a swipe of a massive paw and bury its teeth in his throat?

Neil had no idea, and he was washed over with the helpless sense that even the sheer madness of charging at a tiger with a flaming sword hadn't been quite *enough*.

Muscle flexed under striped fur—and a dart of light shot past the corner of Neil's vision.

An arrow pierced the soil at his feet with a soft *thwack*. Flames licked delicately up the shaft.

Another followed, and then a third.

Neil risked a wild look back into the cavern. In the orange glow of the embers, Subhas was framed by his archers, eyes glinting with purpose and determination.

Jignesh swept another cloth-wrapped arrow through the remains of the campfire, then launched the flaming missile at the tiger's feet.

The tiger took a wary half-step back.

The burning arrows were wisps against the darkness, their light quickly failing against the steady fall of the rain.

The beautiful predator measured all of it. The men in the cavern. The dwindling arrows. Neil. Golden eyes glittered with thoughtful intelligence.

Desperation dragged a ludicrous plea from Neil's lips. "Would you please just *go?*"

The tiger cocked its head as though considering the request—then turned and leaped away into the forest.

Neil stared after the soft crash of its movements, still clinging to the sword as though afraid the wrong gesture would break the spell and bring the animal charging back.

A hand came down on his shoulder. Neil flinched.

"You can put that down now," Subhas said.

The man stood beside him in the rain. Neil wiped his sleeve over his spectacles, momentarily clearing them enough to make out his expression. It was softened with a note of grudging approval.

In the shelter of the cavern, the Adrija embraced each other with a laugh of relief. A few of them shot looks of mingled surprise and wariness at Neil.

He pulled a handkerchief from his pocket with a shaking hand, managing to wrap it around Dyrnwyn's hilt. The sword snuffed out, plunging the camp back into thick orange shadows.

Neil's spectacles were worse than useless. He tugged them off and shoved them into his pocket. He squinted back out at the forest, half afraid he would see the tiger staring back at him.

The trees remained dark and still.

The branch on the ground by his boots caught his eye. The length of strong green wood was as long as Neil's arm and perhaps an inch thick in diameter, thickly covered with leaves.

The end was cut cleanly, as though severed by a razor—if razors could slice through a solid inch of strong green wood.

Strange, Neil thought with a queasy uncertainty.

"Neil," Constance called softly.

He turned to where she waited under the overhang, holding out his scabbard. Neil joined her there and took it with a still-unsteady hand. He sheathed the blade.

Relief washed over him alongside a shaking sense of delayed terror. "It might have pounced on me. Or pushed past me into the camp. I just put myself in the way of all the men who knew what they were doing. I—"

Constance set her hand on his arm. At the warmth of her touch through the wet fabric of his shirt, Neil's words evaporated.

"That was very well done," she declared softly.

Neil had no idea how to respond, locked in the steady warmth of her gold-touched eyes.

As her look lingered, the tenor of it shifted in a way that sent an odd tingle dancing over Neil's skin.

Or maybe that was just his bad vision.

Definitely his vision, Neil thought firmly.

"Back to sleep, both of you," Subhas warned. "We have a long day ahead of us—and I expect you to keep up."

"Yes, sir," Neil replied automatically.

"Sir?" Subhas echoed dryly—then clapped him on the shoulder and laughed as he walked away.

TWENTY-SEVEN

$\mathcal{D}$R. NEIL FAIRFAX looked different as Constance descended the slope into the broad green valley with Subhas and the Adrija. Nothing had actually changed about Neil. He was still good old Stuffy, dressed in a slightly-worse-for-wear shirt and a brown waistcoat. The scabbard for Dyrnwyn was strapped across his back, and his spectacles were firmly in place. But Constance's eyes hitched against the sculpted line of his forearm under the rolled-up sleeve of his shirt as he rubbed at the sweat that lightly glistened on the nape of his neck.

She vividly recalled how Neil had looked the night before, standing in the downpour with his sword burning in his hands as he confronted the most beautiful monster she'd ever seen. His soaked shirt had clung to his movements, eloquently displaying every line of his torso. His long, sensitive hands—made for lovingly turning through the pages of old books—had gripped the bone hilt of the flaming sword as his jaw tensed with both fear and a fierce determination.

The man had admittedly always been attractive. Even as Ellie's scrawny older brother, there'd been something appealing about the perfect cut of his cheekbones and the way his over-serious eyes mingled hues of brown and forest green.

When Constance had finally run into Neil again as an adult, she'd been surprised to see how well he'd filled out. When she'd landed on him in the thieves' tunnel in Saqqara, feeling the firm plane of his chest under his jacket had even sparked the notion that she might make use of good old Stuffy in her plan to sow a few wild oats before settling down to a respectable marriage.

Since then, Constance hadn't been shy about making a healthy, red-blooded study of Neil's charms when the opportunity presented itself. And why shouldn't she take a moment to appreciate Neil's assets when they were on display rather than buttoned up under layers of tweed? She considered herself a connoisseur of the well-formed male physique.

She might even have indulged in musing over what it might feel like to grab hold of his perpetually disheveled hair and drag him down for a kiss.

All of that had been perfectly harmless—nothing one wouldn't expect between friends who happened to be reasonably attractive.

What had been racing through Constance's brain since last night felt somewhat less harmless. The sight of Neil facing down that tiger with his flaming sword in spite of a very deep natural aversion to danger had *done things* to her.

Things that did not seem to be easy to undo.

She was having *notions*.

It had taken an act of sheer will for Constance to hand Neil back his scabbard without dragging the man down to the floor with her. She'd had to fight to resist running her hands over his chest when he'd stripped off his soaked shirt to hang it up to dry. As she had finally lain down on her blanket beside him and tried to go back to sleep, she had been tormented by thoughts of climbing onto Neil to kiss him senseless.

She was having the bloody notions again right now, and all Neil had done was pause to take a swig from his canteen.

Subhas stood right beside him, bare-chested and frowning—a look that undeniably suited the Adrija law student very nicely. Constance would normally have made a point of stopping to appreciate that sort of thing.

She barely spared him a glance. Her attention was locked on Neil's Adam's apple as it bobbed against the pale column of his throat with his swallow. She was suffused with the urge to rise up on the toes of her boots and lick it.

Constance had always admired Neil. Even when they were children and she'd made it her purpose to find ways to rile him up, she'd been mostly motivated by the fact that he was just so terribly clever. It made winning his attention away from his piles of books—even his mortified or exasperated attention—feel like a boon.

Her respect for him had only grown since they'd become reacquainted. Neil had grown into an exceptional man. He was far from perfect—he'd done some absolutely infuriating things in the brief weeks since they'd become reacquainted—but he wasn't afraid to admit it, and he genuinely worked to do better. He listened. He thought about things. He *cared*.

There was nothing respectful about the way Constance thought of him at the moment.

Everything would've been fine if not for that blasted tableau—Neil, all lean and scholarly and not at all the conventionally heroic type, standing in the rain as he faced down a gorgeous deadly beast with a mythical sword glowing in his hands. Constance was quite sure the image would be emblazoned in her mind till her last breath. How could it not?

It was no wonder she was having lustful thoughts. If she hadn't been, someone ought to check her pulse.

Constance definitely had a pulse.

What she needed—rather urgently, it would seem—was to find a way to settle things back to normal. She could hardly run around consumed by the urge to lick Neil's Adam's apple, could she?

There must be a way for her to exorcise these demons and get back to the comfortably abstract desire she'd enjoyed for the last several weeks.

Thankfully, Constance had a plan for that—one that she intended to execute just as soon as the opportunity presented itself.

She was looking forward to it.

A short distance later, Constance pushed through the brush to reveal a carved stone archway that towered over her between the trees.

Neil gripped her arm as he stared up at it. "It's a torana—a ceremonial gateway! Connie, there's a torana here!"

His hand was hot on her skin through the thin fabric of her blouse.

"Look at the fluting on those columns!" Neil rambled on. "If that's not Persian, I don't know what would be. I knew there must be some Achaemenid influence on later Indian architecture!"

He could lift me up against that ceremonial gateway and kiss me senseless, Constance thought distractedly.

She scowled with frustration. This was intolerable. "It's a very nice torana, Stuffy."

"Henduko, Abbaya. Kōnja!" Jignesh exclaimed cheerfully.

Constance plucked Neil's too-distracting hand from her arm. "Kōnja?"

"It's our clan name," Subhas replied, mildly amused. "It means 'monkey.' They're on the arch."

She realized that the weathered carvings on the stones weren't just ornamental decoration. Lanky limbs and curving tails wove through depictions of thick leafy vines heavy with fruit.

"It really is Kishkindha!" Constance burst out excitedly.

"Kishkindha?" Neil echoed distractedly, still studying the torana.

"The monkey kingdom? Hanuman's home?" Constance pressed.

"Kishkindha's a myth," Neil replied automatically. "Monkeys don't have a kingdom."

"I know they don't have a literal kingdom, Stuffy," Constance retorted impatiently. "But they're all over the stonework!"

"Animal motifs appear frequently in early Indian art and architecture." Neil bent over the base of the archway. "I wonder how deeply these foundation stones are buried."

Constance hauled him up by the back of his waistcoat and forced him to face the arch. She jabbed a finger toward the stone simians.

"*Let his midday shadow point you to the ruins of the most loyal kingdom.* That's Kishkindha—the monkeys were Rama's fiercest allies. And now we are staring at an archway covered in monkeys!"

Neil's eyes widened. "Oh!"

"Are we going in?" Subhas prompted.

The rest of his men lingered around him with varying expressions of amusement and impatience.

"Of course, we are." Constance reached back and grasped Neil's hand… which was a perfectly friendly thing to do.

His long fingers instinctively wrapped around her own, the heat of his palm warming her skin.

Constance suppressed a shiver.

Neil looked down at their clasped hands with a blink of surprise.

"Come on, Stuffy," she ordered and dragged him through the gateway.

To Constance's eyes, the ruins that followed were slightly disappointing. She had been hoping for towering palaces draped with vines, hiding secret chambers packed with treasure. Instead, tumbled piles of stone grew plucky flowers. The structures that did remain intact weren't very large, consisting of maybe a room or two across a single story.

She bit back a sigh of disappointment.

Meanwhile, Neil exploded with excitement.

"Look at these holes in the paving stones! I'd bet my left foot a substantial wooden structure stood on this terrace." He whirled, pointing to a few rocky squares in the ground. "And these are likely residential structures, based on their size, or maybe storerooms for the temple precinct!"

He pressed forward, hurrying through the ruins.

The trees parted to reveal the column they had glimpsed through the canopy the day before. The scale of it was even more impressive up close. Pale gold stone gleamed in the sunlight that filtered down through the trees.

Neil gaped at it with an air of astonished wonder. "The high gloss of the Mauryan-era stone polishing techniques... The lack of any base adornment..."

His eyes sparked greener with excitement as he whirled to grab Constance by the shoulders. "Connie, this is an Ashoka Pillar!"

Constance reeled from the unexpected contact.

He released her a moment later, circling the monument as he kept rambling. "Ashoka raised these after his conquest of Kalinga, when his guilt over the slaughter of the war prompted him to convert to Buddhism. Which means that somewhere on here, there's going to be..."

He jabbed a finger at the towering shaft of stone, voice rising with elation. "An inscription! In Brahmi script! Can anyone here read Brahmi?"

He looked hopefully to Subhas.

"No," Subhas replied dryly.

Neil visibly slumped with disappointment.

"I thought you didn't know anything about Indian archaeology," Constance accused.

"I don't," Neil replied. "I've only picked up a few things here and there over the years."

"Like Mauryan stone-polishing techniques?"

"Yes?" Neil appeared confused by her wry tone.

The man honestly had no idea. Constance wondered what level of knowledge it would take for Neil to consider himself reasonably well-informed on a topic.

Subhas shook his head.

Neil traced his fingers reverently over the script on the column. "The other structures aren't Mauryan. I'd estimate they date from the eleventh or twelfth century, along with the torana. The presence of the Ashoka Pillar indicates this was originally a Buddhist site, but I suspect it was resettled by Hindus sometime after its initial abandonment." He clambered over to a jumbled pile of rocks nearby. "I wonder if there's evidence of the earlier Buddhist structures in the foundation stones."

"Watch out for pit vipers," Subhas commented mildly.

"Wait—what?" Neil danced back from the ruins as if expecting a snake to strike from behind them at any moment. "Are there pit vipers here?"

Subhas's eyes glinted wickedly. "Keep jumping around in the rocks where they like to hide, and I suppose we'll find out."

Neil went pale.

Constance shot Subhas a glare.

Subhas answered it with a wink. "Let's go find your waters. Jignesh! Ziju aanaha!"

"Waters?" Neil contemplated his beloved foundation stones as though torn between the urge to clamber over them and a natural aversion to being bitten by a deadly snake.

"The Waters of the Son of the Wind?" Constance reminded him. "You know—from Tulsidas's clues?"

"But... the foundation stones..." Neil cast a mournful gaze back at the jumbled rocks.

Constance hooked a hand through his arm and dragged him from the pillar. "The rocks will wait for you, Stuffy."

TWENTY-EIGHT

*A*DAM WAS IN hell.

"So then I told him—that shows what you know about Herodotus!" Dawson continued. "And yet that blasted journal published his paper instead of mine—a clear instance of favoritism if I have ever seen it."

"Uh-huh," Adam vaguely agreed.

They had been hiking for hours through the towering forest that covered the rising slope of the ridge. The heat of the day was thick and humid despite the haze overhead. Lizards darted through the undergrowth while birds flitted between soaring trees where flowers hung heavily from fragrant branches.

Subedar Singh Rao had broken up the camp while the sky was still gray with dawn, setting a hard pace. None of the men complained. Adam suspected that had more to do with Singh Rao's leadership than any general respect for Borthwick.

They had reached the Shiva stone on the ridge before noon, right where Adam had said they would find it.

When he'd blurted out the location of the landmark the night before, he'd been acting on desperate impulse, driven by the terror of what Borthwick's whip could do to Vanika. The consequences of that split-second decision had come home to him as the colonel studied the slender pillar of pale stone that pierced the distant canopy below their perch.

Adam was leading Borthwick straight to the damned astra.

"And that's why I make it a point to steer clear of mollusks," Dawson concluded authoritatively.

Dawson had glued himself to Adam's side like a barnacle on a pier. The guy was desperate for someone to talk at, and Adam was his best prospect now that the professor was convinced they were on the same side.

He'd been yammering the whole way up and down the damned mountain.

Ellie rode at the back of the line with the rest of the mules carrying the equipment. Adam hadn't tried to connect with her. There wouldn't have been any point. It wasn't as though they'd have any privacy for a chat with Dawson clinging to Adam like a burr on his shorts.

Normally, Adam would enjoy thinking of creative ways of getting rid of the man, but his hands were tied. He couldn't afford to disabuse Dawson of his belief that Adam had 'come to his senses' and sided with the Order of Albion, or he'd send his plan straight to hell.

Not that it was much of a plan.

Adam knew he'd have his best chance of getting Vanika out if he waited until after nightfall, but he'd messed things up good when he'd outed the girl's bluff the night before. When he had caught her eye briefly earlier that morning, she had treated him to a single glare before resolutely looking away. He needed to find a way to convince her that she could still trust him—without letting Jacobs know that Adam cared about her.

Fix things with the kid. Avoid Jacobs. Play nice with Dawson. Keep from rousing Borthwick's suspicions.

And hope the damned Brahmastra was far enough away to give him time to make his move.

Adam might've managed worse situations before… but not *much* worse.

"The climate here is truly terrible." Dawson wiped his sweating face with his handkerchief. "I don't know how the local people tolerate it. Perhaps they have different glands."

Adam moderated his tone by sheer force of will. "Pretty sure we've all got the same glands."

Jacobs glanced back at them from further up the line. His mouth stretched into a slightly gloating smile.

The man clearly meant to make Adam's life as difficult as possible. Adam had to admire the Machiavellian skill in the way he'd found to do it.

"And I have broken out in a rash in four different places!" Dawson whined.

Adam could've escaped from Dawson—if he'd walked with Borthwick. Dawson was as wary of the colonel as a kicked dog. If Adam caught up to the spy chief, Dawson would finally leave him alone.

But to do it, Adam would have to slip into that other skin again—the one he'd worn back in San Francisco. The notion made him feel like he was standing on the edge of a cliff. His palms slicked with sweat as his pulse jacked up, and he fought the urge to either punch something or run away.

No—he wouldn't go back to that again if he could possibly avoid it. Even if that meant putting up with Dawson.

Adam just hoped he could manage it without kicking the man down the mountain.

"So then I said—that's what you *might* think… if you didn't know the first thing about Phoenicians!" Dawson finished triumphantly.

Singh Rao's deep, steady voice cut through Dawson's rambling. "Mr. Bates."

The subedar was equal to Adam in height, his features elegantly stern over his well-groomed beard. His shoulders were broad and fit under his khaki uniform. The blade on his belt wasn't military issue. Adam guessed it was ceremonial in purpose, perhaps related to his Sikh faith.

"Apologies for interrupting. If I might speak with you for a moment?" Singh Rao's request was smoothly courteous in a way that made it impossible to refuse.

Dawson opened his mouth to try anyway.

"Of course," Adam offered quickly. He forced himself to give Dawson an apologetic look. "We can keep talking later."

Adam tried not to let it sound like a prison sentence.

Singh Rao motioned for Adam to join him, and the two men used their longer pace to leave Dawson behind.

Adam could feel the professor's annoyed glare on his back.

He felt an involuntary burst of gratitude toward the Sikh officer—not that he believed Singh Rao had done any of this for Adam's benefit.

Singh Rao's question was tactfully phrased. "You and the professor are… friends?"

"Something like that," Adam muttered. "What'd you want to talk to me about?"

The subedar's gaze was quietly assessing. "You wanted to intervene in the tent yesterday when the colonel threatened the girl."

Adam's pulse kicked up along with his sense of threat. He wondered if he had just walked into a trap.

He briefly considered whether he could fight his way out and quickly dismissed the idea. He wasn't sure he could take on Singh Rao even if they hadn't been surrounded by his soldiers. The man exuded strength and competence.

His mind whirled desperately as he tried to think of how to respond. The answer came to him from somewhere else—his gut.

Which had always done a better job of steering him right anyway.

Tell the man the truth.

Adam forced himself to meet the officer's gaze. "That a problem?"

Singh Rao didn't answer.

Borthwick glanced back from ahead of them. His eyes stopped on Adam for a breath, then moved on, unconcerned.

The subedar hadn't pulled Adam aside for an interrogation. They were walking amid the other soldiers. From where Borthwick stood, it probably looked like the pair of them had just ended up in the same part of the line.

Had Singh Rao done that because he didn't want Borthwick to notice that they were talking?

Singh Rao studied the line of men marching in front of them as he spoke. "I am an officer of the Indian Army. I took an oath to be loyal to the crown and to follow orders. I take my oaths very seriously, Mr. Bates."

"I don't doubt that," Adam replied—and found that he meant it.

Singh Rao paused as the trail climbed a steep ladder of stone. "That does not mean I always agree with those orders."

Surprised understanding hitched in Adam's chest. "You didn't like what he was doing."

Singh Rao's words were careful. "I did not like what he was doing."

"Would you have stopped me?" Adam pressed.

He was following his damned gut again… which was telling him, strongly and against all common sense, that this man was not his enemy.

"Yes," Singh Rao replied flatly.

Adam took a bigger risk. "And what if they come into conflict? Your oath to protect the crown—and your orders?"

"That would be a very unusual circumstance," Singh Rao returned deliberately. "One that I should not expect to meet on this expedition."

Adam heard the warning that lay between the subedar's words.

Borthwick was Singh Rao's commanding officer, and the bar for betraying that—and subjecting himself to a potential court-martial—was going to be pretty damned high.

Singh Rao might not personally agree with Borthwick's methods or his mission, but he wouldn't move against it.

Not unless things got very damned *unusual.*

Singh Rao nodded. "Mr. Bates."

"Subedar," Adam returned—and watched the man walk away.

As they crested the ridge once again, Singh Rao signaled to his men with crisp gestures, and low whispers moved down the line. The sepoys readied their rifles, slipping between the thinning trees until they reached the top. Once there, they crept forward through the sparse grasses and low brush until they reached the place where the mountain fell away steeply in the remnants of an old landslide.

The mules lingered behind a little further down the slope. Ellie dismounted and joined Adam where he stood at a nice, healthy distance from the drop.

He noticed the slight hitch in her pace. "How's the leg?"

"A little sore, but nothing more than that. I don't see why I have to be stuck in the back with the luggage. I'm perfectly capable of walking."

"I'm sure you'll be running around looking for things to blow up before you know it," Adam quipped.

Ellie's eyes twinkled before sobering. "Are you managing all right?"

Adam didn't pretend to misunderstand. "I'm managing. Hell, we might even make it out of this, if things can just stay moderately predictable for the next few hours."

Borthwick's voice cut to them from across the ridge. "Bates!"

Adam stiffened with a snap of dread as Borthwick motioned to him from where he lay at the edge of the cliff.

Ellie's mouth tightened with worry. "Are you sure that's a good idea?"

"I'll be fine," Adam assured her.

"Will you?" Ellie countered skeptically, looking from Adam to the cliff.

Adam sighed and rubbed a tired hand over his face. "Gonna have to be."

He steeled himself and walked over. His brain began to protest as soon as he came within a few paces of where the ridge sheared away.

Green, thickly forested valley sprawled below him, pierced by the pale finger of the pillar he'd seen from the Shiva stone. The monument was much closer now.

Adam dropped to his knees as the view went a little tippy. He supposed it was a good thing that he was clearly meant to crawl sneakily forward to where Borthwick crouched beside Singh Rao. If he had stayed on his feet, he probably would've fallen over.

Just don't look down, he told himself as he reached the edge… not that he could really avoid it. There was nothing *but* down in front of him.

Borthwick extended a leather-wrapped telescope to Adam. "What do you see?"

Adam wondered whether facing a hundred-foot drop through the instrument would be less taxing on his fear of heights. Wouldn't the ground seem closer? Couldn't his brain just pretend he was actually down there?

He put the telescope to his eye and twisted the lenses to bring them into focus.

Adam's throat tightened with nausea. His brain was not going to pretend that he was down there.

He followed the line of the stone column down to its foundation, which was visible through a break in the canopy. The lens scanned over tumbled stones and a pale terrace.

A handful of roughly dressed figures moved past the glass, and Adam's gut twisted in a manner that had nothing to do with his altitude.

Had Borthwick seen it?

Of course, he had seen it.

"Looks like there are some people down there," Adam reported numbly.

"Natives," Borthwick elaborated. "I count roughly a dozen. Subedar?"

"The same," Singh Rao replied.

"Khond, presumably," Borthwick continued casually. "There are several villages a day's march from here, across the river."

Though the focus wasn't tight enough for Adam to make out the details of the faces below him, he found that he had absolutely no doubt what village they had come from.

"Should we regard them as hostile?" Singh Rao asked.

The question was briskly professional. Adam thought of the thirty armed, disciplined men behind him.

Someone else stepped into the steady circle of the lens, slightly blurred by the mild imperfections of the instrument.

Pale skin framed a brown waistcoat. Gold rims glinted around his eyes.

"They're always hostile," Borthwick pushed back easily as Adam stared down at the oblivious figure of his best friend. "Prepare the men for an engagement."

TWENTY-NINE

$\mathcal{W}$ILD FASCINATION MINGLED with an aching sense of regret as Neil moved through the ruined city. He ought to have been surveying all of it one square foot at a time, studying old road beds and looking for signs of agricultural manipulation of the landscape. Could he pick out remnants of civic infrastructure? Maybe a hint of a municipal water system?

A municipal water system would be deeply enticing.

The mossy structures were rich with the promise of all they could teach him about the people who had lived in this place centuries before. He picked out the distinctive foundation imprint of a granary. Another cluster of buildings likely indicated a family compound.

Those were normal, rational leaps of intuition for someone who had trained for over a decade in how to recognize the patterns of previous habitation.

Other leaps of intuition weren't quite so rational—like how Neil knew that lotus blossoms used to grow in the ruined artificial pond that stood beside an overgrown orchard.

He smelled sandalwood. Heard a woman's laugh carry to him on the breeze.

Neil told himself that it could all be his imagination, even as a chill danced up the skin of his arms.

He rubbed at the goosebumps—then whirled at a sound from behind him like the bark of a hoarse, angry duck.

A monkey perched on one of the nearby branches. It coughed at him again, glaring with irritation from a small black face surrounded by soft gray fur.

Constance's eyes widened with delight. "He's adorable!"

She and Neil were alone on an overgrown road. Subhas's men had spread out to cover the rest of the ruins.

"I believe he's trying to threaten us," Neil theorized uncomfortably.

"Do you have any snacks in your pockets?" Constance pressed, ignoring his concern. "I want to make friends."

The langur snorted, then swung away through the leaves.

Neil glimpsed a flash of mossy gray stone through the shifting branches. He pushed through the brush and found himself in front of a simple one-story structure roughly the size of a carriage house, flat-roofed and fronted by a low portico.

Rich vegetation sprawled up the sides of the building, obscuring much of the carvings that decorated the stone facade. Sal trees grew thickly to either side, the air scented with their blooms.

The monkey sat on top of the entrance, flicking its tail with disapproval.

"Stuffy, there are more monkeys here."

Neil hurriedly searched the trees around him with a jolt of nerves at the notion of running into an entire troop of irritable simians.

"Not there—on the building!" Constance corrected.

Neil peered past the foliage and realized that the small structure was decorated much like the torana, with loads of langurs gamboling and leaping across the surface of the stone.

Constance looked from the weathered bas-reliefs to the live animal glaring at them from above the portico. "I think he wants us to go in."

Neil assessed the entrance to the building with a twinge of unease. The interior was shadowed with gloom, obscuring whatever lay within—which couldn't be much.

"Aren't we supposed to be hunting for the Waters of the Son of the Wind?" he pushed back weakly, recalling the clues from the manuscript that had led them to the ruins.

The langur barked impatiently and sprang away.

Constance strolled inside.

Neil hurried after her with a dart of alarm. "Connie, you shouldn't enter these structures until they've been properly assessed for stability…"

His words trailed off as he pushed through the gloom—and realized what lay on the other side.

Where the back wall should have been lay the opening to a stone-walled staircase that descended into a steep channel in the earth. Arched arcades braced the walls in cake-like layers. Green vines spilled down over the lip of the ground. Cool air wafted up strangely from the obscure depths ahead.

"It's so lovely!" Constance's voice was softly breathless as she gazed at the narrow, haunted descent.

Neil's mind spun with scholarly fascination. "But all of this is deliberate! Think of the pressure that must be pushing in on all of this at the soil levels—that's why they built all those arches. They're systematically designed to hold everything in place. Have you any idea the complexity of that sort of engineering? And all of this must have been designed nearly a thousand years ago!

"The engineering is very nice," Constance conceded. "But now let's see where it all goes."

She tugged him onto the stairs. Soft light alternated with deeper shadow as they passed under the stacked arches.

Moss clung to the walls. Small flowers and ferns grew tenaciously from the cracks in the mortar.

The heat of the day faded, replaced by a cool stillness that whispered of damp and smelled of ancient stone.

They passed under another tower of arcades, and Neil craned his neck back to see the layers climb four stories to the distant ground above.

"The calculations that must have been involved…" he wondered wistfully, itching for a theodolite and a measuring tape.

The stairwell fell into a tunnel carved through solid bedrock. Neil tore his attention from the marvels overhead to follow Constance inside. Gloom fell over him and then receded as the tunnel ended—and they reached their destination.

Neil found himself at the base of a shaft cut into the earth. It soared up to a distant square of light dimmed by the far green leaves of the trees. Galleries lined the space at each level, ornately carved pillars framing shadowy recesses carved into the stone.

At his feet, a few short steps led down to a landing that ringed a deep pool of still, green-tinted water.

Old readings burst back to life in Neil's brain, filling him with both recognition and a wild sense of wonder.

"Municipal water systems!" he burst out, his voice choked with excitement.

"What's that?" Constance frowned at him from where she was making her way around the lower gallery, examining the structure.

Neil waved his hand at the towering shaft. "It's a stepwell! We're standing in a stepwell!"

Constance's eyes flashed with amusement. "You're going to have to elaborate on that, Stuffy."

Neil quickly circled the pool as he craned his neck at the distant opening overhead. "They're meant to provide access to water during times of drought. Indians have been building them since ancient times, but I've never actually seen one before, only read about them."

A quick flapping sounded from behind him. Neil whirled toward it, nearly losing his footing and tumbling into the water. He managed to right himself as a sparrow darted out of the shadows of the gallery. The bird made a frantic circle of the well before disappearing between the pillars of the upper level.

Something about the shadows where the bird had emerged tugged at Neil's attention. He moved closer, and a figure emerged from the gloom.

Neil startled, his hand automatically flailing for his sword until he realized that he wasn't looking at an intruder but rather a shape carved from pale gray stone.

The statue was straight and still, its hands pressed together over its chest in a gesture of prayer. The stone form was decorated with carved beaded bracelets, armbands, and necklaces, but it was the distinctive features of its face that made Neil's eyes go wide with surprise. They reminded him of the irritable langur that had guided them to this place—with the wise gaze and rounded jaw of a monkey.

"Oh, it's Hanuman!" Constance darted over for a better look. "He must be here to mind the well. He's meant to be very devoted and courageous because of how loyal he was to Lord Rama."

Neil pulled up what he could recall about the god. He had been Rama's companion, as close as a brother to him, standing by his side and lending aid throughout Rama's quest to free his wife from the demon Ravana.

But Hanuman had also turned out to possess supernatural powers of his own, thanks to his unknown history as the…

"Son of the Wind!" Neil blurted out.

"Are you cursing?" Constance prodded.

"No…" Neil stammered. "I'm talking about Hanuman—in the Ramayana. It's some sort of divine conception, which is most likely a metaphor for—"

"Stuffy," Constance warned.

"Vayu, the wind god. That's Hanuman's father. He's the Son of the Wind."

"This is it, then!" Constance bounced with excitement. "The Waters of the Son of the Wind! This is where we'll find the next clue!"

"But what are we looking for?" Neil asked as he studied the softly gloomy hollow of the well. His voice sounded loud against the deep silence that surrounded the still green water.

"Someplace *where nobility of spirit is never untouchable.*"

"How on earth are we supposed to know what that means?" Neil grumbled.

Constance didn't answer. Instead, her gaze fell to Neil's shoulders—then drifted down his chest.

Neil glanced down at his shirt and waistcoat. They didn't appear any filthier than they had that morning. The shirt just clung to him more closely, slightly damp with the humidity.

"Is there something on my…" he began.

Constance's eyes jerked back up. She blinked at him innocently. "Hmm?"

A bizarre theory burst into Neil's mind. Had she just been *distracted* by him?

The idea was frankly ludicrous. Why would the fiercely gorgeous, blazingly confident Constance Tyrrell have been distracted by the sight of Neil Fairfax in a slightly sweaty shirt?

"I'll just look around," he hurriedly suggested.

"Good idea," Constance agreed. "Keep your eye out for any secret passages."

"Secret passages? What on earth would those even look like?"

"You'll know one when you see it," Constance assured him.

Neil slowly circled the gallery. The pillars were silent sentinels keeping watch over the still water. They framed a deeply shadowed recess cut out from the stone, likely intended as a place where visitors to the well could rest and cool off on hot summer days.

Constance poked her head into an opening cut into the wall on the far side. "I think I found the stairs to the upper level."

She ducked inside.

Neil started to follow her—and realized another doorway stood in the stone behind the Hanuman statue. He slipped around the god to peer inside, where he could barely make out a narrow alcove carved into the stone

"There's something here too, but I can't see it very well," he called up.

Constance stepped onto the gallery above him. "Stuffy, you have a flaming sword."

"Oh! Right."

Fighting back a now-habitual sense of unease, Neil drew Dyrnwyn from the scabbard on his back.

Cool, silent flames bloomed up its length.

Neil stood in a space a little bigger than a dressing room. A stone bench along the far wall suggested it might have been a more private retiring room, perhaps for members of the local nobility.

The walls were richly decorated with bas-relief carvings. Dyrnwyn's flames danced over a warrior fighting a pack of wolves, a crowned goddess riding a dolphin… and a couple tangled in a frankly erotic embrace.

Constance poked her head around Hanuman's form to peer inside. "See anything interesting?"

Neil dropped the sword, plunging them into gloom.

"You were upstairs," he blurted out desperately.

"Yes," Constance returned with exaggerated patience. "And then you told me you'd found a secret room."

"It's nothing," Neil asserted quickly. "Everything's fine."

He could just make out Constance's skeptically arched eyebrow in the gloom and felt himself start to sweat. "Not that it wouldn't be fine. It's just a closet. And then I dropped my sword. Because you surprised me."

"Are you going to pick it up again?" Constance asked with careful patience, shadow cloaking the details of her expression.

The bas-relief from the wall blazed through Neil's brain—of a woman's head turned back for a kiss while the fellow behind her lifted her leg and…

"Please no," he pleaded, and then winced. "I mean—I will. In a minute. After I… cool off."

"Uh-huh," Constance returned skeptically.

To Neil's infinite relief, she moved away.

He waited for her to step back out into the well, then yanked his handkerchief from his pocket and used it to safely retrieve Dyrnwyn, shoving it back into the scabbard.

Darting past Hanuman, he leaned against the wall and gave a shaking sigh of relief.

Constance studied the carvings on a pillar nearby. "Aren't some of these scenes from the Ramayana?"

Neil joined her as she moved between the columns, pointing out scenes from the famous story.

"The stringing of Shiva's bow," she listed. "The betrayal of Kaikeyi. Exile into the forest."

Her fingers brushed against the stone garments of a woman who lingered behind Rama at the edge of the trees, her body partially obscured by his own.

Constance named her. "Sita."

The uncertain note in her voice finally wrenched Neil's attention from his own mortification. "Why do you say it like that?"

Constance threw him a slightly rueful look. "Oh, it's nothing. Only that

I've always thought Sita was a bit useless. Letting her husband be exiled. Getting herself kidnapped. Sitting around waiting for him to come and rescue her. But…"

Her expression was uncharacteristically solemn in the soft, deep light of the well as she traced the lines of the thousand-year-old carvings. "Aai reminded me that there's always more to the story for women. Things we have to hide because the world isn't ready for everything that we really are."

Something tightened inside Neil's chest at her words.

He thought of all the things that Constance had to hide from the world. Her dreams of a life of adventure and purpose. Her courage and audacity. The part of her heritage that was woven into the marvel of engineering that surrounded him.

How much more might there be that he hadn't even discovered yet?

The degree to which she lived as her true self in the face of relentless opposition frankly awed him—and a new feeling unfurled inside of him in response.

It was bigger than awe, and Neil recognized that it was far more dangerous, even as he struggled to put a name to it. The feeling bloomed until he felt as though he would crack open if he didn't find a way to let it out. But what could he possibly say?

That he wanted to know everything—all the dreams and hopes and fears she kept hidden inside herself. That she was magnificent. That if the world was too small for her, it should get out of her bloody way.

And like that, the careful stories Neil had been telling himself for the last several weeks splintered, shivering away like the walls of Jericho falling to the cry of the trumpets. Destruction stripped him bare, leaving only a raw and undeniable truth in the place where his defenses had been.

One that he knew very well how to name.

She was an endless night in a labyrinthine library. A pyramid complex rife with secrets. A world that Neil wanted to explore in all its stunning depth until he lost himself inside of it.

This wasn't just lust. This was something else—something that electrified him with terror.

He was her *fake fiancée*. At some point in the not-so distant future, they would have to find a way to break that off—and where would that leave them? Could they possibly find some way to save their friendship in the face of that?

Two months ago, the notion of being Constance's friend would have sent him running for the hills in fear of having his site reports set on fire.

That friendship had become desperately important to him. It was still important—even if it had also grown dangerously complicated.

He knew Constance cared about him, but he was just Stuffy to her—Ellie's stick-in-the-mud brother with his nose stuck in books and his head full of dead languages.

And if he gave voice to this reeling, dizzying epiphany welling up inside of him, who would he be then?

Just another person demanding more from Constance than she wanted to give.

I can't, he thought desperately. *I won't.*

Constance had moved to one of the pillars beside Hanuman, oblivious to the tumult silently raging through Neil's heart. Her brow furrowed thoughtfully. "Hold on. Isn't this Shabari?"

"Shabari?" The word came out in a croak.

"Here—look."

She tugged him over by his sleeve. In the carvings on the column, Neil identified the figure of Rama by the noble lines of his face and the mala necklace draped over his bare chest. He could feel the hero's stoic endurance across the thousand years since the artist had set his chisel to the stone.

A woman knelt beside him, her face weathered with her advanced years. She held an offering out to Rama in humble hands, her head bowed with reverence.

Constance brushed her finger over the aged figure. "This one happened while he was on his quest to save Sita after she was kidnapped by Ravana. You can see Shabari here giving Rama berries, but Lakshmana tells Rama not to take them. He says the berries are tainted because Shabari had tasted them—she'd done that to make sure that she only gave him the ones that were sweetest. Only Rama accepts them anyway because they've been offered with love." She shook Neil's arm with excitement. "Neil, Shabari was a low-caste woman. She would have been considered…"

"Untouchable," Neil filled in. "*Where nobility of spirit is never untouchable.* You're right, Connie. You found it."

Constance frowned irritably. "Only I have poked all over this carving, and not one bit of it serves as a trigger to open a secret tunnel."

Subhas's voice sounded from behind them. "Secret tunnel?"

Neil turned to see the Adrija leader watching them wryly from the other side of the well.

"There aren't any secret tunnels," Constance complained. "But we did find the next clue."

Subhas circled the gallery to join them. He studied the carving thoughtfully. "It's damaged."

He was right. A fragment of the pillar had sheared off, lost to an ancient fault in the material. A pair of carved mountains framed whatever piece of the story had fallen away.

"Maybe the carving itself is the clue, telling us where to go next," Constance mused. "But does that mean the path to the astra isn't here anymore?"

"That might be for the best." Subhas met Neil's astonished look. "If the clue is gone, Borthwick can't find it. This artifact of yours could just stay hidden forever."

Subhas was probably right. Maybe it was for the best if the secret of the Brahmastra remained hidden forever... even if Neil's heart ached at the sense of a mystery only half unfolded.

A subtle sound broke through his thoughts, soft as a whisper.

Tap.

Neil looked up. The sparrow he had startled earlier was perched on the upper gallery. It blinked down at him, head cocked, and returned to pecking at the stone.

Tap. Tap. Tap.

The sound changed in Neil's awareness, shifting in tone and location.

He thought of tiny chips of stone dusting the ground at the base of the pillar. The notion was whimsical, entirely out of context with what was going on around him, but it struck him with a particular itching intensity... one that Neil was starting to recognize.

His gaze swung back to the carving of Rama and the Untouchable woman, snagging on the blank space above their heads where the pillar had been damaged.

The itch turned into a buzz like a hundred boxed-up bees.

"Something changed," Neil blurted.

The sparrow pecked at the upper gallery again. Neil heard the sound like the snap of a chisel against stone.

"What do you mean, Stuffy?" Constance prodded gently.

Neil stared helplessly at the pillar as the feeling grew stronger. "Something changed about the carving."

"Part of it fell off," Subhas reminded him with a hint of mischief.

"No," Neil bit back sharply. "Not that. Before."

Subhas arched a surprised brow.

Constance's eyes widened. "You're doing it right now, aren't you? Using your magic."

"I'm not… It isn't…" Neil twisted between his complete discomfort with the word and the undeniable truth that rang through him like a struck tuning fork.

The tapping echoed in his ears, hollow and relentless.

Neil gritted his teeth.

A warm hand closed over his own. He looked down, startled to see Constance's fingers entwined with his.

"It's all right, Neil," she softly assured him. "No one here is going to judge you for it."

He met her steady gaze and knew that at least part of that was true. Constance would never judge him for what he was. She'd soak it all up with curiosity, wonder, and a childlike excitement.

Subhas's expression was less reassuring, but his skepticism fell into a tired look of chagrin. "Just… do your thing."

Neil faced the missing piece of the carving. "I still don't know what that is, exactly."

"Try saying whatever comes into your head," Constance suggested.

How could that possibly be enough? It felt mad… but so was all of this.

Neil closed his eyes, opened his mouth, and let the words spill out.

"Bas-relief works in ancient India weren't painted the way they were in the Mediterranean regions. Sculptures like these were intended as devotional and teaching aids more than decor."

Blurting out the ephemera of years of random books and journal articles probably hadn't been what Constance had in mind—but she'd told him to say whatever popped into his brain.

Helpless and slightly desperate, Neil kept going. "The Ramayana was a religious tale meant to instill a sense of wonder at the power of the gods while also teaching the principles of dharma, or one's proper path in the universe, with Rama's actions serving as a model for righteous living. And there was something else between those mountains."

He stopped, thrown by his own words.

"What do you mean? What was between the mountains?" Constance prompted.

Subhas watched them thoughtfully.

Neil studied the two peaks that framed the missing piece of the carving. They were roughly but not precisely even in height, lower in profile like the rambling slopes of the ridge that framed the valley.

He shook his head, feeling dizzy.

Something between the mountains…

An image popped to life in his mind like a jack-in-the-box.

"Horns?" Neil burst out.

He felt like a lunatic… even as his instincts sang with recognition.

"Horns," he forced himself to say again as he followed the thread, the image burning more brightly inside his brain. "They're poking up out of the ground. Enormous, curving horns. Wait…" He caught himself, frowning. "It's not just horns. It's…"

The word that floated to his lips sent a chill over his skin.

"Bones," he finished awkwardly. "It's a valley of giant bones."

Subhas's face blanked with shock. He looked from the sheared piece of stone to Neil. "None of that is here."

Neil rubbed a tired hand over his face. "I know how it must sound."

"But you recognize it," Constance filled in cannily. "What Neil described—it's a real place, isn't it?"

Subhas's expression was tight as he nodded.

Neil reeled. Nothing on the pillar would have prompted him to intuit what once filled that broken space—and yet he had done it, drawing the truth from the blank stone.

"Where?" he rasped.

"It's not a place my people go," Subhas warned. "I haven't been to it myself, but those mountains in the carving—they're three miles to the southwest. There's a stream that runs between them. You can follow it to the pass that will take you there."

"Three miles?" Constance pressed eagerly. "We could be there by this afternoon!"

A response sounded from across the hollow air.

"How very convenient," Colonel Charles Borthwick commented as he stepped into the light.

THIRTY

$\mathcal{A}$DAM STARED INTO a secret world painted with streaks of filtered golden light, surrounded by soldiers and helpless with dread.

The stepwell was the sort of place he could imagine exploring for days, listening to Ellie ramble on about underground aquifers while she made him survey each arch and angle.

Adam wouldn't be doing any surveying now. Instead, he was watching everything go straight to hell.

Singh Rao had been the first to descend the ridge, slipping into the ruins with a hand-picked detachment. Adam had followed behind with Borthwick, Dawson, and Ellie. When they'd caught up to the advance force, they'd found themselves on the heels of a successful ambush, with Singh Rao's men guarding a dozen disarmed and battered Adrija.

Jignesh had been among them, his wrists bound. The wiry old hunter's eyes had flashed with recognition when Adam stepped into view, but he'd kept silent.

Seeing the Adrija caught had brought home how much more now depended upon Adam's ability to maintain his thin and uncomfortable set of lies.

When one of Singh Rao's men had reported hearing voices rise from an opening in the ground deeper in the ruins, Borthwick had left the Adrija under guard and navigated his way to the stairwell. Adam had joined them as they silently descended through the labyrinth of soaring arcades, fearing the worst—and then finding it. In the heart of the well, Borthwick's soldiers had fanned out along the gallery and pinned Subhas, Constance, and Neil with their rifles.

The clatter of cocking hammers echoed off the high walls and pillared galleries. Constance's hand froze at the pocket of her trousers, where Adam knew her knives were hidden at her thighs. Subhas's expression was grimly determined, but he made no move to reach for the antique Enfield slung over his shoulder.

Neil looked scared.

He should be scared. The place was a dead-end trap.

Ellie moved into view overhead, staring down into the well with an expression of terrible worry. Kalb hovered by her legs. The dog didn't look worried—but then, he probably just figured that Adam would solve the problem. Kalb had complete and abiding faith in the man who snuck him sausages.

Adam had no idea how to solve this.

Borthwick descended to the landing that framed the still pool of green water, pacing casually. "I was wondering whether you two would turn up again. I must say, I will appreciate the opportunity to find out who sent you here to try to steal my arcanum. And I'm sure you'll tell me, given the right degree of persuasion."

Borthwick's hand dropped to the coil of his whip, and Adam's skin went cold.

Of course, the colonel assumed that Neil and Constance must be working for someone who wanted the astra for themselves—a perfectly natural leap of logic for a secret policeman to make.

He'd peel the answer out of Neil's skin—and expose Constance's family to the full wrath of the Raj.

Blowing Adam's cover to hell in the process.

At the sound of Borthwick's coolly echoing words, Jacobs stepped to Ellie's side at the lip of the well.

He took in the scene below with a glance—and smiled.

New fear layered over the tension already twisting Adam's guts. Jacobs would like nothing more than to have Neil and Constance within his reach—giving him all the leverage he needed to force Adam and Ellie to bend to his will.

All of this was extraordinarily bad.

Borthwick was still talking.

"I'm sure we can make this all much easier if you'll agree to cooperate, Dr. Culpepper."

Adam frowned. *Culpepper?* What the hell was that about?

Neil's cheeks flushed with embarrassment. Constance looked a little smug.

Dawson's voice resounded irritably from Adam's back.

"Doctor *who?*"

Adam whirled like a man trying to stop a falling vase from breaking, but Dawson had already pushed past him. The professor stomped down to the edge of the pool and jabbed a self-righteous finger across the water to Neil.

"That man's not Culpepper. That is Dr. Neil Fairfax—though he hardly deserves the title. The man's grasp of Akkadian is absolutely wretched."

From above, Ellie made a choked sound as she bit back a protest—probably related to the abysmal quality of Dawson's own skills with ancient Semitic languages.

Adam felt the situation veer wildly out of his control.

In a moment, Borthwick was going to demand how Dawson knew Neil. The ginger twit would tell him—which would make it very damned obvious that Ellie and Adam hadn't just randomly happened upon Borthwick's expedition.

He was about to lose whatever slim chance he had of trying to talk his way out of this situation. He took a desperate step forward, flailing for a way to intervene.

His brain coughed up nothing. Dawson opened his big mouth to answer, and Adam ran out of time.

So he did what he did best and tossed the self-important ass into the water.

A subtle bump was all it took to send Dawson tumbling into the green pool with a splash that washed over the toes of Borthwick's boots. The professor rose a moment later with an astonished splutter as the soldiers all turned to stare.

Subhas used the distraction. Darting into the cover of one of the pillars, he whipped his Enfield from his shoulder and let off a shot.

The sepoys dove for cover and returned fire.

Constance grabbed Neil by the back of his waistcoat, hauling him into the shadow of a monkey-faced god. She whipped a dagger from her torn-out pocket and threw it at the first soldier who charged toward her.

The man ducked back, raising his rifle with new caution.

Adam read the odds. They weren't good. He readied himself to wade in, hoping a machete and lousy instinct for self-preservation might be enough to swing the balance.

Then he realized Dawson was drowning.

The professor's head had sunk below the surface of the pool, his hands flailing uselessly at the surface—because the damned fool couldn't swim.

"Hell," Adam bit out as guilt wrenched through him—and he dove into the water.

He snagged a handful of Dawson's coat as the professor continued to sink.

Dawson grabbed at him wildly, wrapping a desperate arm around Adam's face.

Adam sank too, murky water blinding him.

He wrenched himself free of the professor and gripped the man around the chest, kicking for safety. They burst through the surface, and Dawson gasped in a breath. He was still trying to climb Adam's body like a tree, and Adam fought to keep from sinking again.

"Take him, dammit!" he barked at a nearby sepoy, half choking on a mouthful of green water.

The soldier dropped his gun to dash forward and haul the professor from the pool. Dawson landed on the paving stones in a wheezing puddle.

Kalb barked overhead, and Adam ducked as a bullet whizzed past his face.

Soldiers ringed the gallery on both sides, using the pillars for cover as they worked to pin their enemies down. On the right, Singh Rao's men had figured out that Subhas had to reload between shots. They charged. Subhas swung the antique gun at them like a club, but the men overtook him, pinning him down.

Another pair of soldiers pushed in from the left, emboldened now that Constance was out of knives.

From behind the monkey god statue, Neil whipped out his sword. Flames burst up Dyrnwyn's length.

In the flare of light, Adam could just make out a dark opening hidden in the shadows of the wall at Neil's back.

Borthwick eyed the fiery blade with avaricious interest.

The sepoys regarded the weapon with a less eager hesitation.

"Don't just stand there!" Borthwick snapped. "It's only a bloody sword!"

The men rushed in from both sides.

Constance braced her back against the wall, planted her legs on the statue's rear end—and shoved.

Hanuman toppled from his platform. The massive stone figure rolled toward the soldiers, who stumbled back.

Then it crashed into the columns supporting the gallery.

The pillars burst into splinters, shards of rock flying like shrapnel. Adam flinched back, raising an arm to shield his face where he still floated in the water.

The dust hadn't settled when a deep, ominous crack echoed dully off the walls of the well. Adam looked up—and watched the columns of the upper gallery pop like firecrackers.

Hands grasped the back of his braces and hauled him out of the water, sliding him onto the stones like a beached fish. Singh Rao's face hovered over him.

"*Back!*" the subedar shouted with a furious wave toward the tunnel that led to the stairs.

The soldiers ran, shoving Subhas with them. Dawson hovered in their path, dripping wet and gaping as the floor of the upper gallery began to tilt.

Constance's face blanked with shock. Neil paled with horrified understanding—then grabbed her and threw her into the darkness behind them.

"Adam!" Ellie screamed from the top of the well, where Jacobs held her back with an arm around her waist.

Singh Rao yanked Adam to his feet, shoving him into the tunnel. Adam half fell into cover as a crash roared through the well.

Dust rolled over him like a cloud, choking his lungs. Adam coughed as he staggered back to his feet and spun to see what had happened.

The back half of the upper gallery had collapsed. A mountain of stone covered the place where Neil and Constance had been.

Adam pushed toward it, and Singh Rao caught his arm.

"Wait!" the subedar ordered, holding him back.

Adam's instinct was to fight, but before he could take a swing, another piece of the gallery fell, stone cracking against the floor of the well in an explosion of debris.

He forced himself to hold for a single, terrible breath as the rubble slowly settled, then wrenched himself free of Singh Rao's grip. Fear pounded through his chest as he skidded around the well to the broken heap of stone.

Neil had taken Constance toward the door Adam had glimpsed from his position in the well. Had they made it inside? Had anyone else seen that shadow-cloaked opening in the wall?

He had to think. He had to be careful, even as his heart screamed for him to start hauling away the stones and shouting to wake the dead.

Reveal nothing. Not the door. Not his connection to the people who might be trapped inside. Adam had to keep every advantage he could get—and pray it would be enough.

"Culpepper?" he called, his voice catching roughly on the false name as he waited desperately for an answer.

THIRTY-ONE

$\mathcal{N}$EIL LAY ON the ground beneath Constance in the near total darkness. At Adam's call, she felt his chest fill as he drew in a breath to respond.

She clamped her hands over his mouth, whispering quickly at his ear. "Careful!"

Neil's sword had gone out, tossed from his hand as they'd fallen into the narrow room carved into the rock at Hanuman's back. Dust still coated Constance's skin and hung thickly in the cool, still air.

A wall of rubble filled the space where the door had been. Whispers of light slipped through slim cracks near the top of the pile, providing just enough illumination for her to make out the ghostly circles of Neil's spectacles.

He nodded.

Constance climbed free of him and picked her way over to the wreckage of the upper gallery. She kept her voice to a low hiss through the tiny gaps in the debris.

"We're here! Everyone is fine—but don't tell them anything! Lead them off, and we'll dig our way out to come and find you!"

A sliver of Adam's jaw came into view as he moved his head closer to the cracks.

"Sure about that?" he murmured back, his lips barely moving.

Constance glanced back over her shoulder at Neil, who had climbed up from the floor. His face was dusty, pale, and distinctly nervous.

"Absolutely," she whispered back to Adam—ignoring the twinge of unease under her skin.

Borthwick's voice echoed down to her from farther away. "Mr. Bates?"

Adam's face disappeared as he moved away. "Nothing. I don't see any way they could have made it."

His voice was flat as though he were talking about the untimely demise of a pair of strangers.

Neil grasped Constance's arm, his grip tight with worry. "What about Jacobs?"

Constance felt a quick jolt of fear. She had forgotten that the man who loomed above them could tell when someone was lying.

She waited for him to intervene—for that smooth, cold voice to call out Adam's falsehood.

Jacobs said nothing.

"He needs Adam alive," she reasoned aloud, still close by Neil's side by the blocked door. "He can't say anything or he'll risk Borthwick deciding to shoot Adam on the spot."

Neil didn't look particularly reassured. Constance supposed that was fair. Their situation was admittedly a bit precarious.

Borthwick's voice took on a tinny edge as it filtered through to where Constance stood on her toes, pressing her ear to the gap in the rubble.

"Pity."

His clipped tone reminded Constance of what the colonel had said before about *persuading* her and Neil to reveal their secrets.

She felt queasy.

"Let's move on," Borthwick ordered. "I want us in that valley by sunset."

Relief washed over her, along with a flicker of hope.

Borthwick's next words tainted the feeling with unease.

"Mr. Singh Rao—I believe it might be prudent for Mr. Bates to have an escort for the remainder of our journey."

The officer answered with a note of hesitation. "Sir?

"The ground ahead is likely to be treacherous," Borthwick elaborated.

The response was tactful, but Constance had no doubt about his meaning. Adam's actions in the well had crossed the line into rousing Borthwick's suspicions.

He had just been put under guard—which admittedly made her situation a touch more complicated.

The stern Indian officer called out an order, and the crunch of boots on stone signaled that the soldiers were moving away. Still, she kept her hand on Neil's arm, warning him to silence. She kept it there until long after the last footsteps had faded.

Then she sprang into action. "Where's your sword? We need light to figure out how to dig our way out of here!"

Neil felt his way along the floor, and a moment later, flames bloomed up

Dyrnwyn's iron blade.

The room came to life—and Constance found herself staring at a massive slab of stone.

It was the floor of the upper gallery. The entire piece had hinged down to slam across the door to their chamber.

Constance's twinge of unease grew deeper as she faced it.

Neil looked queasy. "How are we supposed to dig through that?"

Constance smothered her growing fear with a forceful optimism. "Adam must have seen that this was here. He'll know to bring the necessary tools to break it up with him when they come back for us. Or perhaps Ellie can move it with a small explosion."

"When they come back for us," Neil echoed dully, staring at the rock.

"They'll find a way to get free of Borthwick," Constance insisted, willing herself to believe it. "We're perfectly fine in here in the meantime. There's air getting inside, and we're hardly going to starve in a day or two."

"We would die of dehydration before we starved." Neil let out a tight, nervous laugh. "I might die of dehydration inside a Somavamshi stepwell."

Alarm thrilled through Constance at his words. "There is really no reason to panic."

"Why would I be panicking?" Neil began to pace the narrow confines of the room, Dyrnwyn flaming in his hand. "We're only trapped inside a thousand-year-old closet waiting for our currently imprisoned friends to dig us out. What could possibly go wrong in that scenario?"

His voice hitched up at the end of the words as his breathing went tight.

Constance put her hands on his shoulders and pushed. "Sit. Now. And put your head between your knees."

Neil dropped to the ground and obeyed, still holding the sword awkwardly in front of him. He drew in a few shaking, uneven breaths.

Constance patted his back reassuringly. "We're going to be just fine. Your sister and your best friend are not going to leave us here, and they are both exceptionally resourceful people."

Neil lifted his head and ran a shaky hand through his disheveled, dust-streaked hair. "You're right. Of course, you're right."

"We just need to find a way to pass the time that doesn't involve contemplating our possible slow and painful deaths," Constance asserted.

Neil went a bit green. "Like what?"

Constance suddenly found herself more aware of everything around her—the light pall of dust on her skin. The cool stillness of the stone-scented air. The way Dyrnwyn's pale light flickered across the carvings that covered the walls.

"Now that you mention it, I might have an idea," she mused.

"Oh?" Neil pressed hopefully.

Her gaze traced the length of Neil's arm where he gripped the sword, following it up to the firm, straight line of his shoulders. Stubble lightly dusted the sharp angle of his jaw, and the arch of his cheekbone was scraped under the curve of his spectacles from their tumble into the carved room.

"It's just a little... *experiment* I've been considering."

Neil perked up. "What sort of experiment? Is it geological? Perhaps something related to hydrology?"

Constance stood up and held out a hand. Neil took it, and she levered him to his feet. He brought the sword with him, its dancing light bringing the carvings on the walls to life.

The maneuver put them in quite intimate proximity. Neil loomed over her. His shirt and waistcoat were scuffed with dust, one of his buttons lost at the collar.

She stood right at the level of his Adam's apple. "It's not related to hydrology."

Neil swallowed thickly. Electricity singed through Constance at the subtle movement in his throat. "Then what is the—er—subject matter?"

Beyond the gold frames of his spectacles, his eyes were touched with green and brown like a forest in riot.

Yes, she thought distantly. Her idea was really a stroke of genius—an eminently sensible solution to their problem.

"Kissing," she reasonably replied.

THIRTY-TWO

$\mathcal{E}$LLIE MARCHED TOWARD the waiting soldiers, her heart pounding in her chest. Jacobs' presence was a cold threat at her back.

Borthwick had gathered his forces around the small building that served as a gatehouse for the stepwell. Ellie quickly picked out Adam's figure among them. He wasn't bound and still had his machete, but two men stood at his back with rifles in their hands—leaving her with no illusions as to whether or not he had gone from a curiosity to a prisoner.

The colonel faced another captive, one whose hands had been lashed behind his back.

"Subhas Kōnja," Borthwick said smoothly. "I've had my eye on you for a while now. Always suspected you were something more than just a law student. Leading an armed band of revolutionaries against an official military expedition is certainly evidence enough to brand you a criminal—along with the rest of your village."

At his final words, Subhas's air of mutinous calm burst into fury. He pulled against the men who held him as Borthwick circled him like a newly caged tiger.

"These hill villages are like wasp nests, you see." Borthwick spoke as though for an audience, but Ellie wasn't sure who was meant to be listening. The milling sepoys, who didn't speak English? Singh Rao, who watched the proceedings with stoic silence?

Perhaps it was Adam, whose expression tightened with barely concealed disgust.

He had never been much of an actor. Ellie rather liked that about him.

Borthwick faced Subhas with distant contempt. "There's always violence seething under the surface."

Ellie recalled what a declaration of criminal status would mean for a

"

community like the Adrija—forced relocation and controlled movement as everyone's livelihoods and homes were stripped away from them.

Helpless fury washed through her.

Borthwick waved a dismissive hand. "Put him with the others."

The soldiers hauled Subhas away. He didn't struggle any longer, but his gaze found Ellie as he was taken, hard with determination and rebellion.

She read the promise in that look. Subhas wasn't done yet—and they were still in this together.

Ellie let herself be reassured by that, even if the odds were still increasingly overwhelming.

Everything had happened too fast.

The events in the stepwell had only taken minutes to unfold. Ellie had barely had time to realize that Neil and Constance were there before Dawson was tumbling into the well and the place started falling apart.

She knew that her brother and her best friend must be relatively safe. Adam wouldn't have casually reported them crushed if it had been true. He wouldn't have been capable of it.

Jacobs' lip had twitched with irritation at Adam's words—because he'd also known that Adam was lying.

In a terrible moment of tension, Ellie had waited to see whether Jacobs would call him out—but as much as he must have wanted Neil and Constance in his clutches, he'd known that exposing Adam's real motives would put all the control in Borthwick's hands.

Jacobs wasn't ready to risk that—not when he still needed them alive—but the situation was locked in a precarious state of balance that might easily tip into disaster.

The weight of that sat like lead in Ellie's gut right alongside her worry for Neil and Constance. She and Adam would have to find a way to go back for them, and soon—but she had no idea how they were going to do it.

There were too many people at risk. It felt like juggling fire.

Sitting by Ellie's boots, Kalb perked up his head as a soldier passed by munching dried rations. The dog made a low, grumbling whine of desire in the back of his throat.

Ellie glared down at him. "You have not been even remotely lucky."

Kalb wagged his tail at her, panting hopefully.

All of this would feel far less desperate if she had another ally, someone else in Borthwick's camp who might possibly lend them aid… or at least look away at the right moment.

There was one person here who might serve that purpose—if Ellie could convince him that loyalty to Borthwick wasn't really in his best interests.

Which meant that she needed to know what his interests were.

Ellie had already been itching for the answer to that question. She had been locked into a dance of violence for months, and she was done navigating it half-blind.

She sought out the place where Jacobs walked among the trees.

"Come on," Ellie ordered, firming with determination.

She stepped forward—but Kalb didn't follow. The dog froze instead, his attention fixed on a lightly quivering stand of brush.

Ellie recognized the special gleam in his eyes.

Oh no...

The shrubbery rustled, and Kalb bolted. Leaves shook furiously as the lanky golden-haired beast crashed through the growth after some small helpless animal.

"Kalb!" Ellie shouted uselessly after him.

One of the passing sepoys chuckled at her plight, calling over in sympathetic Punjabi.

"Yes, I know he'll bloody come back eventually," Ellie grumbled to herself in response.

She was torn. Should she try to go after him?

The blasted dog could run nearly forty miles an hour. She didn't stand a chance.

Leaving Kalb to his own ill-behaved devices, she set off after Jacobs.

She found him at the far edge of the makeshift camp, leaning against one of the ruined buildings and watching the soldiers with a disinterested glare. His black eyes flicked to Ellie as she arrived, cold and deeply unwelcoming. "Here to ask me to help your friends?"

The words were light, but Ellie could hear the threat in them. She refused to let it intimidate her. She was done playing games with this man.

She set her hands on her hips and glared at him. "Why are you here?"

His tone was smooth as he answered. "That's hardly a mystery, is it? I'm just a bloke doing his job."

"You aren't the sort of *bloke* who'd take a job that involves licking Borthwick's boots," Ellie countered.

His glare heated with a flash of temper. "Careful, *Eleanora.*"

The sound of her name on his lips made her shudder. It was meant to. Jacobs wanted her to leave.

Ellie stepped closer instead. "You're after justice. That means someone wronged you."

Something flashed behind the perfect control of his expression.

"Or maybe not you," Ellie deduced, her mind whirling with furious calculations as she read the dark nuance of his look. "Someone you cared about. A man like you doesn't have friends. Family, then. A sister? A mother?"

The anger in him sharpened at the sound of the word.

"It *was* your mother," Ellie spilled out with a burst of surprise.

Jacobs seethed with threat as he loomed over her. She might as well have been baiting a cobra—but she had to keep going. If Ellie could get to the heart of Jacobs' motivations, she might find the key to getting him to help her… help that could mean the difference between saving the Brahmastra and rescuing her friends.

She would solve this mystery, once and for all, using all the power of her reasoning to pry it from Jacobs, whether he liked it or not.

"You aren't a man who had the care of a loving parent," Ellie reasoned. "Whatever happened to your mother, it took her from your life a very long time ago—but you don't know who did it. You would have killed them already if you knew. You're trying to find out who it was—only you must have some idea, or you wouldn't know where to search. And where are you searching? British Honduras? Egypt?"

She read the rage on his face and knew she was pushing him—but it didn't matter. She wasn't going to stop. Not this time. Not until she'd learned what she needed to know.

"No. It isn't about the places the Order has sent you," she pressed. "It's the Order itself—who they are. What they can grant you."

More of the picture took form—and started to make sense.

"Your accent. The way Borthwick treats you. You were born poor. That's why the Order matters. There's one thing they can grant you that you can't find anywhere else—access to the upper echelons of society. They'll let you get closer because they need a tool—a weapon. You don't know who killed your mother… but you know he's powerful. That he's one of *them*."

A fragment of Ellie's other life tumbled into place, woven through with memories of purple sashes and wooden placards. The suffragists had advocated for more than just women's right to vote. Desperate people had been drawn to them, hoping that perhaps a group of ladies brave enough to go up against Parliament would be able to save them from threats more intimate and terrible than disenfranchisement.

Ellie recalled what she had learned from that experience with a wrenching burst of sympathy. "Most women are hurt by someone they love."

His face washed over with an uncharacteristically raw rage, and Ellie knew that she had gone too far.

Jacobs yanked her around the corner of the building, put his hand to her throat, and pinned her against the stones.

With a twitch of his fingers, his grip tightened.

Ellie couldn't breathe. Instinct took over, and she clawed at his hand where it held her.

His eyes were wild. She had stumbled into a secret that had shattered what little tolerance the man had left for her… and unleashed murder.

With an awkward rustle of leaves, Dawson stumbled around the corner of the building. He stared at Ellie and Jacobs like a startled deer.

For a moment, Ellie felt a desperate, irrational hope that he would intervene—that this weak-willed, self-absorbed man might actually do something to save her.

Dawson took a step back. "I didn't… That is…"

He turned and ran back into the trees.

A battle raged inside of Jacobs, fury wrenching against his iron habit of control. Ellie watched him pull himself back from the brink. It happened slowly, with immense effort, as the need for air consumed her, blackening the edges of her vision.

Jacobs slammed her violently against the ancient stones, and then let her go.

Ellie fell to her knees in the dead leaves at his feet, gasping rawly.

A storm roiled behind his eyes as he stared down at her. The control he had just regained had been hard won—and remained dangerously precarious.

Without another word, he turned and walked away.

Adam burst around the corner and dropped to the ground. "Ellie!"

She reached for him, and he pulled her into his arms, only vaguely conscious of the soldiers shouting at his back.

Rifles cocked, then went still as Singh Rao's authoritative voice called out an order. The sepoys moderated their pose, still wary but no longer actively threatening.

Her throat hurt. Her lungs burned. She could feel the quick thrum of Adam's heartbeat through his shirt as she clung to him.

"What happened? I saw Dawson running like a bat out of hell…" His gaze dropped to the red marks on Ellie's throat and darkened with low-burning fury. "Who was it?"

Singh Rao stood at Adam's back, taking in the scene with a frown.

Ellie grasped Adam's arm and gave it a warning squeeze. "It's nothing," she said quickly. "Everything is fine."

Adam's look was mutinous, but he wouldn't contradict Ellie in front of the subedar and his men. He helped her to her feet instead, keeping her at his side as he walked back to where the soldiers were assembling for their march.

Ellie picked out Jacobs stalking alone at the head of the line. Her muscles stiffened on instinct.

Adam felt it, and his hand tensed where he held her waist.

Ellie caught a handful of his shirt, anchoring him to her side. "It was my fault," she said quickly.

"Your *fault?*" Adam seethed incredulously.

"I pushed him into it," Ellie hurriedly explained. "I wanted to learn why he's here—and I think I succeeded."

Adam pulled Ellie out of the line of men. He whirled her around to face him, his eyes burning like blue fire. "Let's get one thing straight right now, Princess. Nobody gets to hurt you. *Nobody.*"

They weren't just words. They were a vow, one laced with danger and heat. A tension in Ellie loosened at the sound of it.

Singh Rao flashed them another wary look, and Adam guided her back into the march.

"You stay with me from here out," he ordered as they started to walk, his hand steady on the small of her back.

A knee-jerk instinct prompted Ellie to protest, but it quickly withered. Adam's words weren't about possession or control.

And she still remembered what it had felt like not to breathe.

"I will," she promised.

"Good," Adam bit back. "Because we're getting everybody out of this mess alive. *Everyone.* That clear?"

Ellie took in the stubborn set of his jaw with a soft glow of admiration. "It's clear."

At her warm tone, Adam cast her a rueful sideways look—and then led her on.

THIRTY-THREE

$\mathcal{N}$EIL STOOD IN the narrow, blocked-up chamber. Sword light flickered over the carvings on the walls.

He was fairly certain he had missed something. His brain was having trouble processing whatever Constance just said. Perhaps his ears were still ringing from the rock-fall.

"Sorry?" he asked.

Constance's reply was mildly exasperated. "I *said* I think we should try kissing each other."

His first thought was that it would be a terrible idea.

His second thought was that he very much wanted to do it.

Then his thoughts stuttered to a stop altogether.

Constance's gaze drifted over Neil like a caress. "It's only that I've been paying far too much attention to your Adam's apple lately. Among other things."

Neil swallowed thickly. Constance's eyes tracked the involuntary movement of his throat.

The look was *hungry*.

Neil started to sweat. "I'm, ah… I'm not quite sure that I…"

"It's just an experiment, Stuffy! You needn't go all pink at the ears about it."

Neil felt his ears go pink.

"But an experiment requires a hypothesis about a projected outcome," he protested.

Constance raised her hand to his shoulder. Her touch grazed over the fabric of his shirt. "Of course," she replied, clearly only half thinking about the words.

Neil's nerves sparked with a hissing, unruly awareness at the subtle movement of her touch.

"Then what's the hypothesis?" he asked, holding himself very still.

"Oh!" Constance returned vaguely as her fingers drifted over the line of Neil's bicep. "That it won't be particularly good."

Bolts of delicate fire burst across his skin at each point of contact. The distraction made him take an extra moment to process what she had said.

"Hold on—that it won't be good!?"

"We're friends, Stuffy." Constance's absent-minded exploration reached the exposed skin of Neil's forearm.

He couldn't move it. He was, after all, using it to hold a flaming sword.

Her touch blazed across his skin.

Friends.

She reached his hand and traced her fingers over the knuckles of his grip on the hilt of the blade.

"I suspect it will all be rather dull," Constance concluded.

"Dull?" Neil returned vaguely—and his mind flooded with visions of just how dull it would be.

Visions that had started the moment Constance had crashed into his tomb in Saqqara, lovely and dangerous and terrifying. Visions triggered when she irritably ordered him to undress in a cave at Gebel Tukh.

Visions sparked by the erotic carving on the wall of this very room—which was still right behind him, where Constance must certainly be able to see it if she troubled to look past his shoulder.

Please don't look past my shoulder, he thought desperately.

Not that it mattered. Neil was already lost.

Heat roared up, fierce and hungry. It blasted him with even more filthy, delicious visions. Of his hands in her hair. Of his mouth on her throat. Of her gasping his name as he pulled her legs around his waist and took her in a manner that had absolutely nothing to do with years of childhood torments and a softly burgeoning friendship based on shared history and surprising mutual respect.

His throat turned to sandpaper as any semblance of coherent thought fled from his brain.

She was still touching his hand.

Dull, he thought numbly.

It was a terrible idea. He couldn't kiss her. He *wanted* her. His desire for Constance was a raging, dangerous beast stalking him like a tiger in the rain.

"But what if it goes wrong?" he burst out desperately.

"If it isn't any good, then we'll know," Constance returned with a shrug.

She hadn't understood him. She thought he was afraid he wouldn't like it.

That was not remotely what Neil was afraid of.

Belatedly, his mind caught up with the rest of her words. "Wait. Know *what?*"

"Whether it's worth doing it again, silly."

Again.

The word made Neil dizzy.

Constance set her fingers against the flat surface of Neil's chest. With the slightest pressure, she propelled him backward until his spine bumped against the wall.

She stood close enough that the swell of her breasts under her blouse brushed against Neil's torso. The movement of her breath was an exquisite form of torture. His self-control fractured dangerously in response.

Her hand rose to the top of his shirt, where her fingers traced his collarbone, drawing trails of fire over his skin.

"We're trapped in a hole in the ground," he pointed out tightly.

"Obviously," Constance retorted.

"Shouldn't we be doing something more…"

He trailed off, at a loss for what word he had meant to say.

"We're just passing the time, Stuffy," Constance retorted. "Think of it like charades."

Nice, harmless charades.

This did not feel like charades.

Neil knew what he ought to do. He should remove her hand from his skin and gently set her back a step. It would only take a few words to straighten things out between them and return their relationship to its nice, safe status quo. Doing that would demonstrate respect for Constance's family, who had taken him into their home and their lives with a warm and easy welcome. It would honor her relationship with Neil's sister, whom he loved dearly and never wanted to hurt.

Constance would be disappointed. She would probably make his life miserable for a while in revenge for thwarting her whim, but it was clearly the sensible thing to do.

Neil had always preferred things to be sensible.

"Just a kiss," he blurted out.

Which was not the right answer at all.

Constance's mouth curved with wicked triumph. "I'm sure that will be sufficient."

He could do this, Neil thought distantly. It wasn't really that momentous.

It was just a kiss. Constance's experiment would be concluded, and they could go back to the way things had always been.

And for at least one brilliant moment in his life, Neil Fairfax would have known what it was like to touch her.

Almost like a real fiancée.

Not her lips, Neil thought in a last desperate attempt to retain his sanity. *Not yet.*

Constance's head came to the height of his chin. She had tilted it back to look at him, eyes sparkling with victory and anticipation.

Neil lowered his mouth to her cheek and brushed his lips over the silken curve of it.

He fought back ragged impulses as he drifted lower, tracing another kiss along the perfect line of her jaw.

Constance's hands rose to his shoulders as she pressed herself closer to him, generous curves melting against the harder surfaces of Neil's body—and setting every inch of him on fire.

He grazed over the sensitive skin at the base of her ear. The soft heat of a gasp brushed his throat.

The beast inside of him tugged more wildly at its leash.

Constance shivered in his grip—and then her pliant surprise shifted to a dangerous determination.

Her hand tangled in the cropped brown hair at the nape of his neck. "That doesn't count," she accused darkly... and took his mouth with her own.

Her lips delved hungrily. Her hands gripped his shoulders as she arched herself against him.

Want blasted through Neil like a hot wind, shattering the last vestiges of his self-control.

He used his greater strength to spin her around and press her against the wall instead. Then he plunged his fingers into the thick silk of her hair, tugged her head back, and devoured her.

His teeth grazed over her lower lip, tugging it before he moved in to catch the low groan that escaped from her throat in response. He dipped his tongue into her mouth, dancing it over her own.

She tasted like jasmine and nutmeg, honey and heat.

He wanted more.

He was only half aware of the flaming sword he still held in his hand. He slammed it into the wall to hold it out of the way. His mind vaguely registered that there was something odd about the blade's angle.

Neil brushed the irritating thought aside like a fly. He would rather not have been holding the damned thing at all. Then he could have put both of his hands on Constance. He *needed* them on her—but they also needed the light.

The last delicate tendrils of his moral decency slipped through his fingers. "Connie," he pleaded—and then forgot what he was begging for as Constance traced her tongue up the sensitive length of his throat. "*Dear God.*"

"I have been wanting to do that," Constance reported, gloating. "You know, you've almost got a bit of stubble back here."

She clarified by running her hand along the nascent beard roughening the edge of his jaw.

Neil groaned with a mix of mortification and lust, then kissed her again.

His free hand moved to her hip, feeling the strong curve of it under his grip as she fitted herself to him and explored his mouth with her tongue. It was like holding a river in his arms—power and suppleness, curves and strength.

Constance flexed against him in response to his touch, and friction exploded fireworks against the back of Neil's eyelids. His reason degraded to a strangled sound in the back of his throat.

He wanted the rest of her—all of it. Right there, in a Somavamshi stepwell where they were very possibly going to meet their doom.

And he was fairly certain she would jump at the suggestion.

Constance didn't give a damn about her virtue. She had frankly admitted to considering taking him as a lover in the past.

But you'd be ruining her, the rational angel on his shoulder reasonably pointed out.

Worth it, the devil in his trousers returned.

The war raged inside of him. Neil was momentarily consumed by it, teeth gritted with the effort it took to resist.

One thought, finally, rose above the others, fighting its way clear with an unexpected ferocity.

Not like this.

He took his hand from her hip and set it against the stone instead. "Connie…"

She paused at the desperation in his voice, her lips plump and red with kissing. Hair tumbled in abundant waves around her shoulders. Somehow she'd lost a pair of buttons, exposing the soft curve of the top of her breasts where they pressed up against the line of her corset.

Neil wanted to put his mouth there.

He tore his gaze from Constance's breasts, searching for anywhere else that he could look—anywhere that wouldn't end up with him reaching for the fasteners on her damnable trousers.

His eyes fell on the flaming sword in his hand—which had been driven several inches into the wall.

Neil's brain struggled to absorb it. How could the sword be in the wall?

The thought solidified, becoming stark.

The sword is in *the bloody wall.*

Panic sparked through him, and Neil let go of the hilt.

The temple plunged into complete, utter darkness.

He could feel the puff of Constance's surprised breath against the open collar of his shirt. In the darkness, her heat, her touch—the sound of her clothing sliding against her skin as she adjusted her position—were all amplified into an exquisite torture.

"Stuffy," she said carefully. "Why did you put out the light?"

Neil swallowed thickly. "I'll fix it."

He made himself reach out through the blackness. His hand remembered well enough where it needed to go. His fingers brushed against the bone hilt, and he made himself clasp it once again.

The sword flared back to life.

Constance's grip on his shoulder tightened. "Neil, why is your sword halfway through the wall?"

"It must have fallen into a… a seam in the rock."

Constance's eyes narrowed with suspicion. She disentangled herself from Neil's body to give the elaborately carved stone surface a better look. "There's no seam, Stuffy. There's only a slice in the middle of these carvings—right where your sword went in."

Neil's horrified thoughts shot back to a severed branch on the ground the night before—and earlier, to the slice in the column of the garden pavilion in Nandapur.

The three incidents wove together into a conclusion that held all the reasonableness of pure logic… except that it was impossible and entirely horrifying.

Neil took a half step away—which was as far as he could get without letting go of the hilt and losing the light again. "Ha ha ha. But that would be… You can't possibly be suggesting…"

"Pull it out," Constance ordered.

Neil was suddenly very uncomfortable with where this was going to lead.

He forced himself to draw back the sword.

It slid from the stone without a breath of friction. Neil stared at the flaming metal with a rising sense of horror.

Constance faced him with an air of unmitigated challenge and pointed to the wall. "Stick it back in. Someplace new."

Neil laughed nervously. "Connie, you can't possibly be suggesting…"

"Put the sword in the stone, Stuffy."

Neil didn't want to do it. But what possible reason could he give for refusing?

He slowly drove Dyrnwyn's flaming point forward. It slid into the surface as though the rock were made of butter.

Terror and dismay iced his veins.

"Well, that settles that," Constance concluded cheerfully. "Your sword can cut through stone."

"But that's impossible."

"You are doing it right now," Constance reasonably countered.

Neil yanked the blade from the wall.

Once again, it came out without a whisper of resistance. Where it had been, a perfect slice marred the space below a bas-relief carving of a set of dancers.

Constance looked dangerously thoughtful. "Have you tried cutting through anything else?"

"No!" Neil burst out quickly. "I mean, possibly it cut through part of a tree. But that was… It might simply have been…"

Constance's expression twisted with mingled horror and intrigue. "Could it cut through a person?"

Neil blanched. "I fervently hope that I never have any reason to find that out. But none of this makes any sense! Dyrnwyn is only supposed to flame! That's the story—when anyone well-born or worthy holds it, it lights on fire!"

"Aren't there other old stories about swords that can cut through anything they like?"

"Of course there are," Neil retorted automatically. "There's Durandal, the sword of Roland. And the Juuchi Yusamo of Muramasa. Tyrfing, the blade of Odin's grandson Svafrlami, was said to be able to—"

"Well, there you are," Constance concluded.

"But no one ever said anything like that about Dyrnwyn!"

Constance eyed him cannily. "Didn't you tell me once that the king who owned it kept offering it to people, only none of them wanted to take it because of the sword's great power?"

"Rhydderch the Generous," Neil mumbled uncomfortably.

"A sword that just lights up isn't really that intimidating—certainly not as scary as lopping off one of your own limbs with it by accident."

Neil still held the flaming sword in his hand. He froze. "That isn't helpful."

"I'm sure you aren't going to cut your own legs off," Constance quickly assured him. "It's not as though you're swinging the thing around in battles."

Neil fought for a way to refute Constance's confident theory. "If it's capable of slicing through anything it touches, why didn't it cut through my sword when Julian was fighting me with it back in Egypt?"

Constance smirked. "You must be more worthy than he was."

Neil's palm was sweating. His skin felt slick against the bone of the hilt. He would very much like to put the sword down and walk away from it forever. "But I'm not some mighty mythical warrior! I'm just a... a weak-kneed academic!"

Constance glared at him imperiously. "You are quite a bit more than that, Neil Fairfax."

Neil wanted to protest, but it wouldn't be fair to Constance. Her opinions mattered to him—even if they were opinions *about* him.

A question tinged with desperation came out instead. "What on earth am I supposed to do with it, Connie?"

Her gaze softened. "I think you'll know when you're ready." Her expression brightened with delighted inspiration. "But right now, you can use it to slice our way out of this room!"

"I can?"

Constance waved her hands at the pile of rubble that imprisoned them. "Stuffy—*it cuts through stone.*"

"Oh. *Oh!*" He stared at the flaming blade in his hand. For the first time, he saw it not just as an object of vague terror, but as something that might actually be *useful.*

Constance grasped his shoulders, turning him toward the slab of fallen gallery that blocked their way out. "Start from the top," she instructed authoritatively. "So there's less chance of the rest of the gallery coming down on top of us."

"What?!" Neil protested, his voice rising with alarm.

"Quickly, Stuffy!" Constance urged impatiently. "We have an astra to save!"

THIRTY-FOUR

$\mathcal{A}$DAM HIKED UP the pass under a sky turned to heavy gray lace by the soaring branches of old-growth teaks. Two rambling peaks framed his way while clusters of wildflowers and ferns whispered around his boots.

He was under armed guard. He had lost his dog. Two of his best friends were buried alive in a thousand-year-old stepwell.

All in all, he felt like hell.

His fear for Neil and Constance was only moderated by the strength of his determination to go back and dig them out. He wasn't bound, and he still had his knife. Both of those things helped his odds, but he also stood in the middle of a platoon of capable soldiers. If he tried to make a run for it now, he'd be shot down or tackled before he could take two steps.

He didn't doubt that he could find a way to get loose later. He just wasn't sure what he would have to leave behind when he did—or what staying alive in the meantime would cost him.

Ellie stayed close, clearly shaken by her encounter with Jacobs. Adam was shaken by it, too. He had always known the man was dangerous, but his attack on Ellie had felt like a different kind of violence—one that wasn't remotely purposeful or controlled like all the rest of his actions.

Ellie had said that she had been poking at the truth behind Jacobs' mysterious quest for justice. That she thought she had started to get close to it when he attacked her.

Adam guessed she was probably right.

Bruises darkened the skin of her throat. The sight of them made Adam want to hurt someone—not that he was in any position to do it. Instead, he was pretty sure he owed it to Dawson of all bloody people that Ellie hadn't actually been throttled to death.

Adam wasn't sure how to feel about that.

Dawson trudged along ahead of him. Every now and then, the professor cast a huffy glare over his shoulder. He obviously felt betrayed to discover that Adam hadn't really been his friend.

Adam didn't feel too bad about that.

Jacobs trailed behind. Adam tried not to look at him. If he did, he wasn't sure he'd be able to resist going back there to pummel the man—and then his situation would get even more damned complicated.

They neared the top of the pass, and Adam pulled his compass from his pocket.

It had been elegant once, a gentleman's accessory sheathed in gold and beautifully engraved. The gold was scratched and battered now. Rust showed at the hinges. Adam should have sold it off to a jeweler and bought himself something more practical a long time ago.

He still wasn't sure why he hadn't.

He flipped it open and stared at the inscription inside the lid.

To A. May you always know your path—GB

Adam pushed the words from his mind and focused on calculating their distance from the stepwell where Neil and Constance were waiting for a rescue.

Three miles. Thirty degrees southwest.

He snapped the compass shut.

An odd hiss rose through the whispering of the trees. The sound was familiar, though Adam failed to place it.

He scrambled up the last stretch of the climb and stared down into another world.

A deep, ragged gorge lay below him, framed by soaring cliffs of ocher stone. A massive silver curtain raced down the face of the steep bluff at the far end, feeding the turquoise waters of a quick-moving stream that curved through the base of the ravine.

The waterfall was alive with the flood of the monsoon. Flowering vines hung around the cascade, clinging to irregularities in the cliffs.

It was achingly beautiful... and decidedly strange. Dark openings peppered the walls of the gorge like the hives of some insect—except that they were Adam's size and clearly made by men. While some of the holes were simple ovals that almost looked natural, others were carved in rectangular lines, framed by false door jambs or shadowy colonnades.

"Rock-cut chambers," Ellie breathed with an air of numb wonder as she stopped beside him. "It's like the ruins at Udayagiri or Barabar. Probably a monastery or ashram. These should all lead to residential cells carved from the rock, interspersed with temple structures."

Her brain hauled up more details from her reading. "There's an ashram in the Ramayana—Valmiki's ashram. Sita is sent there after Rama exiles her from his court… but that was supposed to sit on the banks of the Ganges." She straightened, grasping Adam's arm. "Only Sita didn't stay there. Valmiki sent her to live with a group of female ascetics, somewhere secret and safe. That's what this must be. It's Sita's ashram. That's where Tulsidas has been taking us!"

At her words, a gust of wind ripe with the scent of a coming storm stirred the trees that crowned the ridge. The whisper of the leaves mingled with the sibilant rush of the waterfall.

"Great," Adam replied queasily.

Ellie looked disappointed by his response—until her eyes widened knowingly. "Oh. We are quite high up, aren't we?"

"Sss'fine," Adam assured her.

Ellie kept hold of his arm, her concern for his state warring with virulent curiosity. "But what's that all over the ground?"

"Bones," Adam replied.

Across the floor of the ravine, enormous skulls and massive ribs lay in tumbled piles, draped with moss and verdigris. A great tusk, thick as Adam's chest, pierced through the growth to point up at the roiling gray sky.

Adam had recognized the distinct shape and unique scale of the remains the moment he had spotted them. "They're elephants."

The animals must have been coming to this place for ages, drawn by the presence of water during times of drought or the gorge's relative insulation from predators. Ill, injured, or aged to exhaustion, they had lain down by the stream and died.

Adam thought of the stories he had heard about this forest—a place haunted by gods and monsters.

He recalled the word with an uncanny chill. *Rakshasas.*

The bones started to spin. Ellie firmed her grip on his arm as he swayed.

"We should probably get you off the ridge," she suggested pointedly.

"I'd rather go down on my boots than my face," Adam agreed.

She kept her hold on him as they descended the pass, trailed by his guards.

Singh Rao directed his men to a broad, sandy bank at the edge of the stream. The space was relatively flat and free of the undergrowth that sprawled through the rest of the floor of the gorge, tangling with the massive elephant bones. A red-hued cliff rose up behind the site, pockmarked with several of the man-made caverns.

Ellie studied the openings worriedly. "The Brahmastra must be here. We need to get back to Constance and Neil—but we can't just leave the arcanum for Borthwick to find."

Adam felt a bit steadier now that he was on the ground. He surveyed the irregular walls of ruddy stone. "There's gotta be nearly fifty of those caves. It'll take him a while to search them all, assuming whoever put the thing here didn't just leave it lying out in the open."

"But it *could* turn out to be in the first place he looks," Ellie countered, her voice aching with worry.

The weight of all Adam's responsibilities pressed down on him.

Armed guards stood at his back. A platoon of soldiers surrounded him. He was starting to lose track of how many people were depending on him—Ellie, Vanika, Constance, and Neil. Subhas and the rest of his men, who had been left bound and under guard by the ruins. The whole damned Adrija village that Borthwick intended to go after as soon as he'd gotten what he'd come for. Adam needed to do something about all of it, and yet he remained shackled by the need to keep meeting Borthwick's expectations.

"I don't have a plan, Princess," Adam confessed, his voice rough.

"Since when has that ever stopped you?" Ellie challenged.

Adam was thrown. When *had* it stopped him?

He'd been doing stupid things against overwhelming odds for most of his life. It came as naturally to him as swinging a machete or forgetting to change his socks. Hell, his father had spent years trying to batter the trait out of him.

Maybe for once in your life, you might actually stop and think before you do something stupid.

Ellie put her hand on his arm. The touch was gentle but firm, just like the look she gave him. "You told me when we got here that you'd have to be someone else in order to keep us both alive. And it worked, Adam… but maybe now it's time for you to be the man you really are again."

Her words made him feel like he was back on the ridge again. The world went into a slow, dizzy spin.

"Reckless and irresponsible?" he quipped back awkwardly.

Ellie didn't flinch. "Exactly. That's the Adam we need right now. *My* Adam."

Something inside Adam quietly shivered open. He felt it like a drop of rain on his skin or a lit window against the night.

Like hope.

Worry still lingered. "Ellie, we're outnumbered and under guard. The wrong move here could get us both killed. "

"We've been under guard before."

"Yeah—but this time, we don't have a couple of friends on hand to steal you my knife."

Ellie's eyes glinted with mischief. "You still have your knife."

"That's one knife against a whole lot of rifles."

"Is that really your biggest obstacle?" Ellie pressed knowingly.

Adam ran a hand over his face with an air of resigned exasperation. "No."

"Then what is?" Ellie's question was implacable.

Adam didn't search for the answer in his brain. He found it in his gut—where it had been waiting for him all along.

He looked across the camp to where a small, skinny figure sat on a boulder with a rifleman at her back.

"Vanika," Adam replied bluntly. "I'm not leaving here without her. And I broke any trust she might have had in me."

Ellie lifted her hand to his face. "Then go fix it."

The simplicity of her answer cut through the morass of uncertainty clogging up Adam's brain.

Go fix it.

There were legitimate reasons why he hadn't tried. He couldn't let Borthwick or Jacobs know that he had any interest in the girl. Staying away from her had been the pragmatic, reasonable thing to do.

But Adam knew that wasn't the whole truth. A wretched part of him had embraced the excuse because he had wanted to avoid talking to Vanika—because he was ashamed of what he'd done to her in Borthwick's tent.

He didn't *deserve* her trust after all that... but Ellie was right.

"Hell," he muttered under his breath. He cast a pointed look at Ellie. "I don't know where this is gonna go. Be ready."

Ellie cocked a playful eyebrow. "Aren't I always?"

Adam grinned back at her. The gesture was warm and familiar—and he wondered just how long it had been since he'd done it. "With a broken pencil and a bottle of third-rate hooch?"

"A bit of third-rate hooch would be handy at the moment," Ellie grumbled.

"There's still plenty of ethanol in that medical kit."

Ellie brightened with an air of wicked inspiration. "There is, isn't there?"

Adam's mad love for this woman glowed inside him like a sun. "Go get 'em, Princess."

Adam's two guards trailed him as he crossed the camp. Most of the men were setting up. Borthwick leaned over his folding desk with Singh Rao as they developed a plan for surveying the cliff chambers.

The colonel barely spared Adam a glance. As far as Borthwick was concerned, whatever problem Adam might pose had been resolved when he'd been put under guard.

Singh Rao was more careful, but the subedar didn't intervene as he watched Adam approach Vanika.

The girl stared at the ground, shoulders slumped and legs kicking listlessly. She looked like a lost, scared, twelve-year-old kid.

Because that's exactly what she was.

Adam's heart wrenched in his chest.

He risked everything by being here now, even though the steady rush of the waterfall at the end of the gorge would drown out their words to anyone who might actually understand them.

He decided he didn't care. He should've done this sooner, and to hell with the consequences.

"Hey," he said.

Vanika's head jerked up. Her eyes flared with recognition—and a mingled twist of hurt and fury.

The hurt gutted Adam most.

"Mind if I join you?" he asked.

"Yes," Vanika retorted.

Adam sat down next to her anyway.

Vanika scooted as far away as she could.

Adam let her. For the first time since he had come to this damned forest, he didn't feel like he was second-guessing himself, wondering how he was going to get it wrong.

"I owe you an apology," Adam confessed. "I thought if I pretended to be on Borthwick's side, I'd be able to keep you safe. Pretty sure that was the wrong move."

Vanika glared at him, cautious and defensive. "Pretending to be on his side was *my* idea."

"It was a good one. Might've even worked. But there's a guy here who can always tell when someone's lying. I'm not gonna tell you who," Adam warned as she opened her mouth to ask. "I don't want to catch his attention at the moment."

Vanika huffed with disapproval. "Why are you telling me all of this now?"

Adam studied the organized detachments of sepoys moving out to search the nearby caves. "Because I'm pretty sure things are about to go to hell around here, and I need to make sure you know we're still on the same side."

Vanika's eyes shimmered with angry tears. "You were going to let him whip me."

Adam forced himself not to flinch. "I wanted to take him down just for threatening it, but I thought it would be safer if I could find another way to stop him. *I would not have let him hurt you.*"

A tear carved a path over her cheek. Vanika dashed it away with a quick, defensive flick of her hand.

"I'm sorry for it—for all of it." Adam made the words a plea. "But I'm going to get you out of here. Just as soon as I come up with a plan."

"As soon as *you* come up with a plan?" Vanika countered tartly. "What makes you think that I don't already have one?"

Adam cocked an eyebrow. "Do you?"

He watched a rapid calculation take place behind the girl's sharp features as she studied the shape of the landscape and the relative positions of the soldiers.

Her gaze dropped to Adam's belt, and Vanika lifted her chin defiantly. "I need your enormous knife—and a distraction."

Adam's hand reflexively dropped to the hilt of his machete. "My knife. And a distraction."

"A good one," Vanika pushed back.

He could read the challenge in her eyes. This was a test—his chance to prove that he meant what he had said. "If I do that, will you promise me you'll get out of here?"

"No," Vanika retorted. "I'm going to free the Adrija."

"Absolutely not," Adam replied flatly.

Vanika pinned him with a glare. "Are you saying you don't think I can do it?"

"Borthwick left six armed men back there. How're you gonna overcome those guys with one knife?"

"I don't need to overcome the guards." Vanika's eyes glittered dangerously. "I just need to free my cousin."

Adam considered his brief but potent impression of Subhas Kōnja and wavered.

But he'd be sending a twelve-year-old kid into danger on her own.

"You still need to get your friends out of the well," Vanika pressed mercilessly.

"Yeah, but…"

"And you plan to try to stop that demon from getting Rama's weapon," she continued without waiting for him.

"Might've been considering it," Adam mumbled.

"You are not the only one here who can do things."

Hell, Adam thought ruefully. He couldn't ask for Vanika's trust without granting it to her in return.

The fierce, scrawny girl beside him waited for his response.

"Why do I feel like you're scolding me?" Adam complained.

She rolled her eyes. "Because I am. Now take your knife out and drop it into the grass."

Adam yanked the knife from his belt. He hesitated. "Will you at least promise me that you'll back off if it looks dangerous?"

"Are *you* going to back off if it looks dangerous?" Vanika pushed back.

"Probably not," Adam admitted.

Vanika waited.

Adam muttered a curse under his breath and let the knife go. The blade sank into the tall grass at the base of the boulder and disappeared.

He checked the camp to see if anyone had noticed. After a few suspicious looks when he had first sat down, the soldiers had gone back to ignoring them. Even Adam's guards didn't consider his conversation with a child to be much of a threat. They were watching their colleagues as though wishing they had a more interesting assignment.

He glanced past them to the far side of the camp—where a pair of black eyes studied him with coal-hard intensity.

And like that, the rest of Adam's plan snapped into place.

Not that it really qualified as a plan. It was more like a patently insane impulse—one that he'd likely reconsider if he stopped to think about it.

Good thing he didn't plan to stop.

Jacobs strode toward them through the soldiers.

Adam rose to his feet. "Here comes your distraction, kid," he muttered under his breath.

Vanika's eyes went wide as she looked from him to Jacobs.

Adam wasn't going to lie. As stupid as he knew this was… part of him was going to enjoy it.

Jacobs drew closer, and Adam stepped out to meet him.

Thick clouds roiled with silent threat above the valley of bones. Jacobs studied Vanika with cold interest where she sat on her boulder with a purposefully innocent expression.

"Not just here for the astra, are we?" he noted silkily. "That does simplify things."

Adam beat him to the words. "You're about to threaten to hurt the kid if Ellie and I don't walk away. Only that's not going to work out quite the way you think."

Jacobs tilted his head mockingly. "Isn't it?"

A handful of the nearby soldiers cast them curious glances, sensing tension.

That was a start. Adam needed more.

He pitched his voice to be heard across the camp. "Say that again to my face!"

Confusion flickered across Jacobs' features.

For one final moment, Adam pulled that other persona back around himself, dredging up every tattered fragment of the self-righteous sense of privilege he'd once had mercilessly drilled into him. He let it seethe through his voice as he stepped forward and drove his finger into Jacobs' chest. "The problem with you is that you keep forgetting your place."

The sepoys stopped what they were doing and stared.

Adam had been counting on that. Men on a long mission through the wilderness were bound to be starved for entertainment.

The nearest of the soldiers instinctively formed a loose circle, already sensing where this would go.

Jacobs stilled. "Whatever game you're playing, Bates, I don't think you're going to like how it turns out."

"Probably not," Adam agreed.

He yanked loose his belt and tossed it aside—hopefully before anyone noticed that the sheath hanging from it was already empty.

"No guns. No knives," Adam called out succinctly. "Just fists. Sound fair enough?"

It was Borthwick who answered, taking in the scene as he looked up from his map table. "I should say it does—even for a gutter rat like him."

Jacobs stiffened, hands twitching into fists.

"Well?" Borthwick prompted with an air of arrogant impatience.

Jacobs' fury was palpable. Adam could feel it through the air even from six feet away.

He'd made plenty of men mad before. Hell, he had something of a knack for it, even when he wasn't really trying... but he wasn't sure he'd ever made somebody quite *this* mad.

He had to give Borthwick credit for that.

Jacobs yanked a pistol from inside his jacket. For a moment, Adam wondered if his plan was about to go sideways in the form of a bullet to the head.

Jacobs threw the gun to the ground.

A switchblade from his pocket followed. Another knife fell from his sleeve.

He took out a third.

"How many of those things do you carry around?" Adam burst out in spite of himself.

Jacobs' eyes flashed with recollection of all the times he and Adam had clashed in the past. "Not enough."

He shrugged out of his coat and tossed it aside. His waistcoat followed, and he faced Adam from across the makeshift ring of sepoys, who were already passing around their bets.

Adam had never seen Jacobs in his shirtsleeves before. He was not surprised to discover that the man was as hard as a bloody rock—lean, lithe, and dangerous.

It made sense. He was a goddamned killer.

Adam was taller than Jacobs and heavier by a stone or so. It should have given him an advantage—but he'd fought Jacobs before. His opponent was taut and focused with a whipcord readiness. Adam wasn't even close to certain that he would come out on top of this.

Thankfully, he didn't have to.

Adam pictured the bruises around Ellie's throat and swung his fist at Jacobs' face. He felt the impact of his knuckles on bone.

Jacobs countered with a punch to Adam's gut.

Adam caught the motion just in time to ready himself for it, which saved his diaphragm from collapsing. He offered up a momentary burst of gratitude that he had managed to keep his breath—but Jacobs was still moving, fists jabbing with controlled power. Adam ducked one, shoving aside another. He made his own strike at Jacobs' side, but Jacobs stepped into it, robbing the momentum from the blow.

He grasped Adam's arm, wrenching it at an expert angle. The move forced Adam into a twist.

Adam pulled back, drawing on every ounce of his advantage in size and strength to stall the move. The hold shifted into a stalemate—and then Adam threw himself at Jacobs' body, knocking them both to the ground.

He was only vaguely aware of the cheering and catcalling of the soldiers that surrounded him. Borthwick watched the fight with an air of distant amusement. Dawson stared with horrified fascination, gaping at them open-mouthed from behind the colonel.

How long had it been since it had all started? The taunting, the disarming, the explosion into blows… had it taken three minutes? Four?

How much time did Vanika need?

Jacobs gripped Adam's jaw, forcing his head back until Adam's neck screamed in protest.

Adam slammed the heel of his hand into the crook of Jacob's elbow, buckling his hold.

The two men rolled free of each other, and Adam scrambled back to his feet. The ground was still damp from the previous night's rain. Sand clung to his trousers and the back of his shirt.

He took a slight consolation in the fact that Jacobs was just as disheveled. A bloody abrasion marred his cheek, and his knuckle was split. Half the buttons on his shirt had ripped loose, exposing a deep triangle of pale skin on his chest—and the smallest sliver of raven black that Adam recognized with surprise as a tattoo.

Adam pushed the distraction aside. He had to keep everyone watching. "That all you got?" he taunted—if a little breathlessly.

With a flash of vicious determination, Jacobs ran at him.

Adam twisted to avoid the full force of Jacobs' impact, but it still pushed him to the edge of the stream, where his boots splashed into the shallow water. He moved to counter with a punch, but Jacobs pivoted, and the blow glanced off his kidney. Adam knew from experience that the hit would still hurt like hell, but Jacobs weathered it with a soft grunt of discomfort.

He thrust his leg between Adam's thighs, tripping him into a fall. A knee drove into Adam's spine as his arm twisted into a hold that made his shoulder scream in protest.

With his other hand, Jacobs pressed Adam's face into the water.

Adam inhaled a surprised snort of the stream. It burned in his nostrils before he managed to turn his head and catch a breath.

He tried to push himself up with his free hand.

Jacobs twisted his arm tighter. Adam coughed out a curse as the tension threatened to wrench his shoulder out of its socket.

Jacobs leaned in, using the full weight of his body to force Adam's head back into the sandy shallows. The moist earth gave under his cheek. Water splashed up over his face again.

Borthwick's voice cut through the hiss of the current and the roaring of the crowd. "*Enough.*"

Jacobs' breath was a hot pulse against Adam's cheek. The fury roiling through him tightened at Borthwick's haughty command.

"Did you not hear me?" Borthwick snapped.

Jacobs bit out the words with a grunt of effort as he pushed Adam deeper. "He needs… to bloody… *learn*."

Water flooded his mouth, and Adam wondered, with a vague surprise, whether Jacobs actually meant to kill him.

A crack sounded through the hot, still air, loud and sharp as a rifle shot.

Jacobs froze.

Something dripped onto Adam's skin, warm and slick in contrast to the cooler water of the stream.

Adam's shoulder howled with relief as Jacobs loosened his grip. He lifted his head from the water, coughing out what he had inhaled.

Propping himself up with a shaking arm, he glanced at the boulder at the edge of camp.

The rock was empty. Vanika was gone.

Victory rushed over him giddily as he staggered to his feet, clothes plastered to his body with water and sand.

The feeling died as he looked at Jacobs.

The man's shirt was torn. Where the fabric parted at the back of his shoulder, pale skin was marred by a bloody red gash.

Borthwick faced them with his whip casually unfurled at his side.

"Jesus Christ," Adam breathed out as shock washed over him.

Ellie watched from behind the circle of soldiers, her face drawn with horrified surprise.

Borthwick had given Jacobs the full fury of his flail. The injury needed stitches—dozens of them. The scar would be there for the rest of Jacobs' life. Adam couldn't even imagine how much pain the man was in right now.

Not that he showed it. All Adam could read on Jacobs' face was cold fury as tension stretched between him and Borthwick like the plucked string of a cello.

A whip wasn't meant to be used on a man like that. Adam wouldn't be able to stand by and let Borthwick strike out with it again—not even against a man like Jacobs.

That left him wondering, bizarrely, if he was about to throw himself into a fight to protect a man who had just tried to kill him.

Jacobs' shirt had pulled open to the waist. The tattoo on his chest was fully visible now, covering the flat surface of his left pectoral.

A pair of swords crossed beneath a broken tower. Over it, a Latin motto blazed in blocky capitals.

PER ARDUA

Adam had always had a knack for Latin. He translated the words by reflex. *Through difficulty.*

The soldiers watched Jacobs like a feral animal that had just wandered into their camp. A few put their hands on their rifles.

Blood glazing down his back, Jacobs pinned Borthwick with a glare that would've turned Adam's blood to ice.

It felt like a promise.

Then he walked away.

Singh Rao came to Borthwick's side. "Colonel, the girl is missing."

Borthwick's attention fixed on Adam with an intensity that stripped him bare. "Tie him up. The woman, too."

A pair of men stepped in to follow the order, others cocking their rifles at Adam's head. He let them wrench his arms behind his back and lash them there… and tried not to worry that his likelihood of surviving the day might now lie in the hands of a twelve-year-old girl.

THIRTY-FIVE

A HOT GUST of wind churned the dark clouds over Neil's head as the trees that thickly crowned the ridge whispered with the promise of a coming storm. He lay beneath them on his stomach in the long grass as he stared down into the startling beauty of the ravine, where rock-cut chambers peppered the soaring ocher walls over an uncanny sprawl of bones.

As he watched, Adam and Ellie were shoved to the ground at the edge of Borthwick's camp. Worry for his sister and his friend twisted through him.

Constance flopped down beside him, and Neil's worry mingled with an electric awareness of her proximity.

Cutting their way out of prison in the stepwell had been relatively uncomplicated, if nerve-wracking. Neil had managed to carve off part of the stone slab that blocked their way without dropping any of it on his toes, which he considered rather an accomplishment. The sheer terror of using Dyrnwyn now that he knew the sword could cleave him in two had even managed to distract him from thinking too hard about the fact that he had kissed Constance.

Thoroughly.

And she had liked it.

Neil wasn't used to being an object of amorous interest—or at least, not that he'd ever noticed. Adam had occasionally tried to point out that a bar maid was flirting with him, but Neil had never had the courage to do anything about it.

He supposed knowing that he inspired Constance's sensual instincts should have put him on top of the world. Instead, he felt wretched.

Before he had plunged into a mythical forest with Constance, everything had been fine. Yes, he'd been tormented by occasional fantasies of doing utterly improper things with her, but he could manage that. He'd known they were only that—wild, unrealistic fantasies. He could box them away in a corner of his disobedient brain and go on acting like he and Constance were simply very good friends.

But then she had to go and look at him like the last bonbon in a chocolate box. Put her hands on him and open up her lips and melt into him like she wanted everything.

Only Constance didn't want everything. She wanted a lark. And Neil was convenient—someone reasonably attractive that she felt comfortable with.

In another life, Neil might have been fine with that. He hardly abounded with sexual experience himself. They might have explored that together, and then cheerfully gone their separate ways when they were done.

That wasn't an option anymore—not for Neil. He wanted Constance too much to have her and then watch her walk away.

Which meant that he needed to make certain that he never had her at all.

This had to stop. Neil shouldn't have indulged Constance's experiment at all, but there was nothing he could do about that now. He would simply have to make it clear to her that there couldn't be any *again*. They had to go back to the way things had always been, where he was just Ellie's stick-in-the-mud older brother and she was the danger gnome who enjoyed subjecting him to the odd torment.

And they would—just as soon as Neil was no longer pretending to be her fiancé.

Constance wriggled closer, her hip bumping against his side as she angled for a better view of the gorge.

Neil closed his eyes and prayed for strength.

"There are only two guards, and they aren't really looking," she whispered, pitching her voice just loud enough to be heard over the constant rush of the nearby waterfall. "It shouldn't be any trouble to sneak down there, cut Ellie and Adam loose, and make a run for it."

Neil dragged his thoughts from their fake engagement, his deeply conflicted emotions, and the brush of her sleeve against his side. He needed to fix his full attention on the task that lay before them—if he didn't want someone to end up getting hurt.

"How would we get there without being seen?" Neil pressed.

"We'll just sneak through the bones."

"Sneak through the bones," Neil muttered unhappily. "Why not?"

"The more important question is where we go once we've done that." Constance punctuated the remark with a significant look.

She was uncomfortably close. Her hair was still loose, as there hadn't been a hope of finding her pins in the stepwell, even with the light of the sword. Little bits of grass were caught in her thick black curls.

Neil wanted to pick them out. He was rather afraid that if he did, he was going to start kissing her again.

"What do you mean—where we go?" he whispered back.

"We have to find the astra, Stuffy. We can't let Borthwick get it." Constance waved at the dark openings that pockmarked the walls of the ravine. "And we can't run about searching all of these caves without being seen."

Neil's stomach dropped. "You want me to do it again. Use my…"

He trailed off. He still didn't know what to call the impossible, inconvenient, irrational ability that lurked inside of him.

"You are going to have to think up a name for it at some point," Constance warned.

"I don't think I'm quite ready for that yet," Neil confessed.

He felt Dyrnwyn's weight on his back as he faced the gorge again. Soldiers clad in khaki moved among the flowering vines and soaring rib bones that lined the sandy stream.

Borthwick stood in the center of it, surveying his domain.

In the Ramayana, Valmiki had described a weapon of apocalyptic power— one that could turn a nation into a desert and bring down the most powerful demon in the world.

Neil thought of an arcanum like that falling into the hands the man that he had faced over Tulsidas's manuscript back in Puri.

Constance was right. They couldn't let Borthwick get the astra—no matter what that required of them.

He studied the holes in the face of the ridge. There were dozens of them, from simple ragged openings to chambers fronted by elaborate colonnades. Somehow, he had to use an ability he barely understood to figure out which of those doorways led to wildly dangerous arcanum.

Constance squeezed his hand. "You can do this. I have complete faith in you."

Neil realized with a jolt that she really did. Constance was easily confident that he could do this, even though he'd only done it once before—on purpose, anyway.

"I haven't the foggiest notion where to begin," he confessed.

"What did you do last time?"

Neil tried to remember. "It was the bird."

"The bird?"

Neil shook his head to clear it. He'd gone over a bit vague at the memory. "There was a bird in the stepwell. I heard it tapping at the stones. It felt… important."

"What looks important down there?" Constance nodded at the valley—which held a platoon of soldiers, a sadistic secret police chief, Neil's vulnerable sister and friend, and a forest of bones.

"Everything?" Neil offered back weakly.

"Stuffy…" Constance's tone was dark with warning.

"I'll try," Neil countered. "I'm trying."

He drew in a breath, readying himself to do the impossible.

Constance wiggled next to him as she inched closer to the edge.

Neil's nascent attempt at concentration fractured.

He scooted away from her and forced his focus back to where the openings in the cliffs gazed at him like dark eyes.

Start with whatever feels important.

An impulse rose up in Neil—one that ran so contrary to his normal instincts, he knew with a sinking sense of unease that it had to come from somewhere else.

"I need to get closer," Neil admitted uncomfortably.

Constance frowned. "We are safer up here on the ridge."

"It's… *important,*" he ground out.

Constance arched an eyebrow, then made a study of the landscape of the ravine.

"There." She pointed to a place where the gorge was split by a sharp jut of stone. "If you stay close to the wall, you should be able to look out without being seen from the camp."

The notch Constance indicated lay slightly to the left below them. She was likely right about it offering cover, but they would be exposed for a few seconds while they scrambled down.

That tugging, uncomfortable instinct told Neil that he needed to chance it.

Borthwick's sepoys were fanning out in groups, moving to the nearby caves with organized precision. A couple of sentries remained behind by the camp, holding their rifles with the loose distraction of routine.

The soldier facing their way turned around. Heart thudding, Neil slipped from the grass, skidding down the steep, ruddy shale until he landed in the deeper shadow of the outcrop.

He froze, waiting for a cry of alarm to go up, but the rush of the nearby waterfall cloaked the sound of the shifting debris of his passage.

Constance dropped into place behind him.

"You shouldn't be here!" Neil hissed.

Constance rolled her eyes. "Just get on with it, Stuffy."

Neil repressed a groan. It wasn't as though he could send her back.

Pressing himself to the wall, he peered out into the gorge. His instinct had been right in one respect. He could see more of the rock-cut chambers from his current angle. His scholarly brain whirred as he studied them. A guess put the ruins at roughly two thousand years ago, when this area would have been part of the ancient kingdom of Kalinga.

Neil's attention danced over carved columns and narrow flights of stairs. Moss-covered bones rose from softly swaying stands of bamboo.

Something felt off.

I should close my eyes.

The impulse was a teasing whisper at the edge of his consciousness. Neil's rational mind rebelled against it. How would seeing into the past be facilitated by closing his bloody eyes?

The instinct compelled him regardless.

Bugger it, Neil thought and obeyed.

Storm-scented air tugged at the fabric of his shirt. Birds chirped, wings beating softly through the nearby brush. The damp of the waterfall drifted to him on the breeze, a cool kiss against the exposed skin at his throat.

Worries spun through his mind—about what lay between him and Constance. About how he could possibly help Ellie and Adam. About Vanika, Subhas, and the rest of the Adrija. Those newer fears mingled with older emotions—a lingering pang of guilt for how he had failed Ellie during the years when she had fought to make her own path in the world. Gratitude for the moment Adam had chosen him as a friend. An ache of nostalgia for hours spent crouched in tombs with Sayyid, arguing over Middle Egyptian pronouns.

Neil let the feelings wash over him. What would be the point in fighting them? They were all real.

He smelled earth and ancient stone, flowers and the heat of an imminent storm.

Now, he thought.

He opened his eyes.

The mossy bones and ocher cliffs lay before him in vivid color, the ravine painted with sunlight. Borthwick's men were still there, but Neil was only half aware of them. It felt as though they were shadows—vague, unimportant ghosts flickering across the landscape.

All that mattered—all that was real—was Neil's powerful sense that a woman used to stand on the far side of the gorge.

The feeling was like memory, wistful with longing… except that Neil had never been to this place before.

He still knew exactly how she would have looked framed by the carved stone pillars of the colonnade that fronted her chamber.

Bare feet were brushed by the hem of a sari dyed with saffron. A red bindi blazed from the warm skin of her forehead. Fine lines accented the corners of her eyes and the perfect curve of her lip.

Beautiful, Neil thought distractedly.

She was unutterably beautiful.

The breeze gently tossed the locks of her glorious hair. The woman—the memory—raised her eyes to meet Neil's stare from across the mossy bones and the gurgling stream. Something in her expression—faithful, enduring, and fierce—reminded him of his sister.

Song and laughter mingled with the clash of iron. The copper tang of blood danced through the fragrance of blooming flowers.

Her gaze blazed with flame, binding Neil with a rope of gold—body and mind, soul and desire. In that moment, he belonged to her so completely, it threatened to break him apart with joy and terror.

She carried something in her hand, her grip loose and restful. Neil still understood, beyond any doubt, that she knew exactly how to use it.

"She has a bow," he croaked, forcing the words from his lips.

"Who?" Constance pressed.

"The woman with the stars in her eyes," Neil rasped in return.

The vision who owned his soul raised up her other hand. She held it at the height of her shoulder, palm facing out—a solemn salute that pierced him from across space and time.

Neil lifted his hand in return, mirroring her gesture.

It felt like a promise.

Her gaze was black and wild, howling with rage and justice and hope.

Something itched at the corner of Neil's eye. He blinked against the feeling, and the woman was gone.

"Neil?" Constance pressed from beside him.

Tears traced down his cheeks, cool against the warmth of the afternoon. Neil dashed at them automatically, then stared down in surprise at the moisture on his hand.

Constance watched him carefully. "Why were you making a mudra?"

"A mudra?" Neil echoed, lost.

"With your hand." Constance raised her arm, turning her palm out to face him. "Aai taught it to me. This one is for fearlessness—and protection."

Her gaze flicked to Neil's shoulder, where Dyrnwyn's hilt poked up from its scabbard.

Neil reeled. "She did it. The woman. I… I just…"

Constance touched his arm. "What woman? Who did you see?"

His hands were shaking. He stared down at them in surprise as the answer burst out of him. "She was the most beautiful thing I've ever seen. And she was terrifying."

Constance gazed across the ravine as though she could see some echo of what had once been there. "That sounds like… someone I might have heard of before."

Neil's mind burned with eyes like flame and a beauty that could have cut through him, bone and flesh and sinew, and still leave him aching for more.

"Whoever she was," he replied carefully, "I feel rather certain that she has what we're looking for."

The columns by the rock-cut chamber across the gorge were cracked and weathered with time. The sunlight was gone. Charcoal clouds roiled overhead as Borthwick's men moved past the curving shadows of the bones.

Constance's eyes flashed with determination. "Then let's get our friends and find it."

THIRTY-SIX

*E*LLIE LEANED AGAINST a boulder at the edge of Borthwick's camp, her ankles bound before her and her hands tied behind her back. The stream rushed past a few steps away. Ancient tusks and ribs curved overhead between tall thickets of bamboo. Beyond them rose the steep silver bluff of the waterfall.

Borthwick had gone, hiking off with a detachment of his men to start exploring some of the caves. Singh Rao remained behind to organize the others.

None of them paid her and Adam much mind. And why should they? The pair of them were trussed up like geese.

Bruises were already forming on the familiar lines of Adam's face from his fight with Jacobs. His jaw was scraped, and his soaked shirt sported watery crimson stains. Adam caught her looking at them.

"I started it," he admitted.

Ellie voiced the question that had been itching at her since she had seen the fight break out. "Why?"

"It gave Vanika a chance to get away."

Even though he was filthy, bruised, and exhausted, a familiar brightness gleamed in his eyes.

"You're happy," Ellie pointed out.

Adam cocked a skeptical brow. "We're tied up and completely at Borthwick's mercy."

"I know," she replied significantly.

He leaned back against the boulder. "Maybe it just feels good to be myself again—even if it's landed us in a pretty big heap of trouble."

"I don't mind being in trouble with you. And we've been in worse situations," Ellie asserted.

"Like what?"

"Nearly being poached alive in a room full of Mesoamerican death gods?"

"That was pretty bad," Adam allowed.

"Ambushed in a tomb full of crimson death sand," Ellie listed.

"The tomb wasn't full of death sand. Just the sarcophagus."

"We had to flee a collapsing cave system."

Adam smirked. "You did that one on purpose."

"That was not *on purpose*. I didn't know precisely what was going to happen when I threw all of Padre Kuyoc's dynamite into that hole in the ground. You got us out of all of that trouble by being who you really are."

"I *contributed*," Adam corrected her. "Seems to me, we've frequently benefited from a hell of a lot of help."

"We might be a bit short on help at the moment," Ellie admitted. "Neil and Constance are trapped in the stepwell. Subhas is tied up and under guard with the rest of his men. What about Vanika?"

"I told her to get the hell out of here."

Ellie racked her brain. "I suppose there's the dog," she offered with a grimace.

"Good point." Adam's mouth quirked mischievously. "I'm sure he'll sort it all out once he turns back up."

"You have an inordinate amount of faith in that animal," she grumbled.

"That's because he's a good boy."

A voice hissed from behind the boulder at their backs. "Whatever you do, don't turn around!"

Ellie immediately twisted her body to peek around the stone—where a familiar figure crouched between the slender stalks of bamboo. "Connie!?"

Constance waved a furious hand at her. "Shh! You're going to ruin the plot!"

Ellie quickly pulled herself around to face forward—just as one of the sepoys glanced over at them.

She flashed him a reassuring smile.

The man frowned.

Ellie pitched her words so that they wouldn't be heard over the constant rush of the waterfall. "But how are you here?"

"It's a bit of a long story," Constance whispered.

"Guessing that means it's a good one." Adam's voice was warm with relief.

Worry darted through Ellie. "But where's—"

She was cut off by a slight crash in the bamboo. The stalks above her swayed violently.

"Bugger," her brother bit out under his breath.

"Neil!" Ellie exclaimed, her voice catching.

"Hello, Peanut," he replied feelingly from behind the boulder.

Constance piped in. "We can cut you loose, but we'll need a distraction."

Ellie perked up. "It's possible I might have prepared for that."

"I know that tone," Adam said warningly. "That's your practical chemistry tone."

Ellie frowned. "I have a practical chemistry tone?"

"What'd you set to blow up, Princess?" Adam pushed back dryly.

"You're the one who told me to do something with that ethanol!"

Adam's eyes rose to the churning gray clouds overhead as though looking for strength. "And what did you do with the ethanol?"

"Nothing yet," Ellie returned pertly. "I only put it aside in a safe place along with a deposit of potassium crystals that I chipped out of the ridge on our way here."

Adam stared at her. "You just randomly collected a bunch of potassium."

Ellie stiffened defensively. "Potassium has many useful chemical applications."

"Like?" Adam prompted.

Her cheeks flushed. "Like creating hydrogen gas when combined with high proof spirits, which is just a little explosive when ignited in a contained environment."

Adam stared at her.

"What? If there are no proper combustibles on hand, one has to make do." She directed the rest behind the boulder to Constance. "I emptied out one of the supply trunks and stole a bit of fuse as well."

"I'll take care of it," Constance confirmed eagerly. "I'll just need Stuffy's sword."

Neil's horrified voice hissed at her from behind the rock. "You can't use Dyrnwyn for that!"

"Why not?" Constance retorted crossly.

"It's completely covered in flames! If any of that hydrogen leaks out of the seams in the trunk, you could blow yourself up before you get to the fuse!"

Constance made a distinct noise of dissatisfaction. Ellie couldn't entirely blame her.

Adam shuffled himself closer to the edge of the rock. "Matches. In my pocket."

Constance poked her head out to assess the scene. Her hair hung loose and tangled, peppered with bits of leaves. She was missing a few buttons at the top of her blouse, exposing a slice of well-formed cleavage. Satisfied, she plucked the tin from Adam's trouser pocket and ducked back into her hiding place.

The suspicious sepoy whirled at the flicker of movement, his eyes narrowing.

Ellie tried her best to look innocent. Adam smiled as the flowers danced at his side.

The soldier called across the camp, and Ellie chilled with alarm as Singh Rao approached.

The subedar loomed over them, framed by one of the moss-draped elephant bones. Unlike Ellie and Adam, he still appeared entirely well put together, with his turban perfectly wrapped and his beard brushed.

"One of my men said you were talking to someone," Singh Rao accused.

"Just the two of us here," Adam returned lightly.

"He thought he heard someone else."

"Maybe it was a ghost," Adam quipped. "This place seems pretty haunted."

Singh Rao looked pained. "You seem to have a knack for causing a great deal of bother."

"Can't really argue with that." Adam dropped his insouciance. "Do you know what your colonel is actually here for?"

"Yes."

"Really think it's a good idea for him to get it?"

"Some old artifact?" Singh Rao returned with tired skepticism.

"What if it's not just an old artifact?" Adam pushed back.

Singh Rao shook his head. "You choose strange things to risk your life for, Mr. Bates."

Adam let out a low, dry chuckle. "Ain't that the truth."

Across the stream, a burst of hot blue fire whooshed up from the forest of bones.

With a giddy thrill, Ellie calculated the height and velocity of the explosion. That feldspar she had collected must have had a very high proportion of potassium indeed. It was good that she had placed her little chemistry project in a sheltered, rocky location, or even with the moisture of the monsoon, she might've succeeded in lighting the whole ravine on fire.

Singh Rao dropped into an instinctive crouch, whipping his sidearm from the holster and aiming it at the explosion. The soldiers around him did the same, weapons clattering as everyone took up defensive positions.

The subedar's eyes snapped back to Adam.

"Don't look at me." Adam shifted his torso to show Singh Rao how his wrists were still tied behind his back. He added an insouciant wiggle of his fingers.

Singh Rao's mouth tightened with exasperation. He signaled to his men, and a handful took up secure positions to offer cover while he led the rest across the stream.

Everyone was focused on the potential threat across the water—and not the pair of scruffy prisoners by the boulder with their hands and feet still bound.

Neil scrambled out from behind the rock.

He was filthy. His waistcoat was scuffed and his shirt smudged with dirt. He hadn't shaved—not that it mattered all that much with Neil. The lightest shadow of a beard accented the line of his jaw. Relief washed through Ellie at seeing him intact.

"Get her behind the rock!" Adam ordered, already shuffling himself in that direction.

Neil hooked his hands under Ellie's armpits and hauled her around the boulder. He tugged quickly at the knots binding her ankles.

Adam collapsed to the ground beside them, his cheek kissing the gravel. "This would go a little faster with a knife," he pointed out urgently.

A shout of alarm rose from the camp.

Neil stared at the knots he had barely started to undo and winced.

"Please hold very, *very* still?" he pleaded.

He whipped out his sword.

Flames shot up Dyrnwyn's length. Neil brought the weapon down between Ellie's legs—and the ropes fell away.

Adam stared at the perfectly severed strands piled around Ellie's feet. "How sharp is that thing?"

"You *really* don't want to know," Neil returned feelingly, then cut Adam's ankles free as well.

Yanking Ellie upright, Neil pushed her into the forest of bamboo. Constance burst through the slender trunks from the other direction, her eyes bright with excitement.

"I had no idea chemistry could be so much fun!" she exclaimed brightly.

"Talk about it after we run," Adam countered.

Ellie plunged through the leaves and branches, sprinting awkwardly with her hands still bound behind her back. Her boots slipped on moss-covered bones. Adam tripped along beside her, Neil at his heels with his sword now safely sheathed. Shouts rang out from behind as Singh Rao's men organized a pursuit.

Adam jerked his head toward the silver torrent of the waterfall. "This way!"

They sprinted past the moon-like curves of massive ribs, and the bamboo gave way to tall ferns and woody shrubs. Ellie shoved through them with her shoulder as the air cooled with damp spray.

Adam scanned the cliff that rose in front of them, then hurried toward a spot near the edge of the cascade where the ruddy stone was thickly covered with vines and flowering creepers. He plunged into the foliage—and then through it, to where Ellie now saw a dark opening cut into the face of the rock. She stumbled after him, feeling a chill splash of water as she ducked through the edge of the falls. She pressed herself against the damp wall inside as Neil and Constance followed.

"Quiet," Adam warned lowly.

Soldiers moved closer, their voices just audible over the rush of the water. The sounds drew near… and then crashed off in another direction.

Ellie slumped with relief.

"Wanna get the rest of these off?" Adam turned to offer his wrists to Neil.

While Neil took out his sword and cut Adam loose, Ellie studied where they had landed.

It was one of the rock-cut chambers of the ashram. The space was sized like a deep, narrow alcove, rich with shadow thanks to the vines that nearly obscured the entrance. In the low light, she could just make out a beautiful relief carving on one of the longer walls, where Vishnu reclined on top of a many-headed serpent as he waited for the moment when he would wake to usher in a new age. He wore an expression of restful peace on his face under his heavy crown.

"Peanut?" Neil offered, Dyrnwyn flickering in his hands.

"Oh!" Ellie turned her back to him. Her shoulders flooded with relief as the bindings around her wrists fell away and blood pulsed back into her fingers.

Now that her arms were free, she threw them around her brother. "I'm so terribly glad you're safe!"

Neil frantically thrust Dyrnwyn out of the way of her embrace. "Careful of the sword!"

Ellie eyed the weapon skeptically. "Why? Will it set me on fire?"

"Possibly?" Neil hedged. "But I'm more worried about it slicing one of your arms off."

She froze with a quick jolt of alarm. "What on earth would it do that for?"

"Apparently, Stuffy's sword is exceptionally good at cutting through things," Constance answered cheerfully, shaking the moisture of the waterfall out of her hair. "That's how we got out of the stepwell. Neil carved through the rubble."

"How about we talk about this after you put the damned thing away so it doesn't serve as a nice handy beacon telling the bad guys where we are?" Adam suggested.

With a flash of mortification, Neil pulled out his handkerchief and wrapped it around the hilt. The sword snuffed out.

Constance tapped her chin thoughtfully. "You should get a glove."

"A glove?" Neil echoed. "As in—just one?"

"Then you could put the sword out without needing to dig through your pockets," Constance elaborated reasonably.

"I'm supposed to run about wearing just one glove?" Neil protested.

"I think it would make you look terribly intriguing," Constance returned authoritatively.

"He ought to have some sort of training with that thing as well." Ellie grimaced warily at the weapon as Neil shoved it back into the scabbard. "Especially if it's capable of lopping people's arms off if you use it the wrong way."

"Most fencing clubs limit themselves to foils." Constance frowned thoughtfully. "Except the one where Julian practiced, of course."

Neil looked aghast. "You want me to learn sword fighting from Julian Forster-Mowbray?"

"Goodness, no. He wasn't even very good at it. I'm sure Mr. Mahjoud could teach you—if he'd stop pretending that he isn't a fearsome warrior."

Adam cocked a skeptical eyebrow at Constance's statement.

Ellie couldn't blame him. She was still far from convinced of Constance's theory that Mr. Mahjoud possessed martial capabilities.

Neil was tired and disheveled. None of what he'd just experienced aligned with his scholarly disposition. Ellie set a comforting hand on his arm.

"I'm sorry I didn't tell you I could see things in the past," he spilled out.

"I have the entire history of Tulan trapped in my mind," Ellie confessed at the same time.

They stopped, staring at each other.

"Tulan?" Neil echoed first.

Adam stepped up behind Ellie and put a steady arm around her waist.

She drew in a breath and said the rest. "I have the knowledge of an entire civilization that died two hundred and fifty years before we were born stuffed into my brain."

Neil blinked at her, wordless with surprise.

"It happened back in British Honduras with the Smoking Mirror. Not that I can get at any of it very easily," Ellie complained. "It only pops up when I'm not really trying. How am I supposed to preserve, record, and study the knowledge of a place that I can only remember when I'm not really trying? But if I don't, so much will be lost. I know there are fragments of Tulan that survived in the practices and origin stories of some of the neighboring cultures—but they're *fragments*. For all of the rest of it, there's just me."

Shame burned. "I should have told you ages ago, only… Well, I don't even know why I didn't. I suppose it's because it all felt so terribly strange and not at all the sort of thing a proper academic ought to entertain as an idea, never mind run around having inside one's brain—"

"I understand," Neil cut in with an aching note in his voice. "I know exactly what you mean."

And he did, Ellie realized.

She was momentarily overwhelmed by how lucky she was to have him in her life. How rare was it that the boy who became her brother just happened to be someone who understood and shared her intellectual passions?

There were things he'd overlooked from within the shell of his own privilege, but he'd learned to recognize that, and he'd done better. Now the two of them shared the burden of these strange gifts, and they had the opportunity to support each other as they learned what it all meant.

"So what's next?" Adam pressed.

"We get the astra," Constance declared stoutly.

"But we don't know where it is," Ellie pointed out.

Neil shifted uneasily. "That's not entirely true."

Ellie narrowed her eyes. "You must know it is absolutely killing me not to be able to ask you a million questions about this mysterious power of yours."

His expression softened. "It doesn't make you think any differently about me?"

"Beyond being extraordinarily jealous?"

Neil looked flabbergasted. "Jealous?"

"You can *see the past*, Neil! Just imagine what you could do with that—what you might discover!"

"But nobody would believe me!" he protested.

Ellie waved a dismissive hand. "You don't have to go about advertising it to them. You could find the physical evidence to support what you saw—

because you'd know exactly where to look for it!"

Neil seemed thrown. "I… I never thought of it that way."

With a sudden impulse, he pulled Ellie into a hug. "Thank you, Peanut."

Ellie soaked up the warmth of the embrace, her brother's chin tucked against the top of her hair.

Adam frowned down at the front of his soaked, torn shirt. "I've got Jacobs' blood all over me."

"That doesn't seem very hygienic," Constance commented with a wicked glint in her eye.

"Doesn't, does it?" Adam shot Ellie an unrepentant smirk.

"Oh, go on!" Ellie huffed indulgently.

He yanked off the shirt and tossed it to the ground, exposing the firm lines of his tanned chest. Ellie's mind momentarily blanked as she soaked up the view.

Constance shot a devilish look at Neil. "Your shirt's a bit worse for wear as well, Stuffy."

"Absolutely not," Neil returned flatly. "Now, are we going?"

THIRTY-SEVEN

CONSTANCE SHOULD HAVE been worrying about the platoon of sepoys on their tail or relishing in the thrill of searching for supernatural artifacts in a legendary ashram.

Instead, her thoughts were glued to Neil.

The results of Constance's experiment in the stepwell had been conclusive. The man had set her on *fire*.

Constance had indulged in her share of flirtations in the past. There had been staid kisses and sloppy kisses, firmly not to be repeated. Other kisses might have had potential if it hadn't felt as though she and the gentleman in question were dancing to different tunes.

There had been nothing out of tune about Neil Fairfax.

Constance could still remember the way his lips had felt grazing and tugging at her own. How his hand had gripped her hip as he pulled her closer, trails of electric heat singeing her skin with every touch.

Constance's attraction to Neil wasn't new. She would hardly have been considering taking him as a lover back in Egypt if she hadn't appreciated the view he offered—but she had never suspected that Ellie's scholarly brother was hiding a sensual beast under that staid, play-by-the-rules exterior.

Now that she knew it was there, Constance couldn't help but see it every time she looked at him.

His shirt was damp from their plunge through the edge of the falls. It clung to the firm line of his shoulders and the curve of his spine.

Constance could run her fingers up that arc until she reached the soft, damp hair at the nape of his neck, threaded her fingers into it, and hauled him down for another go.

He had tasted like coffee and dark spice. Smelled like amber and old books. His eyes grew more fascinating the longer she looked at them, notes of green mingling with stormy gray and earthy brown. The light hint of stubble on his jaw was a touch of ruggedness that belied his proper exterior, hinting at something wild underneath.

Well, she supposed she'd had more than a hint now—and it had only deepened her interest in exploring further.

Not that she'd mentioned any of that to Neil yet. Constance knew him too well to think he'd be comfortable throwing himself into a wild temporary affair. Such a move would also be complicated by the fact that, as far as the rest of the world knew, Neil was her fiancé… at least until Constance was through having Indian princes thrown at her by her well-meaning family.

Then they could break things off—but what would that mean for their relationship? Ladies didn't stay friends with the gentlemen who had jilted them.

Well, Constance would find a way to do it. She was not giving Neil up over this. He was a part of her life now, whether he liked it or not. Whatever rules there were, she would break them—and drag Neil along with her.

It was only a shame that he had refused to take off his shirt.

Adam led them through the forest of bones. Here and there, the voices of Borthwick's men echoed off the pockmarked red walls of the ravine, but Adam steered their party along the cascade, where the rush masked the sound of their movements.

They waded across the stream, water soaking Constance to her thighs. She missed her footing, and the current pushed her into a slide.

Neil threw his arm around her waist to steady her.

His chest pressed against her back. Uneven breath brushed her ear.

Constance shivered.

He quickly released her.

They caught up to the others under a flame-hued poinciana that sprawled near the base of the cliffs. Adam studied the cave Neil had identified from their hiding place. The opening sat three stories up from the ground, fronted by a shadowy line of six chipped and weathered columns. A narrow set of steps carved into the stone was the only way to reach it.

"This shouldn't be visible from the camp until we get to the top," Adam concluded.

"It's still a risk," Ellie pointed out. "We don't know where Borthwick's men are looking for us."

"I don't see any other way to get there," Adam admitted apologetically.

Neil warily considered the climb. "Are you sure it's safe?"

"Of course it is, Stuffy," Constance countered.

Before he could argue, she darted onto the steps, scrambling up with easy confidence. Reaching the top, she dodged into the shadow of the colonnade.

The columns fronted a narrow veranda carved from the face of the cliff. Constance pressed herself against the back wall as she studied the landscape below for any shout of alarm or crack of rifle fire.

The gorge remained quiet save for the rush of the nearby waterfall.

She called down the stairs to the others in a pointed whisper. "All clear!"

While she waited for them to join her, she took a moment to appreciate the view—which was stunning. The colonnade was positioned to offer a broad vista of the shimmering silver falls. Majestic walls of ocher stone framed a sky full of silently roiling gray clouds. The cliffs were draped with tumbling clusters of gold and purple blooms that kissed the air with their fragrance.

Neil arrived, leaning against one of the columns as though his knees were shaky. "That was terrifying."

Constance found herself staring at the lingering damp that glistened on the skin of his throat.

She wondered if he would let her taste it.

He peered out from behind the column to take in the view. His expression shifted to one of solemn wonder. "This is..."

Lust shifted into a softly thrilling sense of kinship. Constance knew exactly what he meant. "Yes," she quietly agreed, coming to stand beside him.

A gust of heady wind lifted her loose, tangled hair. A low rumble punctuated the silence, the first promise of the gathering storm.

Ellie stumbled as she reached the veranda.

Neil darted out to catch her. "Are you alright?"

"I'm fine," she assured him with a hint of irritation. "It's only these dashed bite wounds on my leg don't appreciate me walking around quite so much."

Neil paled. "I'm sorry—did you say *bite wounds?*"

"Was it a tiger?" Constance asked, her interest piquing.

"Fish, actually," Ellie returned automatically. She wiped a line of sweat off her brow. "Goodness. That was precarious, even for my tastes. I do hope—"

She trailed off as Adam lurched into view. He threw himself around one of the columns and hung onto it as his knees buckled.

"Ssss' fine," he slurred queasily. "Just... need a lil minute..."

He started to slide off the column. Neil dragged him to safety. Adam remained on his back on the floor, staring up at the stone ceiling of the veranda.

Constance peered down at him. "That's right. You aren't very fond of heights, are you?"

"Nope," Adam replied succinctly, making absolutely no move to get up.

"But were we seen?" Neil demanded nervously.

"I haven't heard any gunshots," Constance replied reasonably.

Neil swallowed uncomfortably. "That's… reassuring."

Ellie moved to the far end of the rock-cut overhang. "The entrance to the chamber is over here."

Constance felt an enticing thrill of imminent discovery. They were standing at the threshold of one of the most important stories in India's history. Who knew what wonders would be inside, waiting for them to discover?

She prodded Adam's bare flank with the toe of her boot, not bothering to hide her impatience. "Can you move yet?"

"Sure," Adam groaned. "I'll get right on that."

Ten minutes later, they finally stepped inside.

The rock-cut chamber was cool and dark. The space was graciously sized compared to the smaller cave they had hid in earlier. Ample light poured through the entrance, illuminating a slab carved into the wall for a bed and a niche that likely served as an altar.

There were no artifacts, only a few old birds' nests and a pile of shelled nuts from some industrious rodent. Thick spiderwebs draped the corners, and bird droppings stained the rock below a natural ledge. Something cooed with mild alarm as they moved deeper into the room.

As she hobbled inside, Ellie blazed with excitement as though the rugged ceiling was the eighth wonder of the world. "This was clearly adapted from a natural formation in the rock!"

"I think these scratches might actually be Indo-Aryan petroglyphs," Neil burst out happily.

"That carving's nice," Adam commented.

He was looking at the wall that faced the entrance, which was decorated with images of tangled vines rich with flowers. Children played with delicate deer while lovers fed each other sweets. The artwork was weathered, time softening its details.

The nesting birds cooed again in the corner.

"If this was Sita's chamber, it doesn't seem very queenly," Constance commented, trying to hide her disappointment.

"Isn't an ashram kinda like a monastery?" Adam asked.

"They are places of contemplation and spiritual work," Ellie offered as she peered under a pile of leafy debris.

Adam shrugged. "Then maybe that's what she was looking for, instead of another palace."

Constance was struck by his words.

She had always thought of Sita as the victim in Rama's story—cast out by her husband, weeping and powerless, over accusations that he'd already known were false. Constance could imagine her throwing herself onto the hard stone bed cut into the wall as she bewailed her terrible fate.

But the woman Neil had seen from across the valley had left him consumed not with sympathy but with a terrified holy awe as he raised his hand in the mudra for fearlessness.

She thought of Aai's words in the Kali temple.

Sita is both more powerful and more complicated than you give her credit for.

A soft, insistent wind blew into the chamber. The dry leaves in the corners stirred, quietly dancing.

"I'm not sure there's anything here," Ellie concluded reluctantly.

Adam leaned against the wall as he continued to recover from his vertigo. "Maybe we should try the other door."

Constance's attention sharpened. "The other door?"

Adam jerked his head toward the deeper shadows at the back of the chamber.

Constance hurried over and realized that one of the shadows wasn't a shadow at all. Instead, the wall of the cave bent sharply to reveal a set of stairs carved into a tunnel that descended deeper into the cliff. Soft gray light painted the red stone at the bottom.

"There's something else down there," Constance said wonderingly.

Neil pressed closer to peer over her shoulder. "What is it?"

His chest brushed against her back as he forgot to keep his distance in his excitement at the discovery. Constance felt a less sacred sort of tingle at his proximity.

Goodness—was he going to have that effect on her all the time from now on?

"Ladies first," Adam offered with a wave.

The sound of the waterfall faded as they descended, replaced by the scrape of boots on stone and the soft whisper of grass in the breeze.

Constance stepped outside to find herself someplace impossible. Walls of mossy red stone rose up to a circular opening forty feet above that framed a patch of stormy gray clouds. The level ground was grown over with softly whispering grass and flowering herbs that scented the air with basil and mint.

Vines tumbled down from above and shade-loving creepers climbed up the walls.

"It's a sinkhole," Adam said, his voice numb with surprise.

"But what's that building?"

Constance pointed at the structure that stood in the center of the natural enclosure. It consisted of a single story, octagonal in shape, with a flat roof. The exterior stonework was carved with false pillars that lent a timeless grace to the building.

The entrance faced them. There was just enough light in the interior that Constance could make out the shape of shadowy columns.

"I think it's another temple," Ellie answered softly.

Wind gusted through the space, gracefully tossing the grass and flowers. The building looked like something from beyond time, as though they had stumbled into one of Neil's visions.

Constance was consumed by the odd sense that a single step forward would break some sort of spell and send ancient, inevitable gears spinning forward.

They fell into a quietly reverent line as they faced the building. Adam stood at the end, bare-chested and battered. Ellie was beside him, the knot of her bun falling into tendrils, her cheeks smudged with dirt.

Constance couldn't be looking any better, with her hair tangled and her shirt open to her corset.

Neil stepped into place beside her, his sword strapped across his back, his spectacles glinting over the scrape on his cheek.

"We probably don't want to waste too much time," he noted nervously.

Another low roll of thunder rumbled from above.

"Then what are we waiting for?" Constance demanded and strode inside.

THIRTY-EIGHT

$\mathcal{E}$LLIE GAZED AT the softly shadowed interior of the temple with quiet wonder.

Up in the cave, she had found it hard to absorb that she stood in a space that had once been inhabited by a legend. The chamber had simply been a fascinating archaeological discovery in its own right, promising to reveal more knowledge of ancient Hindu ascetic practices.

This was different.

Ellie clung to analysis in the face of the growing feeling that she was somewhere not at all scholarly in nature. "Based on the similarity between the carved decorations on the exterior of the structure and the colonnades fronting some of the rock-cut chambers, I would estimate that all this dates from roughly two thousand years ago."

"Quite," Neil agreed inadequately, adjusting his spectacles as he stared around him.

The space was humble. The single room was broken up by a circle of columns that supported the flat slab of the roof. Windows were set into three alternating walls. The other four held carved niches with holy figures.

Hanuman filled the hollow to Ellie's left. He knelt with his powerful mace at his side, his hands pressed together in prayer.

Lakshmana stood to her right. Rama's loyal brother was a straight-backed, youthful figure with a garland of carved stone flowers around his neck.

Across the room, a man with the bearing of a king faced a woman whose body curved with grace and beauty. The details of her face were worn away.

Constance joined Ellie to look at them, her voice softened with awe. "Rama and Sita."

The rest of the players of the Ramayana were carved into the walls. Giant vultures soared over monkey kings. An army crossed the thrashing waves of the sea. Demons ranged in fearsome troops before a ten-headed monster.

The soft gray light from the windows painted an octagonal slab of stone in the center of the temple. Three objects lay there, held up on small braces of stone.

A recurve bow, still strung. A silk-lined quiver. And a single humble arrow.

The bow was formed of layers of gleaming wood tipped with bone, the grip wrapped with cords of pale sinew.

The head of the arrow was pounded iron, shaped like a leaf. A shaft of unpolished bamboo was fletched with black feathers.

Another storm-scented wind shifted through the temple, tugging lightly at the loose strands of hair at the back of Ellie's neck.

"If these date to the same era as those caverns, they shouldn't be this well preserved," Neil noted uncomfortably.

"Maybe someone brought them here more recently," Ellie suggested.

The words rang false. This place had the feel of somewhere that had not seen mortal steps in a very long time.

The objects were simple in the way of well-loved things. Ellie could see where the patina of the wood of the bow was darkened by the grip of someone's hand. "This was used… but I don't remember Sita having a bow."

Constance shot a knowing look at Neil. He coughed uncomfortably.

"Maybe she got it from him." Adam jerked a thumb at the kingly statue that stood behind him.

Ellie studied the arc of polished wood with a surprised reverence. "You think this is *Lord Rama's* bow?"

"The bigger question might be whether that arrow is the apocalyptic weapon of the gods," Adam countered.

With obvious discomfort, Neil crouched by the altar to give the artifact a better look. "It resembles several dozen other ancient arrows I've seen, save for some slight regional variations in the style of the point."

"Well—it would, wouldn't it?" Ellie retorted. "The astra wasn't some specially constructed treasure. It was a power you summoned into any object you wanted. Rama would have called it into whatever arrow happened to be in his quiver."

"Right." Neil sounded shaky. "Because he knew the mantra. You use the mantra to invoke the astra. But then… if none of us knows the mantra, could we even use this? Assuming we wanted to," he quickly corrected. "Which we absolutely don't."

"If we're right about this being what we think it is, someone with the mantra already did summon the astra into it. This invocation of it is just…"

Ellie trailed off, at a loss for the right word.

"Leftovers," Adam offered.

Ellie raised her brows at his casual description.

Adam shrugged.

Constance huffed with frustration. "But how do we *know* whether it's leftovers or just another arrow?"

Ellie studied the artifact with a deep sense of discomfort. "When Sayyid handed me the Staff of Moses, it felt like a dozen bees were stinging my fingers."

"Dyrnwyn doesn't sting," Neil absently countered.

Adam plucked the arrow from its stone braces.

It glowed, tendrils of light whipping out from the shaft in mingling hues of blue and gold, silver and crimson. The shadows of the temple grew longer and deeper around them, and a dry, strange wind rushed through the close space, making the dead leaves on the ground whirl furiously.

Ellie's skin tightened. Blood pounded inside her skull like the uneasy pressure of standing near an imminent lightning strike.

Adam very quickly set the arrow back down.

The glow flickered out. The wind died. The shadows went back to normal. The leaves settled onto the ground with a dry rustle.

"Doesn't sting," Adam reported in a tight voice.

Neil had half collapsed behind the altar. He slowly crawled back up, regarding the arrow with a terrified respect.

"It really is the astra," Constance breathed out.

"If you had dropped that," Ellie said in a strangled voice, "you might have taken out half of Chhattisgarh."

"Guessing that means you don't need to know the mantra to use its leftovers," Adam deduced uncomfortably.

Constance studied the objects on the altar with bewildered wonder. "Aai has been telling me about Rama and Sita for as long as I can remember—but they were always just stories." She turned to Ellie, her eyes wide. "Except they weren't. Because Sita was here. She was *here*, Ellie."

Ellie felt the whispering, uncanny awareness that she had once again brushed up against the imprint an extraordinary woman had made on the world.

She remembered golden eyes and a scarred cheek.

You want to know who we were.

Neil's outburst snapped her back to herself. "But what on earth do we do with it? Borthwick is out in that valley. We can't take the chance of carrying this with us just to have him take it. And there's only one way out of this place!"

Ellie recalled the steep, curving walls of the sinkhole. Neil was right. Their only way out of here was to go back through Sita's cave—and somehow get past Borthwick and his soldiers in the gorge.

"So maybe we don't carry it out with us," Adam said grimly. "Maybe we destroy it right here."

Ellie felt a thrill of horror. "There is no way to destroy it. You can only use it. Which means you'd have to find a target... and that target would be completely obliterated. Even if we just directed it at the ground, we could end up devastating the entire forest."

"Do any of you know how to shoot an arrow?" Adam asked.

"Don't you?" Neil pressed back uncomfortably.

"Why would I? I'm usually carrying around a perfectly good Winchester repeater—when someone hasn't dropped a cave on it," Adam added with a mischievous look at Ellie.

"I did not drop a cave on your last Winchester," Ellie tartly corrected. "Borthwick took it."

"That's fair," Adam allowed.

"I know how to shoot an arrow."

The voice was low, even, and casually threatening.

Ellie whirled toward it to see Jacobs step into the doorway—and level a rifle at her chest.

"And it looks like I have a Winchester as well," he added darkly.

Jacobs' shirt was open to the waist, the fabric torn in places. Blood soaked his back and shoulder. A bruise darkened his jaw, his hair wet and disheveled.

Ellie, Adam, Constance, and Neil froze in a tableau where they were gathered around the altar.

She made a rapid, desperate calculation. Adam's machete was still missing. Constance was out of daggers. The only weapon they had was Neil's flaming sword—which he had no idea how to use.

"That's my gun, isn't it?" Adam nodded to the rifle.

Jacobs answered him with an unapologetic smile.

"How are you even here?" Ellie demanded.

"I followed you lot. You always seem to find your way to what I'm looking for." Jacobs swung the rifle to point at Constance. "Hand me those items from the altar, Miss Mallory, and I'll refrain from putting a hole in your friend."

Constance's expression blazed with fury. "If you were three steps closer, I promise I could make that much harder for you to do."

"I don't need to be any closer to shoot you, Miss Tyrrell," Jacobs reasonably replied. "Now hurry along, Miss Mallory. Or I can kill your friend right now to show you just how serious I am and still have your brother to threaten."

Ellie looked to Adam. His expression was grim. "I don't think this is a bluff we want to call, Princess."

Carefully, she picked up the arrow. It flared with ghostly, dancing light. A hot wind rose once more, the scent of ozone burning in her nose.

She felt something where her fingers met the shaft—not the uncomfortable sting of the Staff of Moses but an electric, humming sense of unimaginable potential.

The feeling was not comfortable. Ellie quickly dropped the arcanum into the quiver.

The bow seemed warm to the touch as she lifted it, as though someone else had only just let it go.

Jacobs balanced the rifle against his hip from the strap over his uninjured shoulder, his finger still on the trigger. He extended his left hand to Ellie, his jaw twitching with pain as the movement tugged on his wound. "Quiver first."

She handed it to him. He slowly lifted the strap over his head. The muscles of his cheek tightened with a wince as the quiver fell into place on his back, just below the vicious wound from Borthwick's whip.

Ellie felt a queasy, involuntary tug of sympathy.

Adam nodded at Jacobs' shoulder. "That must hurt like hell."

"Gloating, Mr. Bates?"

Adam's expression was level. "Might surprise you, but I happen to think it's wrong to whip a man. No matter how much of a bastard he is."

A rich, tense complexity swirled between the two men as Jacobs held out his hand again. "Bow."

Ellie obeyed, and a shudder of pain racked through him as he slid the weapon onto his wounded shoulder.

The movement pulled aside his ripped, bloody shirt, revealing the dark lines of a ruined tower and its twin swords slashed across the pale skin of his chest. Words blazed in black over his heart.

PER ARDUA.

Constance lifted her chin with an air of contempt. "I knew you were a stooge for the Order of Albion, but I didn't think you'd stoop so low as to tattoo Lord Aldbury's sigil on your chest."

Jacobs went deeply, entirely still.

The room froze around him, the air itself holding taut. Even Ellie's blood seemed to slow, pulsing strangely through her veins as her mind scrambled to make sense of what she had just heard.

Jacobs spoke, each word burning like hot iron. *"What did you say?"*

Constance frowned, bewildered by his tone. "That symbol on your chest. It's from Lord Aldbury's ring. He wears it constantly. Surely you've seen it?"

"I have never met Lord Aldbury," Jacobs replied with exaggerated care.

The buzzing in Ellie's brain grew louder.

"He isn't important enough to have met him," she filled in numbly. "He hasn't been let in to their circle."

Constance's brow furrowed. "But then why on earth would he have that tattoo?"

A cold horror ran over Ellie's skin as she met Jacobs' burning black gaze from across the room. "Because he saw it somewhere else. I expect… that he saw it the day his mother died."

Jacobs stalked forward, leveling the Winchester at Constance's face.

Neil lurched toward him, reaching for his sword.

Adam stopped him, holding an arm in front of his chest as he watched Jacobs carefully.

Jacobs glared at Constance above the barrel of the gun. "Tell me about the ring."

Constance looked at Jacobs with genuine confusion. "There's a black cabochon inlaid with gold, showing that falling tower and the two swords. And then the words around the outside—*per ardua.*" She offered the rest to Ellie. "I noticed it when Mother had him over for tea. Probably because I was so bored with the two of them talking over me."

Her expression flattened with shock as her attention shifted back to Jacobs.

Jacobs tensed behind the barrel of the rifle. "Why are you looking at me like that?"

"You resemble him," Constance spilled out.

"Resemble who?" Ellie prompted—even as a chill of understanding crept up her spine.

Constance gazed at Jacobs with dazed recognition. "Lord Aldbury."

Jacobs took a step back, staring at her as though she had just bitten him.

Adam jabbed a finger, forgetting himself out of sheer surprise. "Hold on—*he* looks like Aldbury?"

"Well, Lord Aldbury's a bit taller, and he's gone silver, especially about the temples, but…" Constance trailed off as though seeing a ghost. "It's a bit uncanny, actually."

"But Lord Aldbury is Julian Forster-Mowbray's dad," Adam pointed out wildly.

Constance waved a dismissive hand. "Julian takes after his mother."

Ellie thought of the words she had spilled out earlier that day—the moment before Jacobs had tried to throttle her.

Most women are hurt by someone they love.

The logical, rational conclusion fell from her lips. "The man you've been trying to find—the man who hurt your mother. It's him. Lord Aldbury. *And he's your father.*"

Jacobs took a threatening step toward Constance. His breath was short and uneven. "If you even *think* to try to mislead me…"

"But she can't," Ellie burst out. "*She can't.* You'd know if she was lying!"

His knuckles whitened where he gripped the rifle as though only his hold on the gun was keeping his hands from shaking.

"Hold on." Adam frowned. "Wouldn't that make The Mustache his half-brother?"

Ellie felt dizzy. "*Fiddlesticks.*"

Jacobs began to laugh. The sound tore out of him, harsh and acid, nearly doubling him over. When he raised his eyes to Ellie and Adam once more, they flashed with a new, dangerous sharpness. "Well, then. I suppose now we know how you two were meant to help me along."

Ellie's blood chilled with a quick rush of fear.

Jacobs didn't need them anymore… which meant he no longer had a reason not to kill them.

Adam realized it as well. He tensed, readying himself for a leap—even though it would almost certainly mean suicide.

Forgotten at Jacobs' side, Neil whipped out his sword.

Jacobs whirled at the movement, but Neil was already slashing the blade down, even as flames still bloomed up Dyrnwyn's length. The weapon sliced through the barrel of the Winchester, and the front half of the rifle dropped to the ground with a clang.

For a moment, all five of them stared at the damage with shock.

Neil snapped back to himself, swinging up the sword.

Jacobs recovered faster. He threw the rest of the gun at Neil, forcing him to flinch back.

With a grunt of muted agony, he ripped the bow from his shoulder—and fitted the arrow to the string.

Unearthly light flared up around the bolt in swirling threads. All the air in the room pulled toward it, setting the dead leaves spinning once again.

Jacobs pointed the arrow at Neil, who gripped Dyrnwyn's silently flickering length in his hands. "Drop it."

Adam raised his hands, pleading. "You can't use that thing on him."

"I'll use it on whoever I bloody like," Jacobs snarled in return, threads of silver and gold painting the harsh lines of his face.

"But it only works once!" Ellie insisted desperately. "What about Aldbury?"

"I don't need an arcanum to kill Aldbury," Jacobs snapped.

Ellie stepped toward him, willing him to understand. "You know who you've been searching for now. It doesn't have to be like this anymore!"

Fresh blood streamed down Jacobs chest, fingers of it staining the black lines of his tattoo. His body was rigid with wild, conflicted energy.

Too much had changed for him, far too quickly. The contemptuous lash of Borthwick's whip. The shocking revelation of the identity of the man he'd been seeking for most of his life. The blazing, terrible power he held in his hands. Jacobs was wrenched taut with all of it.

One impulsive blaze of fury could see all of them destroyed. The arrow, after all, could hit a collective target as easily as a singular one. All that stood between Ellie and death was the question of exactly how Jacobs would process the maelstrom raging through his heart.

He moved around them until the arrow pointed through them toward the door.

"Outside," he ordered thinly. "All of you. *Now.*"

Adam took her arm and guided her back to the entrance of the temple, watching Jacobs warily. Neil and Constance followed.

Ellie squinted as they emerged back into the light of the sinkhole—and then froze at the sight of a ring of rifles pointed at her chest.

"There you are," Colonel Charles Borthwick declared smoothly.

Grass whispered around his boots with the breath of a warm breeze. Singh Rao stood to his right, stoic and unreadable. Sepoys framed them, weapons steady in their hands.

The stairs to Sita's cave lay beyond, a distant black promise in the impenetrable wall of red stone.

Jacobs lingered in the shadows at Ellie's back. The cold glow of the astra dimmed to a simmer as he moderated his grip on the weapon—but she still sensed the threat it posed. The danger encompassed all of them—her and Adam, Neil and Constance. Singh Rao and his men. Borthwick, who eyed them with a triumphant contempt.

The feeling was like a lit fuse hissing in her ear. An explosion was coming—but she found she could not begin to guess where it would be directed.

Borthwick hadn't seen Jacobs yet. His gaze was locked on Adam.

"I suppose I shouldn't be surprised you would turn up here," he commented mildly.

Dawson popped out from behind the soldiers. "I knew these people weren't trustworthy! They are a bunch of unqualified riffraff!"

Constance opened her mouth for an indignant protest.

Adam cut in, muttering. "Not worth it."

Borthwick's gaze shifted to the flaming sword in Neil's hand. "I'm a little more surprised to find you still standing. Perhaps that trinket you're carrying has something to do with how you managed to survive. I look forward to examining it more closely, once I've relieved you of it."

Neil's mouth firmed at the implied threat, his hand tightening on the sword's hilt.

"I assume they've been in league with you all this time," Borthwick remarked casually to Adam. "It's an insult, really—that your father would send you out here to cross me with nothing more than a scholar and a pair of women."

Hot, swirling wind gusted through the sinkhole, rippling the wild herbs at Adam's feet. He looked as queasy as he might on a hundred-foot precipice. "You think my *father* sent me here?"

Borthwick's eyes blazed with hot violence. "Don't treat me like a fool, Mr. Bates. I don't take well to it." He moderated his tone as he paced through the grass. "I do give you credit for the sheer audacity of the show you put on in order to insert yourself into my party. I assumed, of course, that you had most likely been sent to spy on us. Even that would have been a violation of the gentleman's agreement that governs this delicate work. But to learn that your actual mission was to try to steal the arcanum out from under my nose—well, that's something else entirely. The relative civility of this little arms race depends upon the understanding that you Yanks have your territory, and we have ours."

Ellie's mind whirled to keep up with Borthwick's words.

You Yanks have your territory…

"What the hell are you talking about?" Adam demanded.

But Ellie already knew.

George Bates's name was recognized across continents. He was as much a lord in his realm as Aldbury, one who ruled both his financial empire and his family with a merciless will and iron-hard expectations.

One who had tried to force Adam into a brutal mold that he had never been meant to fit.

This little arms race…

The high red walls around Ellie seemed to spin. Borthwick wasn't engaging in a leap of groundless paranoia. He was accusing George Bates of trying to steal arcana… because that must be something Adam's father had already done.

"You think I don't know what he's up to in Seoul?" Borthwick drawled. "He's welcome to whatever the Joseon are hiding—but India's treasures belong to the crown."

Seoul, Ellie thought, feeling sick. George Bates was in Seoul.

He's welcome to whatever the Joseon are hiding…

Borthwick's fingers casually tapped against the butt of his whip. The gesture was deliberate—a reminder of how willing he was to resort to violence. "Clearly, repercussions are required. Boundaries must be maintained—but there's no need to make it unnecessarily unpleasant. We are all still gentlemen, after all. Your wife can carry word to your father in Korea while you remain here as my guest until he has provided a guarantee of his future good behavior."

Adam's hands clenched desperately at his sides. "You can't do that. Ellie has nothing to do with this!"

Borthwick's brow rose. "Your wife isn't the one I was threatening to hold on to."

But Adam wasn't a fool. He would have understood that.

He was afraid because Borthwick planned to send Ellie to his father.

An itching, uncomfortable tension crept up her spine.

Adam struggled to rein himself in. "My father won't care what you do with me."

"Nonsense," Borthwick retorted. "George Bates is a man who values his legacy. A son isn't something he'll let go of lightly."

The words echoed hollowly through Ellie's mind.

A son isn't something he'll let go of lightly.

The air around her grew colder.

"Now, if whichever of you is hiding my astra would be so kind as to hand it over?" Borthwick lightly ordered.

The murderer who lurked at Ellie's back stepped into the light, holding the power of the gods in his hands.

Jacobs' expression was unreadable. The black lines of the tattoo on his pale chest were smeared with crimson. The Brahmastra was notched and ready, the arrow dancing with ghostly light.

Ellie's skin hummed with an uncomfortable, electric tension. The wind that tugged at the loose tangles of her hair smelled of ozone.

Borthwick studied Jacobs with dry interest. "This is a surprise. I assumed you'd gone off to lick your wounds, but it would appear that you actually made yourself useful for a change. Bring the astra here—unless you plan to keep skulking back there like an alley thug."

Dawson's eyes widened with horror at the dismissive contempt in Borthwick's tone.

Ellie's fear tightened as though a volatile element loomed at her back, and Borthwick was intent on lighting the fuse.

Singh Rao sensed it as well. He signaled subtly to his men with a flick of his hand, and sweating fingers tensed on triggers.

Not that it would matter against the weapon that flickered silently at Ellie's back.

Jacobs didn't move. The bow remained taut in his grip, the astra dancing with cold flame.

Borthwick had already started to turn away. At Jacobs' lack of response, he frowned. "Did you not hear me?"

"I heard you," Jacobs returned in a voice that Ellie knew uncomfortably well.

Her hand rose to the bruises at her throat.

Clouds swirled dangerously through the gap overhead, thickened to a heavy charcoal. Dawson looked up at them nervously.

Singh Rao waited, tense and ready.

"Have you already forgotten the last lesson I taught you?" Borthwick snapped. "You're the son of an East End whore. What do you think you're here for, exactly?"

Ellie closed her eyes and wondered if they were all about to die.

Jacobs was still as water—and yet the texture of the air around him seemed to deeply, irrevocably shift.

"What am I here for?" His mouth curved into a knife-thin smile. "Nothing. Not anymore."

He loosed the arrow.

Time slowed like water.

The roar of unquenchable flames filled Ellie's ears. Air drew toward the bolt as though sucking into the vacuum of a black hole. Golden light burned at the corner of her eye.

The astra moved past her face with a flash of heat that pulled at the bones beneath her skin—and slammed into Borthwick's chest.

His face twisted with purple outrage as he raised a hand to the shaft protruding from his shoulder. "You stupid bloody fool! That wasn't even a killing—"

The words died as a wild, terrible light burst from the place where the weapon met his flesh.

Borthwick's arms flew wide, his chest pulling toward the sky. His mouth dropped open in a terrible scream.

Ellie couldn't hear it over the roar of the wind in her ears.

The grass bent flat with the force of the tempest, the sky overhead turning to a roiling nightmare pierced by a thousand shards of wild purple light.

Arms snared her waist and hauled her down. Ellie found herself tucked against the temple wall as Adam covered her with his body.

Borthwick glowed with impossible fire. The blaze tugged at his skin, pulling it inward until bone broke through.

Then his bones were burning.

Everything burned… until it was over.

What had once been Borthwick showered to the earth in a fall of white ash.

The grass stilled with a whisper of shifting blades. Silence settled over the enclosure.

The soldiers had dived for cover. Dawson lay flat on the ground, his hands over his head.

Neil held Constance, pressing her to the relative shelter of the temple wall.

The shocked, frozen tableau was broken by the sound of a bow hitting the ground as Jacobs unceremoniously tossed the artifact aside—and began to walk away.

THIRTY-NINE

*D*izzy with shock and horror from within the circle of Adam's arms, Ellie watched Jacobs walk away.

Singh Rao was the first to recover. The subedar whipped his sidearm from its holster as he rose to his feet. *"Halt!"*

His men followed his lead, scrambling upright and leveling their rifles.

Jacobs paused, glancing back at them over his shoulder.

The terrible wound showed through the tear in his shirt. He showed no fear as he stared at the weapons ranged against him—only a cold, unflinching contempt. "I could have killed all of you. I won't say I didn't consider it."

He turned away and kept walking.

Singh Rao's expression flickered with uncertainty—and then firmed. He stepped forward, the pistol steady. "You will need to come with me."

Jacobs didn't stop.

The subedar's lips thinned with frustration, his finger tightening on the trigger.

Wild instinct pushed Ellie free of Adam's arms. Her wounded calf made a hot protest as she stumbled toward them.

A plea burst from her mouth. "Don't shoot!"

Jacobs hesitated at the foot of the stairs—where Singh Rao clearly intended to stop him, whatever that required.

The Sikh officer kept his eyes on Jacobs as he responded to her. "Why?"

The question echoed through Ellie's mind. *Why indeed?*

Jacobs was a ruthless, vicious killer. He had tried to throttle her only a few hours before. She knew without a shadow of a doubt that he was leaving now to go hunt down and slaughter a peer of the realm—one that Ellie felt uncomfortably certain was also a murderer.

Jacobs was dangerous. He would always be dangerous… and he had more or less promised to kill both her and Adam the next chance he got.

The idea of seeing him shot down like a rabid dog still filled her with horror.

Singh Rao waited for her answer with an air of exasperated impatience. The subedar simply wanted to do his job—which obviously included not allowing the man who had just obliterated his commanding officer to walk away.

Adam stared at Ellie with worried surprise. Constance's eyes were wide as she stepped out from the shelter of the temple, Neil at her back.

Ellie had no idea what to say—except that no one deserved to be gunned down like that, not even a killer.

And that she was oddly, uncomfortably certain that her and Adam's story with Jacobs didn't end here.

Singh Rao wouldn't accept either of those explanations.

This could not go well for Ellie and her companions, either. They had been caught red-handed trying to interfere with an official government expedition. That very likely qualified as treason. At the least, a man like Singh Rao would feel obligated to put all four of them under arrest and return them to the colonial authorities in Madras.

Where the Order of Albion was sure to have far more influence than a bunch of disreputable scholars.

They were outgunned and trapped in a hole in the ground. Ellie was consumed by the awareness that they were completely and utterly at Singh Rao's mercy.

He was still waiting for her to speak. So was Jacobs, balanced on the threshold of the stairs.

Ellie had no idea what she could possibly say to either of them.

She opened her mouth to try anyway—and was interrupted by the clatter of arms from above.

Singh Rao jerked his head up… where the circular mouth of the sinkhole was framed by the crouched, ready figures of the Adrija.

Bows and muskets fixed on the soldiers below.

Instinct snapped Ellie's eyes back to the ground—just in time to meet Jacobs' gaze across the meadow.

Dark amusement flickered through his expression… along with a hint of unpleasant promise.

He darted into the passage.

Singh Rao whirled at the movement, barking out an order—and then froze at the crack of a shot from above, dirt exploding from the ground beside his boots.

Subhas Kōnja stood at the edge of the drop, smoke curling from the antique Enfield in his hands.

The army detachment had greater numbers and better weaponry. They would solidly outgun the Adrija in a fair fight—but Subhas's men had the clear advantage in position. Singh Rao had no cover save the temple, where his soldiers would be trapped. They could only escape the sinkhole one at a time through the narrow stairwell.

No matter how the conflict played out, people were going to die.

Singh Rao was quietly calculating. Subhas's white shirt glowed like a banner as golden sunlight burst from beneath the clouds, his men arrayed around him with dangerous anticipation.

Helplessness twisted through Ellie as she realized how little she could do to stop what was about to happen.

Bare-chested, filthy, and weaponless, Adam stepped into the middle of the field.

Several of the sepoys shifted their rifles to aim at the new threat. Overhead, the Adrija shot questioning looks at their leader.

Adam ignored them, focused on the elegant Sikh officer who stood before him. "You don't want to do this."

Singh Rao's jaw tensed. "My last orders were to take you prisoner."

"Can't do that if I'm dead," Adam pointed out helpfully.

Ellie's gut lurched into her throat.

He was insane—her Adam Bates.

And he was glorious.

Adam looked up at Subhas, squinting against the light. "Did you come all the way back here just to rescue us?"

Subhas's relaxed posture still carried a whiff of danger. "Maybe. Or maybe I wanted to make sure that the Indian Army isn't going after my village."

"He's not interested in doing that." Adam glanced over at the subedar. "Are you?"

The sepoys watched the exchange, sensing the tension in it even though they didn't speak the language.

Singh Rao's hands tightened on his pistol. Frustration seethed off of him. Ellie could almost sympathize. The man was trying to do his job—one that he took very seriously—and nothing about this had gone remotely the way he had expected.

The officer met Adam's gaze as he bit out an answer. "That would not be part of my duties, in the absence of an official order... or clear evidence of revolutionary activity."

"Hey, Ellie," Adam called over casually. "You see any revolutionary activity here?"

The question was audacious. Adam delivered it with an air of complete, unflinching confidence.

Ellie's heart burst with pride.

"None at all," she replied with a perfectly straight face as a ring of arrows pointed down from above.

Singh Rao muttered a prayer under his breath in strained tones of exasperation—then waved his hand.

With an uneven, tentative series of clicks, his men lowered their weapons.

Adam turned to Subhas, waiting.

"Ittadu," Subhas ordered, and the Adrija relaxed.

Vanika popped into view at her cousin's side, beaming with smug triumph. "I told you that I would free them!" she called down.

Adam's lip tugged with the urge to smile. "And I thought I said to keep safe."

Vanika rolled her eyes. "Why do you think I did not come to the edge while you were all trying to shoot each other?"

A new voice cut in, distinctly cultured and ringing with mischief. "Tell me that I haven't missed *all* the fun!"

Constance darted out to join Adam under the opening of the sinkhole. "Uncle Vijay?!"

Her royal relative strode into view, beaming down at her. Vijay was a sight. He wore an elegant white sherwani with a gold-embroidered purple sash around his waist, his head wrapped in a turban secured with a jeweled pin. A curved sword hung from his belt alongside a wicked-looking dagger.

"There you are, you mad thing!" he exclaimed happily.

"What on earth are you doing here?" Constance demanded.

"Looking for you, of course," Vijay returned.

"But how could you possibly have found us?" she pushed back.

"I just followed the dog."

"The dog?" Ellie echoed with a lurch of surprise.

Kalb skidded to a stop at the edge of the drop, his tail wagging furiously.

"He found me in the forest and insisted on leading me back here." Vijay gave the happily panting animal a rub on his head.

Adam tossed Ellie a smirk. "Told you he was lucky."

Kalb replied with a happy bark.

Singh Rao studied the glittering figure of Constance's uncle. "You're the lord of Nandapur."

"Heard of me, have you?" Vijay's words were deceptively light.

"My commanding officer might have mentioned you," Singh Rao returned dryly.

Vijay's eyes twinkled with dark amusement. "Did he? And where is your colonel now?"

Ellie instinctively looked to a pile of pale ash in a charred circle of grass.

"No idea," Adam replied with a suspiciously straight face.

Understanding flickered through Vijay's expression. He seemed to grow taller, wrapping an air of glittering authority around himself like a well-tailored coat. "But why such stiff faces? After all, we are here for the same reason."

"And what reason is that?" Singh Rao demanded skeptically.

Vijay's expression was uncharacteristically serious. "The good of India."

"I think we might have different notions of what that means," Singh Rao returned.

"I disagree," Vijay countered, his eyes glittering significantly. "We may have looked for it in unlike places—but I doubt that what we ultimately seek is all that far apart, Subedar."

Singh Rao's face softened as the maharaja's words struck him.

Vijay's posture relaxed as he returned to his usual bright insouciance. "But that's all beside the point. We're just travelers bumping into each other by pure fortune—my niece and her friends, Mr. Kōnja and his companions, and me with a modest little personal guard."

"Personal guard?" Singh Rao echoed tiredly.

Vijay's features schooled into an expression of sober innocence. "One really can't be too careful these days."

A bizarrely unexpected sound trumpeted through the cliffs.

Neil's face drained. "Why did that sound like an elephant?"

"Because it was an elephant," Vijay replied with a blinding white grin. "How else do you think we got here?"

Ellie limped onto the colonnaded veranda in front of Sita's chamber as the sun slanted between the ridge and the heavy gray clouds of the monsoon, painting the ravine with gold. Silver water tumbled down the bluff while flowers framed the turquoise ribbon of the stream.

Doves burst from another rock-cut chamber, soaring over the moss-covered bones.

The room that Sita had called home was undeniably humble, but it had still possessed a view fit for a queen.

That view was currently quite crowded. By the bank of the stream, the men Singh Rao had left behind to guard his camp sat in a circle, disarmed and subdued. They were surrounded by other soldiers dressed in rugged green uniforms. The newcomers carried modern weapons and wore boots with puttees.

Behind them loomed a half dozen massive gray animals decked out in steel-plated leather, iron helmets framing their skulls.

"He actually brought the elephants," Ellie said numbly, staring at the enormous creatures as Adam joined her on the veranda.

One of the largest lifted her trunk and bellowed.

Singh Rao took in the scene with a reflexive twitch of his jaw. "A modest personal guard."

"His Highness likes to feel *really* safe." Adam's expression sobered. "Just how much of this are you going to report when you get back to your base?"

Singh Rao studied the gorge. Ellie weighed how much rode on his response. The subedar had to be feeling torn between the strict interpretation of his duty and his more pragmatic instincts.

"Jacobs shot the colonel. A warrant will be issued. I do not believe that I need to complicate that report with... *incidentals.*"

"Thank you," Adam said genuinely.

Singh Rao's look turned dry. "Maybe I just prefer to avoid the extra paperwork."

He descended the stairs to where the rest of his men had gathered—along with Dawson, who had firmly attached himself to the soldiers, demanding an escort back to Madras.

Ellie wished the subedar luck with that.

Adam tilted queasily. "Pretty glad that didn't involve more talking."

Ellie recalled where they were—on a narrow ledge three stories above the ground. "Drat."

She hooked a hand through Adam's arm and hauled him back against the wall.

He slid down it until he sat on the ground, closing his eyes. "I'll be fine in jusss a minute. Ssoon as things stop..."

He made a vague circling motion with his hand.

Neil and Constance stepped out from Sita's cave. Neil had sheathed his sword, carrying the bow and quiver from the temple instead. His eyes widened with alarm behind his spectacles as he took in Adam's position.

"Are we going to have to carry him down?"

Ellie's calf protested at the idea.

"There's only room for one at a time on the stairs." Constance brightened. "Maybe we could just tie him up and lower him over the side."

"Not a chance in hell," Adam replied flatly.

"What if we blindfolded him?" Ellie suggested.

"Tried that once," Neil replied shortly. "He lost his supper on a constable."

"Wasssn't *on* him," Adam corrected him woozily. "Missed him by a good foot."

Ten minutes and a few harrowing moments later, they got Adam back to the ground—where a blur of golden fur crashed into them from the underbrush.

Adam caught the impact, woozily falling to the grass. Kalb licked his face furiously, and Adam hauled the dog into a hug. "That's right—who's the best boy? You are! You're the best boy!"

Kalb sprang away from Adam, whirling to Ellie. He froze, quivering with barely contained excitement as he whimpered up at her.

Ellie gave in. "Oh, fine. Yes, you were a good boy."

She gave him a pat on the top of his head, and Kalb took that as an invitation to smash himself between her legs, wriggling like a live trout. Ellie nearly tripped from the impact—and then the dog froze at a suspicious rustle from the nearby brush.

"Not again!" she groaned.

With a burst of raucous barking, Kalb bolted.

"He'll be back," Adam asserted from where he remained sprawled on the ground.

"I am starting to actually believe that," Ellie grumbled.

She limped over to him.

"That leg'll feel better once you stop walking on it," Adam pointed out helpfully.

"I think we're about to be a bit short on mules," Ellie countered.

She turned at a sound from behind to see Constance's royal uncle rappel down the face of the cliff, landing with enthusiastic agility. He loosed the ropes from his belt with a practiced tug.

"This really is an absolutely splendid piece of geography." His expression grew dangerously thoughtful. "One might find it an excellent spot for a winter retreat."

Subhas slid down another set of ropes beside him, shooting the maharaja an exasperated look that already carried an air of weary practice. "I don't think Tari Penu would approve of that," he warned tersely.

Vijay winked. "Well, if the goddess wouldn't approve, I'd best not chance it. Plenty of other waterfalls around." He turned to Ellie and the others, setting his hands on his hips. "So, the Brahmastra has been disposed of. It's the best possible scenario, really—for everyone but the poor colonel, obviously."

"We still need to decide what to do with this." Neil awkwardly held out the bow.

Vijay accepted it with an air of uncharacteristically subdued reverence. "Is this what I think it is?"

"Well, it would be difficult to establish a reliable provenance without a written record…" Neil began hesitantly.

"It's Lord Rama's bow," Constance asserted confidently.

Tears gathered in Vijay's eyes as he ran his fingers over the place where the wood had been darkened by use. His expression was firm with determination when he looked up again. "This will be kept secret and safe until the day when India can claim her own treasures once again."

Ellie was washed with a warm sense of relief.

Adam regained his feet. He slid his arm around her shoulder, pulling her to his side. Ellie let herself lean against the warmth of his chest.

Vanika shouted down from the ridge above. Light glinted off the blade in her hand. "Mr. Bates! Can I keep your enormous knife?"

"Absolutely not!" Adam called back. "But if you bring it back, I'll teach you how to throw it!"

Ellie stared at him. Subhas groaned.

Vanika's approving whoop echoed off the ravine.

Vijay clapped his hands with delight. "Now that's all settled—who needs a ride?

The elephants trumpeted again.

Adam gave Ellie a telling look as her leg continued to throb.

"Fiddlesticks," Ellie cursed—and Adam laughed.

FORTY

CONSTANCE STOOD AMID a noisy crowd of elegant silk-clad bodies in the Rani Salon of her uncle's royal palace. The spacious room glittered with mirrors, crystal, and Maratha tile.

It had taken them three days to reach Nandapur, including a stop in Vanika's village where they had joined a raucous celebration of the girl's safe return. For most of the trip, Constance had been too exhausted to think. When they finally returned to the palace late the night before, she had collapsed into her bed and slept until two in the afternoon. That little lie-in had left her with just enough time to dress before her nephew's birthday party.

The festivities were extravagant. The salon was packed with glittering dignitaries and extended family, all chatting and laughing. The men were decked out in gorgeous kurtas and silk trousers while the women wore brilliantly patterned saris or gem-studded shalwar kameez. Hues of peach and saffron mingled with peacock blue and emerald green.

Constance's own gown was a new acquisition that her Aunt Parvati had secretly ordered for the party. The costume was cut like a fashionable British evening dress with capped sleeves and a structured bodice, but it had been made with a beautiful sambalpuri weave in royal purple and sunset gold—the royal family colors.

She might have teared up a bit when Parvati had presented it to her.

The guest of honor, the now-ten-year-old Arjuna, held court in his jeweled turban and gold slippers, receiving the cheerful well-wishes of his guests with the regal air of a future maharaja… until Vanika popped up from behind his chair to drop a lizard down his shirt.

Arjuna leaped up with a howl of righteous outrage, tearing after her as Vanika darted away, her dress tunic and trousers still giving her ample flexibility for a sprint.

Ellie squeezed through the crowd to join Constance by the window. She clutched a book to her chest and only slightly favored her wounded leg. Her bite wounds had calmed down during the rest provided by her three-day ride home—not that Ellie had been remotely happy about being stuck on top of an elephant.

"I don't think I have ever been introduced to this many people at once in my life," Ellie complained.

Her emerald dinner gown had been tidied and repaired since its romp through a bat-infested attic. The color drew out the earthy tones in her hazel eyes and the slightly mortified flush to her cheeks.

She and Adam had been relieved of their dog for the evening in the interest of keeping the Seluki off the tables of food that packed the adjacent chamber. The animal had been hauled away by a sighing servant as he sniffed the air for treats.

Constance took a sip from her flute of champagne. "I hear there's going to be dancing later."

Ellie frowned. "I didn't go to finishing school, Constance. I don't know how to dance."

"You should try anyway. It works differently here in India."

Ellie cast her a skeptical look.

Adam slipped up next to them. Even though he wore an ordinary jacket rather than a dinner one, he appeared perfectly dashing—if one ignored the bruises on his face and the eighteen-inch machete hanging from his belt.

"Are you really wearing that to a child's birthday party?" Ellie nodded at the blade with a note of exasperated indulgence.

"What?" Adam pushed back. "Some of her uncle's guys here are wearing swords."

"Those are ceremonial," Constance pointed out.

Adam gave the hilt of his knife a possessive pat. "Who says this one isn't ceremonial?"

Constance shrugged. She was hardly going to call him out for carrying a weapon around. She had two knives in her garters as they spoke. "What are *your* thoughts on dancing?" she asked instead.

"Love it," Adam replied.

Constance shot Ellie a challenging look. "You have to dance if Adam's going to."

"Why?" Ellie retorted.

"Well, I can't dance with him," Constance countered. "I have to partner with my… er…"

Her gaze shifted to her fake fiancé.

Neil had cleaned up. His shoes were polished and his jaw clean-shaven—not that it made a great difference. He wore the saffron dupatta that Constance had bought for him at the Jagannath festival over his dinner jacket and white waistcoat.

He was pinned to one of the settees by a pile of Arjuna's elegantly dressed younger siblings. A six-year-old boy sat beside him with an enormous book, pointing at it and peppering Neil with questions that held an air of royal command. Neil adjusted his spectacles as he held the tome up for a better look.

A two-year-old crawled up his shoulder to pluck at his glasses. She started to slip, and he caught her automatically with his free arm.

She succeeded in snatching the gold wire frames from his face, which she promptly put into her mouth.

Neil handed the book back to the boy. He plucked his eyewear from the toddler's grip, substituting it for a spoon, which she happily accepted as an alternative object to gnaw.

A five-year-old girl with a jeweled nose ring pressed a treat at him with a sticky hand. Neil accepted it distractedly, gave it a cursory examination, and popped it into his mouth.

Constance's stomach felt a bit fluttery.

It must have been the champagne.

Adam's voice called her back to herself. "Princess, you can't read at a party."

Constance drew her attention back and saw that Ellie had stuck her nose in the book.

"I most certainly can," Ellie retorted.

Constance checked the writing on the spine. "*Mystical Powers of the Hindus?*"

Ellie snapped the book shut and shielded it against her bosom. "It's a very interesting subject."

"Does that mean you finally found Uncle Vijay's library?"

Ellie's reply was clipped with frustration. "Not yet. Someone was using this one as a paperweight."

"Hope they weren't important papers," Adam quipped.

Constance couldn't blame Ellie for wanting to learn more about the world of supernatural wonders they had all recently plunged into. Her friend was a scholar, after all. Even Constance, who had always had a fairly open mind about such things, had been surprised by the wondrous discoveries of the last few weeks… including those that related to people rather close to her.

She looked back at Neil.

He was trying to stand up. The children responded by clinging to him like monkeys. She saw the moment when he gave up and allowed them to use him as a climbing gym.

Her view was cut off by her royal uncle as he walked past with Mr. Chowdhury. Vijay was gorgeously decked out in a sherwani richly embroidered with purple and gold. For once, Mr. Chowdhury also wore Indian dress, though his kurta and trousers were a more soberly elegant dark blue silk.

Ellie stepped out to intercept them. "Your Highness, have you any more books like this one?"

She held out *The Mystical Powers of the Hindus.*

Vijay held Mr. Chowdhury's arm, his eyes merry. "That one's not even mine."

Ellie seemed thrown. "It isn't?"

"That mad Scotsman left it here four years ago." Vijay looked to his companion. "You remember him. Don't you, Nawaz?"

"Your pet hermit?" Mr. Chowdhury returned dryly.

"He made a very charming addition to the eastern gardens," Vijay explained.

Mr. Chowdhury's voice held a note of affectionate exasperation. "He only meant to be here for a month."

"I'm sure I would have convinced him to stay on if he hadn't wandered off in the middle of the night," Vijay complained.

"What else did you expect a pet hermit to do?" his companion retorted.

"Who are you two going on about?" Constance demanded.

Mr. Chowdhury answered. "The gentleman in question was a traveler interested in studying the region's ascetics."

"Looking for swamis who could float," Vijay elaborated helpfully. "How did he put it? 'A study of individuals possessed of exceptional mythic abilities,' or some such thing. I gather he'd made it his beat. He'd been over half the world digging up dusty manuscripts and hunting for monks holed up in caves living on a single grain of rice."

Ellie's arms tightened around her book.

Adam glanced down at her thoughtfully. "This guy still in India?"

Vijay sighed. "Alas, no. He rejected my hermitage after he had interrogated all the half-naked gurus of the hills and moved on to someplace else."

"He was in Korea, last I heard," Mr. Chowdhury filled in.

Adam went still.

Ellie didn't seem to notice. Constance wondered if she had even heard the rest of the conversation. Her expression had grown fiercely thoughtful as soon as Uncle Vijay had mentioned that the traveling scholar had been looking for strangely powerful gurus.

Vijay cocked his head at his companion. "How do you know where my uncooperative hermit is?"

"Because he keeps writing to ask you to forward him his books," Mr. Chowdhury smoothly retorted.

The maharaja cast a slightly guilty look at the volume in Ellie's arms.

"We'll get around to it," he concluded lightly.

"But who was he?" Ellie demanded urgently.

Vijay frowned. "The hermit? I can't say I recall. It was something dreadfully Scottish."

"Cairncross," Mr. Chowdhury filled in.

Cairncross. The name sent a tickle up the back of Constance's neck.

What an odd fellow he must be.

"Whatever would I do without you?" Vijay gave his companion a wink.

The stoic solicitor's lip quirked with affection as he set a gentle hand to the maharaja's back, steering him toward a cheerful greeting from across the room.

Padma's authoritative voice rang through the salon. "Kondi!"

"Go on," Adam said with a nod.

Ellie shook her head, coming out of a momentary fugue. "Yes, don't mind us."

With a curious frown, Constance left them behind.

Padma looked perfectly regal in a mauve sari with a Rajput drape. Jewels glittered at her nose, ears, and wrists. She dismissed a bevy of other bejeweled aunties with a few gracious words before drawing Constance aside. "Why do I feel like you've been avoiding me?"

"I wasn't avoiding you," Constance protested. "I was sleeping! It has been a very busy week, Aai."

Padma's eyes glittered like the gold at her wrists and ears. "You and your companions did well."

Constance set her hands on her hips with a righteous flash of temper. "Then where does the favor tab stand?"

Padma's expression was as serene as the goddess Lakshmi as she responded. "I believe we can call it even."

Constance felt a wash of relief.

"And have you learned anything from your adventures here in India?" Padma casually pressed.

"Of course. I know a great deal more about municipal water systems. And Subhas's friend Jignesh showed me some very interesting new knife maneuvers."

Padma's gaze drifted over to where Neil was buried under an additional three children. "That is not exactly what I had in mind."

Constance's nerves jumped. "It's not?"

"Oh!" Padma exclaimed lightly. "That's the nephew of the Maharaja of Sonepur over by the dessert table. Not too hard to look at, is he?"

Constance involuntarily jerked her head toward the fellow in question, an admittedly handsome man with gleaming hair and a white smile.

"It's too bad you are set on your English scholar, as Mr. Naru is exceptionally wealthy with an excellent pedigree," Padma continued. "Though you might at least have a little chat with him. It isn't too late for you to change your mind, after all."

Panic whirled up in Constance at her grandmother's casual suggestion.

Aware that Padma was watching her, Constance plastered an empty smile on her face. "Dr. Fairfax and I are thoroughly devoted to each other, so there's no need for any of that. If you'll excuse me?"

The storm inside of her hadn't settled—only tightened. Constance needed air.

She pushed through the crowd, nearly bumping into Vijay's younger brother on her way.

She spun past him as he struggled to right his plate of chenna poda. "Sorry, Uncle Balaram! Lovely party!"

Neil glanced up at her with a frown from beneath the pile of her cousins. Constance ignored him, bursting out the door into the night.

She found herself on a pillared passage that overlooked another wing of the palace, framed by a silent courtyard and clandestine gardens. The only light came from a lamp at the far end of the walkway, cloaking Constance in beneficent shadows as she grasped the balustrade and willed her pulse to steady.

The air was softly cooler than it had been in the salon, the sky violet with the gloaming. Distance dulled the roar of the party to a muffled murmur.

The pounding pressure in her head lingered, refusing to release her.

A footstep sounded against the floor.

Constance whirled, instinctively moving into one of her jiu jitsu stances— only to see Neil standing behind her in his saffron scarf and dinner jacket.

"Are you all right?" he asked carefully.

Constance dropped her martial pose. "I'm fine."

Neil regarded her with a hint of wariness. "If I join you, are you going to try to throw me onto the floor?"

"What would I do that for?"

"You have before."

Soft moonlight glinted off his spectacles. The fine lines at the corners of his eyes were drawn with concern.

The tangled nest of emotion inside of her twisted uncomfortably.

Constance turned away from him, planting herself at the railing.

Neil rested his elbows on the stone beside her as he gazed out over the palace. "It is a bit much in there—in a perfectly lovely way, I mean. But one does occasionally feel the need to reassert one's personal space."

Constance absorbed the familiar lines of his profile as she plucked a piece of chenna poda from his hair. "You're very good with them."

"With who?"

"Children."

Neil gave her a wary look. "I can't say I've had a great deal of experience."

"Then I suppose you're a natural."

The comment was light and easy, the sort of thing Constance might naturally say to her best friend's brother.

Good old Stuffy.

Any further tease caught against the sudden tightness in her throat.

Silence stretched, itching up into tension. Constance fought to understand where it came from. She had never been tense around Neil before.

Perhaps it was because she had kissed him, wildly and with ferocious abandon.

"Have you given it any thought, then?" Neil asked awkwardly.

Given it any thought?

She thought about kissing him all the time.

"How we're going to end this," Neil elaborated.

It felt as though she hit the ground.

The jarring impact took her breath—not that it wasn't a reasonable question. Their arrangement was only meant to last until the threat of a forced marriage was behind her, and the question of how they might reasonably extricate themselves from it still remained. Neil was perfectly within his rights to ask about it.

So why did the question make her feel so wretched?

She ought to tell him that her Aai had only just renewed the threat a moment before. Or she might reasonably put things off. *Let's just give it another two weeks,* or *perhaps we can worry about that when we leave Nandapur.*

Instead, with a flare of anger and an incongruous stab of hurt, Constance gave an answer like a jab from one of her knives. "However you like, I suppose."

Neil straightened from the railing. "However *I* like? I'm not the one who asked for this."

His response added fuel to her anger—which was a far more comfortable emotion than the others roiling inside of her.

Constance embraced it. "As I recall, I very clearly told you I'd changed my mind."

Neil's expression shuttered as he stepped back. "Right. I made it my mess. So I'll clean it up."

He turned and walked away.

Constance stepped after him. "What's that supposed to mean?"

Neil whirled back. "Does it matter?"

It shouldn't.

The thought felt like a wound—but this fake engagement should never have happened. It had always been a bad idea, and it had been Neil who had plummeted them both into it. Why shouldn't he be the one to get them out?

Constance knew all of that was true—and yet part of her still rebelled fiercely against the idea.

"You might do it wrong," she shot back.

Neil let out a helpless, terrible laugh. His eyes were hollow behind his spectacles.

"Connie, if there is one thing in all of this we can be sure of, it's that I'm probably going to do it wrong."

Anger burst through her. "Don't say that."

"Because it's not true?" Neil pressed mercilessly.

The veranda seemed to grow smaller. Constance's head throbbed. "Why are we even talking about this right now?"

It took Neil a moment to answer.

She raised her gaze to him again as the silence lingered. His face was pale—his shoulders heavy as if burdened with some terrible weight.

"Because I'm a wretched actor. I've never been able to hide what I'm really feeling. And I just don't know how long I can go on doing this."

The words stung her with an exquisitely sharp hurt.

How long I can go on doing this.

"You mean pretending to be engaged to me," Constance pushed coldly.

Neil gazed down at her through the cobalt gloom. "Yes, Connie. Pretending."

The hurt stabbed deeper, writhing its way through years of other hurts—comments about being *difficult*, or *a little too much sometimes.*

Constance lashed out against it with the only weapon she could find. "It didn't feel like pretending in the stepwell."

Neil burst out with the opposite of the reaction she had expected.

"That's exactly the bloody point!" he shouted, throwing out his arms as the words echoed down the empty walkway.

Constance shook her head, grasping the railing. "I don't understand."

Neil's voice was raw and unsteady. "*I know.*"

And just like that, he spun on his heel and walked away.

For a moment, Constance stared after him, frozen in place by surprise. Then the surprise crumbled in a rising wave of furious desperation.

"Oh no, you don't," Constance growled—and ran at him.

She caught him by his golden scarf, whirling him around to face her—and hauled him down for a kiss.

He stiffened with shock for a breath—and then met her with a hot, wild fervor.

His hands plunged into her hair, scattering pins to the stones as he ravaged her lips. Constance groaned into his mouth with desperate approval and tore open the buttons on his waistcoat.

She ran her hands up the fabric of his shirt, feeling the taut planes of his chest—then burned with frustration at the barrier between her and what she wanted.

She yanked the shirt from his trousers and tried again.

Her fingers glided up smooth skin. Lean muscle flexed beneath her touch with bare control.

Neil set his hands to her hips and drove her backwards, Constance blindly stumbling until she bumped up against one of the pillars.

Then he grabbed her thighs and lifted them around his waist.

Blinding, ravenous sensation flooded through her. Constance used the power in her legs to lift herself higher, tugging back Neil's head and plunging her tongue into his mouth.

Neil's scent enveloped her—ink and paper, amber and cinnamon. Hot, strong hands gripped her through the silk of her skirt as he pressed himself closer.

Everything about it felt so bloody good… and Constance wanted *more.*

She hooked her ankles behind his hips and bit his earlobe.

Neil's curse was accented by the soft crash of shattering porcelain.

Constance looked over Neil's shoulder to where Ellie stared at her with wide-eyed shock, a broken plate of pastries lying at her feet.

Adam stepped out from the doorway behind her and took in the scene with a glance.

Constance burned with the knowledge of what he saw.

Neil stood with his shirt untucked and his spectacles askew. Constance's dress was pulled down at the shoulder where Neil had been tracing lines of fire across her collarbone with his lips. Her hair had fallen into an abandoned mess.

Her legs were still locked around his body.

Neil released his hold on her thighs, and Constance's feet dropped back to the floor. She took a quick, shaking step back as she tugged up her sleeve.

Her forced, cheerful tone rang with jarring falseness. "Oh. There you two are."

Neil said nothing. He made no effort to right himself. He just stared at his sister helplessly—and then turned to Constance.

His look pinned her in place as the heat faded from the places where he had touched her skin. She tried to read the poetic lines of his face, wondering urgently what he seemed to want—no, *need*—to say.

Aai's voice sang from the door to the hall. "Kondi!"

Neil spun on his heel and ran.

Constance froze with the sense of being torn in four different directions. All of them felt important—but she knew without a shadow of a doubt which one mattered most.

She looked to her friends urgently.

"Stall for me!" she begged Ellie and Adam. "Please!"

Then she bolted after Neil.

FORTY-ONE

$\mathcal{E}$LLIE WAS STILL gaping after her departed friend and her brother when Adam hooked a hand around her waist and propelled her back into the palace.

They ran directly into Mr. Mahjoud. The impeccably dressed dragoman stared down at them with an air of tired exasperation.

"Connie's in the washroom," Adam burst out before Padma's agent could open his mouth to speak.

He spun Ellie around and marched her down the hall away from both Mr. Mahjoud and the noise of the party. They turned a corner, and Adam steered her through a random door.

Ellie stopped just over the threshold, staring at an array of glassy-eyed beasts. The frozen menagerie included a rhinoceros, a tiger, an ostrich, four different types of deer, and a mongoose. Several large fish were mounted on the wall.

It would all have been quite alarming, had the animals not been stuffed.

A pair of ornate armchairs stood in the center of the display next to an elaborate standing ashtray. Both the furnishings and the taxidermy had been meticulously maintained but felt unused. Ellie was left with the impression that the space had belonged to one of Vijay's more sportsmanlike royal ancestors.

Her impressions didn't go any further, because the rest of her mind was still reeling with what she had just seen. "Adam, they were… Neil was…"

Adam shut the door and planted her in one of the chairs. "Sure looked like it."

"But it was never supposed to be… They shouldn't have been…" Ellie's words choked off. "They were only *pretending!*"

Adam collapsed into the other chair, slumping back against the seat in a posture of stunned surprise. "Don't think they were pretending that."

Ellie pushed to her feet, pacing compulsively between the ostrich and the tiger. "I recognize that these things do happen. I cannot even say I am entirely surprised by it. I did have *some* suspicions after our adventures in Egypt, though both of them insisted there was nothing at all untoward going on. And I recognize that forced proximity can be a powerful force for romantic entanglement."

Adam's gaze dropped appreciatively to the close-fitting lines of her evening gown. "You don't say."

"You are trying to distract me," Ellie accused crossly.

"Now why would I go and do a thing like that?" Adam put his hands behind his head in a way that made his substantial biceps press against the fabric of his jacket.

Ellie threw up her hands. "They have known each other since they were children!"

Adam cocked an eyebrow.

She put her fingers to her temples. "That doesn't really mean anything, does it?"

His expression grew more serious. "How are you feeling about all of it?"

"How am *I* feeling? They are two grown adults. It's hardly for me to comment about what they get up to with each other."

"Didn't ask you to comment." Adam eyed her knowingly. "I asked you how you *felt*."

"How can I know that? I have no idea what's even going on between the two of them, beyond the fact that they're..." She forced the word out as her cheeks flushed. "Kissing."

"That was a bit more than just a kiss, Princess. That looked like wild, unadulterated—"

"Yes, I know!" Ellie blurted out before he could go any further.

She went back to pacing. Adam snagged a handful of her skirt as she passed. He gave it a tug, and Ellie stumbled between his legs, catching herself against the back of the armchair.

Her hands were braced to either side of where Adam sprawled across the velvet cushions. His gaze roamed lazily up her body—pausing significantly on her bosom. He lifted his eyes to her face as her cheeks burned.

"Pretty sure you do," he finished with a smirk.

"You're incorrigible," Ellie accused breathlessly.

Adam chuckled.

Ellie gave up on regaining her balance with any sort of dignity. She sat down on his knee instead. "But do you think it's serious?" she asked, sobering.

"I think serious is the only way your brother knows how to do things," he pointed out gently.

Ellie groaned. "Of course, you're right. But Constance…"

"…cares about him," Adam filled in deliberately. "She's cared about him for a while now, even when she was justifiably furious at him back in Egypt. I know she's talked about running off to have an affair with a trapeze artist, or a pirate captain, or whatever the hell else, but I don't think that's what this is to her. And not just because Neil's about the furthest thing you could get from a pirate captain."

Ellie thought of what Neil's sock drawer looked like—extremely organized—and how many hours he could spend poring over Herodotus before looking up, blinking like a man waking from a thousand year sleep and wondering what century he had landed in.

"True," she concurred with a grimace.

Adam slipped a comforting arm around her waist, and Ellie finally voiced the bigger fear that lurked inside of her. "What if she breaks his heart?"

"If she does, it'll heal."

"You sound awfully sure of that."

"That's because I am. But I don't think that's what's going to happen."

"You don't?"

Adam's hand traced up her back in long, soothing strokes. "Nope. If I were a betting man—"

"—which you are," Ellie dryly inserted.

"I'd put my money on the two of them getting married, and then having a whole lot of—"

"Don't say it!" Ellie queasily pictured Constance's legs around her brother's waist.

"—kids," Adam finished with an unapologetic grin.

Ellie stilled.

His prediction was perfectly reasonable. If Neil and Constance were involved in a more serious way, then children might very well be in their future—but not just any children.

They would be Ellie's nieces and nephews. Her *family*.

The picture bloomed to vivid life in her mind.

Sturdy legs crawled over ruined funerary chapels in a sprawl of sand. Neil would be yelling at them to be careful, and Constance would show them where to find even more dangerous things to get into.

Ellie could hear exactly the groan her brother would make. She knew how he would give in with helpless laughter as one of those children—a little girl with a mane of gorgeous ebony hair—jumped into his arms and demanded a hug.

The vision was so vivid—so *real*—that it stole Ellie's breath, squeezing her heart like a clenched fist.

Adam lifted a scarred, calloused hand to gently brush the moisture from her cheek.

Ellie startled at the touch, bringing her own hand to her face. "Why am I crying?" she gasped out, her voice breaking.

"I think you've gotta tell me that," Adam replied softly.

Ellie let herself fall against him, curling into his side in the chair with her legs across his lap. His arm cradled her warmly as she rested her face against his broad shoulder.

The words spilled out of her like a confession. "I want that for them. Adam… I want it for them so badly, it *hurts*."

"Guess we know how you feel about it, then," Adam commented warmly. "Though I thought you didn't like kids."

"I would like *their* children!" Ellie countered defensively. "I can do that, you know, and still not want any of my own."

"Makes perfect sense to me," Adam cheerfully agreed as he held her. "For what it's worth, I think you'll be a great aunt."

"I don't know about that," Ellie grumbled skeptically—even as a more rebellious part of her brain gleefully imagined what that role might be like.

She could offer the children helpful instruction with their Latin conjugations. Lead them on an excursion across the Saqqara plain, pointing out the various layers of habitation visible in the exposed structures.

Of course, as these were Constance and Neil's children, some of them would wander off in search of cobras to befriend, while others would get stuck on a single panel of hieroglyphs and refuse to move until they had translated them in their entirety.

But that would be all right, Ellie decided comfortably as she nestled against the warmth of Adam's shoulder—more than all right, really. In fact, Ellie found that the notion made her happier than almost anything she had ever thought of before.

A terrible new worry burst into her brain, and Ellie sat up. "What if they muck it up? Neil is terrible at this sort of thing!"

"He's not *that* bad." Adam read her expression and let out a breath. "All right—maybe he is that bad. But Constance sure as hell gets what she sets her sights on."

"What if she gets him and then realizes she doesn't really want him?" Ellie fluttered with panic at the notion.

"I don't think that's going to happen."

"Why not?!"

Adam stroked his knuckles over her cheek. "Because your brother's a damned good man, Princess."

Moisture welled up in her eyes once more at the certainty in Adam's voice.

"He might not always get it right the first time," Adam continued. "Hell, he's practically got a knack for putting his foot in things—but his heart always steers him true in the end, no matter what he's gotta go through to get there."

Tears streamed readily down Ellie's cheeks. She couldn't quite manage to speak at first, nodding instead. "You're right," she finally warbled out, her voice ridiculously uneven.

Adam laughed helplessly at the sound. He raised a pleading hand. "I'm sorry. I'm just not sure I've ever seen you like this before."

"That's because I am not prone to fits of feminine weeping!" Ellie protested stoutly—even as the cursed tears kept streaming down her cheeks.

"Nothing feminine about a good cry," Adam asserted authoritatively.

"You *would* say that," Ellie grumbled back irritably.

Adam's hand smoothed over her back. "She's your best friend."

"She is!" Ellie wiped away more tears.

"And he's your brother." Adam's hand continued to move in slow, tender strokes along her spine. "And not one that you had all along, which I'm guessing means you remember what it was like before he got there."

Ellie couldn't answer him. She gazed at him helplessly as the tears kept falling.

He brushed the pad of his thumb over the damp staining her cheek. "It all makes perfect sense to me."

"Of course, it makes sense to you," Ellie countered, warmth and a helpless irritation mingling in her words. "You're Adam Bates."

She kissed him, holding the rough texture of his cheeks gently between her hands. Her skin was cool with the echo of her tears as she grazed her lips tenderly over his own.

"Think you're ready to face the party again?" Adam gently prompted when they were done. "Because it's starting to feel like all these dead animals are staring at us."

Ellie recalled herself. It did seem like the ostrich, the rhinoceros, and the tiger were pointing their beady eyes right at where she and Adam were sitting. "That is rather unsettling, once one notices it."

"Let's go get some treats," he asserted and hauled her to her feet.

FORTY-TWO

Constance chased Neil through the palace.

The man's legs were too bloody long. In his few seconds' lead on her, he had managed to disappear, turning around a corner that led off in three different directions.

Thankfully, Constance wasn't averse to a good sprint.

She made two false starts before determining on the third way, which led her down a set of stairs that spilled out into one of the palace's many secluded courtyards. The pale marble square was lined with white pillars that shimmered in the moonlight. The lights and noise of the party rose softly from beyond a darkened wing of the palace.

Neil was still walking. He had nearly reached the far end of the marble paving stones.

"Where are you going?" Constance called after him.

He paused but didn't look back. "Does it matter?"

Fury replaced the colder fear that had driven her after him. She set her hands on her hips. "Yes, it bloody well does!"

Neil finally turned. He took in her pose and laughed. The sound was dark and helpless. "You looked at me like that thirteen years ago when you were defending using my fountain pen ink to paint the Bayeux Tapestry on one of the bedsheets."

Constance waved dismissively. "You had plenty of ink."

"You took *all* of it," Neil countered.

"It was an expansive mural." Constance crossed her arms defensively over her chest.

The tired flash of humor fell away, and Neil dropped to one of the benches that lined the softly moonlit space. He put his head in his hands.

He looked... *broken.*

Constance had seen Neil frustrated, horrified, or furious. She had deliberately provoked those reactions from him throughout most of their childhood.

She had only seen him like this once before, back in Egypt when he had thought his terrible choices might have cost Adam and Ellie their lives. What could be happening right now that was anywhere near as awful as that?

Constance sat beside him. "Neil… can you tell me what's wrong?"

He kept his palms pressed to his eyes under his spectacles. His voice was raw in his throat. "I don't think that I can, Connie."

Fear tangled inside of her again. "Why not?"

"Because it wouldn't be fair."

"Fair to whom?"

Neil's face was drawn in the moonlight as he finally raised his head. "To *you*."

Constance stood and faced him, planting her hands back on her hips. "I don't care if it's unfair, then. I want you to say it."

Neil's spectacles glinted with silver light as he stared up at her.

"No," he said.

He stood, moving past her to walk away.

Constance grabbed him by his untucked shirt and anchored him in place with sheer stubborn strength. She hauled him closer.

"I will tie your socks into knots. I will cut open the pockets of every single one of your waistcoats. I will hound you through every nook and corner of this palace, night and day and back around again, until you tell me what is wrong," she vowed, her voice seething with threat.

Neil's eyes flickered with a sad shadow of amusement. "You would, too. Wouldn't you?"

His expression shifted, the poetic lines of his face drawn with dismay. "I'm in love with you, Connie."

The pillars that framed the courtyard tilted as Constance's mind blanked with shock. "You're… what? But *why?*"

Neil ran a hand through his soft brown hair and laughed helplessly. "Why? Why do you bloody think?! Because you walk into danger like it's a birthday party. You've threatened me with knives. Put a live trout under my pillow. Saved my life. Kissed me like I was…"

He trailed off, the words catching in his throat. A tear slipped past the line of his spectacles to run down his cheek.

"That's why, Connie," he finished, his voice rough. "That and a thousand other reasons."

Constance felt as though she had just stepped outside to find that the world had turned upside down.

It would *never* have occurred to her that Neil could feel this way—Neil, who had hidden in his room every time she came over. Who'd groaned with exasperation at her deliberate acts of mischief.

But he had been a boy then.

He wasn't a boy any longer.

Neil's green-touched eyes had always been transparent, glittering with excitement when he was rattling on about Ancient Greek grammar or shadowing with guilt when he knew he had made a mistake.

They could hollow with vulnerability—or burn with desire.

Or they might look as they did just then, aching with sadness as Neil waited for Constance to gently tell him why he couldn't possibly be the man she was looking for.

But that wasn't what she wanted to say. Something else rose to her lips instead—a startlingly unexpected notion born of the silent world of moonlight and marble that surrounded her.

"What if we didn't end it?"

Neil looked confused. "End what?"

Constance swallowed. Her mouth was oddly dry.

"Our engagement."

Neil held himself still as he responded. "Why wouldn't we end it, Connie?"

Fear darted through her. "Isn't that what you want?"

Neil's shirt hung loose over the waist of his trousers. The courtyard painted him in tones of subtle blue and silver, giving him the look of a ragged knight stepped out of a fairy tale.

"I need to know what *you* want," he demanded.

The words rumbled from deep in his chest. Constance fought the surprising impulse to press her hand over his heart and see if she could feel the subtle thrum of them.

What *did* she want?

There were so many ways she might answer, visions she had dreamed up for what her life might look like. Galloping across the desert with a tribe of Bedouin marauders. Sailing away on a pirate ship. Discovering a lost civilization on the banks of the Congo.

An affair with a passionate Austrian violinist. Masquerading as a mysterious French art collector. Climbing the Matterhorn.

Those images all scattered from her mind like fallen leaves. Instead, she thought of a man who had thrown her off a boat into the Nile. Of enthusiastic lectures on Demotic and groans of dismay over scorched notepapers.

Remembered scholarly hands tracing over her body and Neil's taste on her tongue—leather and tea and spice.

Words spilled out of her as though they had been waiting at the edge of her lips.

"You have never once asked me to be somebody other than who I am."

Neil's brow furrowed. The familiar expression warmed Constance like a softly crackling fire.

"Not even when I was tormenting you," she continued. "You might easily have done it then. 'Constance, why can't you be just a little less…'"

Her voice trailed off with a pang of remembered hurt. "Other people have. They wished that I were quieter. Less opinionated. More well-behaved. Not quite so Indian."

"I might have occasionally wished you were a little less quick to charge into danger," he admitted. "But then, your complete lack of any sense of self-preservation has worked to my benefit more than once since we became reacquainted—though I won't pretend it doesn't terrify me."

"And then you turned up on me in Egypt," Constance continued. "Or I turned up on you, rather—and you're all… this."

She waved a hand over the lean, strong lines of his body. Neil looked down at himself as though unsure what she meant.

Constance gave a huff of frustration. "A scholarly wizard with a flaming sword."

Neil stared at her as though he was having trouble absorbing her words. "That is… not exactly how I would have put it."

"Well, of course not," Constance retorted. "You never could see your own appeal, outside of being handy with a library card catalog."

Neil stiffened defensively. "I'm very good at libraries."

"You're exceptionally good at kissing as well, though I doubt you noticed that either," Constance retorted crossly.

Neil's stillness took on a different edge—one that felt just a little danger-ous. "Am I?"

"*Yes,*" Constance assured him emphatically.

She raised her hands to the dupatta that hung around his neck and glided them down the saffron silk as she moved closer. "We've managed two stolen moments of perhaps three minutes apiece, and I can tell you with full and absolute confidence that I am nowhere near satisfied with the use I'd like to make of you."

Neil's breath hitched. His head dropped to graze against her unbound hair.

"Blast it, Connie…"

Constance tightened her grip on his scarf as though some part of her was afraid that if she let go, he would disappear. "You will undoubtedly try to remind me that you are an unemployed academic from a family of no account in the world, and I will answer that *I do not care*. I have known piles of men with sterling credentials, and not one of them would ever have admitted when he was wrong, or faced a truth that utterly upended his world when he could just as easily pretend it didn't exist. You haven't the foggiest notion how rare that is. You haven't the foggiest notion how rare *you* are."

The look he gave her was raw with feeling. "You really mean that."

Constance tucked an unruly lock of hair back from his forehead. "Of course I do." Her throat tightened as she continued, her heart thudding wildly in her chest. "If we never broke off our pretend engagement, then we would end up getting married. Is that what you want?"

Neil swallowed thickly. Constance followed the enticing movement of his throat. She wasn't sure why the pulse of his Adam's apple had such an effect on her—but by God, did it ever.

"I don't think I have allowed myself to consider that question," he admitted carefully.

"You must be considering it now," Constance countered impatiently.

"Yes," he answered helplessly.

The word shivered through her body like a caress.

Constance brushed her thumb along the sharp line of his cheekbone, and Neil's eyes fell closed.

"It never occurred to me that something like this was possible," Constance admitted, her fingers tracing the graceful angle of his jaw. "But now that you've put the idea in my head, I will admit that I find it *desperately* appealing."

Neil caught her hand and held it, his words threaded with a fragile hope. "You do?"

"Why wouldn't I?" Constance took a step closer. "You could teach me your history. Show me pot shards and mud bricks and explain how terribly important they are. Take me to Egypt, or Greece, or Persia. I could see the world while you dig up all its lovely, ordinary secrets." She swallowed, her throat suddenly tight. "You could fight for me."

"You're the fighter, Constance."

Constance rolled her eyes. "Did you ever think that maybe I might *like* to have someone who would stand up to the rest of the world with me? Even if they did it with books and pens and stubbornness instead of that sword you don't know how to use. And you would," she added. "Don't even try to pretend otherwise. You defend the things you love, Neil. I have already seen you do it. And there is a very great deal to admire in that."

The lines of Neil's face were drawn in the moonlight. "Is that it, then? You admire me?"

"Hardly," Constance retorted. "I also want to do absolutely *wicked* things with you. The most wretchedly sinful notions have been tormenting me since our experiment in the stepwell—or earlier than that, if I'm to be perfectly honest. I have been itching to get you out of all that tweed for weeks. You are a damnably attractive man, Neil Fairfax."

Neil's gaze darkened with a focus like sunlight through a magnifying lens.

Constance drew nearer until she could feel the warmth of his body through the silk of her gown. A deep, needful shudder moved through him in response.

"Are you attracted to me, Neil?" she asked, deliberately provoking.

"I think you are perfectly well aware of the effect you have on me," Neil retorted tightly.

"Not as aware as I'd like to be." Constance glided her hand down the front of his shirt. "I could be so much more aware… if you'd let me."

"Bloody hell, Connie," Neil rasped. "You can have me any time you want. You don't have to marry me for that."

Constance cocked an eyebrow at this intriguing confession. "I thought you were more of a gentleman than that."

"Not when it comes to you," Neil bit back desperately.

"But you *want* to marry me," Constance clarified thoughtfully as her fingers traced the waistband of his trousers.

Neil closed his eyes, fighting an obvious war of self-control. "Yes."

Constance's hand stilled. "Why do you want that, if you know you could have me anyway?"

Neil's gaze shadowed with vulnerability through the searing heat of his desire. "I think I already answered that."

"Because you're in love with me," Constance filled in.

She slipped her arms around his waist, laying her face against the warm, solid plane of his chest. She fit there very nicely, her head just coming to his shoulder.

He slowly came to hold her in return, as though afraid that if he went too fast, she would startle and run away.

She spoke across his chest. "You know, I think you might really mean it—that you love me, I mean. And not just your own notion of who you'd like me to be."

Neil laughed. The helpless sound hummed against her skin. "Connie, I couldn't pretend you were someone else if I wanted to. You'd set me straight in a heartbeat. Probably in some way that would scorch my eyebrows or require replacing several of my reference books."

Constance lifted her face from his chest to look up at him. "I know," she said—the words coming from someplace deep. "But don't you want me to love you back?"

Neil's expression flashed with vulnerability once again. "I... yes. That's what I want. If you think you could. But it wouldn't have to happen right away. I... We could wait, if you like. To see if you..."

His words trailed off, and he looked up as though searching for strength.

"I mean, I *do* love you already," Constance mused. "I've loved you since we were children. Why else do you think I spent so much time trying to make you miserable? I don't mean in a romantic way, of course," she quickly corrected. "I hadn't any notion what that looked like all those years ago. I loved you because you were my friend—even if you didn't really want to be. And because of Ellie."

"It isn't that I didn't *want* to," Neil protested. "You just made it feel so bloody dangerous!"

"It still would be," Constance warned him. "Just because I fall in love with you doesn't mean I'm going to behave myself."

"I am more than well aware of that," Neil replied dryly.

"You are, aren't you?" Constance gazed up at him wonderingly. "I wonder if you realize how extraordinary that is."

Her hand glided up the back of his neck, her fingers threading gently into the soft waves of his hair. "I already love you. I am *wildly* attracted to you. You know me, and you still want me, exactly as I am—even though it has to frighten you at least a little."

"Yes," Neil confirmed bluntly.

"And you *are* a scholarly wizard with a flaming sword," she pointed out with wicked delight.

"I wish you'd stop calling me that."

"Absolutely not," Constance vowed. "You can see what all of that adds up to, can't you? If that isn't a recipe for falling in love with a person, I don't know what would be. In fact, I wonder if I haven't fallen in love with you already—only I didn't really let myself see it. Maybe because you've been here in front of me all this time, in one way or another. Or because..."

Constance wavered on the edge of someplace more real—more true—than she had let herself go before.

And leaped.

"Because saying it would have made me realize how very much you had come to mean to me. And how terrible it would have been if you had decided to go away."

Neil's voice was rough. "Why would I go away?"

Constance shrugged. "If I wasn't what you really wanted. We are very different, you know."

"I know," Neil confirmed. "But you're what I want, Connie. I hope you can believe that."

"I do," Constance said—and the words swept through her like a revelation.

Happiness bloomed inside of her like something made to fly. She smoothed her hand over Neil's chest again, feeling his solid strength through the fabric—and the way his breath went ragged at her touch.

"So will you marry me, then?" She glanced up at him with wicked slyness. "I promise I'll make it worth your while."

Neil let out a helpless laugh. "Why does that sound like a threat?"

"Because it is." Constance flashed him her teeth. "One that I intend to make good on in the mornings. And over lunch. And on your desk, after I shove all your precious papers onto the floor." She dipped her hands under the loose hem of his shirt and stroked up his skin, her nails lightly grazing the flesh of his abdomen. "I'm going to make good on it until the two of us are so sated we can barely stand."

"I yield," Neil groaned. "Damn it, Connie. Yes. I'll marry you. Even though I was supposed to be the one to ask."

Constance shrugged. "Well, you were leading up to it nicely."

And then—at last—Neil leaned in to kiss her. His hands cradled the small of her back like they held something achingly precious, and his lips glided over her mouth with a taut, eloquent restraint—a perfect balance of hunger and delicacy, heat and reverence.

He kissed her like she was a poem that he held in his arms. It was a promise and an act of worship, aching with bone-deep joy.

All of which was perfectly lovely.

Constance grabbed the lapels of his coat, spun him about, and shoved him down onto the bench.

"Let's try it my way now," she declared as she climbed on top of him.

FORTY-THREE

$\mathcal{T}$HE PARTY WAS moving outside when Ellie and Adam returned to it. They found themselves herded from the salon with the rest of the boisterous guests, entering an adjacent garden where lanterns hanging from archways spilled abundant light over lush hibiscus flowers and golden trumpetbush.

Music kicked up, tabla and sitar picking out a lively beat. Laughter bubbled up into the star-studded violet sky.

"Where are Constance and Neil?" Ellie wondered aloud.

Adam's mouth twitched with suppressed humor.

"Never mind—don't answer that," she warned him.

Adam raised his hands innocently. "Wasn't going to."

Ellie groaned. "But now you've put the notion in my head."

"I didn't say a word!"

"You didn't have to!" She flapped a hand at him. "Give me something else to think of."

Adam nodded to where Constance's uncle and a few other gentlemen were puffing on their cigars. "It smells like Balaram's smoking some really nice stuff over there."

"That's what you have to offer? Tobacco? Tobacco isn't going to make me stop thinking about my brother and… things… that I have absolutely no wish to think about!"

"I'm gonna go have a smoke." Adam's eyes glinted with mischief. "After all, I did win our bet."

Ellie threw up her hands. "I never took your bet!"

"I'm gonna cut way back," Adam assured her as he backed away. "Promise."

"Black lung!" Ellie shouted after him.

"Just one!" he called in return, and then let himself be pulled into the circle of men.

Ellie shook her head—and then startled to realize that Padma stood beside her.

Constance's grandmother glittered with jewels, looking every inch the princess. Mr. Mahjoud had returned to join her, a looming and distinguished presence at her back.

He treated Ellie to an irritated frown—probably because she and Adam had sent him off on a wild goose chase.

"When are you leaving for Korea?" Padma asked lightly.

The garden tipped sideways as Ellie tried to catch up with her words. "Why would I be going to Korea?"

"There is that little matter of George Bates," Padma replied.

Ellie's thoughts shot back to Borthwick's revelation in front of the temple of the Brahmastra.

He's welcome to whatever the Joseon is hiding…

But Padma had been miles away when the colonel had spoken those words.

Suspicion flared. "How do you know about that?"

Padma's expression was serene. "I make it a point to stay abreast of these matters."

Anger snapped through Ellie with a quick heat. "How *long* have you known about it?"

Padma met her glare without a hint of apology. "Longer than you."

The anger burned hotter. Ellie reminded herself that they were standing at the edge of a party. If she started shouting, people would notice.

"Then would you kindly tell me *why you didn't say anything about it?*"

"You needed to focus on the Brahmastra."

Ellie's fists clenched. Her head pounded with the effort of restraining her temper. "That *wasn't* your decision to make."

"Wasn't it?" Padma returned coolly.

Ellie controlled herself with some effort. There were more important things she needed from this conversation than to let Padma know how furious she was. "And what else do you know about Adam's father?"

"He is searching for a place that the Chinese call Mount Penglai."

Ellie's stomach twisted at the words. She knew what Penglai was… and what George Bates must be seeking there.

"You don't have the funds to make the journey on your own," Padma declared flatly. "Your money—such as it is—is tied up in London. Mr. Bates never had any to begin with."

Ellie's fury was a hot, electric wind roiling inside of her. "Are you *blackmailing* us?"

Padma's expression was as placid as a lake in winter. "I believe that I am offering to assist you."

"Because it serves your interests," Ellie accused.

"This is a war, Jhia," Padma snapped. "The men who crush nations under their boots are stealing our own history to help them do it. Did you come here to fight that? Or would you rather go home?"

"That isn't fair," Ellie pushed back.

Padma's eyes flashed with dark, powerful rage. "Neither was what was done to my country. One million dead in Odisha alone, in a single famine, because the Raj destroyed the systems that would have cared for them, offering us telegraph wires and trade restrictions instead. I left because I could not raise my children in a place that reeked of death, and I have never forgiven myself for it. But I am here now, and I will do whatever is necessary to protect my people—along with others like them across the world who are crushed under the boot of empire."

Ellie could not disagree with her. She understood justice. She had fought for it on her own battlefields all her life—but her own anger lingered.

"I do not appreciate having my strings pulled," she warned dangerously. "I won't be a puppet. Not for anyone."

"I am not asking for a puppet."

"What are you asking for, then?"

"Soldiers." Padma's lip curled wryly. "Not that I expect either you or Mr. Bates to be very good at following orders. So let us make it warriors, aligned in a cause… if we are aligned, Jhia."

In the garden around them, children chased across the paving stones, their laughter ringing out into the night air. A group of older women gossiped over tea. Lanterns glittered amid branches heavy with fragrant blossoms, framed by a building with centuries of heritage.

What would it mean if all of that were lost? If men like Borthwick or Lord Aldbury used the powers of the past to sweep it into oblivion so they could remake the world in their own image—for their own benefit?

Ellie couldn't stand aside and watch that happen. She would never feel right doing anything less than her utmost to stop it.

"I want what you want," she replied. "But that doesn't mean I'll be your tool."

"I'm not asking for tools," Padma corrected her. "I'm asking for allies."

"Then I need to know that you will never hide something like this from me again," Ellie snapped.

"I won't promise you that," Padma returned without a hint of apology. "My interest in this goes beyond the personal. Borthwick was the more immediate threat. He had to be dealt with. You might not have had the strength to recognize that, if I'd given you the choice."

Ellie shook her head, shocked. "How can you expect me to accept that?"

"I don't," Padma replied simply. "I expect you to talk to your man about it."

Ellie involuntarily glanced at Adam, who stood smoking and laughing with Constance's uncle and his friends.

He caught her look, and his easy expression narrowed to one of concern.

Padma's mouth curved dangerously. "See what he has to say, and then you may give me your answer."

Her air of martial authority fell into a regal ease as she walked away to join a cluster of aunties gathered by the music.

Mr. Mahjoud gave Ellie an ironic nod before he followed her.

Ellie's head spun.

Adam joined her, looking to where Padma now laughed with the other women. "What happened?"

Ellie gripped his arm as though its solid strength could stop the world from spinning around her. "We need to talk."

Adam slipped an arm around her waist and steered her inside.

They passed through the maze-like halls of the palace, dodging wandering guests and busy servants, until Adam pulled open a door carved in square panels studded with brass.

He guided her inside, and Ellie found herself in Vijay's royal library.

The collection was enormous. Shelves lined the walls to a height of two stories. Cabinets and reading tables were packed with treasures. Cases for scrolls and carvings lay beside tomes with gilded spines in Odia, Hindi, Sanskrit, Arabic, English, Latin, and Greek.

Ellie could have lost herself there for years. "Did you know this was here?"

"Just pulled a lucky door," Adam replied.

Ellie traced her hand over the spines, drawing comfort from them. She had been hunting for this room since she had first come to Nandapur—but she couldn't throw herself into exploring its wonders. Her heart was too heavy with a bigger burden.

She hated what she would need to say next—but she did it anyway.

"Padma believes that we are going to Korea."

Adam leaned against the closed door, his posture deceptively casual.

"Where'd she get that idea?"

Ellie came closer to him. "She already knew about your father."

There were a hundred questions Adam might have asked her. Ellie sensed the significance of the one that rose to his lips first.

"What's he looking for?"

"Penglai Shan," Ellie replied. "The land of the immortals."

The myth of Penglai was Taoist, most well-known through Chinese folklore. It spoke of a mountainous island said to be home to sages whose wisdom had raised them beyond the confines of ordinary flesh to a state of spiritual and physical perfection that granted them immortal life. The method of that transformation varied depending on what version of the story one heard, from a godly elixir to the fruits of a holy tree or more abstract concepts of spiritual energy.

The location of Mount Penglai—if such a place existed—had long been a mystery. George Bates apparently believed it lay to the north in the kingdom of Korea.

Korea had its own myths of immortality and of mountains that hid powerful secrets. They were less well known in the West, but that knowledge could be learned—and might conceal a powerful truth.

Ellie had never met George Bates. She knew him only by his reputation… and by the shape of the scars he had left on the heart of his son.

"We don't have to go."

Adam moved to the window and stared out into the darkness. "It wouldn't be any different than what we've done before. He's just another bastard in a suit."

The forcefully casual words cut at Ellie like a knife.

She crossed to him and put her hand on his arm. It was stiff with resistance.

"No, he's not," she countered gently.

His facade broke at her words. A shudder moved through him, and his face fell into lines of rage and fear. The words tore out of him roughly.

"You don't know what he's like, Ellie."

She thought of Adam's strange reaction to Borthwick's threats back at the Brahmastra temple. "You begged Borthwick not to send me to him. Why? What did you think your father would do to me?"

Adam's eyes were haunted. "He would carve you full of holes."

Ellie stilled with shock.

"Not like Jacobs," Adam elaborated, his face drawn. "He doesn't have to use knives. He can do it all with words."

The enormous room shrank as Ellie felt herself draw closer to something old, dark, and rotten.

"Tell me what that means," she demanded.

His voice was raw as he answered her. "He would take you down, one little piece at a time. Make you doubt everything you thought you knew about yourself. Everything you thought was good. He'd turn it around until all you could feel about any of it was shame, and that still wouldn't be enough. Because even if you tried to be the person he said he wanted you to be, he'd keep showing you all the ways you'd failed. He *breaks* people like that. He breaks you until you're nothing but a kicked dog, cringing from the next blow."

Ellie's mind spun with horror at what Adam had just revealed.

She had known some part of it—glimpses she had intuited through all his careful defenses and unexpected vulnerabilities. But she hadn't understood, not really.

Not until now.

She raised her hand to his face. It was as familiar to her as her own, still shadowed by the bruises he'd won fighting for the people he cared about. Grief and love formed an ache inside her chest. "That's how he hurt you, isn't it?"

Adam looked back out into the darkness. She could see the struggle inside of him.

The pain. The shame.

It tore at her like a wound. She wanted to go back in time and save him from being hurt like that by the person he should have been able to trust most in the world. Make him see his own goodness—his astonishing, unutterable value.

She couldn't, and the scars were part of what made him the man he was—not because of George Bates, but in spite of him.

Because of *Adam.*

She took him by the shoulders and spoke with all the force she could muster. "*You got out.*"

"Not as soon as I should have," Adam pushed back harshly.

"You were a *child* before that," Ellie emphasized fiercely. "But you got away from him and built a life for yourself—your life, on your own terms."

"I left my mom behind," Adam bluntly returned.

"She should have protected you," Ellie shot back.

Adam's expression was lined with grief. "I don't think she could."

Ellie closed her eyes as she absorbed everything those few words meant.

"And your brother?" she asked gently.

She remembered the name he had shared with her once. It was her only knowledge of Adam's younger sibling.

Ethan.

He looked tired. "Dad was never like that with him. I don't know why. Maybe I should've been angry about it or thought it was unfair, but I didn't. All I could think was that it must have meant there was something wrong with me."

Ellie pressed her hand to his heart as she spoke, the words fierce. "There is *nothing* wrong with you."

Adam drew in a deep, uneven breath as he met her look. "I know."

The depth of her admiration for the man before her swept through her like a tide. For everything he had survived. For what he had built himself into in spite of all the violence that had been used to try to crush him.

He gripped her shoulders, desperate. "I don't want you anywhere near him."

Ellie traced the lines of his face. "Then I won't be."

Relief and worry mingled in his expression.

He let her go and began to pace the room. "How could we even do it? Borthwick is nothing compared to what we'd be going up against this time. *Nothing.*"

"We don't have to go," Ellie said again.

Adam braced himself against the wall, his body tense. He shook his head. "We have to."

"Why?" Ellie demanded.

His face was hard. "Because he's my father."

"That doesn't make him your responsibility," Ellie snapped.

She was angry. The feeling seethed under her grief for Adam and her desperate desire to support him—a violent, dangerous rage against the man who had done this to him.

"Padma will have other people she can send," she asserted.

She was certain that it was true. Constance's omniscient grandmother would never leave herself with so few cards to play.

Hot steel flashed behind Adam's gaze. "Nobody else knows him like I do."

A terrible sense of inevitability closed over her. Ellie fought back against it. "How much damage could a person even do with the secret to eternal life?"

"You tell me," Adam demanded.

Irresistibly, Ellie thought of the answer.

She imagined a world where the right to conquer death could be bought and sold. How a race of immortal men might place themselves above everyone around them.

People would be desperate to buy even a taste of that privilege, to cure their diseases or claw a few more years of life for themselves or those they loved. They would give *anything*. And before very long, there would be two species on the earth—two different breeds of human. Those who lived, and those who served, with nothing in between.

What would a man like George Bates do with an arcanum like that?

Ellie already knew.

Whatever would make him more powerful. No matter what it cost anyone else.

Adam read the expression on her face. "Yeah. That's what I thought."

Fear twisted through her as she realized what that meant—and what it would demand of Adam.

Determination snapped through her with the force of a storm. Ellie spoke the words through gritted teeth. "*I will not let him hurt you again.*"

Adam's voice was achingly sad. "I'm not sure that's something you can promise me, Princess."

Ellie twisted her hands into the fabric of his shirt. A tear broke loose from her eye, gliding down her cheek. "I just did," she bit back stubbornly.

Adam cupped her face with his hand, his thumb grazing over her cheek. "There's another reason we need to go to Korea. Your reason."

"Mine?"

"Seems to me there's a failed hermit you need to talk to."

Ellie recalled the name of the scholar who had taken up temporary residence in Vijay's garden.

Cairncross.

"I'm sure that fellow isn't the only person in the world with some knowledge of the things we've been running into lately," she hedged.

"He's the only one we know about," Adam pushed back stubbornly. "You're carrying a lost city around inside of you. Your brother's running around having visions of the past. We've been tripping over bloodthirsty mirrors and Biblical staffs. It's important, Ellie. You deserve to know what that's all about."

Ellie couldn't tell him that it didn't matter. She would have been lying.

"I think we should go," Adam declared firmly.

Love swelled painfully inside of her. With everything he had just revealed—all the reasons he had given for why he felt he had to do this, even though it might cost him terribly—he was still asking.

There was only one answer she could give.

"Then we'll go."

She set her hand to the front of his shirt, gliding it up the hard lines of his chest. "But when we go, I will be traveling with you as your wife." She caught herself. "If you find that arrangement acceptable, of course."

Adam's hands tightened where he held her waist, his grip heating her skin through the silk of her gown. "It's more than goddamned acceptable."

The implication of what they had just said washed through her.

Adam's eyes widened with a dawning surprise. "We just did something there. Didn't we?"

"I… think we did," Ellie agreed, reeling from the realization of what they had just committed to.

It meant hours in tangled sheets without shame or fear. Waterfalls and summer nights and ancient secrets. Rum and mud and laughter.

Adam's strength at her back for all the battles to come. A united front against the myriad forces of the world that stood against them. Partnership and struggle and discovery, side by side, as the years unwound before them like a tumbled ball of yarn.

"Are you all right with that?" Ellie asked with a quick note of panic.

"Are you?" Adam pushed back uncertainly.

The answer came to her as irrepressibly as a hot air balloon. "Goodness, yes!" she breathed out feelingly.

She could hear the joy in Adam's laugh. His arms firmed around her back. "Thank Christ," he groaned with obvious relief.

Then Ellie was laughing too—until she caught his face in her hands and pushed herself up for a kiss.

It was tender and hungry. Ellie drank it in—drank *him*. Her lover and friend. Her companion in life.

Her pretend husband.

She laughed again through the kiss, tears cooling her cheeks—and then Adam spun her around and pressed her against the wall.

After that, she felt something else entirely—something that fully and blissfully consumed her for a spell of breathless time.

FORTY-FOUR

$\mathcal{E}$LLIE WAS FLUSHED, sweating, and sated as she and Adam returned to the garden.

She had needed that time with him after the tumult of their conversation to try to heal some of the pain he had shared with her—to show him how thoroughly she meant to be there for him.

They had come together like a vow.

She kept hold of his hand as they slipped back into the party, daring the world to take issue. Between the joyful chaos of the glittering crowd and the generous shadows between the pools of lamplight, nobody took notice.

Just like nobody noticed the glimmer of Constance's figure as she hurried along a raised bridge that bordered the far side of the garden, connecting two of the palace wings.

Ellie's friend skipped down an open stairwell. Her cheeks were rosy and her eyes glittered. She brightened at the sound of music.

A few relatives spotted her as she reached the ground, sweeping her up into a chattering conversation.

"Wonder where she's been?" Adam mused.

Neil stepped onto the bridge.

The structure was roofed, raised over the garden on pillars. Ellie's brother was cast in shadow, but he seemed at least somewhat more put-together than he had been when she had last seen him.

Had that really been this same evening? It already felt like years.

His shirt was tucked in and his waistcoat was buttoned under the fall of his gold scarf—but his hair was still mussed and his spectacles were crooked.

"You thinking what I'm thinking?" Adam asked.

"Absolutely not," Ellie returned firmly. "Nor do I have any wish to be."

"You should probably go talk to him," Adam helpfully suggested.

"Fiddlesticks," Ellie muttered under her breath.

She wove through the party to climb the steep stone stairs to the bridge. Elegant arches of carved stone marched down the length of the raised walkway to where Neil stood alone.

Her brother didn't look at her. His eyes were fixed on the party. No, Ellie realized—they were on Constance, where she stood amid a gathering of cousins and aunts, her laughter echoing up into the night.

"She looks happy," Ellie noted as she stopped beside him.

Neil jumped. "I… What… How…?"

Ellie reached up to fix his crooked spectacles.

Neil paled—and then firmed with resolution. "We're getting married."

Ellie stilled. "You and Constance?"

"Yes?" Neil answered awkwardly.

"And you've both… talked about this?"

Neil's tone was dry. "That is usually how marriage proposals come about, Peanut."

"I know that," Ellie returned irritably. "Only back upstairs when you were…" She trailed off, choking on the notion of elaborating further. "I have to say it didn't look exactly…"

Neil's ears turned pink. "It only just happened. Now. After that… other bit."

Ellie raised her eyebrows. "You mean that you just now asked her to marry you."

"It was the other way around, actually. She asked me. Or perhaps we were asking each other? I'm… not precisely clear on it."

"You're not precisely clear on how you came to be engaged to Constance?"

Neil ran a tired hand over his face. "Can you honestly say that surprises you?"

"Well… no," Ellie admitted. "But how do you feel about it?"

"Feel?" Neil echoed blankly.

"Are you happy?" Ellie elaborated gently.

His gaze dropped back to Constance. "She's the most magnificent woman I've ever known. And she told me she's falling in love with me. Or maybe that she already had?"

He turned back to Ellie, his face drawn with hope and fear and joy. "Peanut, I am having a hard time understanding how I could possibly have become so lucky."

The words were rich with feeling, and suddenly Neil's quiet bewilderment made a perfect sort of sense.

"Oh, Neil," Ellie breathed out. "I am so ridiculously happy for you."

She threw her arms around him. Neil froze with surprise for a moment—and then hugged her tightly in return.

"Thank God!" He pushed her back to look at her, his hands warm on her shoulders. "I've been terrified that you were going to hate the idea and that it might have muddled things up between us, or muddled things up between you and Connie, and then I would have ruined everything, just because I'd gone and…"

"You don't have to complete that sentence," Ellie quickly offered.

"I wasn't talking about *that!* There hasn't been any…" Neil caught himself, distinctly uncomfortable. "I mean, I suppose there's been some, er… but not the sort of thing you're… Unless you're thinking of…"

He clamped his mouth shut and drew in a breath.

"…fallen in love with her," he finished carefully.

"Are you in love with her?"

The word spilled out of Neil like a confession. "Wretchedly."

Ellie raised her hands to his face, cradling the long, familiar lines of it as a wonderful warmth bloomed inside of her. "You are perfect for her. It's mad I never saw it until now. You are going to make each other brilliantly happy. You have my blessing—not that you require it. But I'm wholeheartedly giving it to you anyway."

Neil's eyes shimmered with tears. "Peanut…"

"But please don't let me catch you mauling each other like that again," Ellie pleaded. "That was *not* an image I want permanently etched into my brain."

"You think my brain isn't already etched with whatever you and Bates are getting up to?" Neil protested. "It's horrifying!"

"Stick-in-the-mud," Ellie accused.

"Harridan," Neil shot back.

"Prude."

"Stumpy."

Ellie narrowed her eyes. "I am *not* stumpy."

"You are a bit." Neil grinned down at her.

At the warm sight of that grin, Ellie felt a shiver of worry.

"Adam and I are going to pretend to be married," she blurted out.

Neil's eyebrows rose.

"You know my feelings on the institution of marriage," Ellie pressed on. "Adam respects all of that very deeply—which is part of why I am so dreadfully fond of him. Only traveling around as though we're merely friends—or that he's your friend, and not even mine particularly—feels absolutely wretched. I don't want to do it anymore. Not when it's so far from the life we really want to be living together." She swallowed, her throat tight with worry. "Could you… understand that?"

"You and Bates living together in sin?" Neil filled in. "I can't say I'm thrilled about the notion, but I'd thought it was already happening, more or less."

"It has not!" Ellie protested, taken aback.

"You mean the two of you haven't been…" Neil started with obvious discomfort.

"Er…" Ellie replied.

The smile she plastered onto her face was halfway to a grimace.

"Never mind. Don't tell me. I don't want to know. It doesn't matter anyway. Well, I mean—it matters, but…" He drew in a breath, working to gather himself. When he spoke again, his voice was clear. "I just want you to be happy. Both of you. If this is how you can do that, then of course I support it." His look of certainty collapsed into one of deep unease. "But what are you going to tell Mum and David about it?"

Ellie thought of her lovely, boring, slightly clueless father and her loud, affectionate, and mildly hysterical stepmother.

"Maybe we can worry about that one a little further down the road? After Adam and I get back from Korea."

"Korea?"

"It's… Adam's father," Ellie explained helplessly. "And there's this scholar there, and the land of the immortals, and…" She gave up with a sigh. "We have to go, but it won't be forever. And we'll be careful—I promise. But what about you? Have you and Constance talked about where you plan to go after all this?"

"No. But there's this notion I can't get rid of, Peanut. About Thinis."

"The lost capital of pre-dynastic Egypt?" Ellie felt a rising pinch of excitement. "But scholars have been searching for it for centuries. No one has ever been able to pinpoint its location."

Neil's reply brightened with a fervor that matched her own. "Except that I found something at Gebel Tukh in the tomb of an Old Kingdom Eighth Nome official—a reference to sealing the royal tombs at Thinis!"

"Fiddlesticks!" Ellie breathed out reverently. "But Neil, if that's genuine… Maspero did theorize that it must be located somewhere near the modern city of Girga…"

"And there are several unexcavated early settlement sites there and a necropolis nearby at Beit Khalif," Neil filled in. "Which strongly indicates that the region was inhabited during the early dynasties of the Old Kingdom." His brow creased with worry. "Do you think Connie would be amenable?"

"To searching for a fabled lost city said to hold the treasures of Egypt's first pharaohs?" Ellie filled in dryly. "No, I don't think you'll have too much trouble on that front."

Neil sobered. "I wouldn't feel right about doing it unless I could convince Sayyid to join me—and not as a foreman. He would need to be a partner… or dash it, I could work for him. Lord knows he's better at all of it than I am."

Ellie squeezed his hand. "I think the two of you would get along very well together."

Neil flashed her a small smile of relief. "Of course, I can't begin to think of how we could manage it. Even a preliminary survey of the region would cost money, never mind an excavation. I have certainly destroyed my relationship with the British Athenaeum for Egyptological Studies, and I think I would be hard pressed to find support from any of the other respectable funders after how I left things at Horemheb's tomb in Saqqara."

Ellie stared at him. "Neil… you do realize that Constance is an heiress?"

Neil blinked at her. "She's a what?"

"Her father has settled a substantial portion on her for whenever she marries," Ellie explained patiently. "And then she'd inherit the entirety of the Tyrrell fortune after Sir Robert and Lady Sabita pass away, as she's their only child. None of it is entailed. I don't know the numbers involved, but I should imagine they're something in the region of…" Ellie trailed off as she took in her brother's blank, astonished expression. "You didn't know?"

"I mean—she's mentioned a thing or two about it, but I suppose I just wasn't thinking about any of that when we were…" He caught himself, his look shifting to one of horror. "What on earth is she doing marrying me?"

"Exactly what she wants," Ellie returned. "Just as she's always done."

"But her family—"

"Will be inordinately pleased that she's finally picked a husband," Ellie finished for him. "One they've known about for years, and who isn't committing acts of piracy or… well, trying to steal Egyptian national treasures for his own nefarious purposes, like her last suitor."

Neil's face was drawn. "So what you're saying is that I'm better than an actual bandit and Julian Forster-Mowbray?"

Ellie slipped her hand through his arm, patting it comfortingly. "I'm sure you'll do fine."

He groaned, and she leaned against him, soaking up the comfort of his presence. She thought of all the peaks and valleys of their relationship—the years where he had pulled away from her and how thoroughly she knew he regretted it. He had worked to fix that, showing a great deal of bravery and determination over these last few weeks since his life had so dramatically and forcibly changed.

She was consumed by the fullness of how much she loved him and how grateful she was to have him in her life… and now he was going to marry one of the other people she loved most in the world.

"I am going to be an excellent aunt, you know," she commented.

"You'll be… *Oh, hell!*" Neil's eyes widened with a new sort of panic.

Footsteps pounded down the walkway, and Constance skidded into Neil's side.

"Enough sibling bonding for now," she declared breathlessly. "They're about to start the dancing!"

She grabbed Ellie by the arm as well, hauling both of them into a dash along the bridge.

Adam waited at the foot of the stairs with a grin. Constance herded them onto the paved square, where the rest of the party-goers hurried into place as the musicians tuned up their instruments.

Children waited beside aunties in glittering saris. Young couples blushed at each other. Uncles clapped their hands, cheering as they waved more people over.

In the midst of it all, Ellie stood sandwiched between her best friend, her brother, and the man she loved.

"But I have no idea how to dance!" she protested.

"I'm in," Adam said cheerfully. "Never minded making a fool out of myself in the name of a good time."

"You aren't going to make a fool out of yourself," Constance assured him with perfect confidence. "You'll catch on in no time. Just ask Stuffy."

"Stuffy?" Ellie turned to her brother.

"I don't really know how it works," Neil admitted. "But back in Puri, I started dancing right along with everybody else! Maybe it's just… India?" he finished uncertainly.

"Are you suggesting that the entire country is infused with some sort of supernatural dancing magic?" Ellie pushed back wildly.

"Guess we'll find out," Adam drawled with a wink.

And the drums began to beat.

A NOTE FROM THE AUTHOR

Ellie and Adam's adventures will continue in Raiders of the Arcana Book 4, *Mountain of Songs*. To stay informed about when the book will be available for preorder, join the mailing list at JacquelynBenson.com/subscribe-to-the-newsletter.

Curious about what Ellie found at the Cairo book bazaar or why an emu knows about Adam's fear of heights? You can find those stories and more at my Renegade Scholars Club on Patreon.

If you enjoyed *Arrow of Fortune*, please consider leaving a rating or review on your favorite book retailer or review site.

ACKNOWLEDGMENTS

I never meant to go to India, but my characters have a habit of overthrowing my best-laid plans. Constance made it very clear to me in *Tomb of the Sun King* that she intended to pay a visit to Odisha—and here we are.

I owe a great deal to the scholars whose insight helped illuminate this fascinating part of the world. Shashi Tharoor and William Dalrymple deserve particular thanks. I am also deeply grateful for the insightful feedback I received from my sensitivity reader, Ritika, while SR Meher provided valuable help with Odia translations and pronunciation. The Kuvi text in the book was taken from several sources: *Notes on Kuvi with a Short Vocabulary* by T. Burrow and S. Bhattacharya; *Kuvi Phonetic Reader* by B. Ramakrishna Reddy, Susheela P. Upadhyaya, and Joy Reddy; and *A Grammer of the Kuvi Language* by Rev. F. V. P. Schulze. Any errors are my own.

Much thanks is owed, once again, to my crack beta reading team: Nicholas Atwater, Rosalie Oaks, Chris Mornick, Kaitlyn Huwe, and Matthew Dow. As always, the book you hold in your hands is better thanks to their early input.

Selkkie Designs is responsible for the beautiful cover art for this third installment of the series, and Averil created the delightful portraits of our four main characters.

The authors of the Lamplighter's Guild continued to offer moral support and much wisdom. My Renegade Scholars are greatly appreciated for their support and enthusiasm for this series (and their love of spicy bonus scenes, which I've had too much fun typing up.)

To all of you lovely readers who keep coming back: knowing how excited you are for Ellie and Adam's next adventure is a big part of what keeps me writing.

And finally, a shout-out to SRK, Chote Nawab, RK, NTR Jr., Big B, and the many other talents who have wildly entertained me. Tomorrow may never come—but we'll have loads of fun in the meantime.

A brief historical note

In this story, as in my other *Raiders of the Arcana* adventures, I've made an effort to ground the fantastical adventure in as much truth as possible. When it comes to the history of the British Empire in India, some of that is inevitably dark. Though the character of Colonel Borthwick is a fiction, the abuses of power by the Thuggee and Dacoity Department described in this book were all taken from fact, including the horrific impact of the Criminal Tribes Act.

The Adrija are an invention of my own, but the Khond as a greater people are not. I have drawn inspiration from several Khond communities to construct Subhas, Vanika, and the other Adrija characters in this story. Vijay's account of being ritually kidnapped by the Khond during his ascension to the throne was taken from accounts of actual practice in the region, and the Khond in Odisha have historically had richly complex relationships with the local princely states. Their forests were, and continue to be, hotly contested sites where traditional stewardship runs up against the pressures of modernisation—or simple greed. Because this, the Khond staged several uprisings against their Raj overlords, which I tried to reflect in this story.

The royal family of Nandapur are a fiction, though I have drawn inspiration for them from various royal estates in Odisha during the nineteenth century. No resemblance to any actual historical royals is intended. The town of Nandapur has been somewhat transformed in my narrative and perhaps bears more resemblance to Jeypore. I hope readers will forgive me the artistic license.

Puri is indeed home to the wonderful Chariot Festival (or Ratha Yatra) of Lord Jagannath, and I have tried to make my descriptions of that tradition as accurate as possible. The Puri Beach Club is an invention, but it was based on other British social clubs of the time period.

Likewise, Odisha and Chhattisgarh claim to contain the Dandakaranya, the legendary forest of Lord Rama's exile. I have based my descriptions of that wilderness on the gorgeous Khanger Ghat National Park. The park is within the general geographical range of the *Bagarius yarrelli*—or bodh—which typically grow to about six feet in length. However, there are wild rumors of some outlier specimens growing up to thirteen feet. (Betting you thought I made that one up.)

The Ramacharitamanas of Tulsidas is a real book—the first vernacular telling of the Ramayana tale. Tulsidas is thought by some to be the reincarnation of Valmiki. The special manuscript of the text with an extra chapter at Jagannath Temple in Puri is my own invention.

I encourage any of you who were intrigued by my description of the *Waters of the Son of the Wind* to look up India's remarkable medieval stepwells. They varied widely in design and are wonderful evidence of just how fascinating historical municipal water systems can be.

Most of my Hindu readers likely recognized many of the events referenced in *Arrow of Fortune*, from Sita's kidnapping by Lord Ravana to her eventual exile on the banks of the Ganges, but were probably surprised to hear me associate her with the goddess Kali. That connection belongs to Valmiki in his *Abdhuta Ramayana*, the book mentioned by Padma during her visit to Kali's temple. This relatively unknown manuscript had a profound impact on me as I was researching this book. I am not the first feminist to have been troubled by Sita's apparent passivity in the traditional scope of the Ramayana. But one should not assume that because power is not exercised, it does not exist—especially in tales about women told through the eyes of men.

And finally, though I cannot say for certain that the entire nation of India is infused with dance magic, once does have to wonder about reliable cinematic accounts of festival crowds, wedding guests, train passengers, and sixteenth century courtiers bursting into perfectly synchronized routines at the tap of a tabla.

THE
RAIDERS OF THE ARCANA

Find the magic artifacts, thwart imperialists, and fall in love with this smart, swashbuckling historical fantasy adventure series.

Book 0
The Stolen Apocalypse
When a manuscript goes missing in a Gothic priory, Ellie
and Constance set out to thwart the theft.

Book One
Empire of Shadows
Archivist Ellie Mallory teams up with roguish surveyor Adam Bates
in a race to find a legendary city.

Book Two
Tomb of the Sun King
Ellie and Adam race through Egypt on a quest to find a
lost tomb and protect an arcanum of Biblical proportions.

Book Three
Arrow of Fortune
Alongside her scholarly brother and danger-gnome friend, Ellie
plunges into a mythical forest in search of an invincible weapon.

Book Four
Mountain of Songs
Coming soon..

Available everywhere books are sold.